VAULT

PUBLISHER - DAMIAN A. WASSEL

EDITOR-in-CHIEF - ADRIAN F. WASSEL

ART DIRECTOR - NATHAN C. GOODEN

EVP DESIGN - TIM DANIEL

MANAGING EDITOR - REBECCA TAYLOR

PR DIRECTOR - DAVID DISSANAYAKE

OPERATIONS - IAN BALDESSARI

PRINCIPAL - DAMIAN A. WASSEL, SR

WRITTEN BY
ZAC THOMPSON & EMILY HORN

DRAWN BY
ALBERTO ALBURQUERQUE

COLORED BY
RAÚL ANGULO

LETTERED BY
HASSAN OTSMANE-ELHAOU

VAULT COMICS PRESENTS

NO ONE'S ROSE

A NOTHING

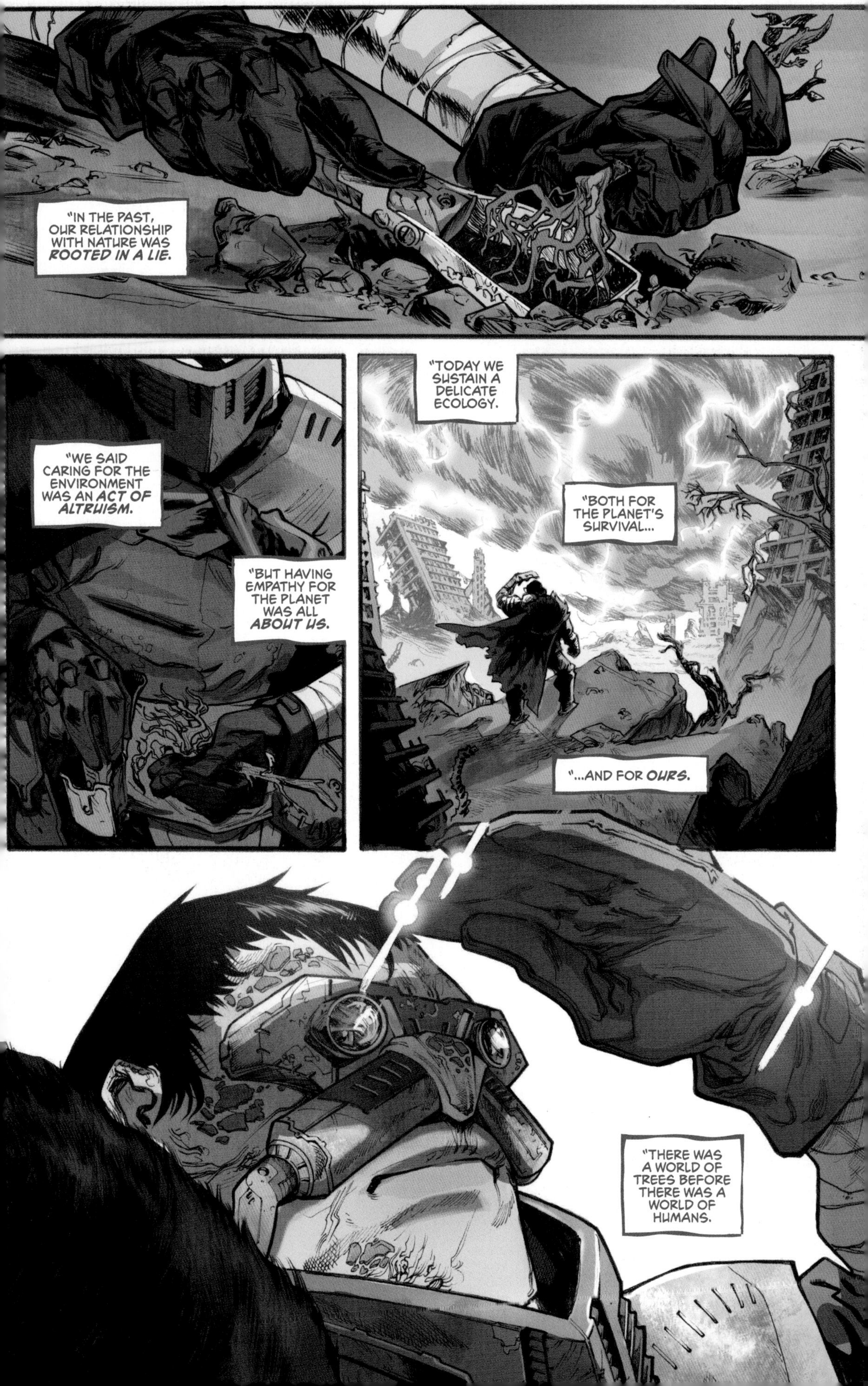
"IN THE PAST, OUR RELATIONSHIP WITH NATURE WAS ROOTED IN A LIE.
"WE SAID CARING FOR THE ENVIRONMENT WAS AN ACT OF ALTRUISM.
"BUT HAVING EMPATHY FOR THE PLANET WAS ALL ABOUT US.
"TODAY WE SUSTAIN A DELICATE ECOLOGY.
"BOTH FOR THE PLANET'S SURVIVAL...
"...AND FOR OURS.
"THERE WAS A WORLD OF TREES BEFORE THERE WAS A WORLD OF HUMANS.

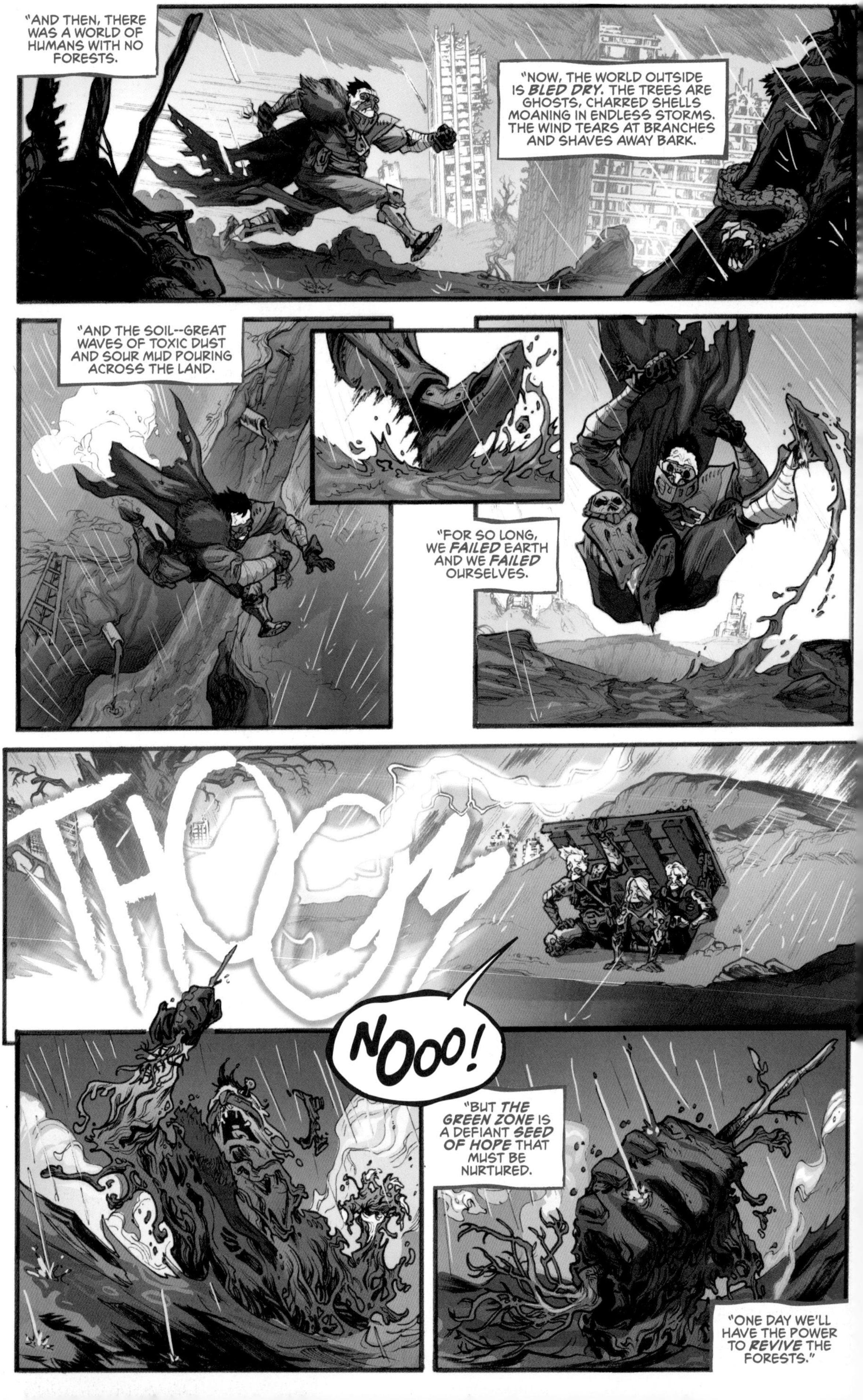

"AND THEN, THERE WAS A WORLD OF HUMANS WITH NO FORESTS.
"NOW, THE WORLD OUTSIDE IS BLED DRY. THE TREES ARE GHOSTS, CHARRED SHELLS MOANING IN ENDLESS STORMS. THE WIND TEARS AT BRANCHES AND SHAVES AWAY BARK.
"AND THE SOIL--GREAT WAVES OF TOXIC DUST AND SOUR MUD POURING ACROSS THE LAND.
"FOR SO LONG, WE FAILED EARTH AND WE FAILED OURSELVES.
THOOM
NOOO!
"BUT THE GREEN ZONE IS A DEFIANT SEED OF HOPE THAT MUST BE NURTURED.
"ONE DAY WE'LL HAVE THE POWER TO REVIVE THE FORESTS."

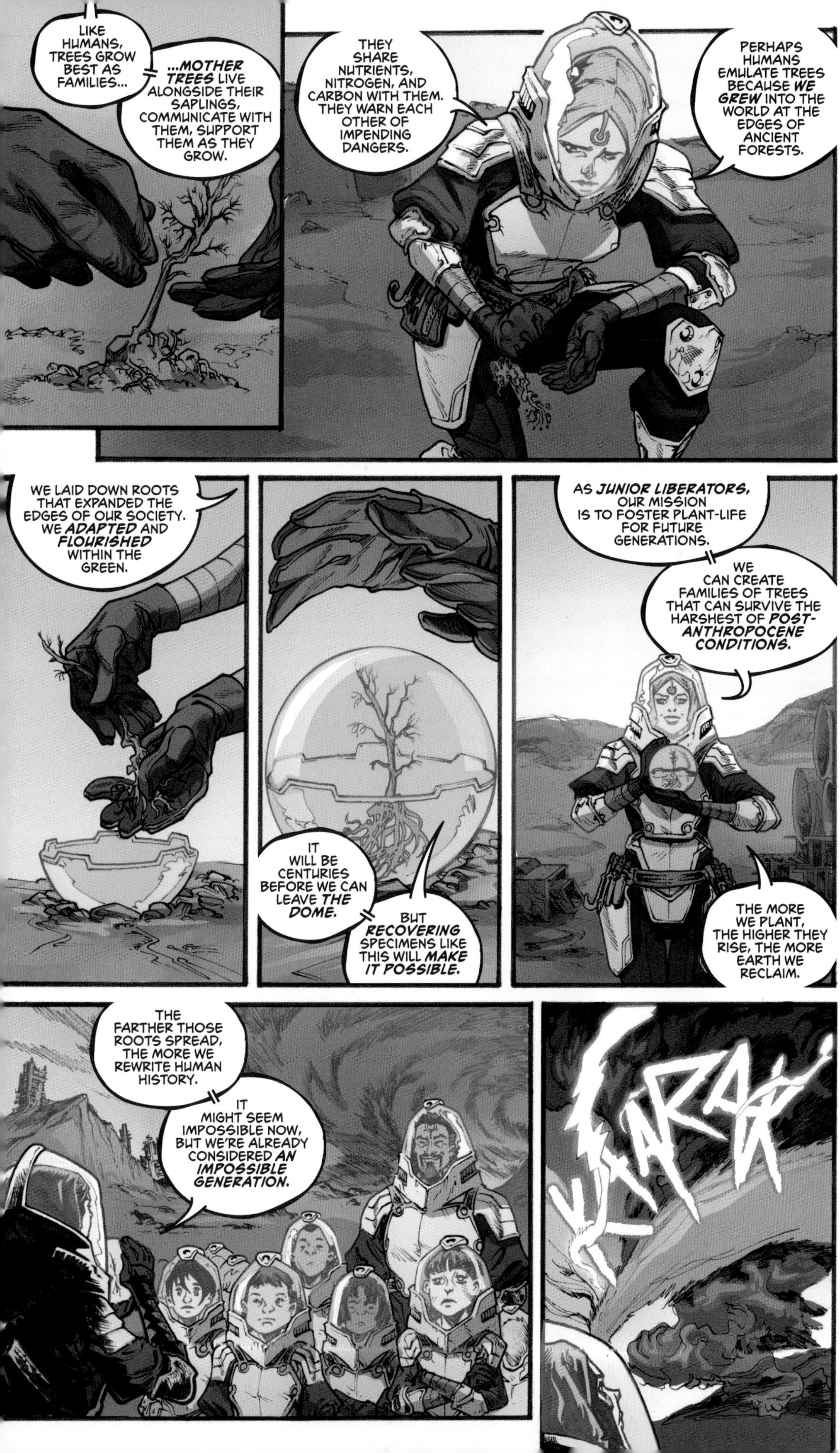

LIKE HUMANS, TREES GROW BEST AS FAMILIES...
...MOTHER TREES LIVE ALONGSIDE THEIR SAPLINGS, COMMUNICATE WITH THEM, SUPPORT THEM AS THEY GROW.
THEY SHARE NUTRIENTS, NITROGEN, AND CARBON WITH THEM. THEY WARN EACH OTHER OF IMPENDING DANGERS.
PERHAPS HUMANS EMULATE TREES BECAUSE WE GREW INTO THE WORLD AT THE EDGES OF ANCIENT FORESTS.
WE LAID DOWN ROOTS THAT EXPANDED THE EDGES OF OUR SOCIETY. WE ADAPTED AND FLOURISHED WITHIN THE GREEN.
IT WILL BE CENTURIES BEFORE WE CAN LEAVE THE DOME.
BUT RECOVERING SPECIMENS LIKE THIS WILL MAKE IT POSSIBLE.
AS JUNIOR LIBERATORS, OUR MISSION IS TO FOSTER PLANT-LIFE FOR FUTURE GENERATIONS.
WE CAN CREATE FAMILIES OF TREES THAT CAN SURVIVE THE HARSHEST OF POST-ANTHROPOCENE CONDITIONS.
THE MORE WE PLANT, THE HIGHER THEY RISE, THE MORE EARTH WE RECLAIM.
THE FARTHER THOSE ROOTS SPREAD, THE MORE WE REWRITE HUMAN HISTORY.
IT MIGHT SEEM IMPOSSIBLE NOW, BUT WE'RE ALREADY CONSIDERED AN IMPOSSIBLE GENERATION.
KRAK

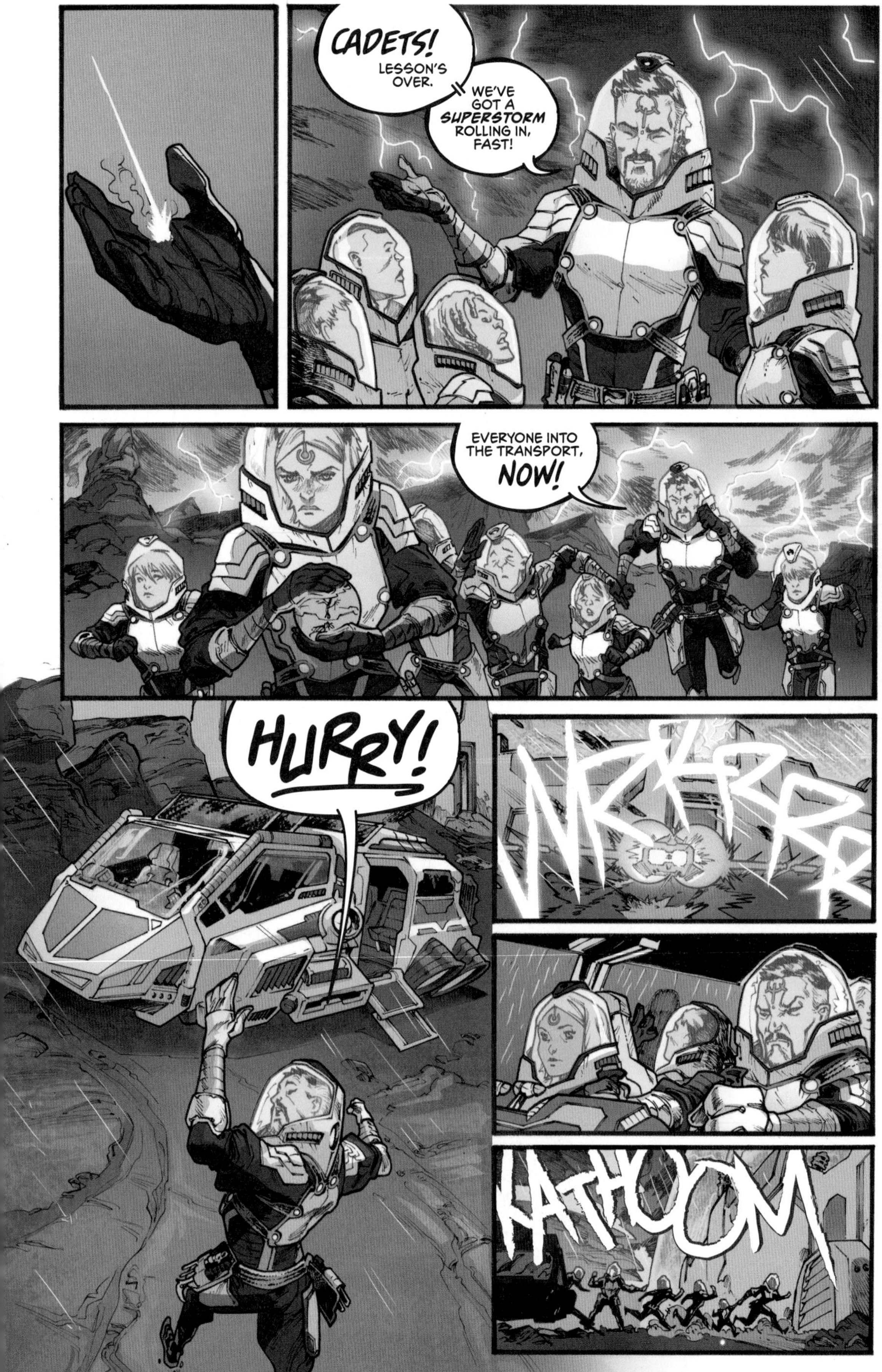
CADETS! LESSON'S OVER.
WE'VE GOT A SUPERSTORM ROLLING IN, FAST!
EVERYONE INTO THE TRANSPORT, NOW!
HURRY!
WRRRRR
KATHOOM

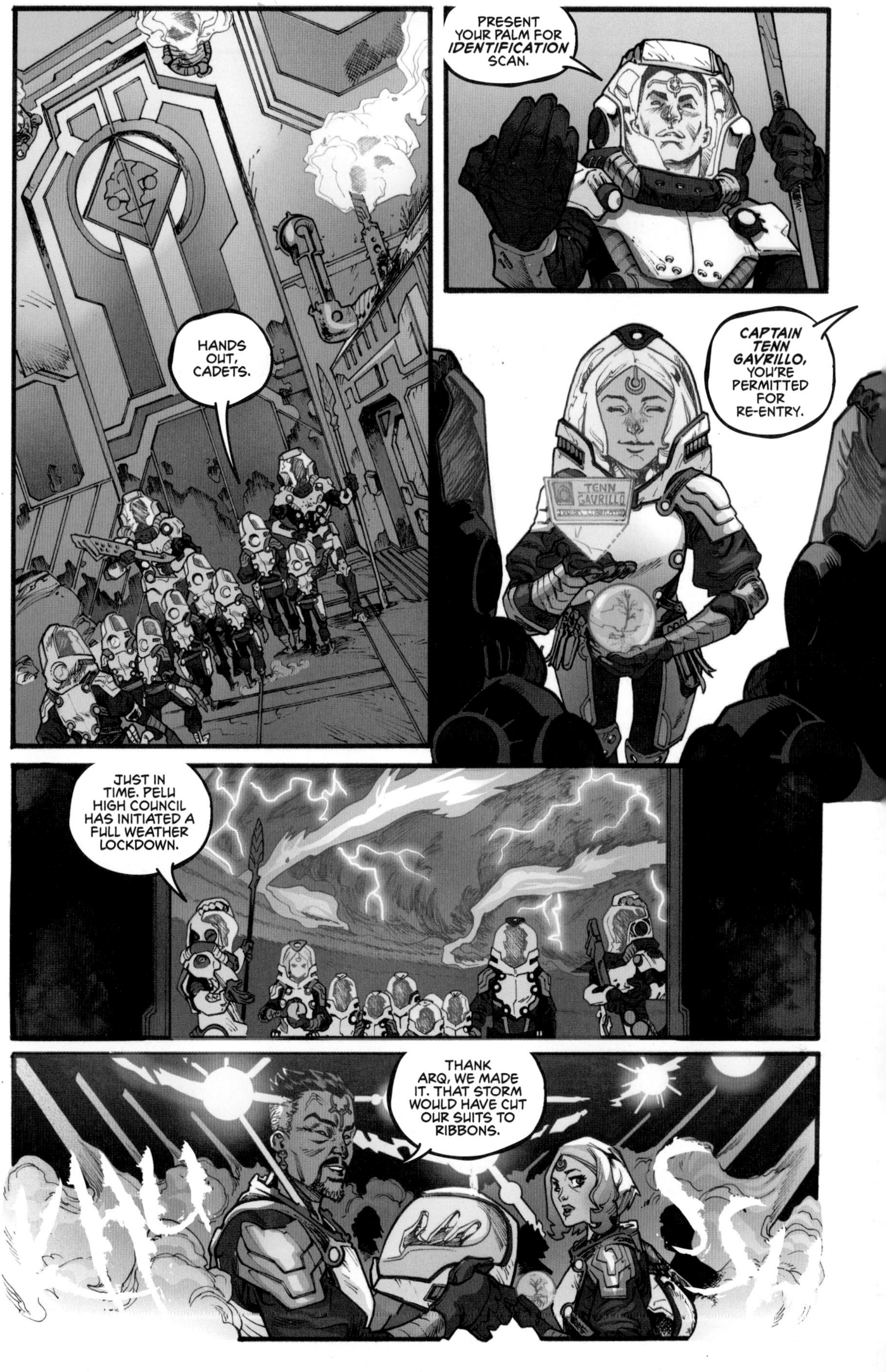
HANDS OUT, CADETS.
PRESENT YOUR PALM FOR *IDENTIFICATION* SCAN.
CAPTAIN TENN GAVRILLO, YOU'RE PERMITTED FOR RE-ENTRY.
TENN GAVRILLO
JUST IN TIME. PELU HIGH COUNCIL HAS INITIATED A FULL WEATHER LOCKDOWN.
THANK ARQ, WE MADE IT. THAT STORM WOULD HAVE CUT OUR SUITS TO RIBBONS.

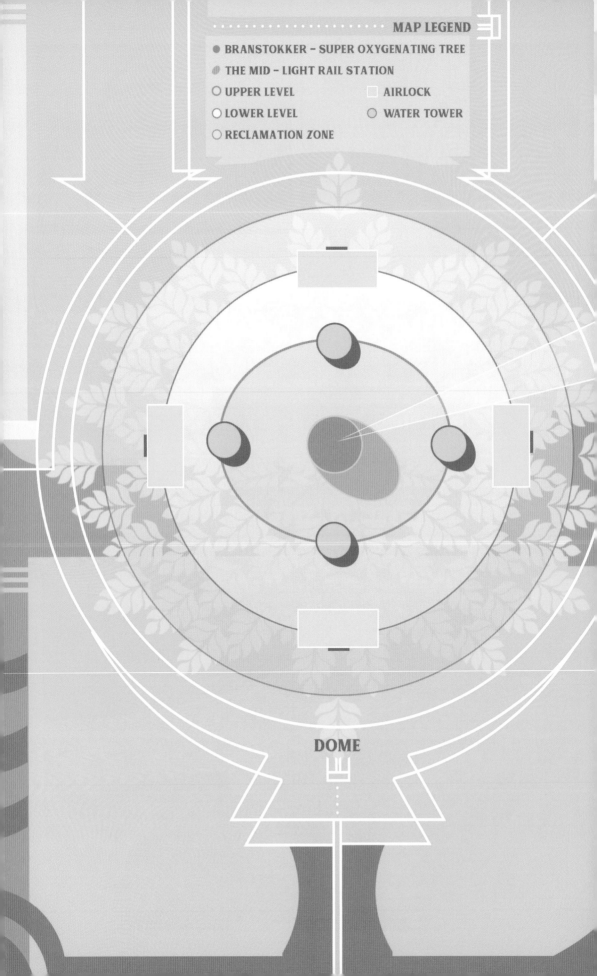

MAP LEGEND

● BRANSTOKKER – SUPER OXYGENATING TREE
◉ THE MID – LIGHT RAIL STATION
○ UPPER LEVEL   □ AIRLOCK
○ LOWER LEVEL   ◉ WATER TOWER
○ RECLAMATION ZONE

DOME

BRANSTOKKER

SUPER OXYGENATING TREE

IN THE LATE 21ST-CENTURY, RUNAWAY CLIMATE CHANGE CAUSES THE ANTHROPOCENE TO COLLAPSE, TRIGGERING EARTH'S SIXTH MASS EXTINCTION EVENT.

DROUGHT, RADIATION, RISING SEA LEVELS, FLOODING, POLLUTION, AND ERRATIC SUPER-STORMS RAVAGE AND RESHAPE THE SURFACE OF THE PLANET. CENTURIES PASS AND EARTH BECOMES A BARREN PLACE, INHOSPITABLE FOR MOST LIFE. AND YET, HUMANKIND ENDURES ON THE BRINK.

THANKS TO THE POST-ENVIRONMENTAL-LIBERATION-UNION A SOLUTION IS GROWN FROM THE DUST: A BIOME WITH HUMANKIND AT THE CENTRE. A FERTILE DOMED CITY BUILT RA-DIALLY AROUND AN ENORMOUS BIO-ENGINEERED TREE. THIS SUPER-OXYGENATING TREE CREATES A BREATHABLE ATMOSPHERE THAT HOUSES OVER 30,000 HUMAN LIVES. THE PEOPLE INSIDE HAVE FORMED A FULLY SUSTAINABLE, ZERO WASTE, AGRARIAN SOCIETY POWERED ENTIRELY BY RENEWABLE ENERGY.

THE ONCE VERDANT FORESTS THAT COVERED OUR PLANET ARE GONE.

ALL THAT REMAINS IS...

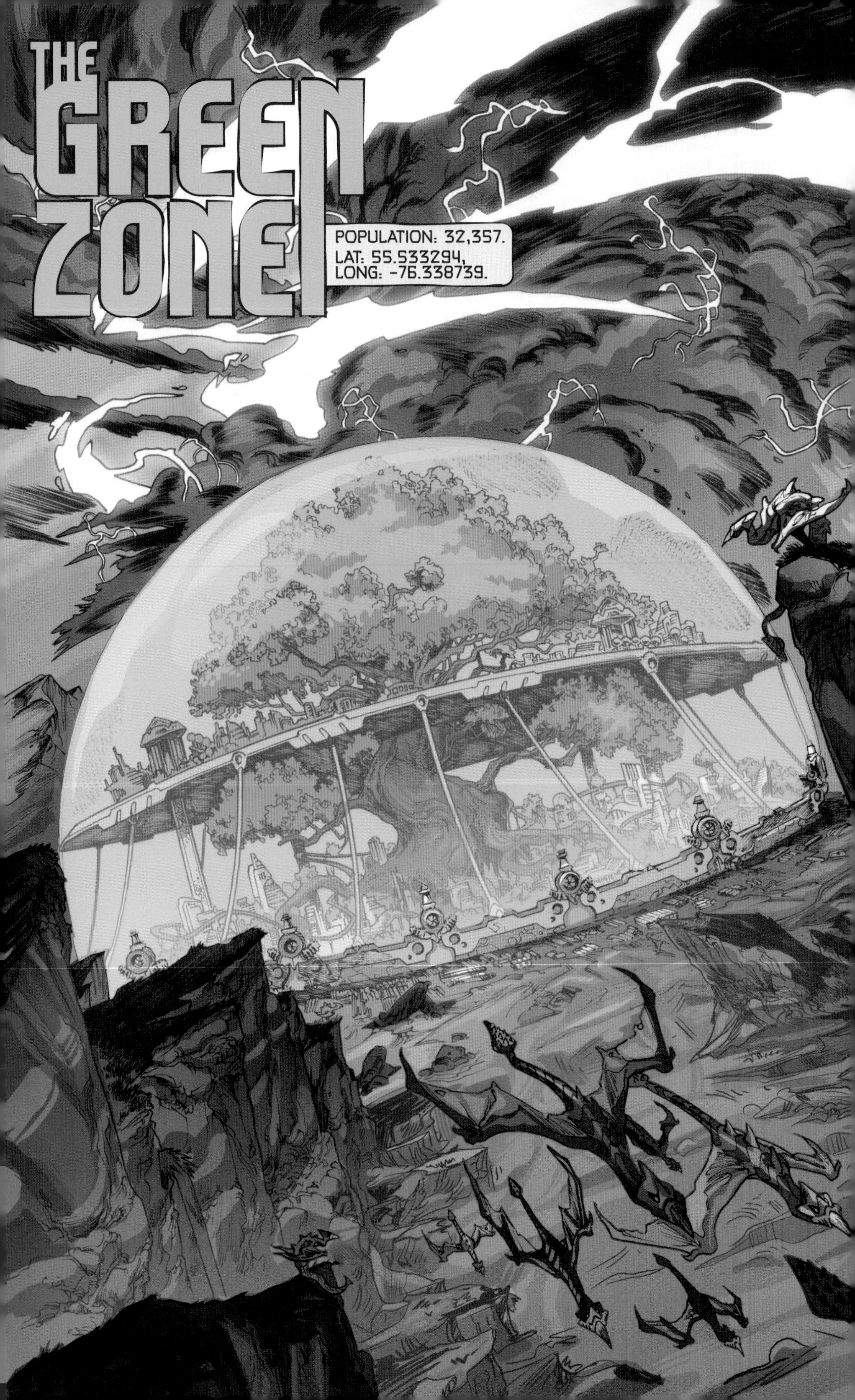
THE GREEN ZONE
POPULATION: 32,357.
LAT: 55.533294,
LONG: -76.338739.

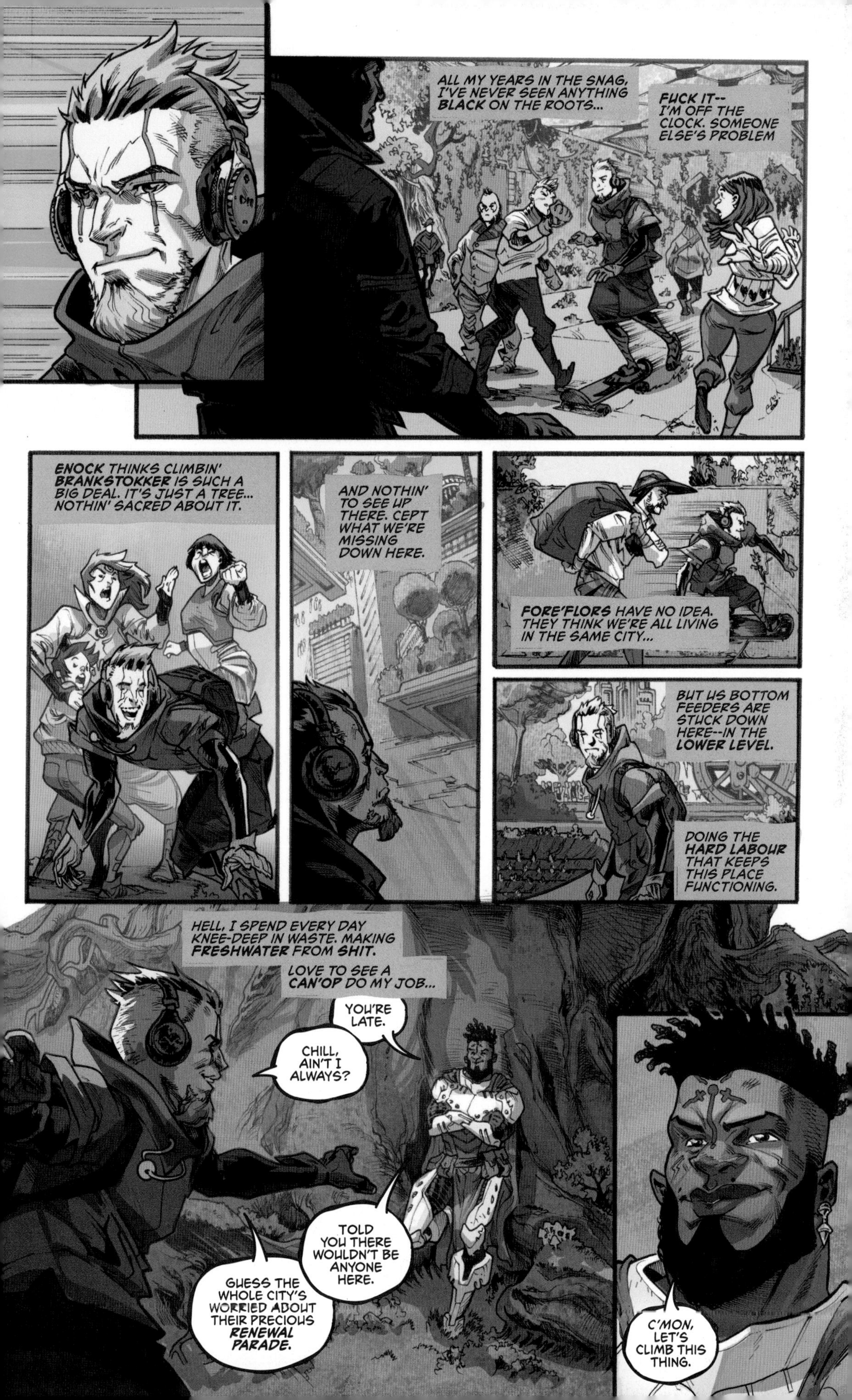
ALL MY YEARS IN THE SNAG, I'VE NEVER SEEN ANYTHING BLACK ON THE ROOTS...
FUCK IT-- I'M OFF THE CLOCK. SOMEONE ELSE'S PROBLEM
ENOCK THINKS CLIMBIN' BRANKSTOKKER IS SUCH A BIG DEAL. IT'S JUST A TREE... NOTHIN' SACRED ABOUT IT.
AND NOTHIN' TO SEE UP THERE. CEPT WHAT WE'RE MISSING DOWN HERE.
FORE'FLORS HAVE NO IDEA. THEY THINK WE'RE ALL LIVING IN THE SAME CITY...
BUT US BOTTOM FEEDERS ARE STUCK DOWN HERE--IN THE LOWER LEVEL.
DOING THE HARD LABOUR THAT KEEPS THIS PLACE FUNCTIONING.
HELL, I SPEND EVERY DAY KNEE-DEEP IN WASTE. MAKING FRESHWATER FROM SHIT.
LOVE TO SEE A CAN'OP DO MY JOB...
YOU'RE LATE.
CHILL, AIN'T I ALWAYS?
TOLD YOU THERE WOULDN'T BE ANYONE HERE.
GUESS THE WHOLE CITY'S WORRIED ABOUT THEIR PRECIOUS RENEWAL PARADE.
C'MON, LET'S CLIMB THIS THING.

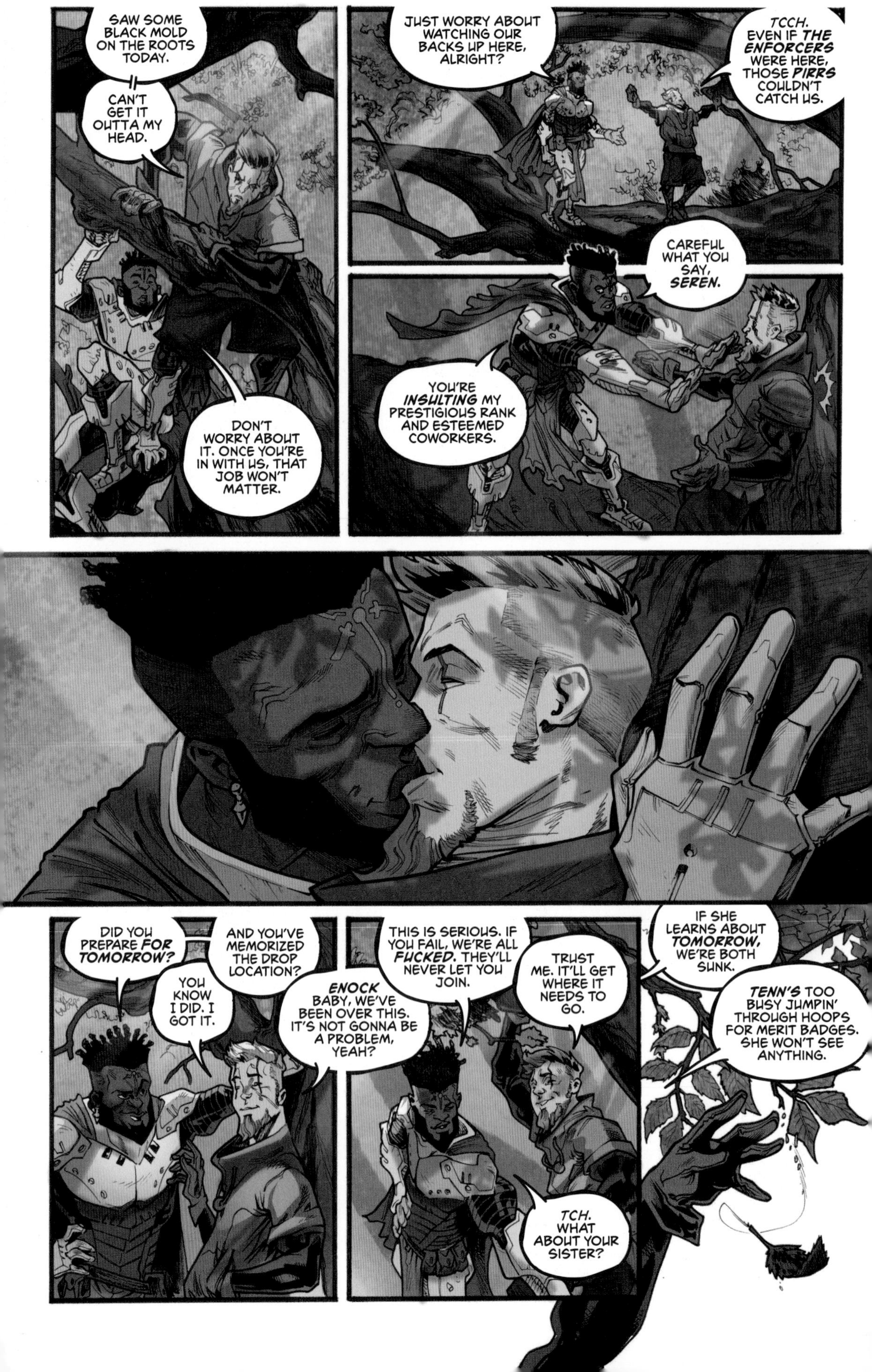
SAW SOME BLACK MOLD ON THE ROOTS TODAY.
CAN'T GET IT OUTTA MY HEAD.
DON'T WORRY ABOUT IT. ONCE YOU'RE IN WITH US, THAT JOB WON'T MATTER.
JUST WORRY ABOUT WATCHING OUR BACKS UP HERE, ALRIGHT?
TCCH. EVEN IF THE ENFORCERS WERE HERE, THOSE PIRRS COULDN'T CATCH US.
CAREFUL WHAT YOU SAY, SEREN.
YOU'RE INSULTING MY PRESTIGIOUS RANK AND ESTEEMED COWORKERS.
DID YOU PREPARE FOR TOMORROW?
AND YOU'VE MEMORIZED THE DROP LOCATION?
YOU KNOW I DID. I GOT IT.
ENOCK BABY, WE'VE BEEN OVER THIS. IT'S NOT GONNA BE A PROBLEM, YEAH?
THIS IS SERIOUS. IF YOU FAIL, WE'RE ALL FUCKED. THEY'LL NEVER LET YOU JOIN.
TRUST ME. IT'LL GET WHERE IT NEEDS TO GO.
TCH. WHAT ABOUT YOUR SISTER?
IF SHE LEARNS ABOUT TOMORROW, WE'RE BOTH SUNK.
TENN'S TOO BUSY JUMPIN' THROUGH HOOPS FOR MERIT BADGES. SHE WON'T SEE ANYTHING.

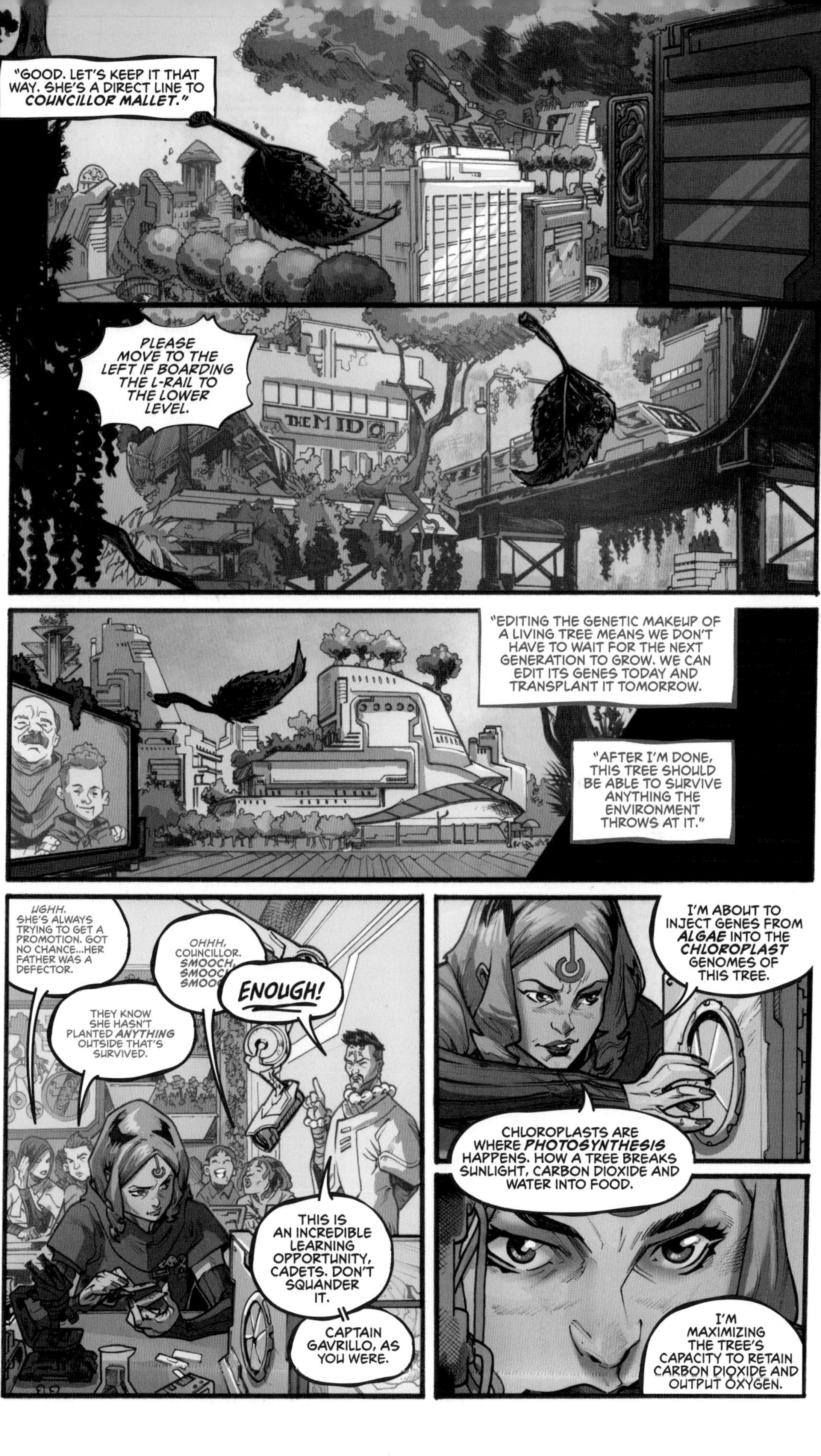
"GOOD. LET'S KEEP IT THAT WAY. SHE'S A DIRECT LINE TO *COUNCILLOR MALLET*."
PLEASE MOVE TO THE LEFT IF BOARDING THE L-RAIL TO THE LOWER LEVEL.
THE MID
"EDITING THE GENETIC MAKEUP OF A LIVING TREE MEANS WE DON'T HAVE TO WAIT FOR THE NEXT GENERATION TO GROW. WE CAN EDIT ITS GENES TODAY AND TRANSPLANT IT TOMORROW.
"AFTER I'M DONE, THIS TREE SHOULD BE ABLE TO SURVIVE ANYTHING THE ENVIRONMENT THROWS AT IT."
UGHH. SHE'S ALWAYS TRYING TO GET A PROMOTION. GOT NO CHANCE...HER FATHER WAS A DEFECTOR.
THEY KNOW SHE HASN'T PLANTED *ANYTHING* OUTSIDE THAT'S SURVIVED.
OHHH, COUNCILLOR. *SMOOCH, SMOOCH, SMOOCH*
ENOUGH!
THIS IS AN INCREDIBLE LEARNING OPPORTUNITY, CADETS. DON'T SQUANDER IT.
CAPTAIN GAVRILLO, AS YOU WERE.
I'M ABOUT TO INJECT GENES FROM *ALGAE* INTO THE *CHLOROPLAST* GENOMES OF THIS TREE.
CHLOROPLASTS ARE WHERE *PHOTOSYNTHESIS* HAPPENS. HOW A TREE BREAKS SUNLIGHT, CARBON DIOXIDE AND WATER INTO FOOD.
I'M MAXIMIZING THE TREE'S CAPACITY TO RETAIN CARBON DIOXIDE AND OUTPUT OXYGEN.

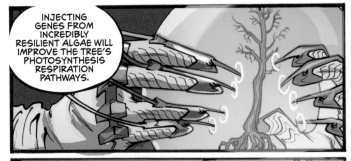

INJECTING GENES FROM INCREDIBLY RESILIENT ALGAE WILL IMPROVE THE TREE'S PHOTOSYNTHESIS RESPIRATION PATHWAYS.

CARBON DIOXIDE TURNS TO CARBON, WHICH IS THE BUILDING BLOCK OF ORGANIC MATERIAL. IF THIS WORKS, IT WILL GROW FASTER AND OUTPUT MORE BREATHABLE OXYGEN THAN ANY OTHER TREE IN THE DOME.

I PERFORMED SIMILAR PROCEDURES ON *EVERYTHING* HERE. EACH WAS RECOVERED FROM OUTSIDE THE DOME. ONCE STUNTED AND *BARELY LIVING,* THESE PLANTS ARE *NOW THRIVING.*

THAT'S IT FOR TIME. YOU'RE DISMISSED CADETS.

TENN, A WORD.

AS *HEAD OF RESOURCES,* I'VE BEEN ENTRUSTED TO SELECT A FEW ENGINEERS FOR ADVANCED FIELD RESEARCH POSITIONS.

PERFECT THE *METHANE UPTAKE* IN CELLULAR RESPIRATION AND THE POSITION IS YOURS.

KEEP UP THE GOOD WORK, THE PARTY NEEDS MORE CAPTAINS LIKE YOU.

THANK YOU, SIR.

I'M HONORED TO SERVE THE *POST ENVIRONMENTAL LIBERATION UNION* AND JORO ARQ AND *YOU* AND--

YOU'RE DISMISSED, CAPTAIN GAVRILLO.

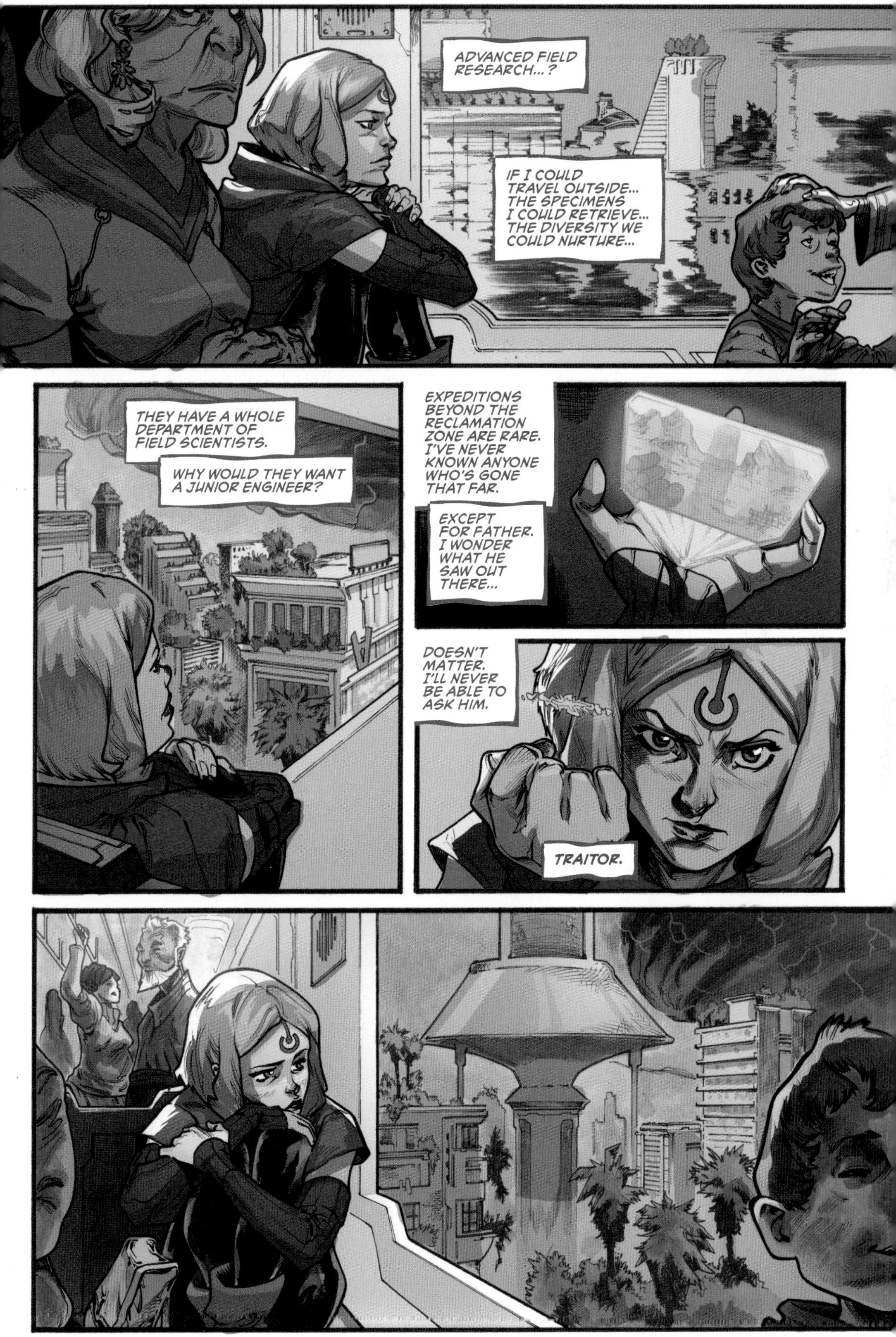
ADVANCED FIELD RESEARCH...?
IF I COULD TRAVEL OUTSIDE... THE SPECIMENS I COULD RETRIEVE... THE DIVERSITY WE COULD NURTURE...
THEY HAVE A WHOLE DEPARTMENT OF FIELD SCIENTISTS.
WHY WOULD THEY WANT A JUNIOR ENGINEER?
EXPEDITIONS BEYOND THE RECLAMATION ZONE ARE RARE. I'VE NEVER KNOWN ANYONE WHO'S GONE THAT FAR.
EXCEPT FOR FATHER. I WONDER WHAT HE SAW OUT THERE...
DOESN'T MATTER. I'LL NEVER BE ABLE TO ASK HIM.
TRAITOR.

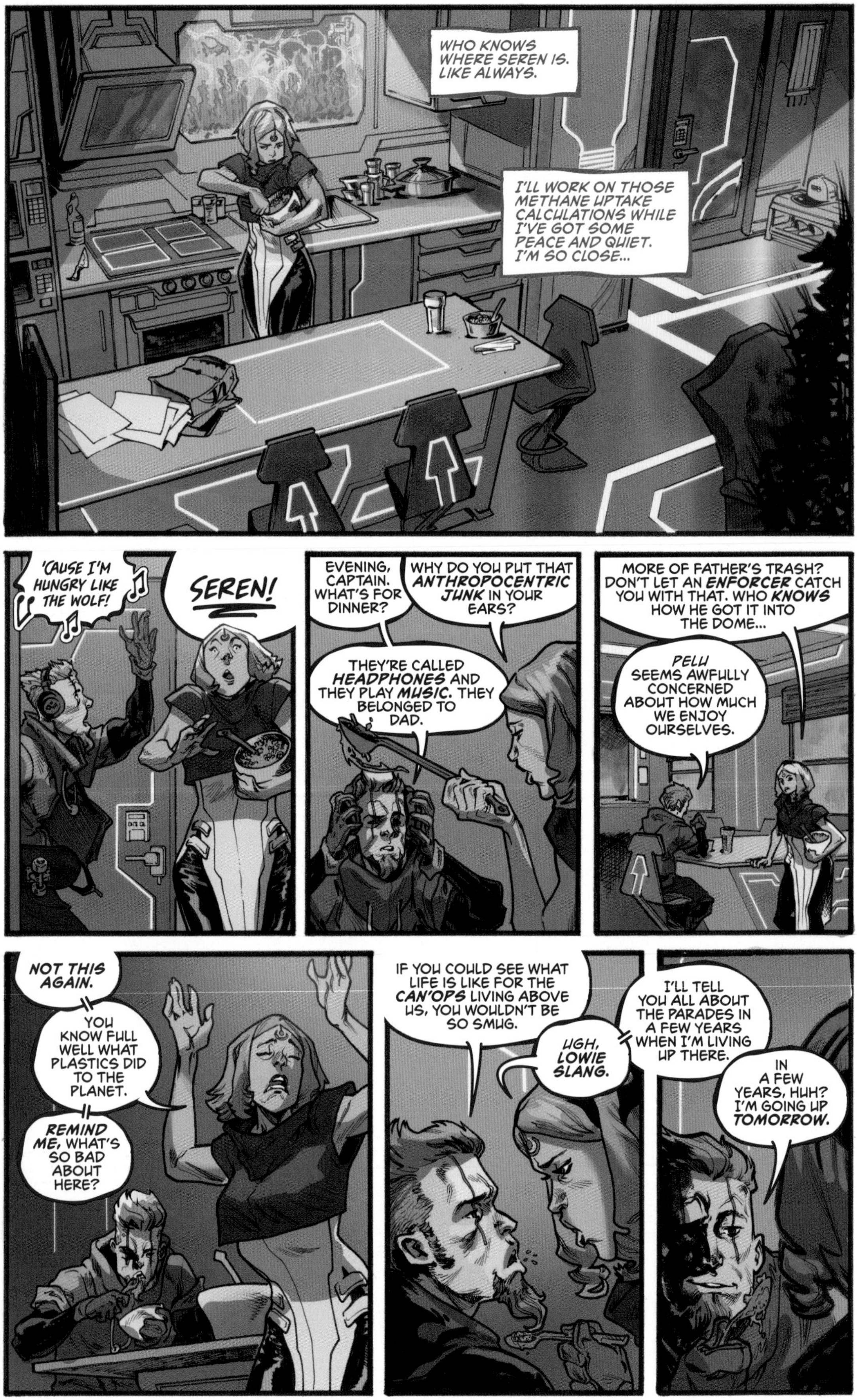
WHO KNOWS WHERE SEREN IS. LIKE ALWAYS.
I'LL WORK ON THOSE METHANE UPTAKE CALCULATIONS WHILE I'VE GOT SOME PEACE AND QUIET. I'M SO CLOSE...
'CAUSE I'M HUNGRY LIKE THE WOLF!
SEREN!
EVENING, CAPTAIN. WHAT'S FOR DINNER?
WHY DO YOU PUT THAT ANTHROPOCENTRIC JUNK IN YOUR EARS?
THEY'RE CALLED HEADPHONES AND THEY PLAY MUSIC. THEY BELONGED TO DAD.
MORE OF FATHER'S TRASH? DON'T LET AN ENFORCER CATCH YOU WITH THAT. WHO KNOWS HOW HE GOT IT INTO THE DOME...
PELU SEEMS AWFULLY CONCERNED ABOUT HOW MUCH WE ENJOY OURSELVES.
NOT THIS AGAIN.
YOU KNOW FULL WELL WHAT PLASTICS DID TO THE PLANET.
REMIND ME, WHAT'S SO BAD ABOUT HERE?
IF YOU COULD SEE WHAT LIFE IS LIKE FOR THE CAN'OPS LIVING ABOVE US, YOU WOULDN'T BE SO SMUG.
UGH, LOWIE SLANG.
I'LL TELL YOU ALL ABOUT THE PARADES IN A FEW YEARS WHEN I'M LIVING UP THERE.
IN A FEW YEARS, HUH? I'M GOING UP TOMORROW.

REMEMBER HOW DAD USED TO SAY, *"THE GREEN ZONE IS LIKE A COLLECTION OF ISLANDS IN THE SEA, SEPARATE ON THE SURFACE BUT CONNECTED IN THE DEEP."*

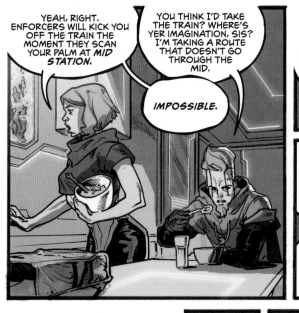

YEAH, RIGHT. ENFORCERS WILL KICK YOU OFF THE TRAIN THE MOMENT THEY SCAN YOUR PALM AT *MID STATION.*

YOU THINK I'D TAKE THE TRAIN? WHERE'S YER IMAGINATION, SIS? I'M TAKING A ROUTE THAT DOESN'T GO THROUGH THE MID.

IMPOSSIBLE.

PELLI'S BUILT A CONTROLLED, SELF-SUSTAINING ECOSYSTEM. EVERYTHING IS LINKED TO EVERYTHING ELSE.

THEY DON'T WANT YOU TO LOOK TOO CLOSELY AT ANYTHING THEY'VE BUILT. *THAT'S* WHAT GOT FATHER KILLED. LUCKILY, YOU'RE THEIR LITTLE PAWN--

OK. ENOUGH WITH THE CONSPIRACY THEORIES. THE RENEWAL PARADE WILL HAVE THE UPPER LEVEL ON COMPLETE LOCKDOWN.

THERE'S NO WAY UP THERE. IF YOU KNOW ONE, THEN SPIT IT OUT. TELL ME WHAT YOU SEE THAT I DON'T.

NAH. YOU COULDN'T HANDLE IT.

HAH, I *KNEW* THERE'S NO OTHER WAY.

YOU DON'T HAVE TO *LIE* TO IMPRESS ME. YOU'RE FULL OF--

WATER.

IT'S THE ONE THING THAT TRAVELS THIS DOME UNCHECKED.

I SPEND EVERY DAY UNDERNEATH THIS CITY, I SEE EVERYTHING MOVE THROUGH THIS PLACE.

THERE ARE FOUR WATER TOWERS IN THE DOME. EACH ONE FILLS EVERY FORTY-FIVE MINUTES AND FEEDS BOTH LEVELS.

THAT GIVES ME PLENTY OF TIME TO GET INSIDE AND CLIMB ALL THE WAY--

I SAID *ENOUGH!*

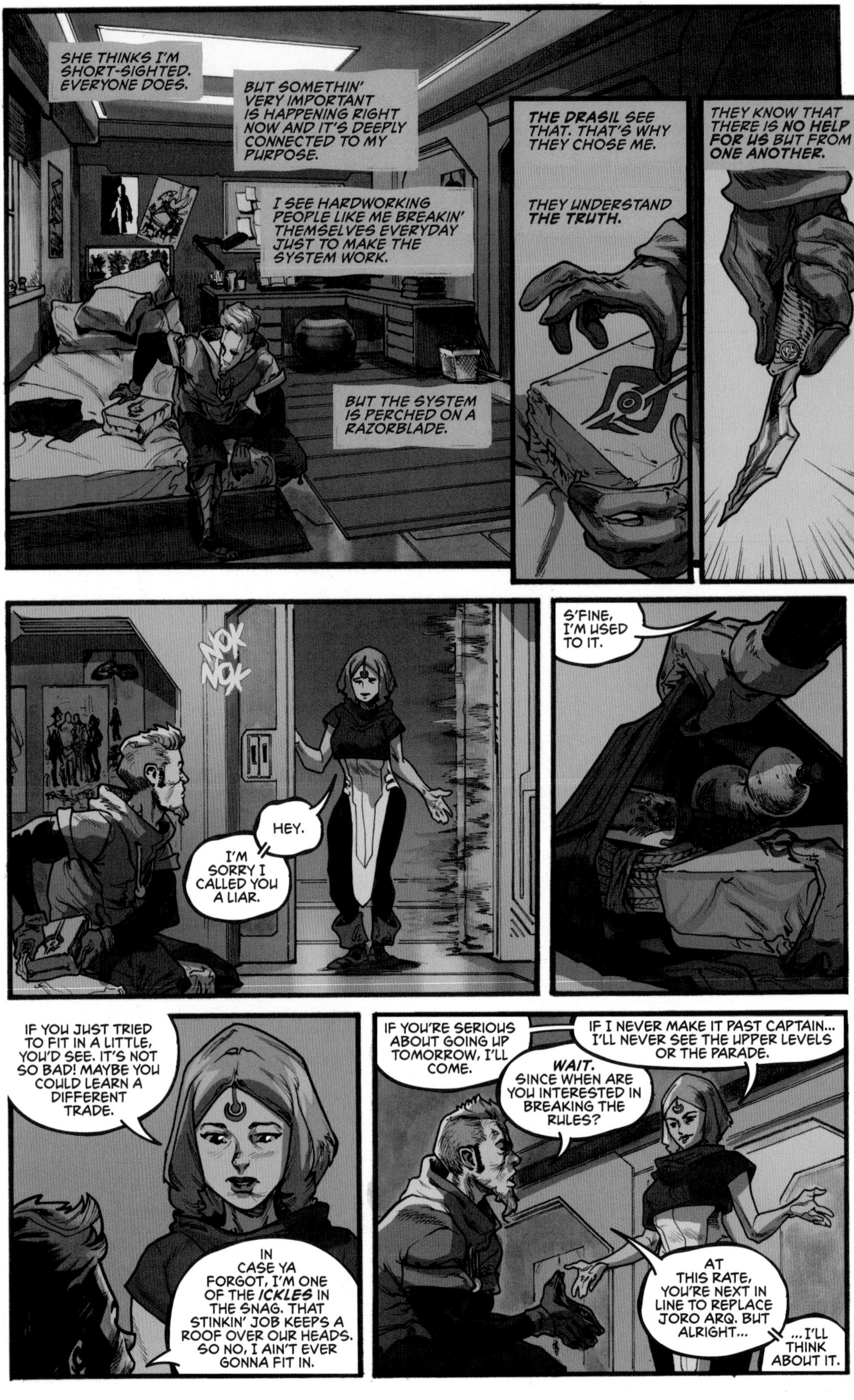
SHE THINKS I'M SHORT-SIGHTED. EVERYONE DOES.
BUT SOMETHIN' VERY IMPORTANT IS HAPPENING RIGHT NOW AND IT'S DEEPLY CONNECTED TO MY PURPOSE.
I SEE HARDWORKING PEOPLE LIKE ME BREAKIN' THEMSELVES EVERYDAY JUST TO MAKE THE SYSTEM WORK.
BUT THE SYSTEM IS PERCHED ON A RAZORBLADE.
THE DRASIL SEE THAT. THAT'S WHY THEY CHOSE ME.
THEY UNDERSTAND THE TRUTH.
THEY KNOW THAT THERE IS NO HELP FOR US BUT FROM ONE ANOTHER.
NOK NOK
HEY.
I'M SORRY I CALLED YOU A LIAR.
S'FINE, I'M USED TO IT.
IF YOU JUST TRIED TO FIT IN A LITTLE, YOU'D SEE. IT'S NOT SO BAD! MAYBE YOU COULD LEARN A DIFFERENT TRADE.
IN CASE YA FORGOT, I'M ONE OF THE ICKLES IN THE SNAG. THAT STINKIN' JOB KEEPS A ROOF OVER OUR HEADS. SO NO, I AIN'T EVER GONNA FIT IN.
IF YOU'RE SERIOUS ABOUT GOING UP TOMORROW, I'LL COME.
IF I NEVER MAKE IT PAST CAPTAIN... I'LL NEVER SEE THE UPPER LEVELS OR THE PARADE.
WAIT. SINCE WHEN ARE YOU INTERESTED IN BREAKING THE RULES?
AT THIS RATE, YOU'RE NEXT IN LINE TO REPLACE JORO ARQ. BUT ALRIGHT...
...I'LL THINK ABOUT IT.

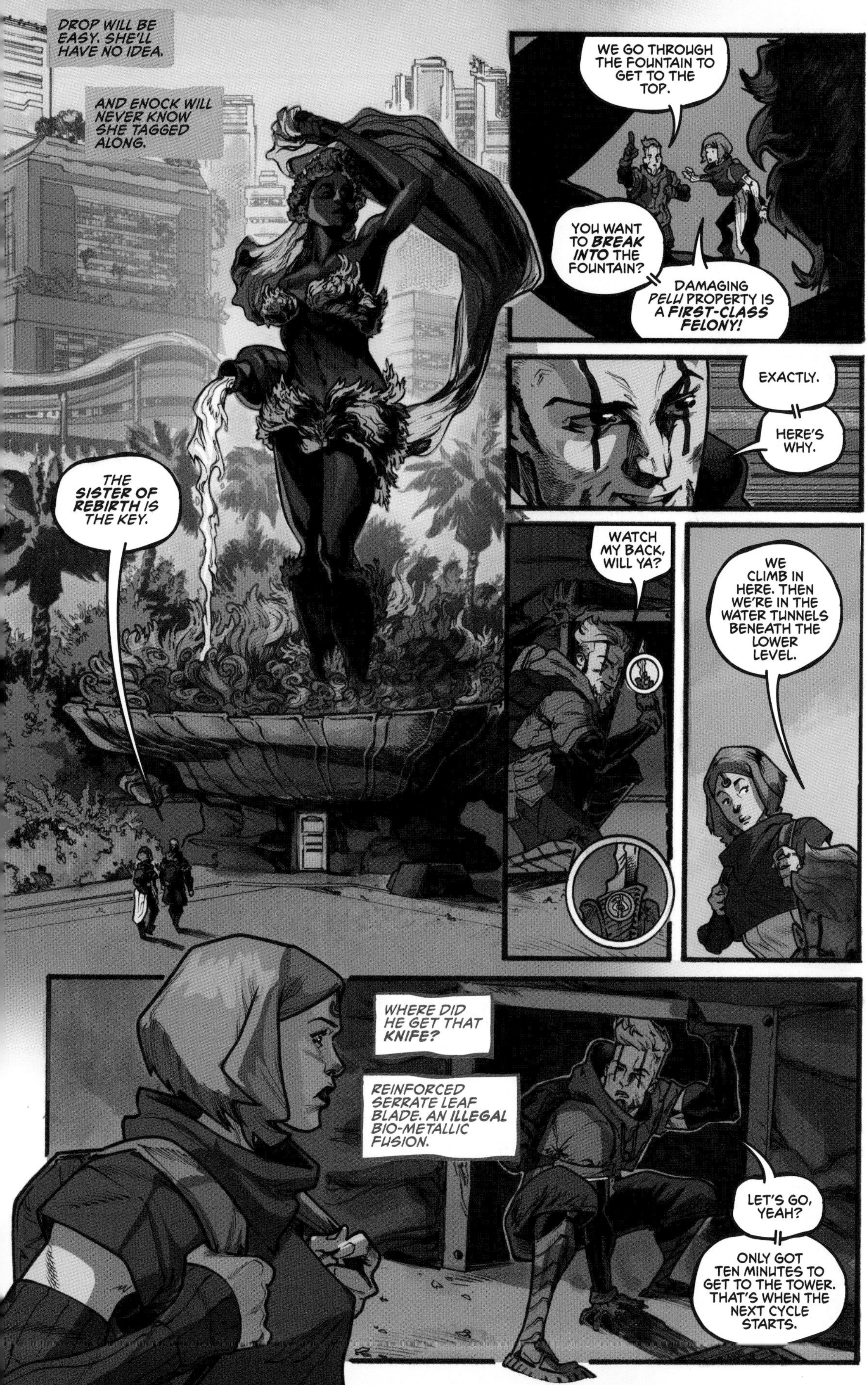
DROP WILL BE EASY. SHE'LL HAVE NO IDEA.
AND ENOCK WILL NEVER KNOW SHE TAGGED ALONG.
THE SISTER OF REBIRTH IS THE KEY.
WE GO THROUGH THE FOUNTAIN TO GET TO THE TOP.
YOU WANT TO BREAK INTO THE FOUNTAIN?
DAMAGING PELU PROPERTY IS A FIRST-CLASS FELONY!
EXACTLY.
HERE'S WHY.
WATCH MY BACK, WILL YA?
WE CLIMB IN HERE. THEN WE'RE IN THE WATER TUNNELS BENEATH THE LOWER LEVEL.
WHERE DID HE GET THAT KNIFE?
REINFORCED SERRATE LEAF BLADE. AN ILLEGAL BIO-METALLIC FUSION.
LET'S GO, YEAH?
ONLY GOT TEN MINUTES TO GET TO THE TOWER. THAT'S WHEN THE NEXT CYCLE STARTS.

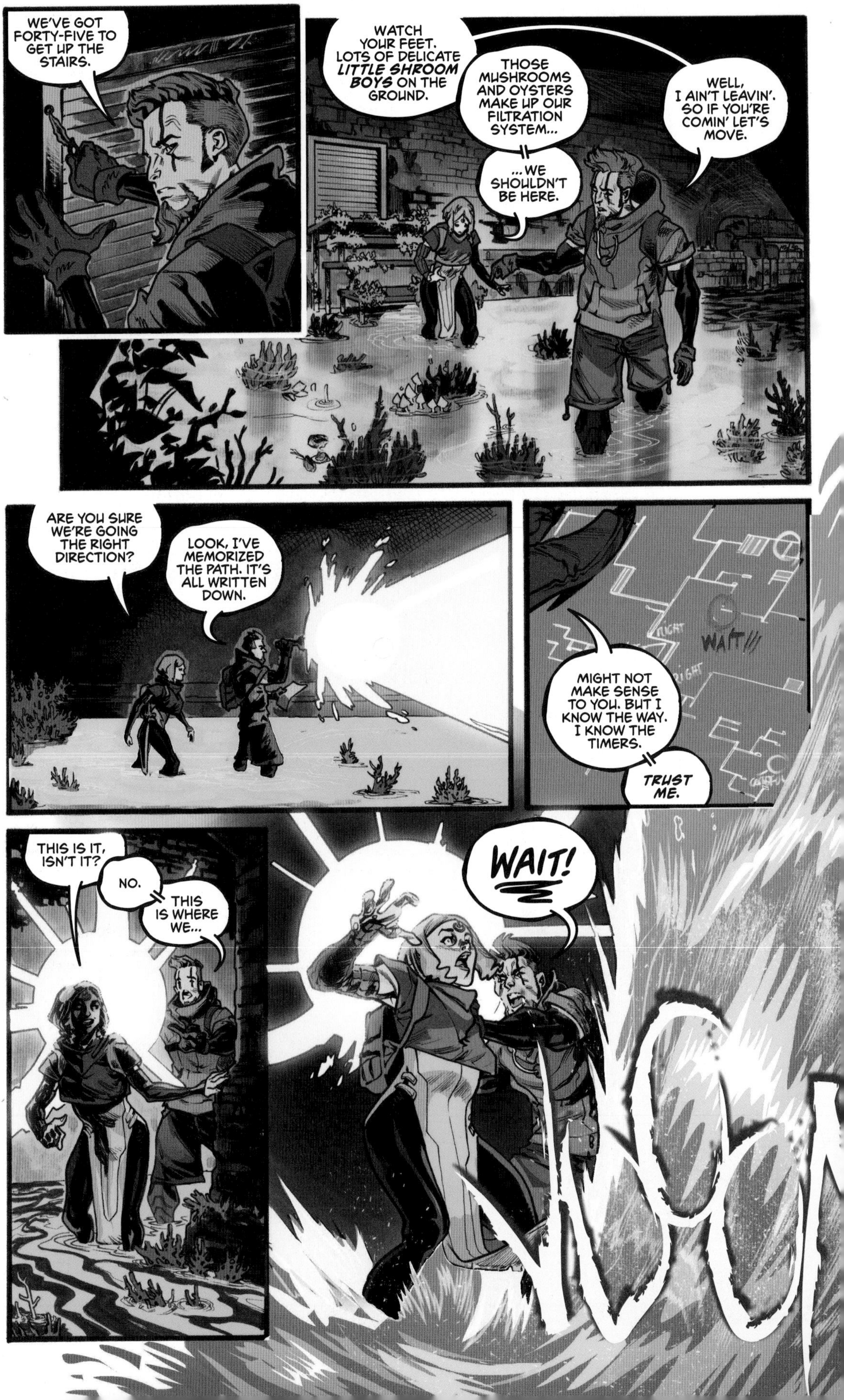
WE'VE GOT FORTY-FIVE TO GET UP THE STAIRS.
WATCH YOUR FEET. LOTS OF DELICATE LITTLE SHROOM BOYS ON THE GROUND.
THOSE MUSHROOMS AND OYSTERS MAKE UP OUR FILTRATION SYSTEM...
...WE SHOULDN'T BE HERE.
WELL, I AIN'T LEAVIN'. SO IF YOU'RE COMIN' LET'S MOVE.
ARE YOU SURE WE'RE GOING THE RIGHT DIRECTION?
LOOK, I'VE MEMORIZED THE PATH. IT'S ALL WRITTEN DOWN.
RIGHT
WAIT!!!
RIGHT
MIGHT NOT MAKE SENSE TO YOU. BUT I KNOW THE WAY. I KNOW THE TIMERS.
TRUST ME.
THIS IS IT, ISN'T IT?
NO.
THIS IS WHERE WE...
WAIT!

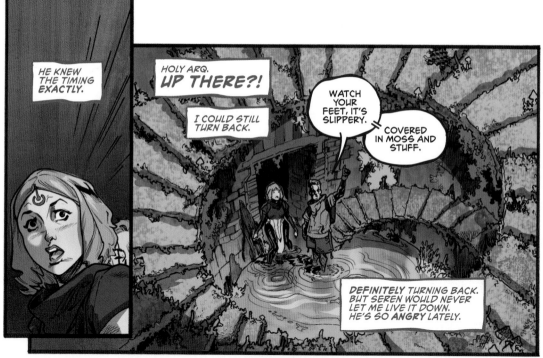

HE KNEW THE TIMING EXACTLY.

HOLY ARQ. *UP THERE?!*

I COULD STILL TURN BACK.

WATCH YOUR FEET, IT'S SLIPPERY.

COVERED IN MOSS AND STUFF.

DEFINITELY TURNING BACK. BUT SEREN WOULD NEVER LET ME LIVE IT DOWN. HE'S SO *ANGRY* LATELY.

HE'S GOTTEN US THIS FAR. ALWAYS LED US IN THE RIGHT DIRECTION, TAKING CARE OF ME WHEN NO ONE ELSE WOULD. BUT, THIS FEELS DIFFERENT...

...WHAT HAVE YOU GOTTEN TANGLED UP IN SEREN?

HE'S MOVING TOO FAST.

I CAN'T KEEP UP.

DON'T PANIC.

ONE STEP AT A TIME.

SEREN!

HUH?

KRSSH

≈GRRGLLE≈

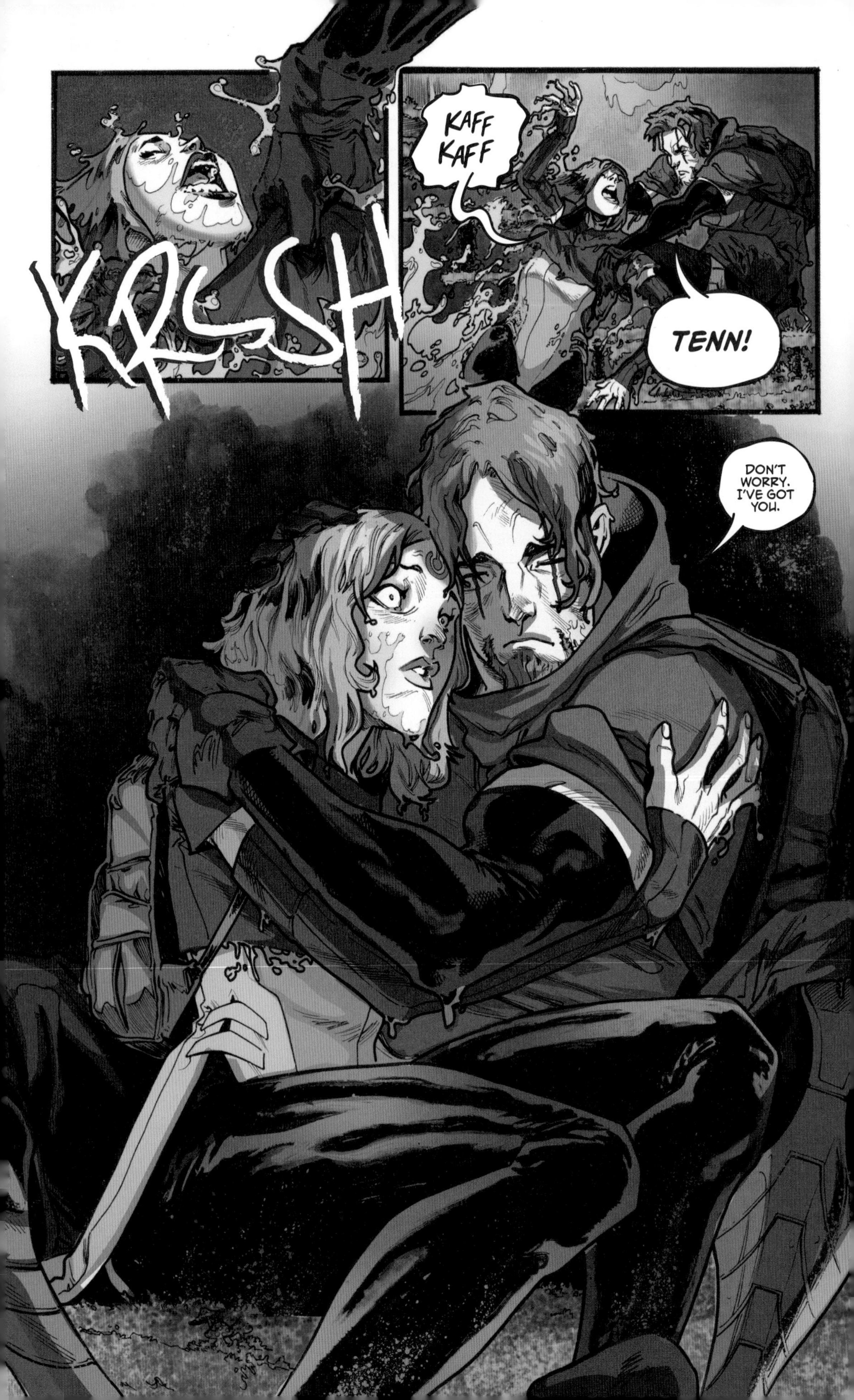
KRSSH
KAFF KAFF
TENN!
DON'T WORRY. I'VE GOT YOU.

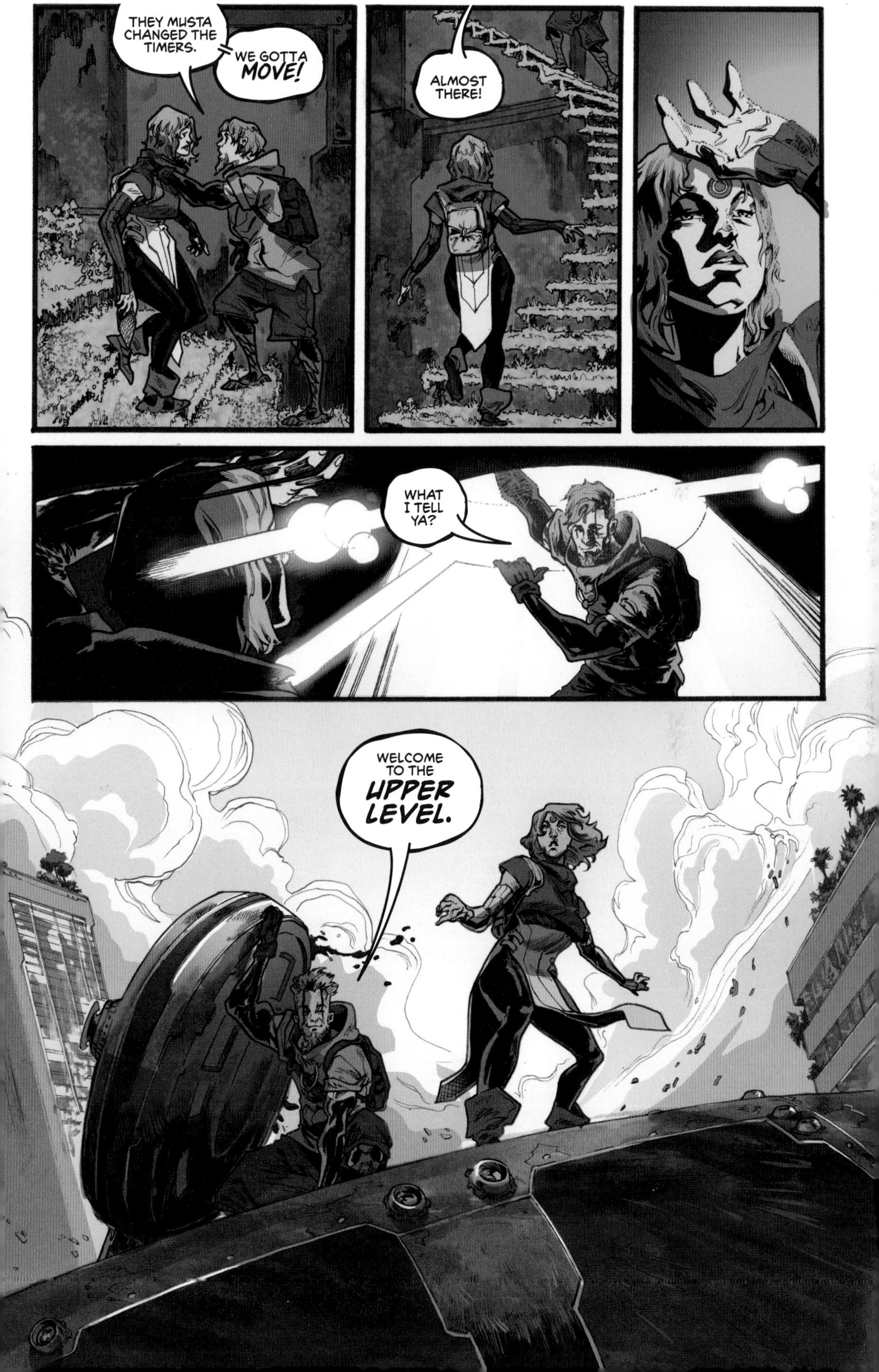

THEY MUSTA CHANGED THE TIMERS.
WE GOTTA MOVE!
ALMOST THERE!
WHAT I TELL YA?
WELCOME TO THE UPPER LEVEL.

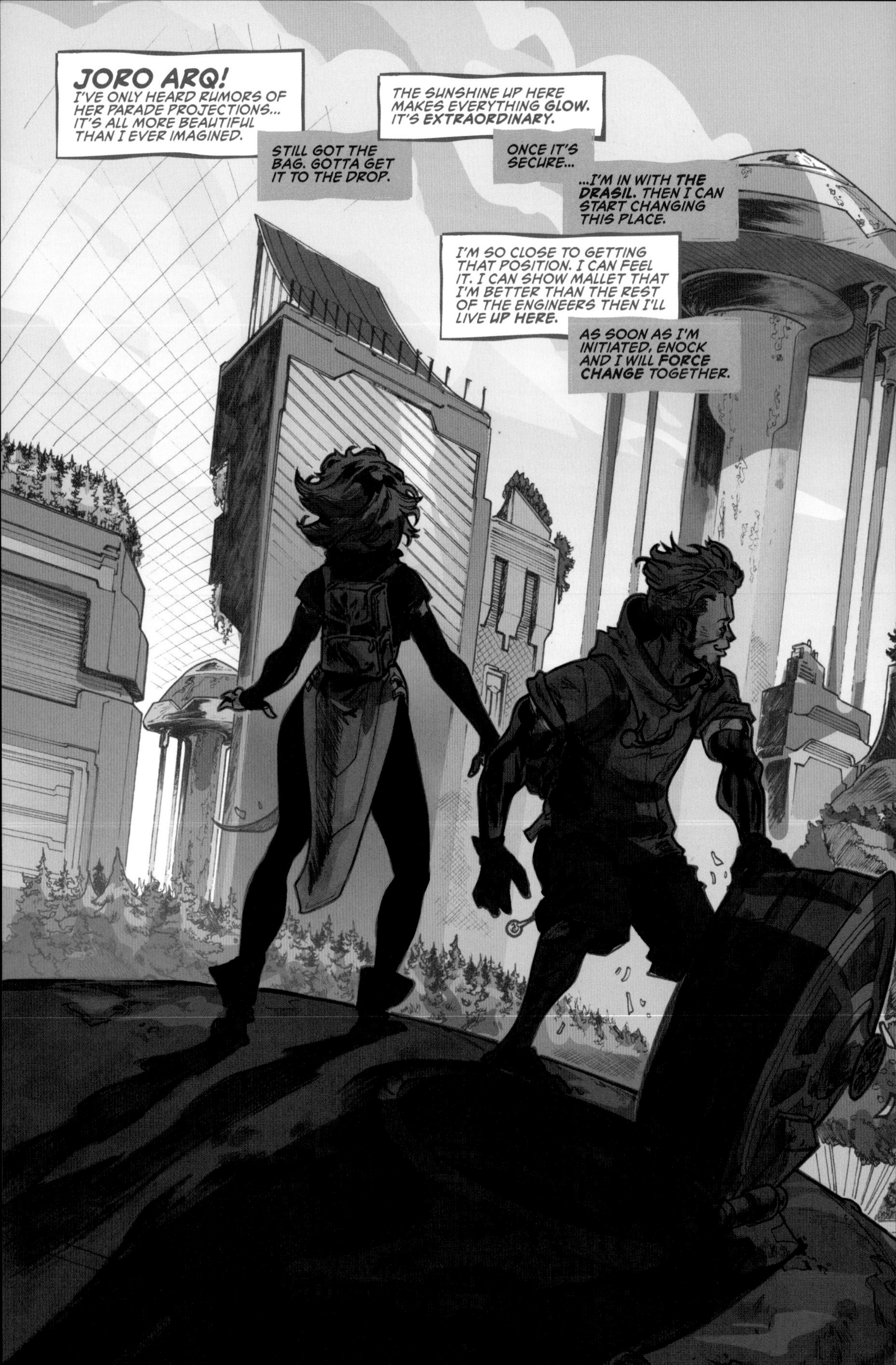

JORO ARQ! I'VE ONLY HEARD RUMORS OF HER PARADE PROJECTIONS... IT'S ALL MORE BEAUTIFUL THAN I EVER IMAGINED.
STILL GOT THE BAG. GOTTA GET IT TO THE DROP.
THE SUNSHINE UP HERE MAKES EVERYTHING GLOW. IT'S EXTRAORDINARY.
ONCE IT'S SECURE...
...I'M IN WITH THE DRASIL. THEN I CAN START CHANGING THIS PLACE.
I'M SO CLOSE TO GETTING THAT POSITION. I CAN FEEL IT. I CAN SHOW MALLET THAT I'M BETTER THAN THE REST OF THE ENGINEERS THEN I'LL LIVE UP HERE.
AS SOON AS I'M INITIATED, ENOCK AND I WILL FORCE CHANGE TOGETHER.

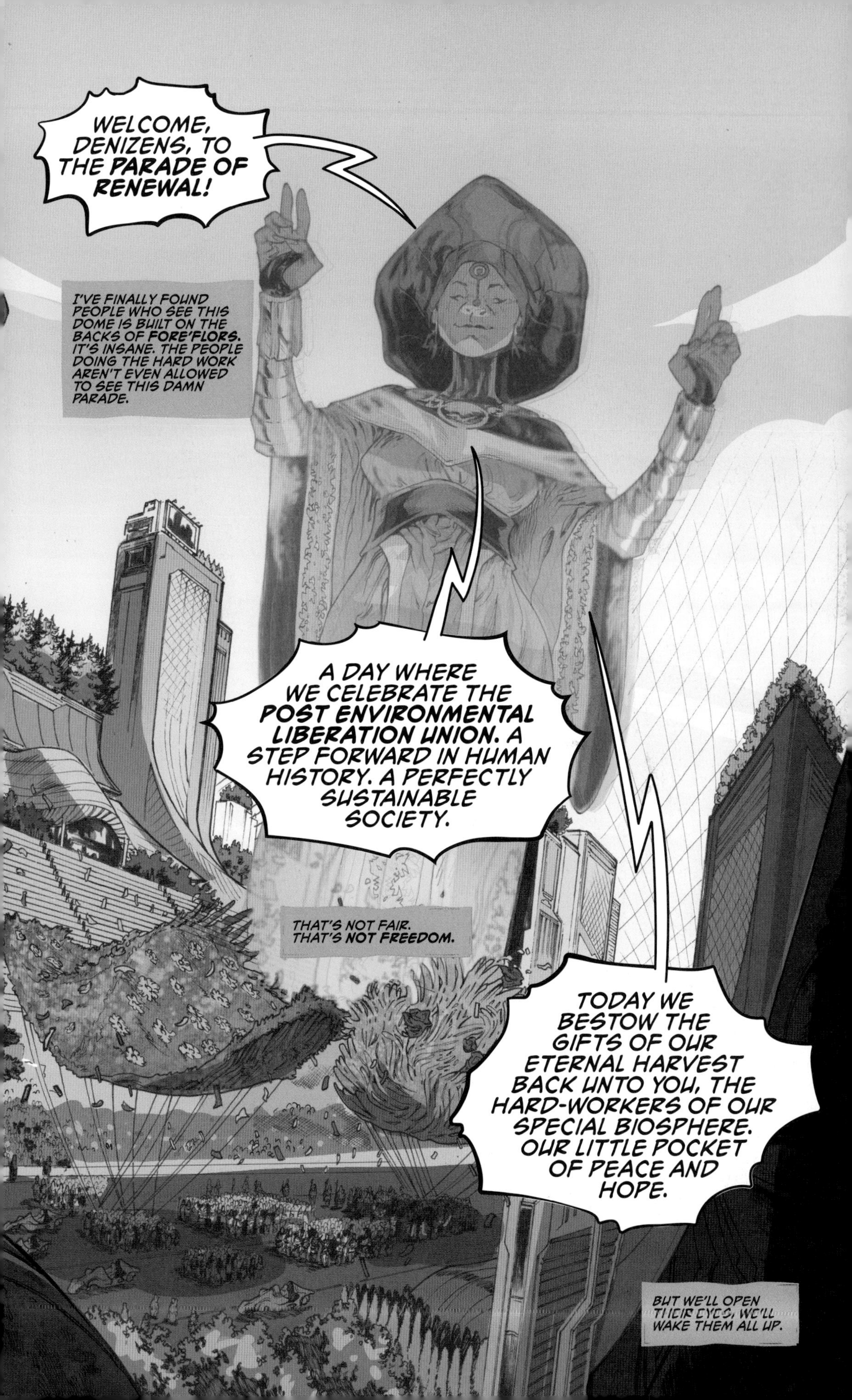
WELCOME, DENIZENS, TO THE **PARADE OF RENEWAL!**
I'VE FINALLY FOUND PEOPLE WHO SEE THIS DOME IS BUILT ON THE BACKS OF **FORE'FLORS.** IT'S INSANE. THE PEOPLE DOING THE HARD WORK AREN'T EVEN ALLOWED TO SEE THIS DAMN PARADE.
A DAY WHERE WE CELEBRATE THE **POST ENVIRONMENTAL LIBERATION UNION.** A STEP FORWARD IN HUMAN HISTORY. A PERFECTLY SUSTAINABLE SOCIETY.
THAT'S NOT FAIR. THAT'S **NOT FREEDOM.**
TODAY WE BESTOW THE GIFTS OF OUR ETERNAL HARVEST BACK UNTO YOU, THE HARD-WORKERS OF OUR SPECIAL BIOSPHERE. OUR LITTLE POCKET OF PEACE AND HOPE.
BUT WE'LL OPEN THEIR EYES, WE'LL WAKE THEM ALL UP.

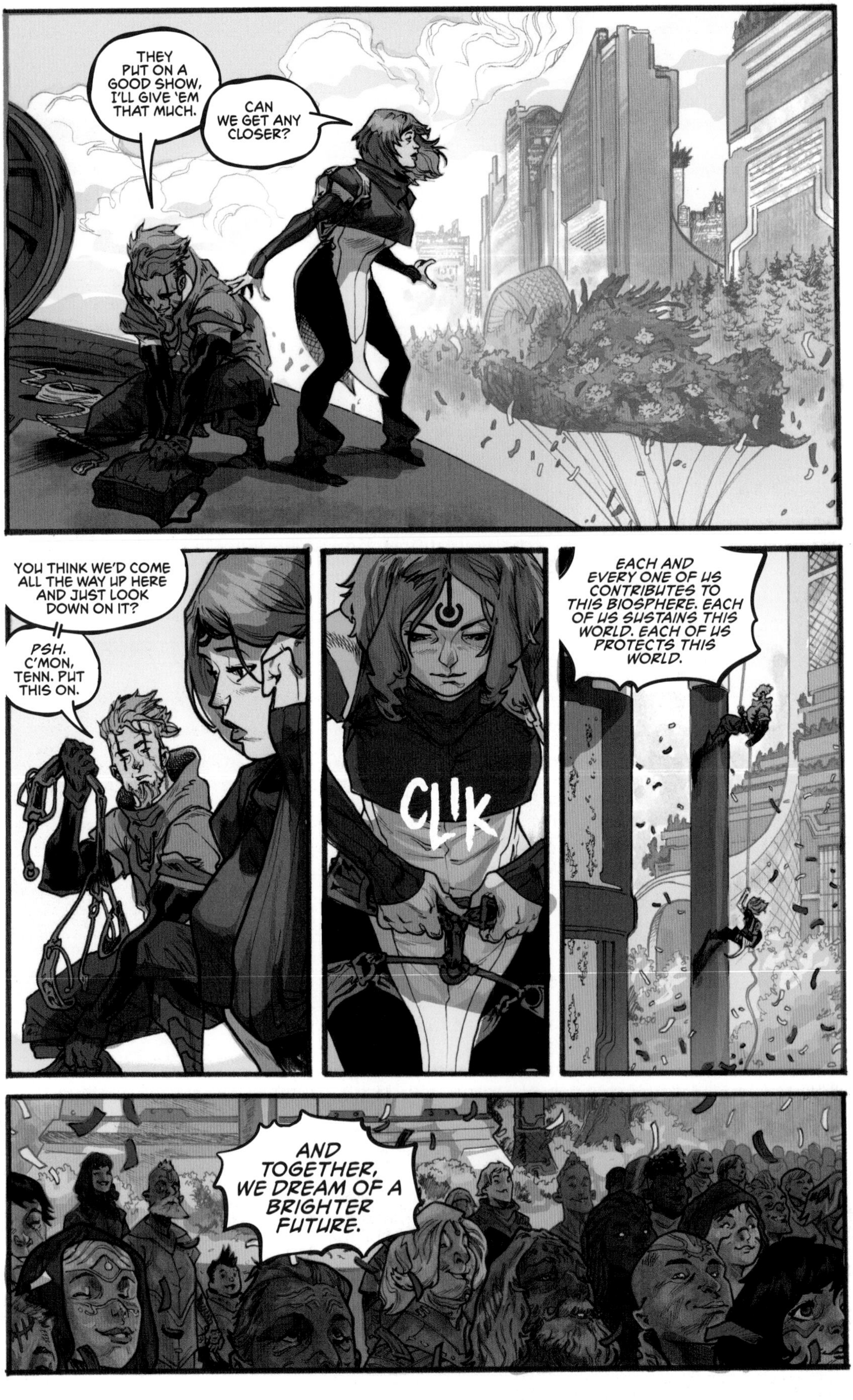
THEY PUT ON A GOOD SHOW, I'LL GIVE 'EM THAT MUCH.
CAN WE GET ANY CLOSER?
YOU THINK WE'D COME ALL THE WAY UP HERE AND JUST LOOK DOWN ON IT?
PSH. C'MON, TENN. PUT THIS ON.
CLIK
EACH AND EVERY ONE OF US CONTRIBUTES TO THIS BIOSPHERE. EACH OF US SUSTAINS THIS WORLD. EACH OF US PROTECTS THIS WORLD.
AND TOGETHER, WE DREAM OF A BRIGHTER FUTURE.

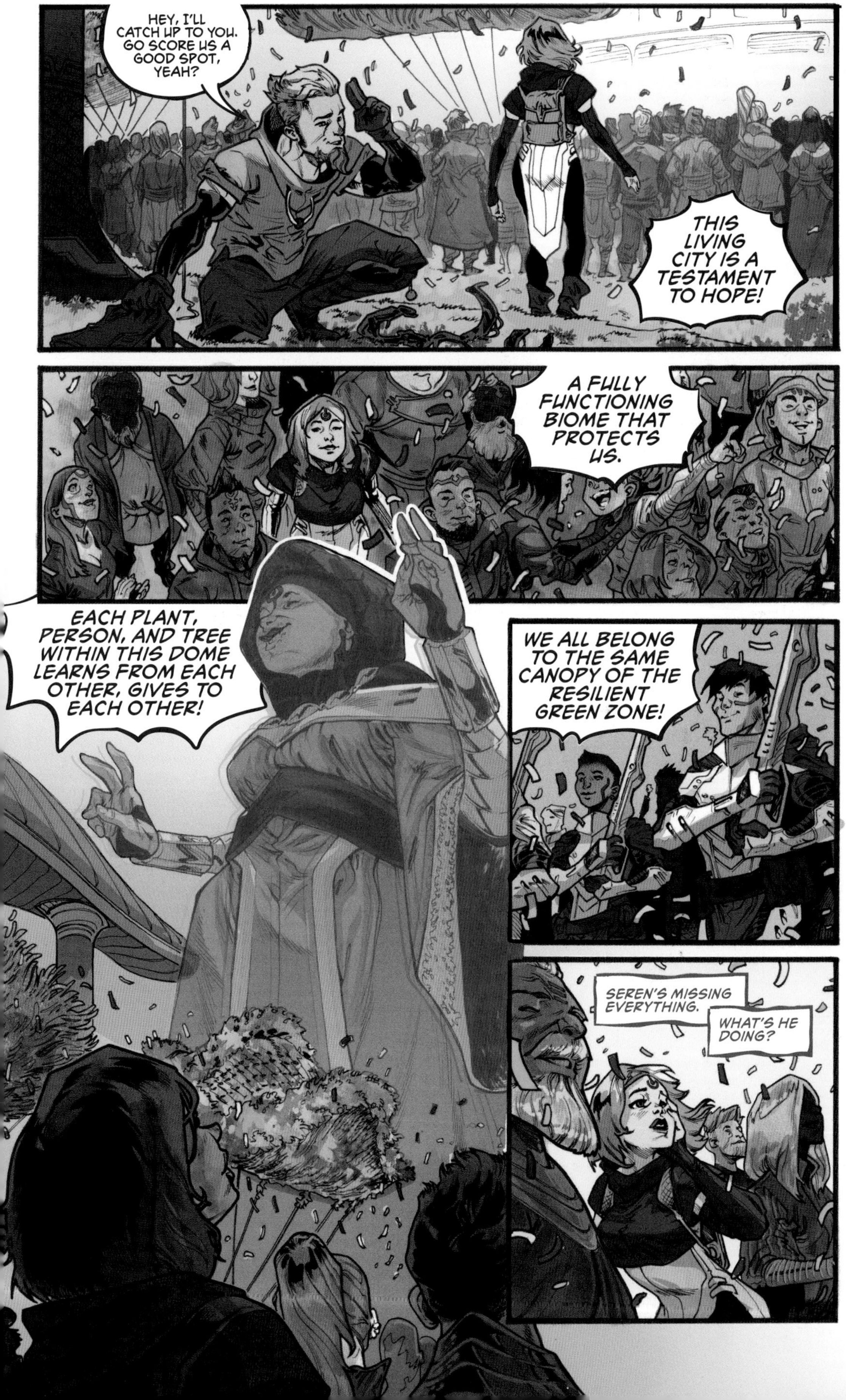
HEY, I'LL CATCH UP TO YOU. GO SCORE US A GOOD SPOT, YEAH?
THIS LIVING CITY IS A TESTAMENT TO HOPE!
A FULLY FUNCTIONING BIOME THAT PROTECTS US.
EACH PLANT, PERSON, AND TREE WITHIN THIS DOME LEARNS FROM EACH OTHER, GIVES TO EACH OTHER!
WE ALL BELONG TO THE SAME CANOPY OF THE RESILIENT GREEN ZONE!
SEREN'S MISSING EVERYTHING.
WHAT'S HE DOING?

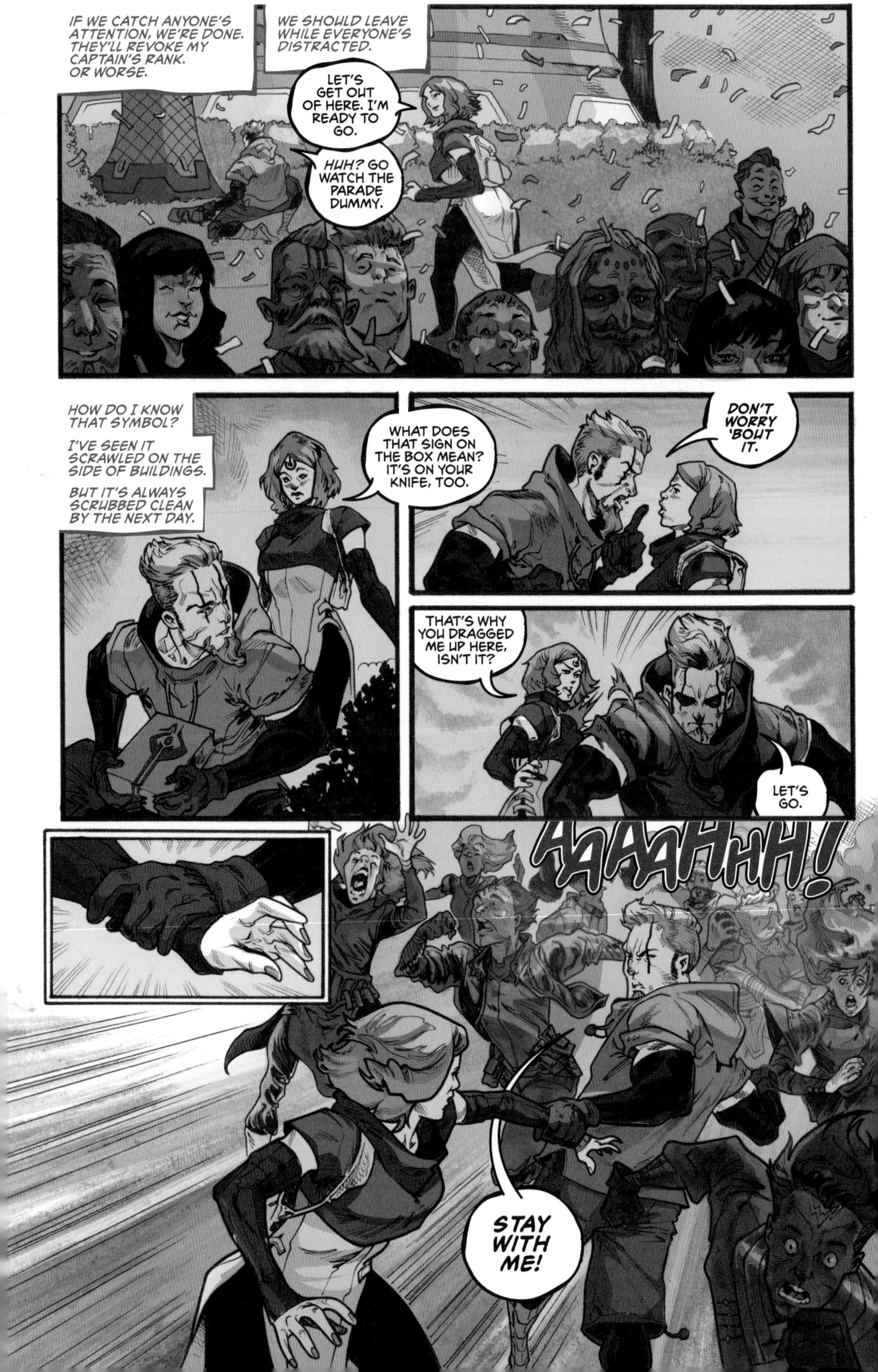
IF WE CATCH ANYONE'S ATTENTION, WE'RE DONE. THEY'LL REVOKE MY CAPTAIN'S RANK. OR WORSE.
WE SHOULD LEAVE WHILE EVERYONE'S DISTRACTED.
LET'S GET OUT OF HERE. I'M READY TO GO.
HUH? GO WATCH THE PARADE DUMMY.
HOW DO I KNOW THAT SYMBOL?
I'VE SEEN IT SCRAWLED ON THE SIDE OF BUILDINGS.
BUT IT'S ALWAYS SCRUBBED CLEAN BY THE NEXT DAY.
WHAT DOES THAT SIGN ON THE BOX MEAN? IT'S ON YOUR KNIFE, TOO.
DON'T WORRY 'BOUT IT.
THAT'S WHY YOU DRAGGED ME UP HERE, ISN'T IT?
LET'S GO.
AAAAHHH!
STAY WITH ME!

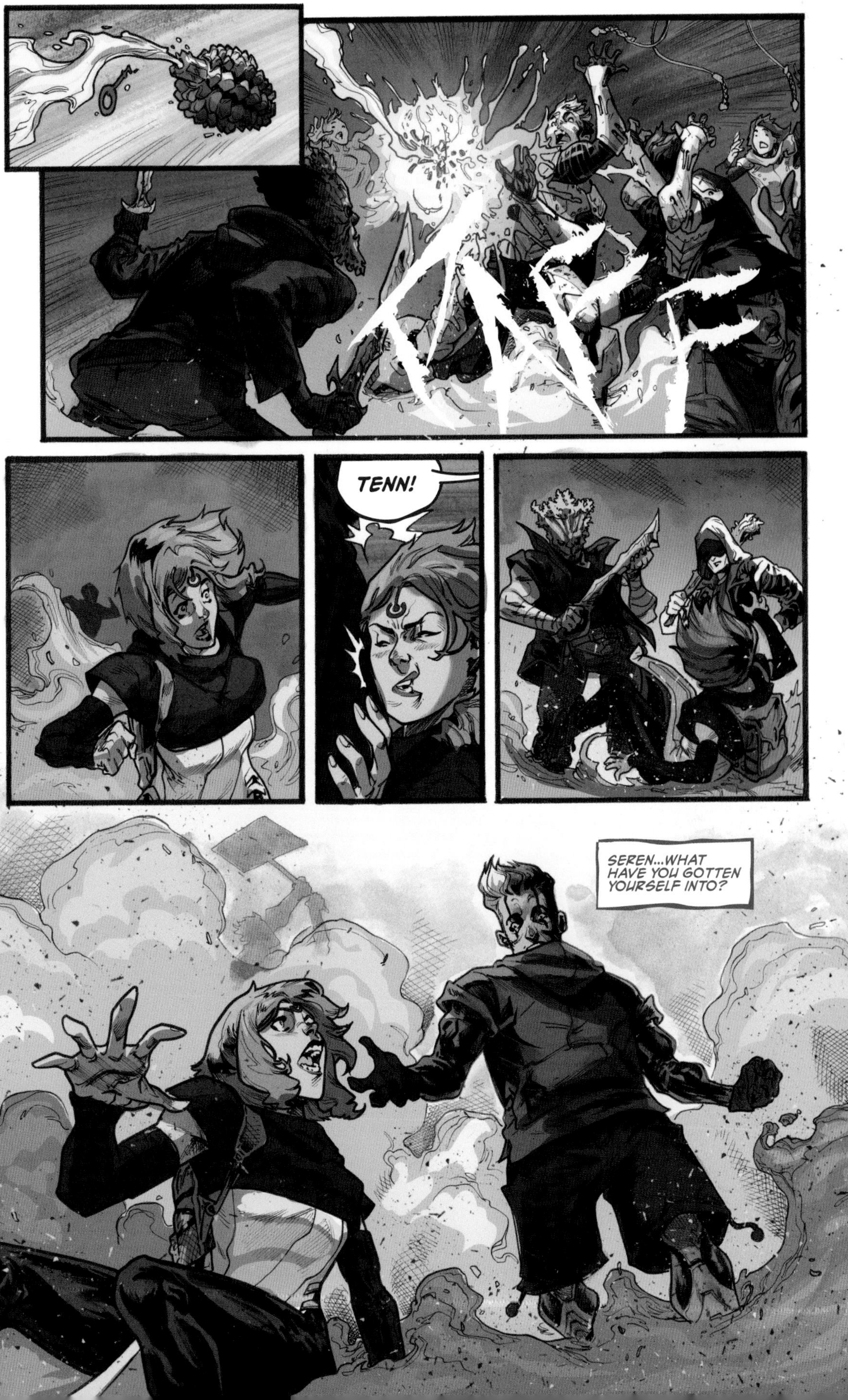
TENN!
SEREN...WHAT HAVE YOU GOTTEN YOURSELF INTO?

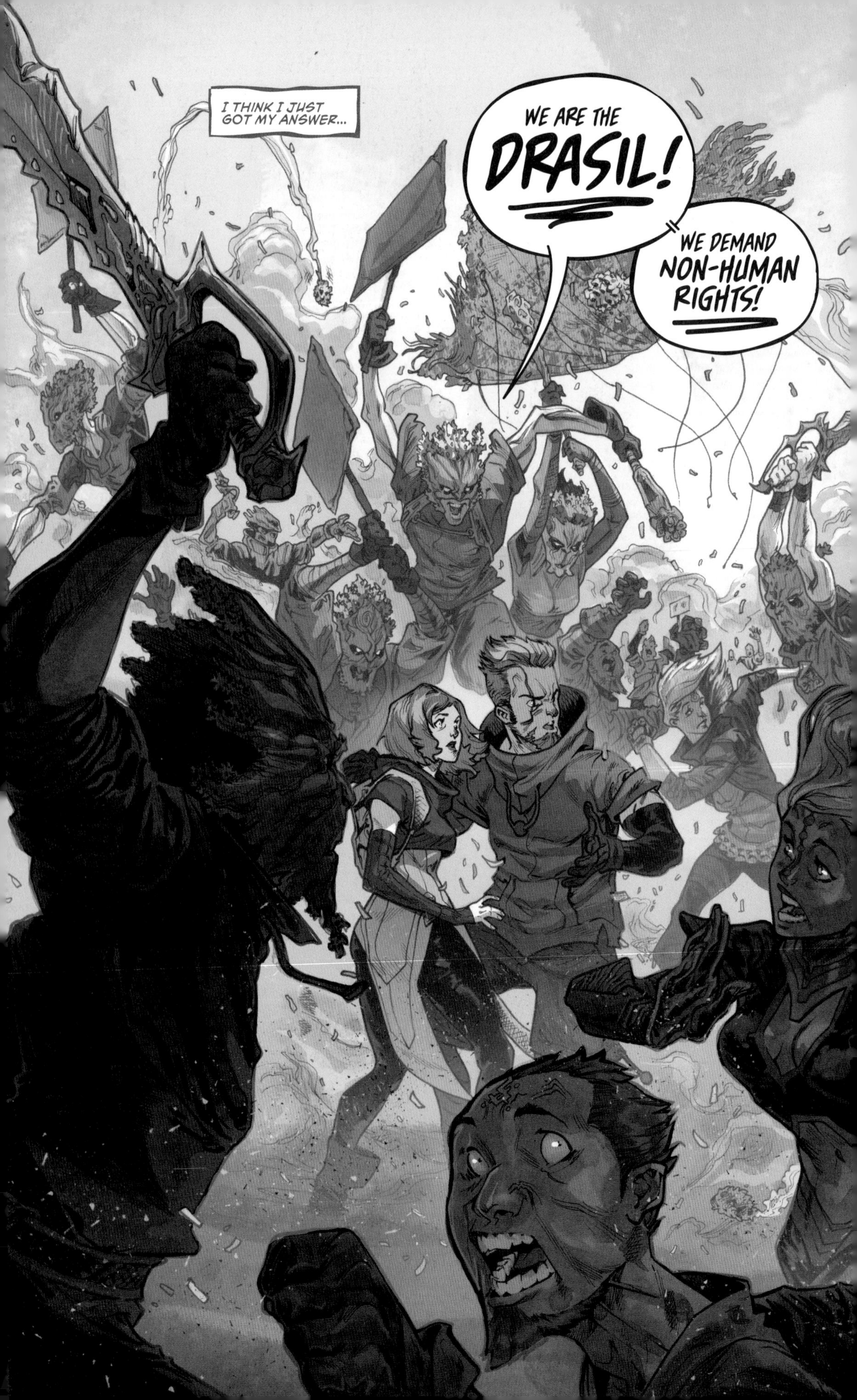
I THINK I JUST GOT MY ANSWER...
WE ARE THE DRASIL!
WE DEMAND NON-HUMAN RIGHTS!

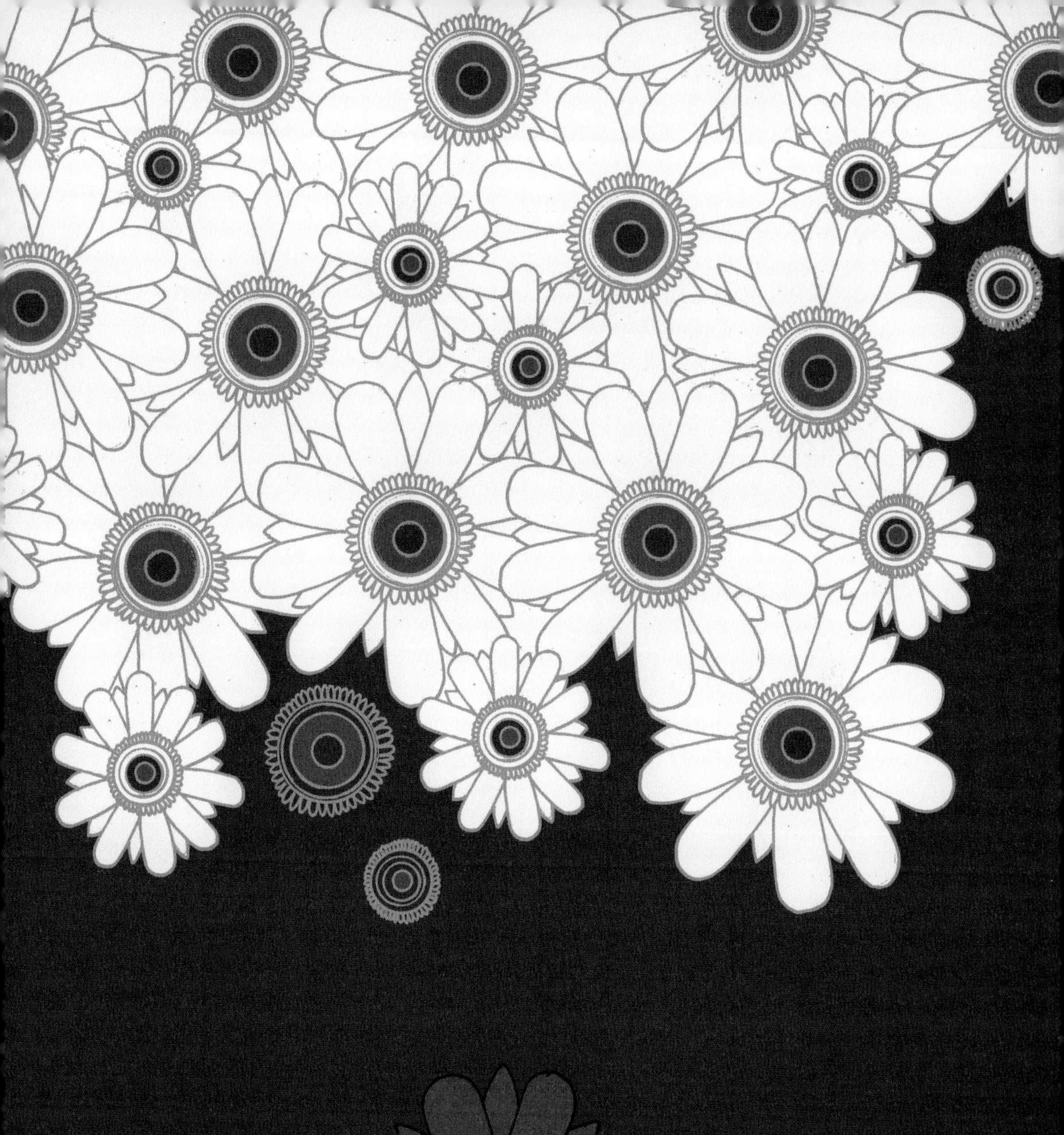

WE WERE, ARE NOW, AND EVER

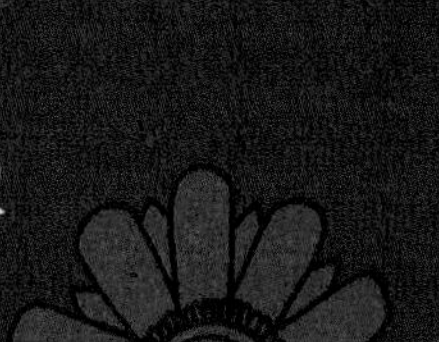

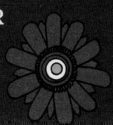

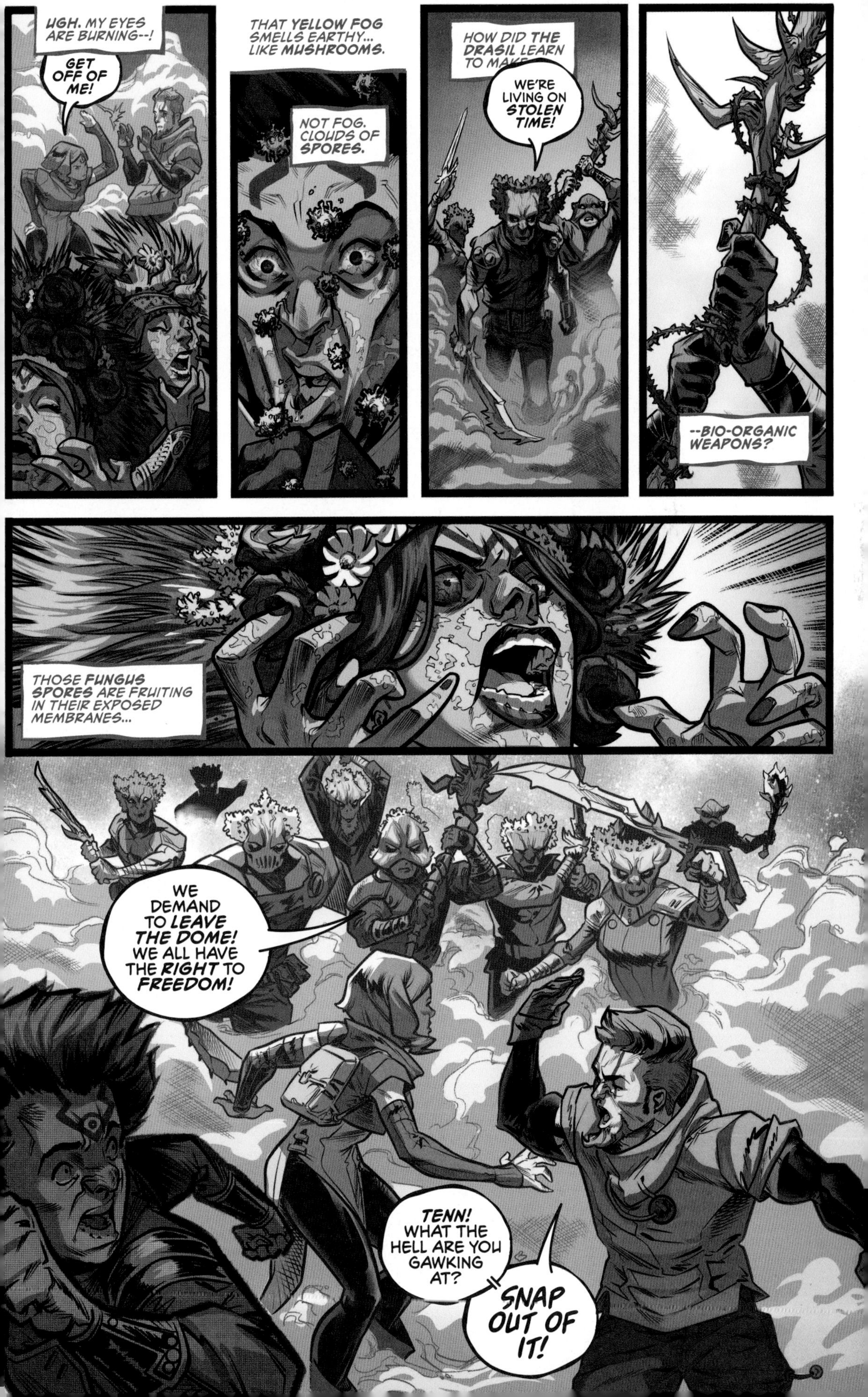
UGH. MY EYES ARE BURNING--!
GET OFF OF ME!
THAT YELLOW FOG SMELLS EARTHY... LIKE MUSHROOMS.
NOT FOG. CLOUDS OF SPORES.
HOW DID THE DRASIL LEARN TO MAKE
WE'RE LIVING ON STOLEN TIME!
--BIO-ORGANIC WEAPONS?
THOSE FUNGUS SPORES ARE FRUITING IN THEIR EXPOSED MEMBRANES...
WE DEMAND TO LEAVE THE DOME! WE ALL HAVE THE RIGHT TO FREEDOM!
TENN! WHAT THE HELL ARE YOU GAWKING AT?
SNAP OUT OF IT!

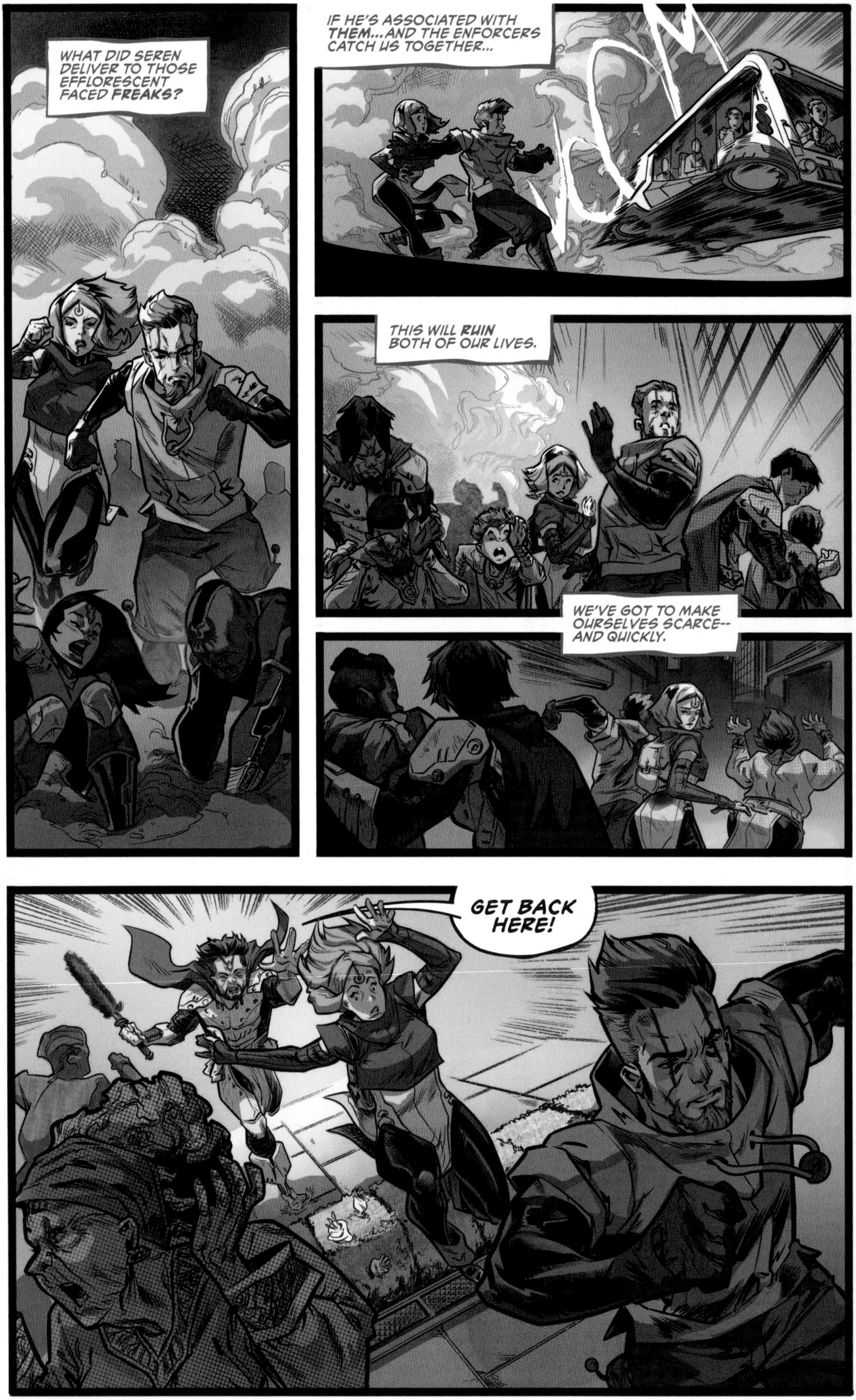
WHAT DID SEREN DELIVER TO THOSE EFFLORESCENT FACED **FREAKS?**
IF HE'S ASSOCIATED WITH **THEM**...AND THE ENFORCERS CATCH US TOGETHER...
THIS WILL **RUIN** BOTH OF OUR LIVES.
WE'VE GOT TO MAKE OURSELVES SCARCE-- AND QUICKLY.
GET BACK HERE!

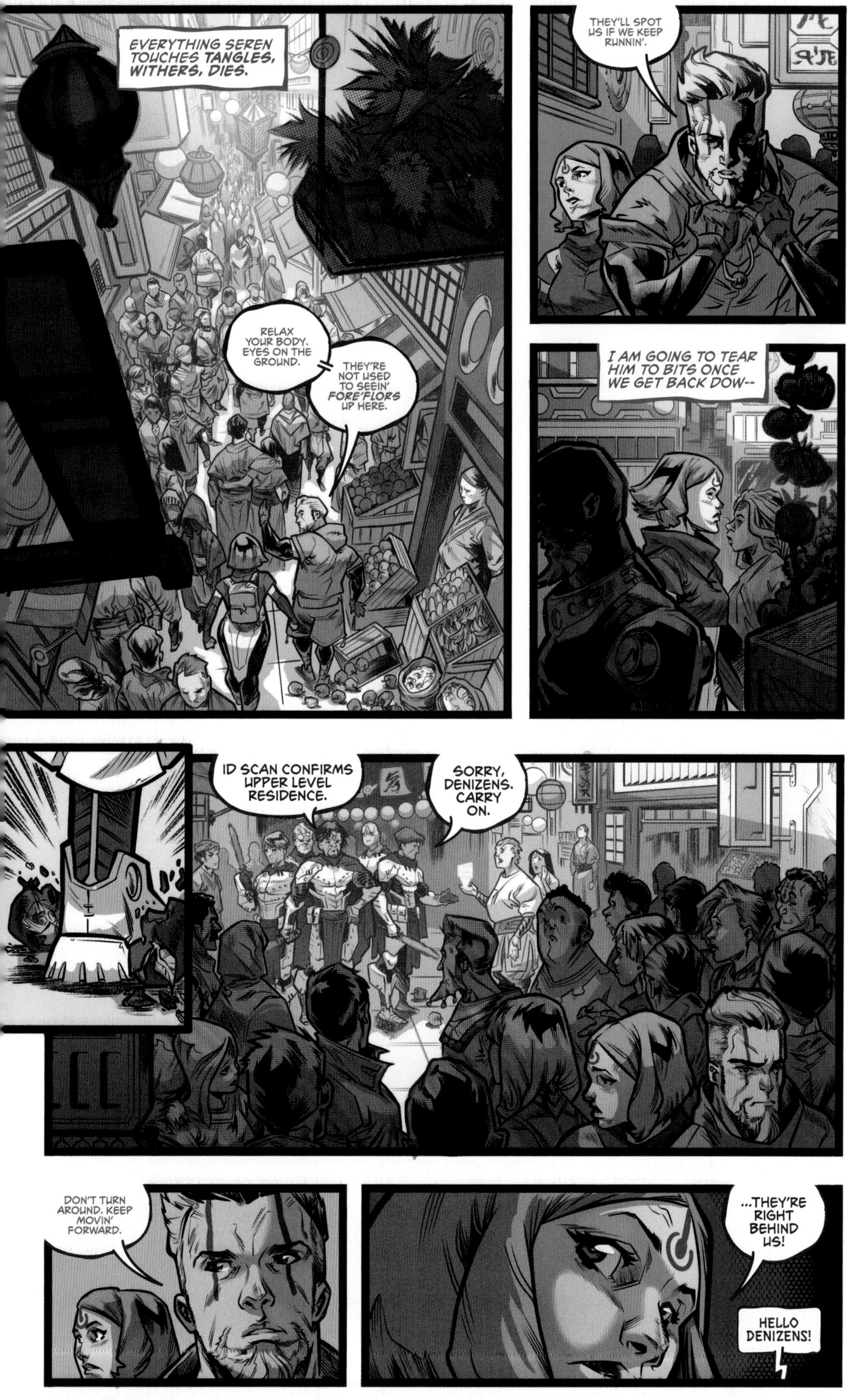

EVERYTHING SEREN TOUCHES TANGLES, WITHERS, DIES.
RELAX YOUR BODY. EYES ON THE GROUND.
THEY'RE NOT USED TO SEEIN' FORE'FLORS UP HERE.
THEY'LL SPOT US IF WE KEEP RUNNIN'.
I AM GOING TO TEAR HIM TO BITS ONCE WE GET BACK DOW--
ID SCAN CONFIRMS UPPER LEVEL RESIDENCE.
SORRY, DENIZENS. CARRY ON.
DON'T TURN AROUND. KEEP MOVIN' FORWARD.
...THEY'RE RIGHT BEHIND US!
HELLO DENIZENS!

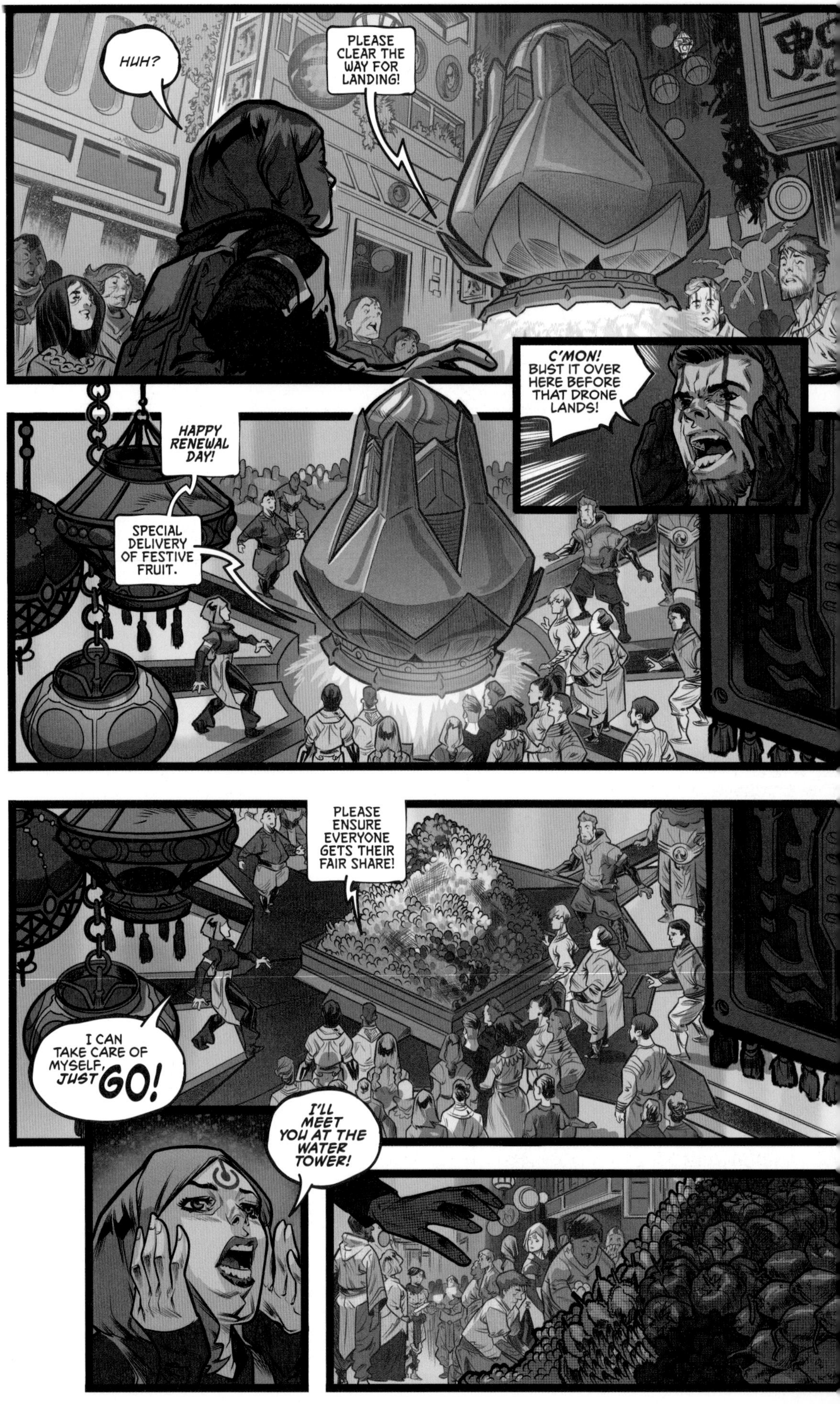
HUH?
PLEASE CLEAR THE WAY FOR LANDING!
C'MON! BUST IT OVER HERE BEFORE THAT DRONE LANDS!
HAPPY RENEWAL DAY!
SPECIAL DELIVERY OF FESTIVE FRUIT.
PLEASE ENSURE EVERYONE GETS THEIR FAIR SHARE!
I CAN TAKE CARE OF MYSELF, JUST GO!
I'LL MEET YOU AT THE WATER TOWER!

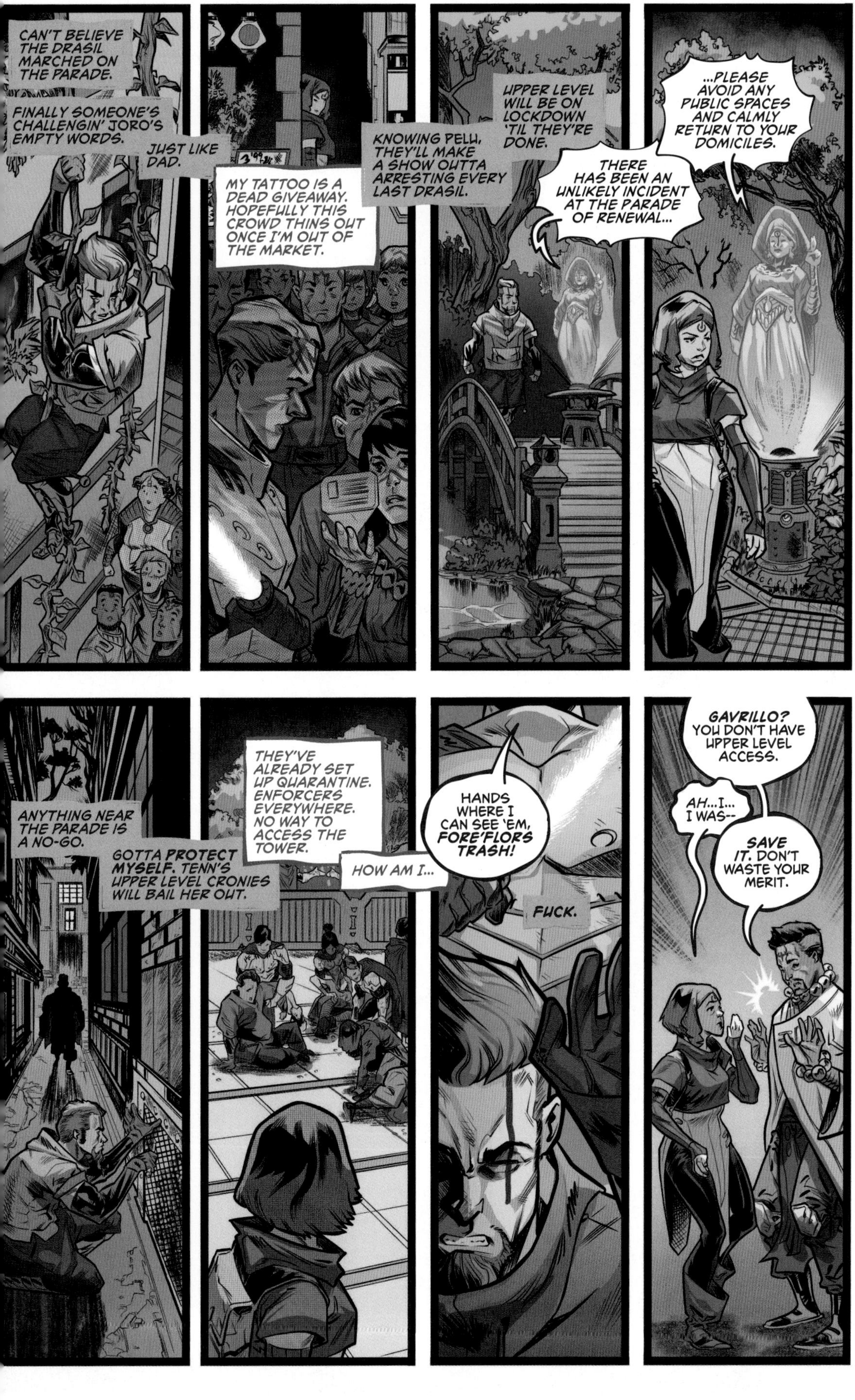
CAN'T BELIEVE THE DRASIL MARCHED ON THE PARADE.
FINALLY SOMEONE'S CHALLENGIN' JORO'S EMPTY WORDS.
JUST LIKE DAD.
MY TATTOO IS A DEAD GIVEAWAY. HOPEFULLY THIS CROWD THINS OUT ONCE I'M OUT OF THE MARKET.
KNOWING PELU, THEY'LL MAKE A SHOW OUTTA ARRESTING EVERY LAST DRASIL.
UPPER LEVEL WILL BE ON LOCKDOWN 'TIL THEY'RE DONE.
THERE HAS BEEN AN UNLIKELY INCIDENT AT THE PARADE OF RENEWAL...
...PLEASE AVOID ANY PUBLIC SPACES AND CALMLY RETURN TO YOUR DOMICILES.
ANYTHING NEAR THE PARADE IS A NO-GO.
GOTTA PROTECT MYSELF. TENN'S UPPER LEVEL CRONIES WILL BAIL HER OUT.
THEY'VE ALREADY SET UP QUARANTINE. ENFORCERS EVERYWHERE. NO WAY TO ACCESS THE TOWER.
HOW AM I...
HANDS WHERE I CAN SEE 'EM, FORE'FLORS TRASH!
FUCK.
GAVRILLO? YOU DON'T HAVE UPPER LEVEL ACCESS.
AH...I... I WAS--
SAVE IT. DON'T WASTE YOUR MERIT.

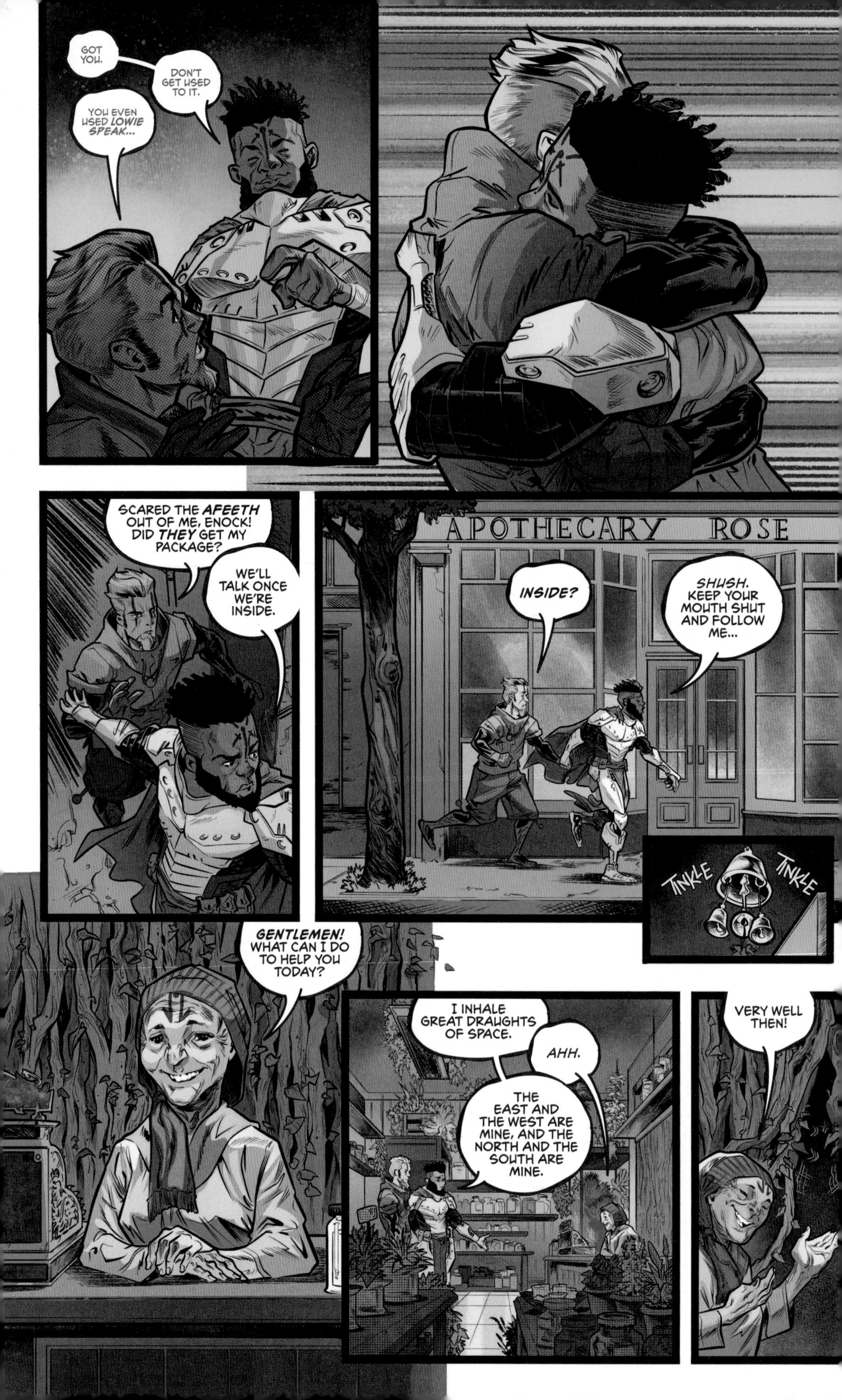
GOT YOU.
DON'T GET USED TO IT.
YOU EVEN USED LOWIE SPEAK...
SCARED THE AFEETH OUT OF ME, ENOCK! DID THEY GET MY PACKAGE?
WE'LL TALK ONCE WE'RE INSIDE.
APOTHECARY ROSE
INSIDE?
SHUSH. KEEP YOUR MOUTH SHUT AND FOLLOW ME...
TINKLE TINKLE
GENTLEMEN! WHAT CAN I DO TO HELP YOU TODAY?
I INHALE GREAT DRAUGHTS OF SPACE.
AHH.
THE EAST AND THE WEST ARE MINE, AND THE NORTH AND THE SOUTH ARE MINE.
VERY WELL THEN!

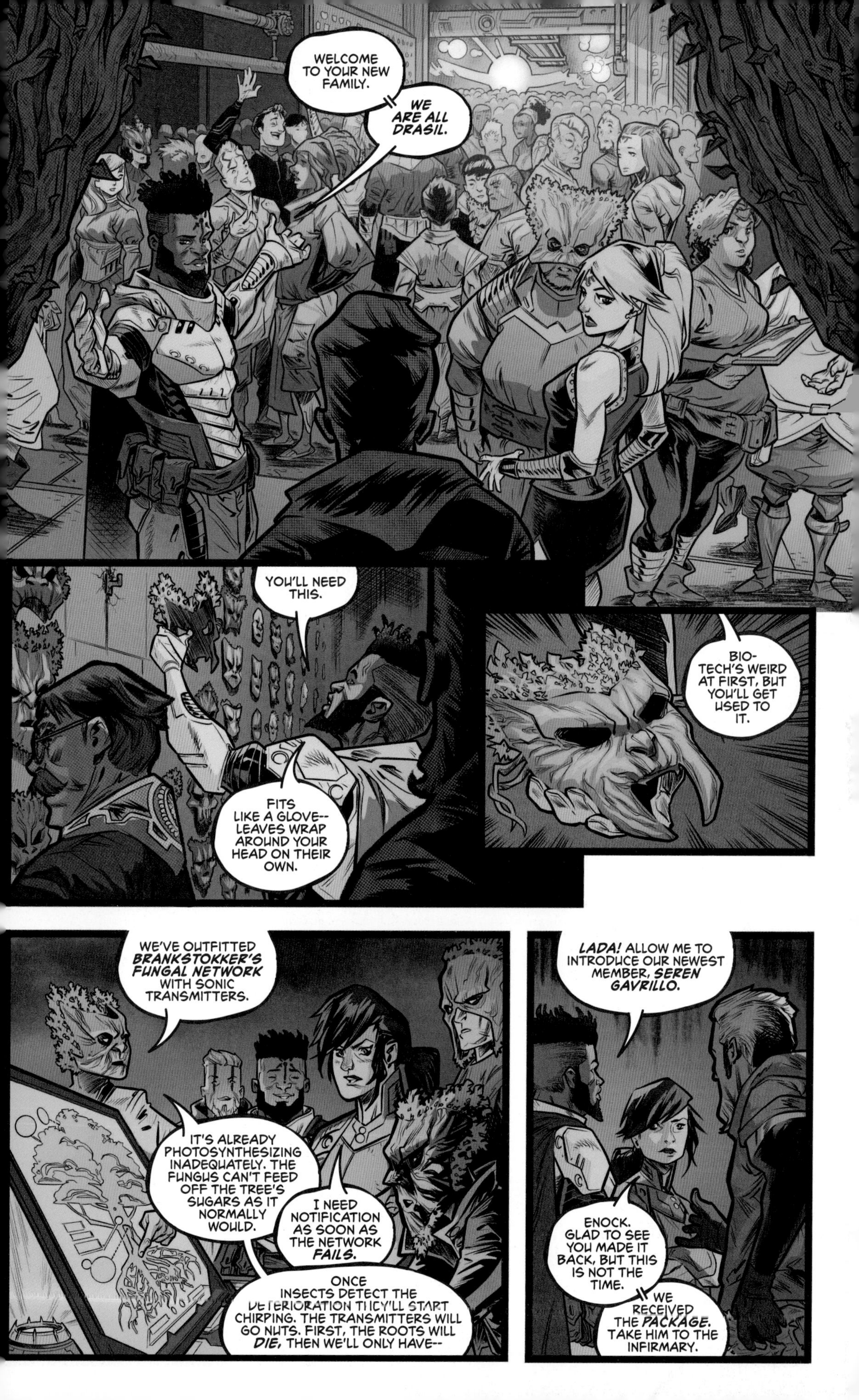
WELCOME TO YOUR NEW FAMILY.
WE ARE ALL DRASIL.
YOU'LL NEED THIS.
FITS LIKE A GLOVE-- LEAVES WRAP AROUND YOUR HEAD ON THEIR OWN.
BIO-TECH'S WEIRD AT FIRST, BUT YOU'LL GET USED TO IT.
WE'VE OUTFITTED BRANKSTOKKER'S FUNGAL NETWORK WITH SONIC TRANSMITTERS.
IT'S ALREADY PHOTOSYNTHESIZING INADEQUATELY. THE FUNGUS CAN'T FEED OFF THE TREE'S SUGARS AS IT NORMALLY WOULD.
I NEED NOTIFICATION AS SOON AS THE NETWORK FAILS.
ONCE INSECTS DETECT THE DETERIORATION THEY'LL START CHIRPING. THE TRANSMITTERS WILL GO NUTS. FIRST, THE ROOTS WILL DIE, THEN WE'LL ONLY HAVE--
LADA! ALLOW ME TO INTRODUCE OUR NEWEST MEMBER, SEREN GAVRILLO.
ENOCK. GLAD TO SEE YOU MADE IT BACK, BUT THIS IS NOT THE TIME.
WE RECEIVED THE PACKAGE. TAKE HIM TO THE INFIRMARY.

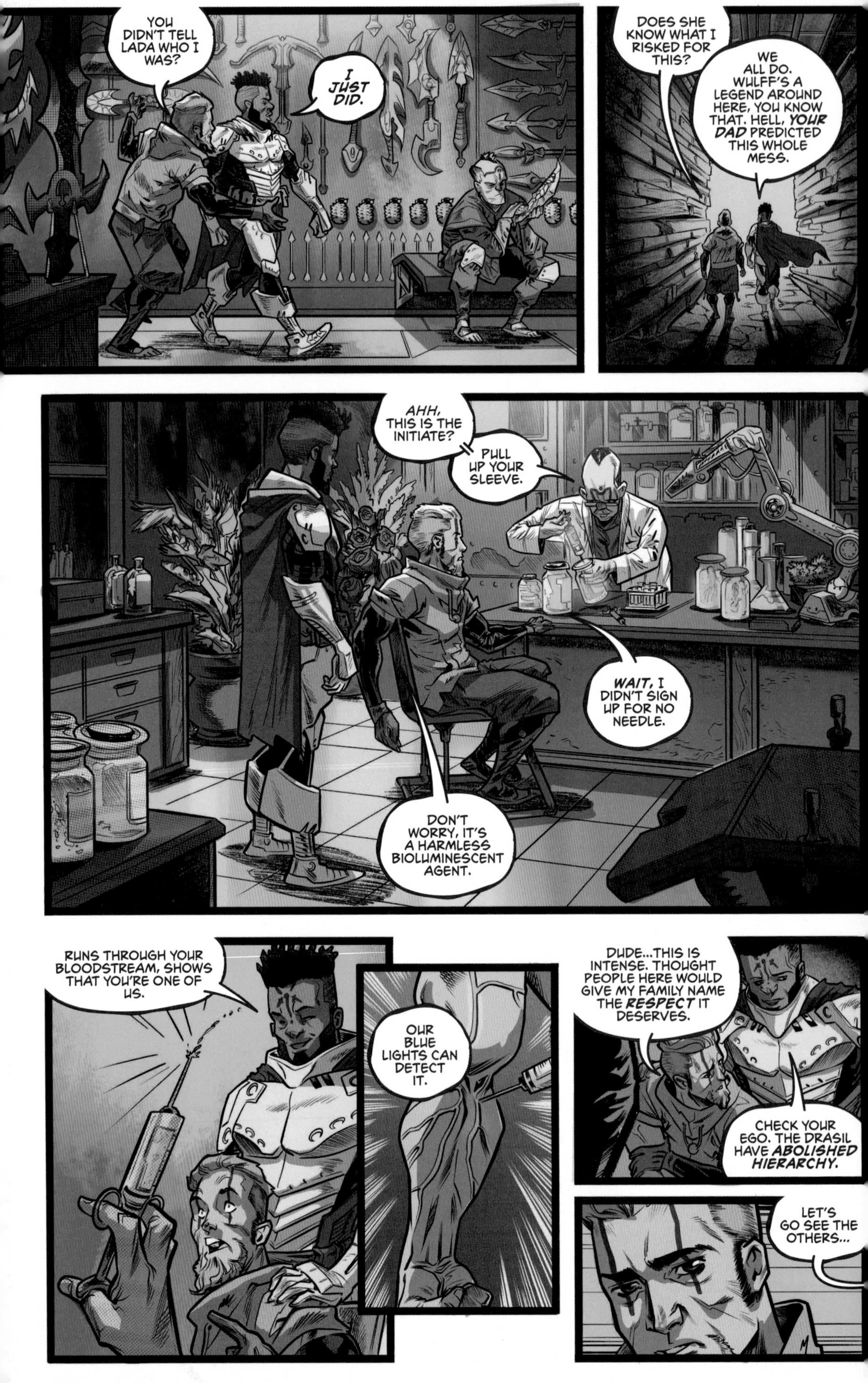
YOU DIDN'T TELL LADA WHO I WAS?
I JUST DID.
DOES SHE KNOW WHAT I RISKED FOR THIS?
WE ALL DO. WULFF'S A LEGEND AROUND HERE, YOU KNOW THAT. HELL, YOUR DAD PREDICTED THIS WHOLE MESS.
AHH, THIS IS THE INITIATE?
PULL UP YOUR SLEEVE.
WAIT, I DIDN'T SIGN UP FOR NO NEEDLE.
DON'T WORRY, IT'S A HARMLESS BIOLUMINESCENT AGENT.
RUNS THROUGH YOUR BLOODSTREAM, SHOWS THAT YOU'RE ONE OF US.
OUR BLUE LIGHTS CAN DETECT IT.
DUDE...THIS IS INTENSE. THOUGHT PEOPLE HERE WOULD GIVE MY FAMILY NAME THE RESPECT IT DESERVES.
CHECK YOUR EGO. THE DRASIL HAVE ABOLISHED HIERARCHY.
LET'S GO SEE THE OTHERS...

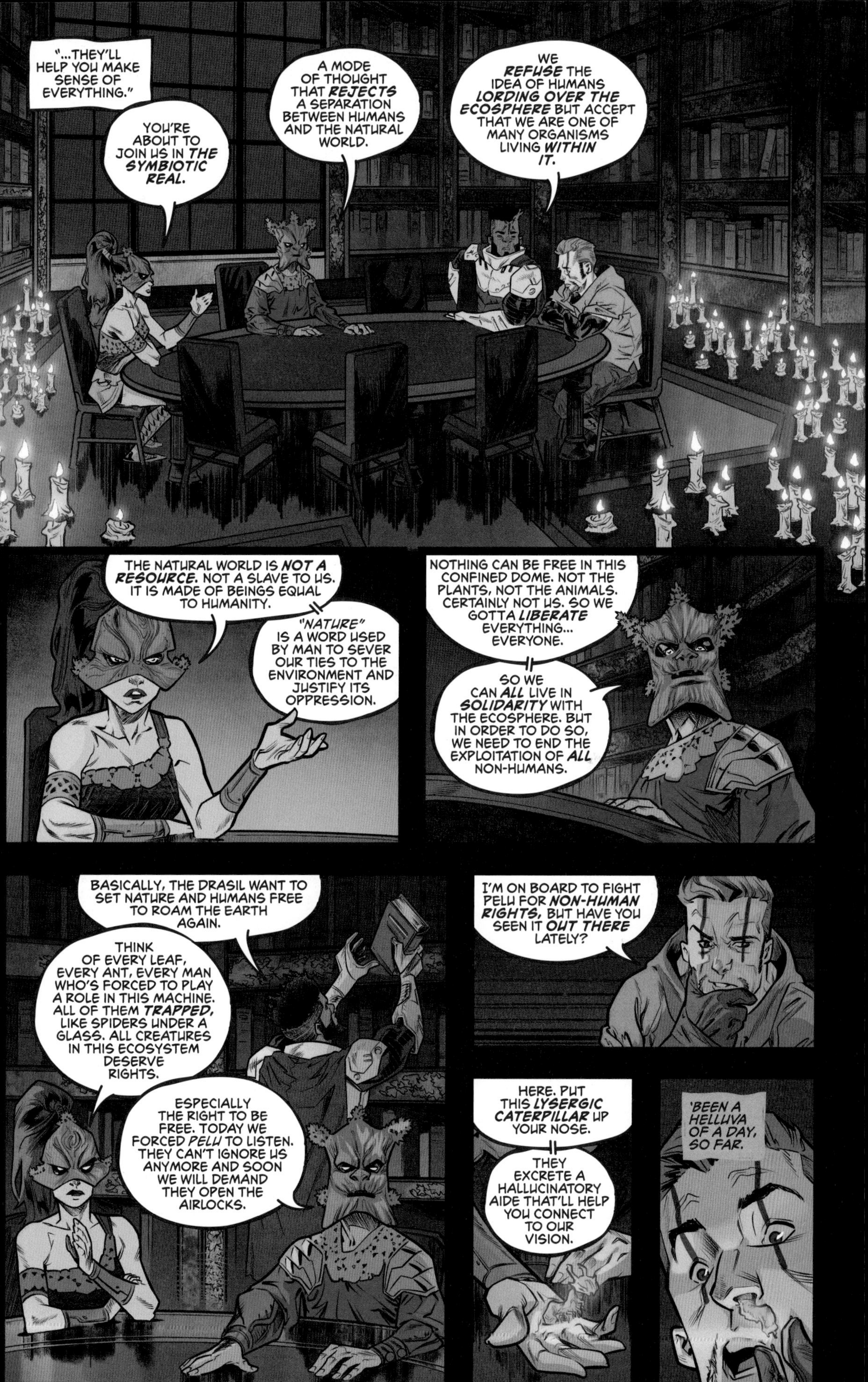
"...THEY'LL HELP YOU MAKE SENSE OF EVERYTHING."
YOU'RE ABOUT TO JOIN US IN *THE SYMBIOTIC REAL.*
A MODE OF THOUGHT THAT *REJECTS* A SEPARATION BETWEEN HUMANS AND THE NATURAL WORLD.
WE *REFUSE* THE IDEA OF HUMANS *LORDING OVER THE ECOSPHERE* BUT ACCEPT THAT WE ARE ONE OF MANY ORGANISMS LIVING *WITHIN* IT.
THE NATURAL WORLD IS *NOT A RESOURCE.* NOT A SLAVE TO US. IT IS MADE OF BEINGS EQUAL TO HUMANITY.
"NATURE" IS A WORD USED BY MAN TO SEVER OUR TIES TO THE ENVIRONMENT AND JUSTIFY ITS OPPRESSION.
NOTHING CAN BE FREE IN THIS CONFINED DOME. NOT THE PLANTS, NOT THE ANIMALS. CERTAINLY NOT US. SO WE GOTTA *LIBERATE* EVERYTHING... EVERYONE.
SO WE CAN *ALL* LIVE IN *SOLIDARITY* WITH THE ECOSPHERE. BUT IN ORDER TO DO SO, WE NEED TO END THE EXPLOITATION OF *ALL* NON-HUMANS.
BASICALLY, THE DRASIL WANT TO SET NATURE AND HUMANS FREE TO ROAM THE EARTH AGAIN.
THINK OF EVERY LEAF, EVERY ANT, EVERY MAN WHO'S FORCED TO PLAY A ROLE IN THIS MACHINE. ALL OF THEM *TRAPPED,* LIKE SPIDERS UNDER A GLASS. ALL CREATURES IN THIS ECOSYSTEM DESERVE RIGHTS.
ESPECIALLY THE RIGHT TO BE FREE. TODAY WE FORCED *PELU* TO LISTEN. THEY CAN'T IGNORE US ANYMORE AND SOON WE WILL DEMAND THEY OPEN THE AIRLOCKS.
I'M ON BOARD TO FIGHT PELU FOR *NON-HUMAN RIGHTS,* BUT HAVE YOU SEEN IT *OUT THERE* LATELY?
HERE. PUT THIS *LYSERGIC CATERPILLAR* UP YOUR NOSE.
THEY EXCRETE A HALLUCINATORY AIDE THAT'LL HELP YOU CONNECT TO OUR VISION.
'BEEN A HELLUVA OF A DAY, SO FAR.

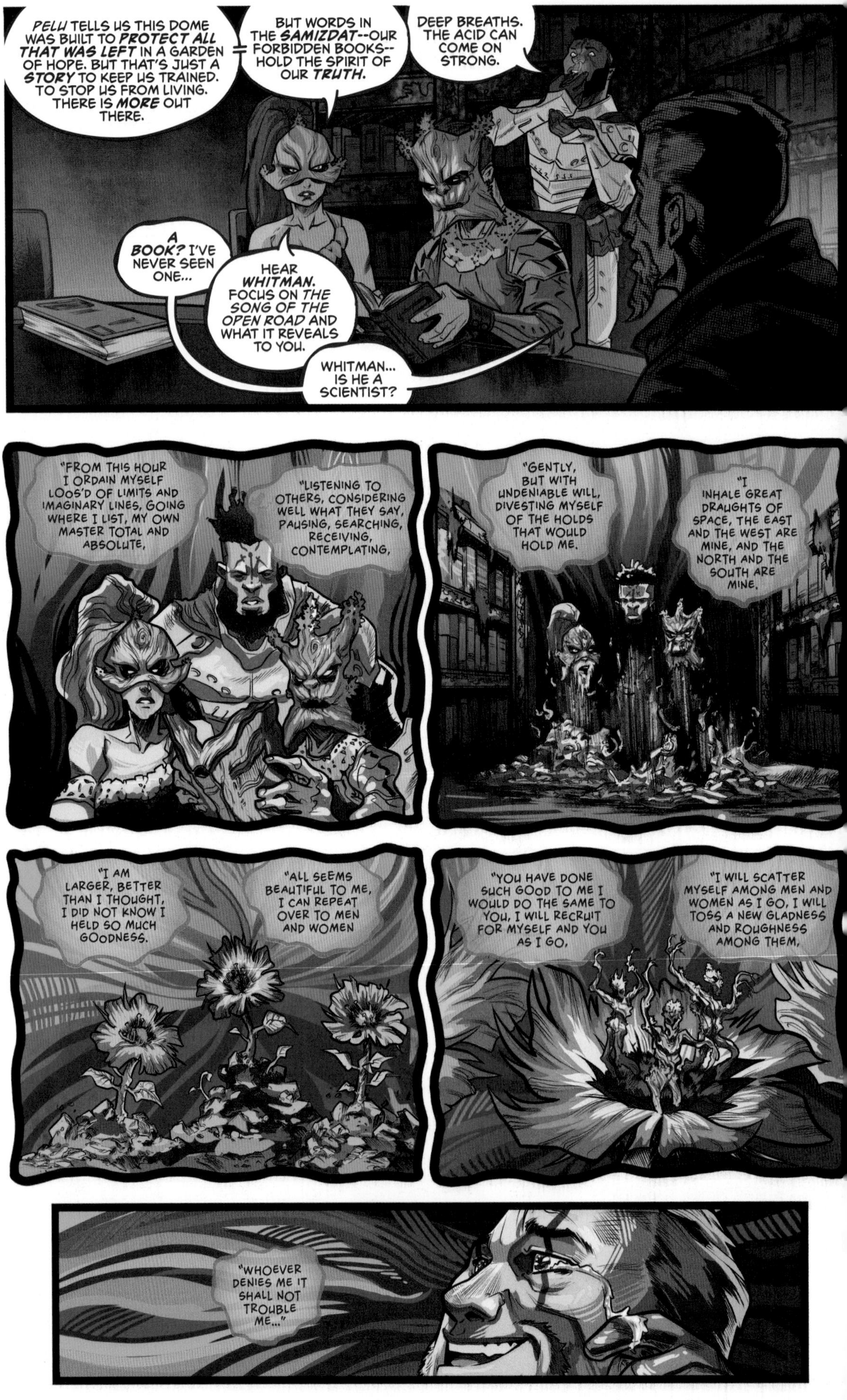
PELU TELLS US THIS DOME WAS BUILT TO PROTECT ALL THAT WAS LEFT IN A GARDEN OF HOPE. BUT THAT'S JUST A STORY TO KEEP US TRAINED. TO STOP US FROM LIVING. THERE IS MORE OUT THERE.
BUT WORDS IN THE SAMIZDAT--OUR FORBIDDEN BOOKS--HOLD THE SPIRIT OF OUR TRUTH.
DEEP BREATHS. THE ACID CAN COME ON STRONG.
A BOOK? I'VE NEVER SEEN ONE...
HEAR WHITMAN. FOCUS ON THE SONG OF THE OPEN ROAD AND WHAT IT REVEALS TO YOU.
WHITMAN... IS HE A SCIENTIST?
"FROM THIS HOUR I ORDAIN MYSELF LOOS'D OF LIMITS AND IMAGINARY LINES, GOING WHERE I LIST, MY OWN MASTER TOTAL AND ABSOLUTE,
"LISTENING TO OTHERS, CONSIDERING WELL WHAT THEY SAY, PAUSING, SEARCHING, RECEIVING, CONTEMPLATING,
"GENTLY, BUT WITH UNDENIABLE WILL, DIVESTING MYSELF OF THE HOLDS THAT WOULD HOLD ME.
"I INHALE GREAT DRAUGHTS OF SPACE, THE EAST AND THE WEST ARE MINE, AND THE NORTH AND THE SOUTH ARE MINE.
"I AM LARGER, BETTER THAN I THOUGHT, I DID NOT KNOW I HELD SO MUCH GOODNESS.
"ALL SEEMS BEAUTIFUL TO ME, I CAN REPEAT OVER TO MEN AND WOMEN
"YOU HAVE DONE SUCH GOOD TO ME I WOULD DO THE SAME TO YOU, I WILL RECRUIT FOR MYSELF AND YOU AS I GO,
"I WILL SCATTER MYSELF AMONG MEN AND WOMEN AS I GO, I WILL TOSS A NEW GLADNESS AND ROUGHNESS AMONG THEM,
"WHOEVER DENIES ME IT SHALL NOT TROUBLE ME..."

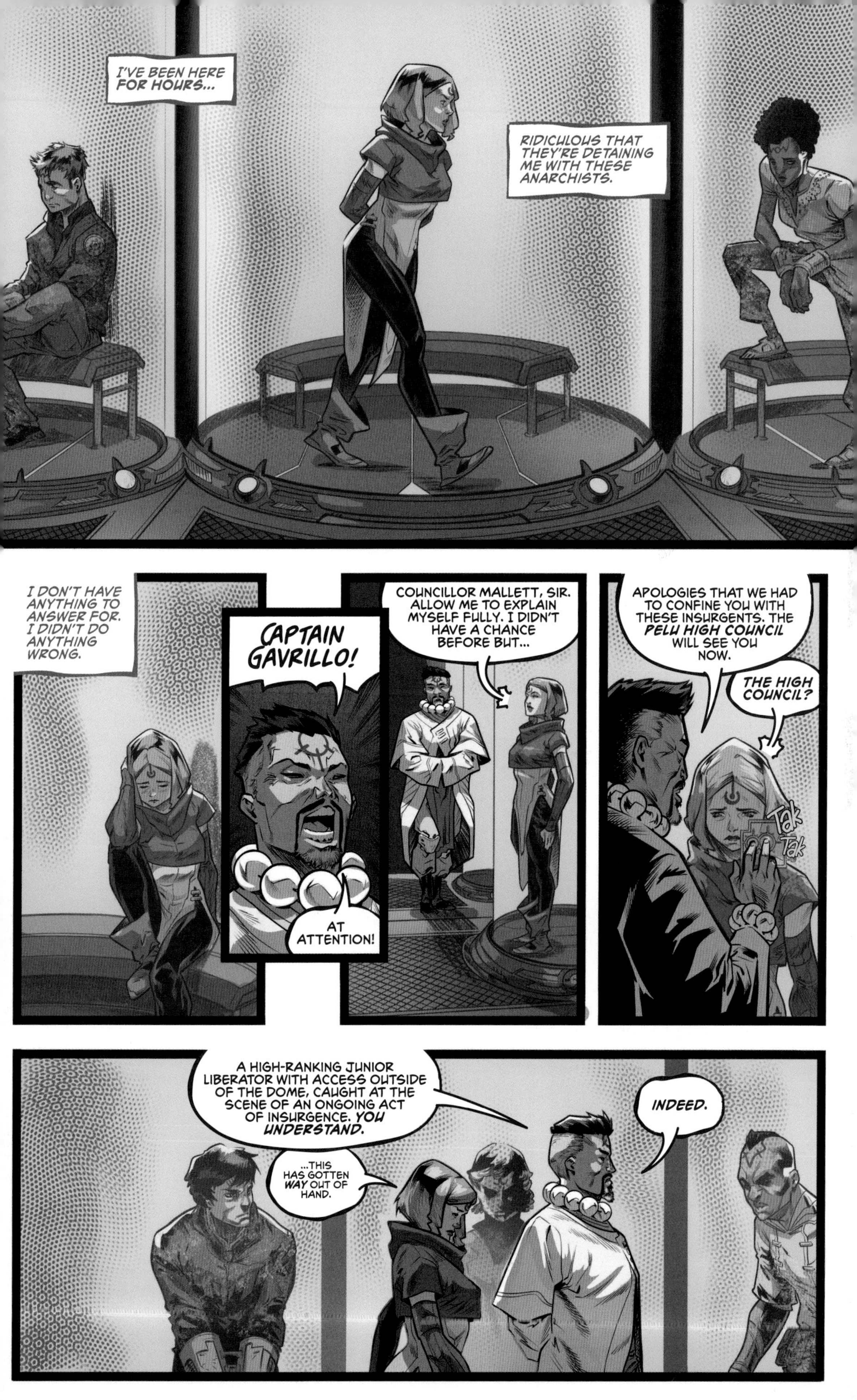
I'VE BEEN HERE FOR HOURS...
RIDICULOUS THAT THEY'RE DETAINING ME WITH THESE ANARCHISTS.
I DON'T HAVE ANYTHING TO ANSWER FOR. I DIDN'T DO ANYTHING WRONG.
CAPTAIN GAVRILLO!
AT ATTENTION!
COUNCILLOR MALLETT, SIR. ALLOW ME TO EXPLAIN MYSELF FULLY. I DIDN'T HAVE A CHANCE BEFORE BUT...
APOLOGIES THAT WE HAD TO CONFINE YOU WITH THESE INSURGENTS. THE PELU HIGH COUNCIL WILL SEE YOU NOW.
THE HIGH COUNCIL?
TAK TAK
A HIGH-RANKING JUNIOR LIBERATOR WITH ACCESS OUTSIDE OF THE DOME, CAUGHT AT THE SCENE OF AN ONGOING ACT OF INSURGENCE. YOU UNDERSTAND.
INDEED.
...THIS HAS GOTTEN WAY OUT OF HAND.

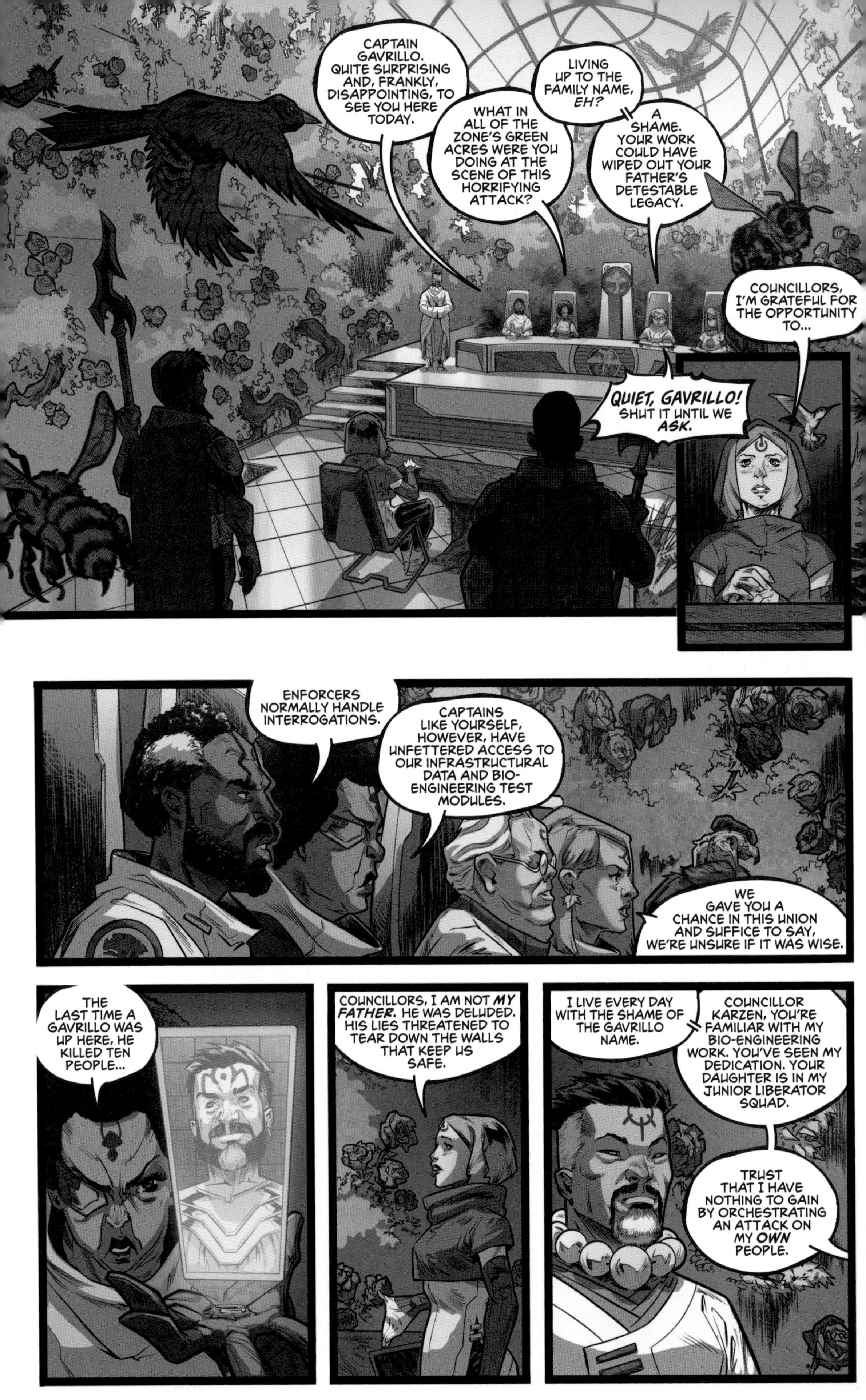
CAPTAIN GAVRILLO. QUITE SURPRISING AND, FRANKLY, DISAPPOINTING, TO SEE YOU HERE TODAY.
WHAT IN ALL OF THE ZONE'S GREEN ACRES WERE YOU DOING AT THE SCENE OF THIS HORRIFYING ATTACK?
LIVING UP TO THE FAMILY NAME, *EH?*
A SHAME. YOUR WORK COULD HAVE WIPED OUT YOUR FATHER'S DETESTABLE LEGACY.
COUNCILLORS, I'M GRATEFUL FOR THE OPPORTUNITY TO...
QUIET, GAVRILLO! SHUT IT UNTIL WE ***ASK.***
ENFORCERS NORMALLY HANDLE INTERROGATIONS.
CAPTAINS LIKE YOURSELF, HOWEVER, HAVE UNFETTERED ACCESS TO OUR INFRASTRUCTURAL DATA AND BIO-ENGINEERING TEST MODULES.
WE GAVE YOU A CHANCE IN THIS UNION AND SUFFICE TO SAY, WE'RE UNSURE IF IT WAS WISE.
THE LAST TIME A GAVRILLO WAS UP HERE, HE KILLED TEN PEOPLE...
COUNCILLORS, I AM NOT ***MY FATHER.*** HE WAS DELUDED. HIS LIES THREATENED TO TEAR DOWN THE WALLS THAT KEEP US SAFE.
I LIVE EVERY DAY WITH THE SHAME OF THE GAVRILLO NAME.
COUNCILLOR KARZEN, YOU'RE FAMILIAR WITH MY BIO-ENGINEERING WORK. YOU'VE SEEN MY DEDICATION. YOUR DAUGHTER IS IN MY JUNIOR LIBERATOR SQUAD.
TRUST THAT I HAVE NOTHING TO GAIN BY ORCHESTRATING AN ATTACK ON MY ***OWN*** PEOPLE.

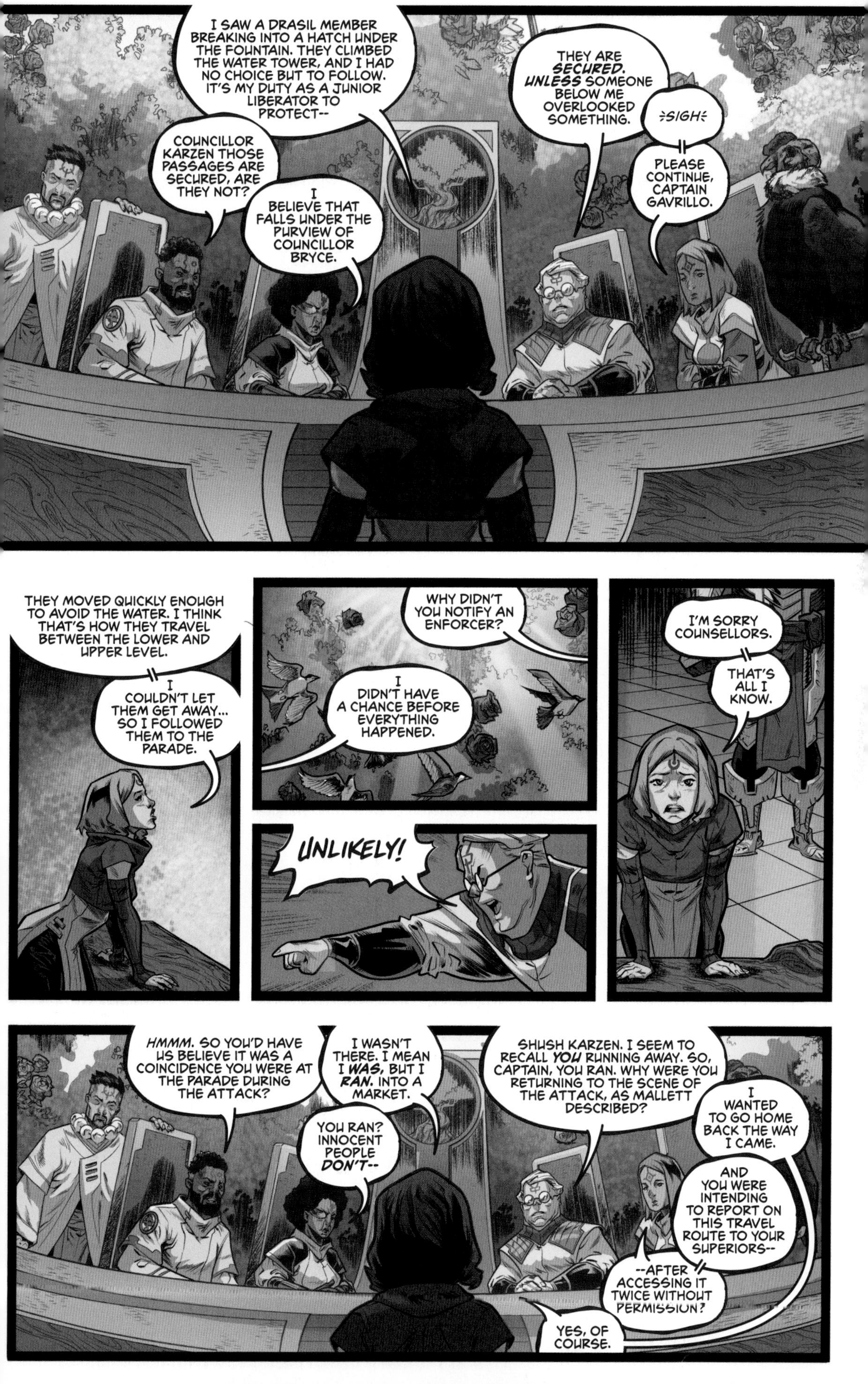
I SAW A DRASIL MEMBER BREAKING INTO A HATCH UNDER THE FOUNTAIN. THEY CLIMBED THE WATER TOWER, AND I HAD NO CHOICE BUT TO FOLLOW. IT'S MY DUTY AS A JUNIOR LIBERATOR TO PROTECT--
COUNCILLOR KARZEN THOSE PASSAGES ARE SECURED, ARE THEY NOT?
I BELIEVE THAT FALLS UNDER THE PURVIEW OF COUNCILLOR BRYCE.
THEY ARE SECURED. UNLESS SOMEONE BELOW ME OVERLOOKED SOMETHING.
SIGH
PLEASE CONTINUE, CAPTAIN GAVRILLO.
THEY MOVED QUICKLY ENOUGH TO AVOID THE WATER. I THINK THAT'S HOW THEY TRAVEL BETWEEN THE LOWER AND UPPER LEVEL.
I COULDN'T LET THEM GET AWAY... SO I FOLLOWED THEM TO THE PARADE.
WHY DIDN'T YOU NOTIFY AN ENFORCER?
I DIDN'T HAVE A CHANCE BEFORE EVERYTHING HAPPENED.
UNLIKELY!
I'M SORRY COUNSELLORS.
THAT'S ALL I KNOW.
HMMM. SO YOU'D HAVE US BELIEVE IT WAS A COINCIDENCE YOU WERE AT THE PARADE DURING THE ATTACK?
I WASN'T THERE. I MEAN I WAS, BUT I RAN. INTO A MARKET.
YOU RAN? INNOCENT PEOPLE DON'T--
SHUSH KARZEN. I SEEM TO RECALL YOU RUNNING AWAY. SO, CAPTAIN, YOU RAN. WHY WERE YOU RETURNING TO THE SCENE OF THE ATTACK, AS MALLETT DESCRIBED?
I WANTED TO GO HOME BACK THE WAY I CAME.
AND YOU WERE INTENDING TO REPORT ON THIS TRAVEL ROUTE TO YOUR SUPERIORS--
--AFTER ACCESSING IT TWICE WITHOUT PERMISSION?
YES, OF COURSE.

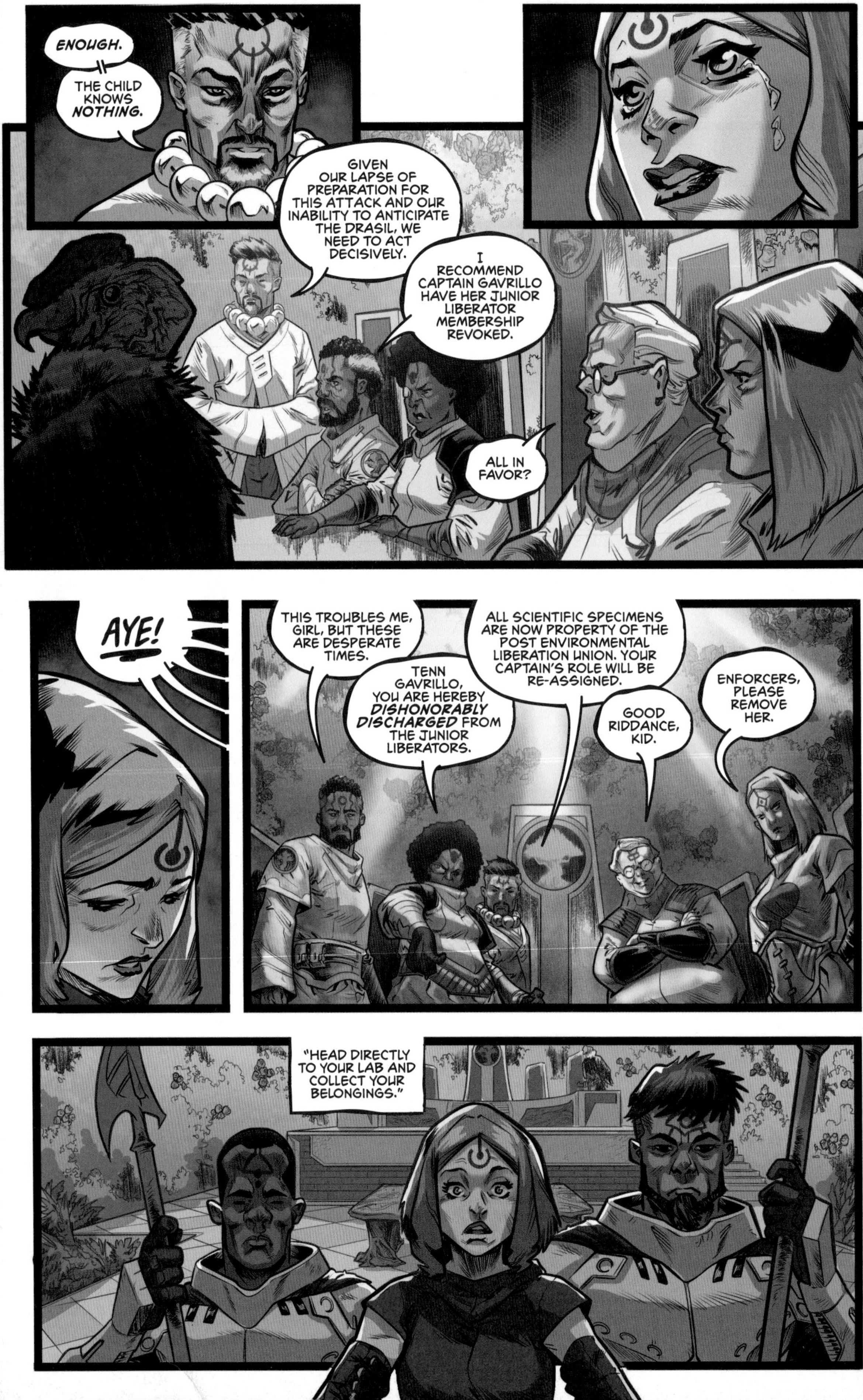
ENOUGH.
THE CHILD KNOWS NOTHING.
GIVEN OUR LAPSE OF PREPARATION FOR THIS ATTACK AND OUR INABILITY TO ANTICIPATE THE DRASIL, WE NEED TO ACT DECISIVELY.
I RECOMMEND CAPTAIN GAVRILLO HAVE HER JUNIOR LIBERATOR MEMBERSHIP REVOKED.
ALL IN FAVOR?
AYE!
THIS TROUBLES ME, GIRL, BUT THESE ARE DESPERATE TIMES.
TENN GAVRILLO, YOU ARE HEREBY DISHONORABLY DISCHARGED FROM THE JUNIOR LIBERATORS.
ALL SCIENTIFIC SPECIMENS ARE NOW PROPERTY OF THE POST ENVIRONMENTAL LIBERATION UNION. YOUR CAPTAIN'S ROLE WILL BE RE-ASSIGNED.
GOOD RIDDANCE, KID.
ENFORCERS, PLEASE REMOVE HER.
"HEAD DIRECTLY TO YOUR LAB AND COLLECT YOUR BELONGINGS."

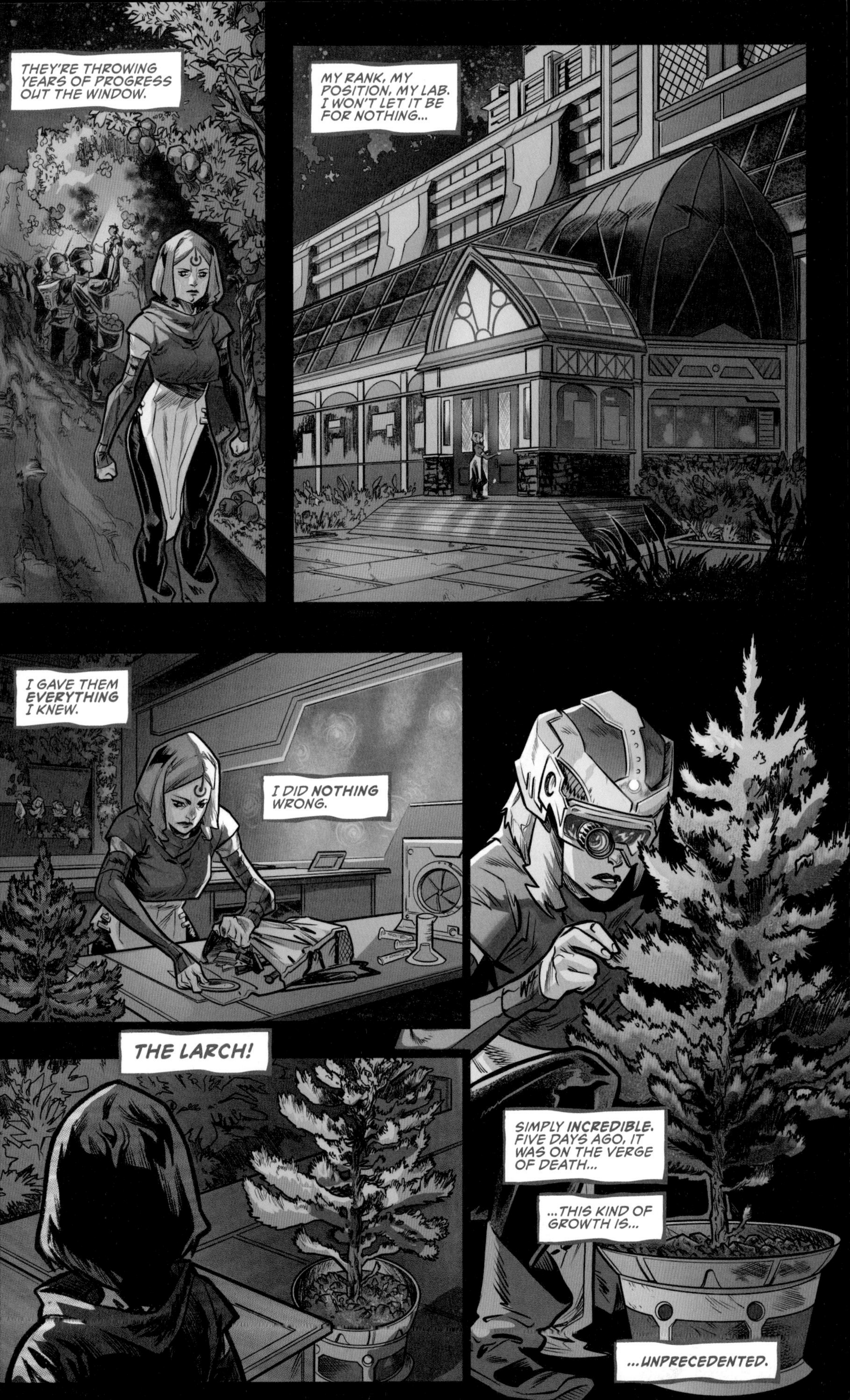
THEY'RE THROWING YEARS OF PROGRESS OUT THE WINDOW.
MY RANK, MY POSITION, MY LAB. I WON'T LET IT BE FOR NOTHING...
I GAVE THEM EVERYTHING I KNEW.
I DID NOTHING WRONG.
THE LARCH!
SIMPLY INCREDIBLE. FIVE DAYS AGO, IT WAS ON THE VERGE OF DEATH...
...THIS KIND OF GROWTH IS...
...UNPRECEDENTED.

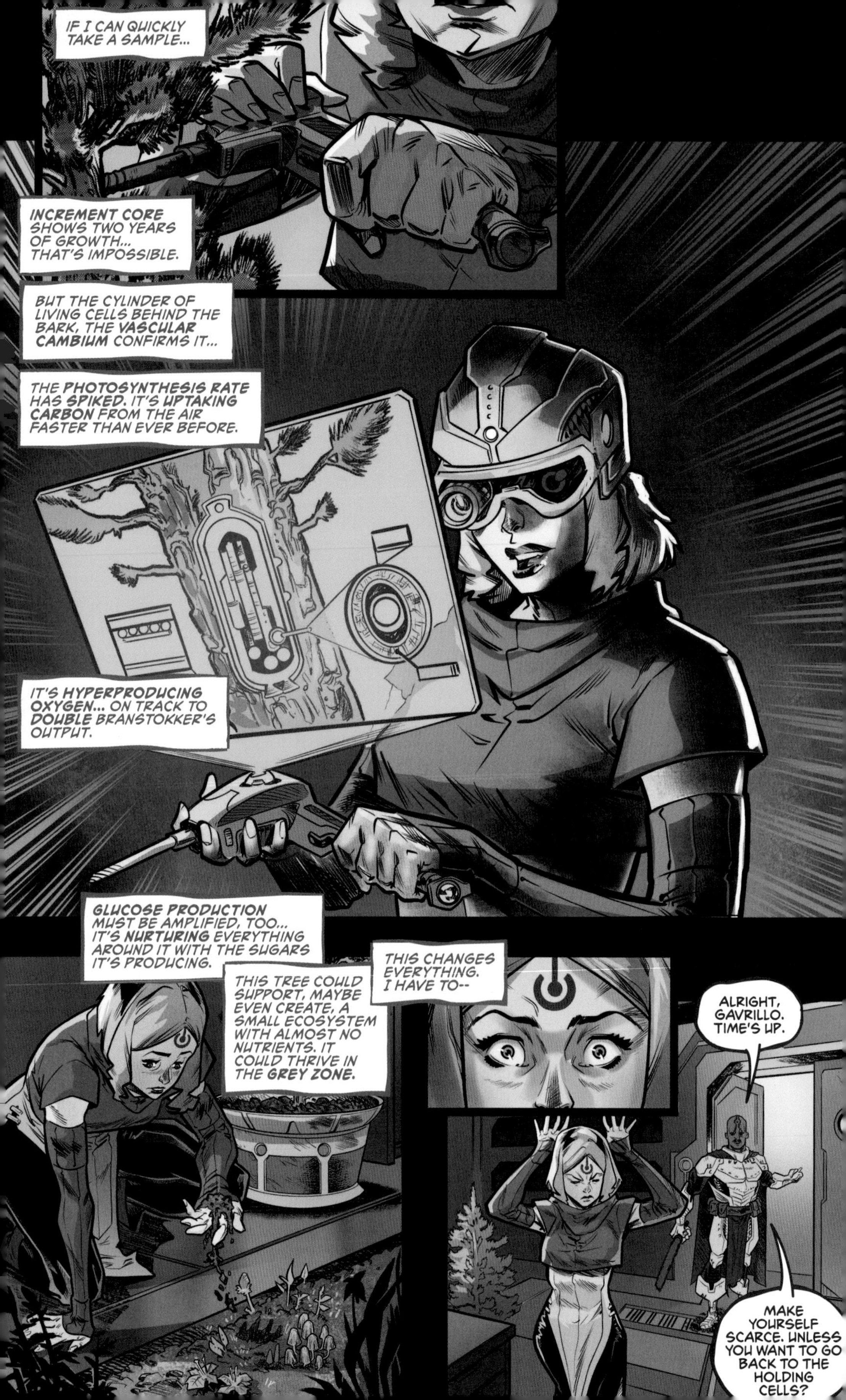
IF I CAN QUICKLY TAKE A SAMPLE...
INCREMENT CORE SHOWS TWO YEARS OF GROWTH... THAT'S IMPOSSIBLE.
BUT THE CYLINDER OF LIVING CELLS BEHIND THE BARK, THE VASCULAR CAMBIUM CONFIRMS IT...
THE PHOTOSYNTHESIS RATE HAS SPIKED. IT'S UPTAKING CARBON FROM THE AIR FASTER THAN EVER BEFORE.
IT'S HYPERPRODUCING OXYGEN... ON TRACK TO DOUBLE BRANSTOKKER'S OUTPUT.
GLUCOSE PRODUCTION MUST BE AMPLIFIED, TOO... IT'S NURTURING EVERYTHING AROUND IT WITH THE SUGARS IT'S PRODUCING.
THIS TREE COULD SUPPORT, MAYBE EVEN CREATE, A SMALL ECOSYSTEM WITH ALMOST NO NUTRIENTS. IT COULD THRIVE IN THE GREY ZONE.
THIS CHANGES EVERYTHING. I HAVE TO--
ALRIGHT, GAVRILLO. TIME'S UP.
MAKE YOURSELF SCARCE. UNLESS YOU WANT TO GO BACK TO THE HOLDING CELLS?

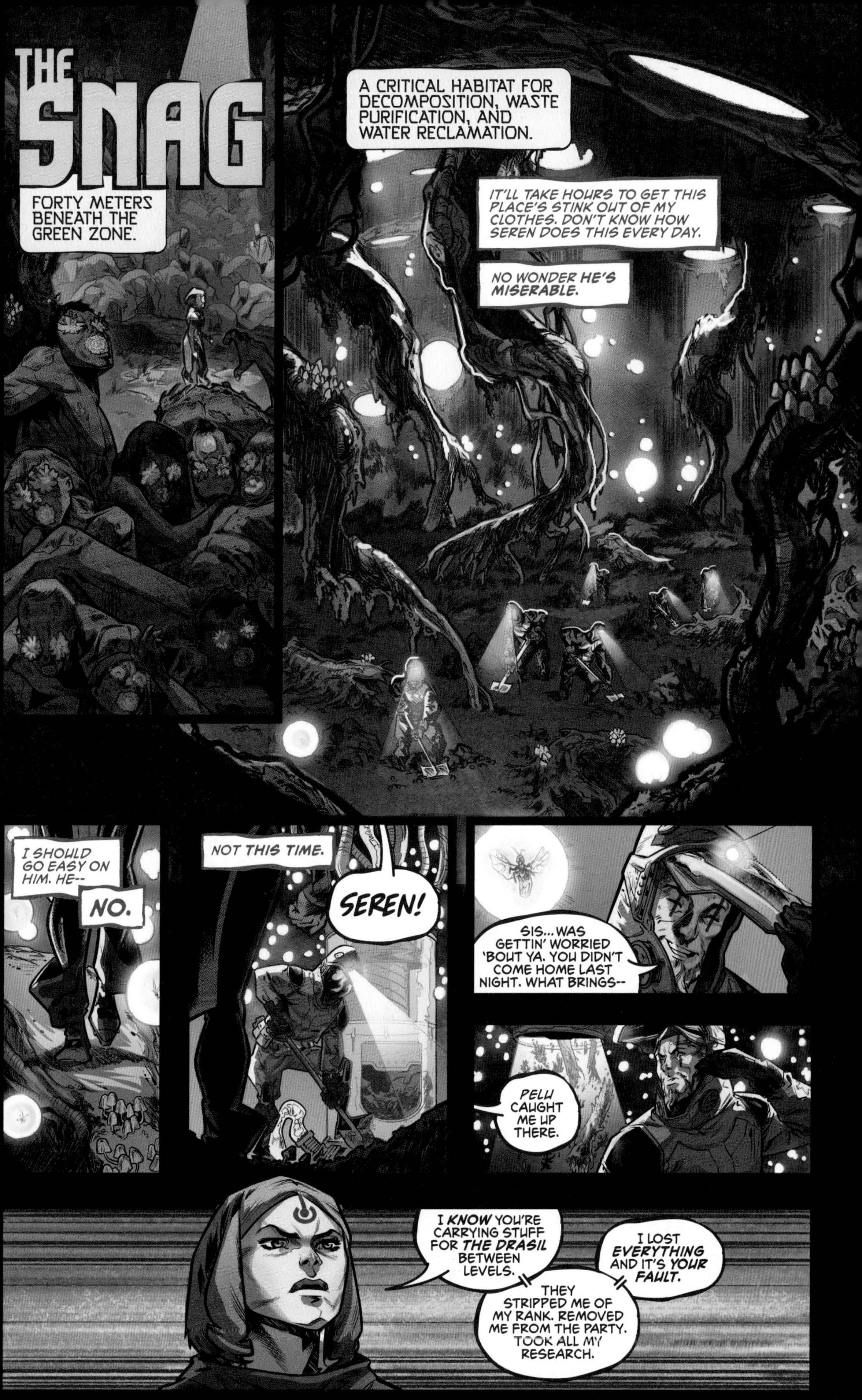
THE SNAG
FORTY METERS BENEATH THE GREEN ZONE.
A CRITICAL HABITAT FOR DECOMPOSITION, WASTE PURIFICATION, AND WATER RECLAMATION.
IT'LL TAKE HOURS TO GET THIS PLACE'S STINK OUT OF MY CLOTHES. DON'T KNOW HOW SEREN DOES THIS EVERY DAY.
NO WONDER HE'S MISERABLE.
I SHOULD GO EASY ON HIM. HE--
NO.
NOT THIS TIME.
SEREN!
SIS...WAS GETTIN' WORRIED 'BOUT YA. YOU DIDN'T COME HOME LAST NIGHT. WHAT BRINGS--
PELU CAUGHT ME UP THERE.
I KNOW YOU'RE CARRYING STUFF FOR THE DRASIL BETWEEN LEVELS.
THEY STRIPPED ME OF MY RANK. REMOVED ME FROM THE PARTY. TOOK ALL MY RESEARCH.
I LOST EVERYTHING AND IT'S YOUR FAULT.

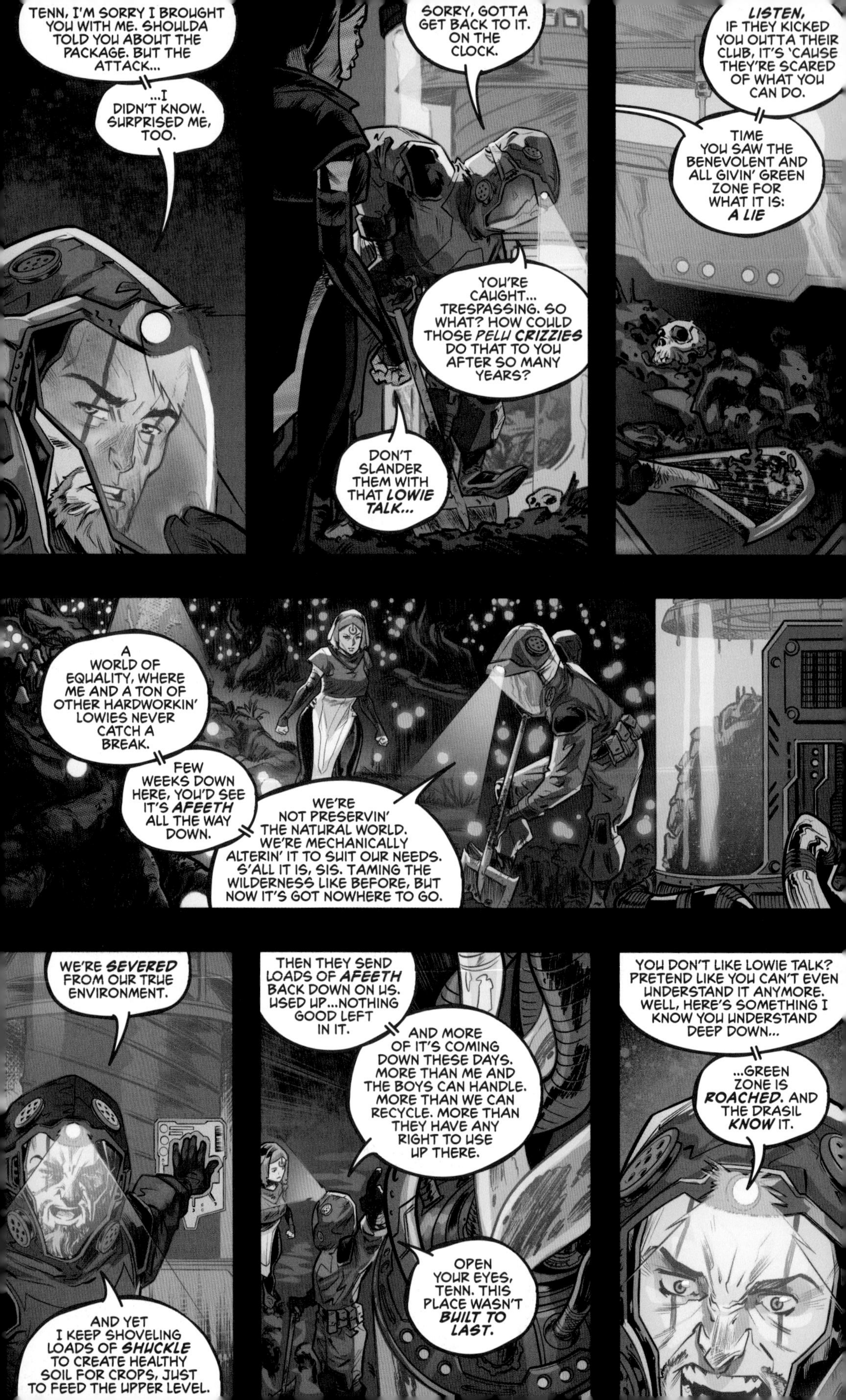

TENN, I'M SORRY I BROUGHT YOU WITH ME. SHOULDA TOLD YOU ABOUT THE PACKAGE. BUT THE ATTACK...
...I DIDN'T KNOW. SURPRISED ME, TOO.
SORRY, GOTTA GET BACK TO IT. ON THE CLOCK.
YOU'RE CAUGHT... TRESPASSING. SO WHAT? HOW COULD THOSE *PELU CRIZZIES* DO THAT TO YOU AFTER SO MANY YEARS?
DON'T SLANDER THEM WITH THAT ***LOWIE TALK...***
LISTEN, IF THEY KICKED YOU OUTTA THEIR CLUB, IT'S 'CAUSE THEY'RE SCARED OF WHAT YOU CAN DO.
TIME YOU SAW THE BENEVOLENT AND ALL GIVIN' GREEN ZONE FOR WHAT IT IS: ***A LIE***
A WORLD OF EQUALITY, WHERE ME AND A TON OF OTHER HARDWORKIN' LOWIES NEVER CATCH A BREAK.
FEW WEEKS DOWN HERE, YOU'D SEE IT'S ***AFEETH*** ALL THE WAY DOWN.
WE'RE NOT PRESERVIN' THE NATURAL WORLD. WE'RE MECHANICALLY ALTERIN' IT TO SUIT OUR NEEDS. S'ALL IT IS, SIS. TAMING THE WILDERNESS LIKE BEFORE, BUT NOW IT'S GOT NOWHERE TO GO.
WE'RE ***SEVERED*** FROM OUR TRUE ENVIRONMENT.
AND YET I KEEP SHOVELING LOADS OF ***SHUCKLE*** TO CREATE HEALTHY SOIL FOR CROPS, JUST TO FEED THE UPPER LEVEL.
THEN THEY SEND LOADS OF ***AFEETH*** BACK DOWN ON US. USED UP...NOTHING GOOD LEFT IN IT.
AND MORE OF IT'S COMING DOWN THESE DAYS. MORE THAN ME AND THE BOYS CAN HANDLE. MORE THAN WE CAN RECYCLE. MORE THAN THEY HAVE ANY RIGHT TO USE UP THERE.
OPEN YOUR EYES, TENN. THIS PLACE WASN'T ***BUILT TO LAST.***
YOU DON'T LIKE LOWIE TALK? PRETEND LIKE YOU CAN'T EVEN UNDERSTAND IT ANYMORE. WELL, HERE'S SOMETHING I KNOW YOU UNDERSTAND DEEP DOWN...
...GREEN ZONE IS ***ROACHED.*** AND THE DRASIL ***KNOW*** IT.

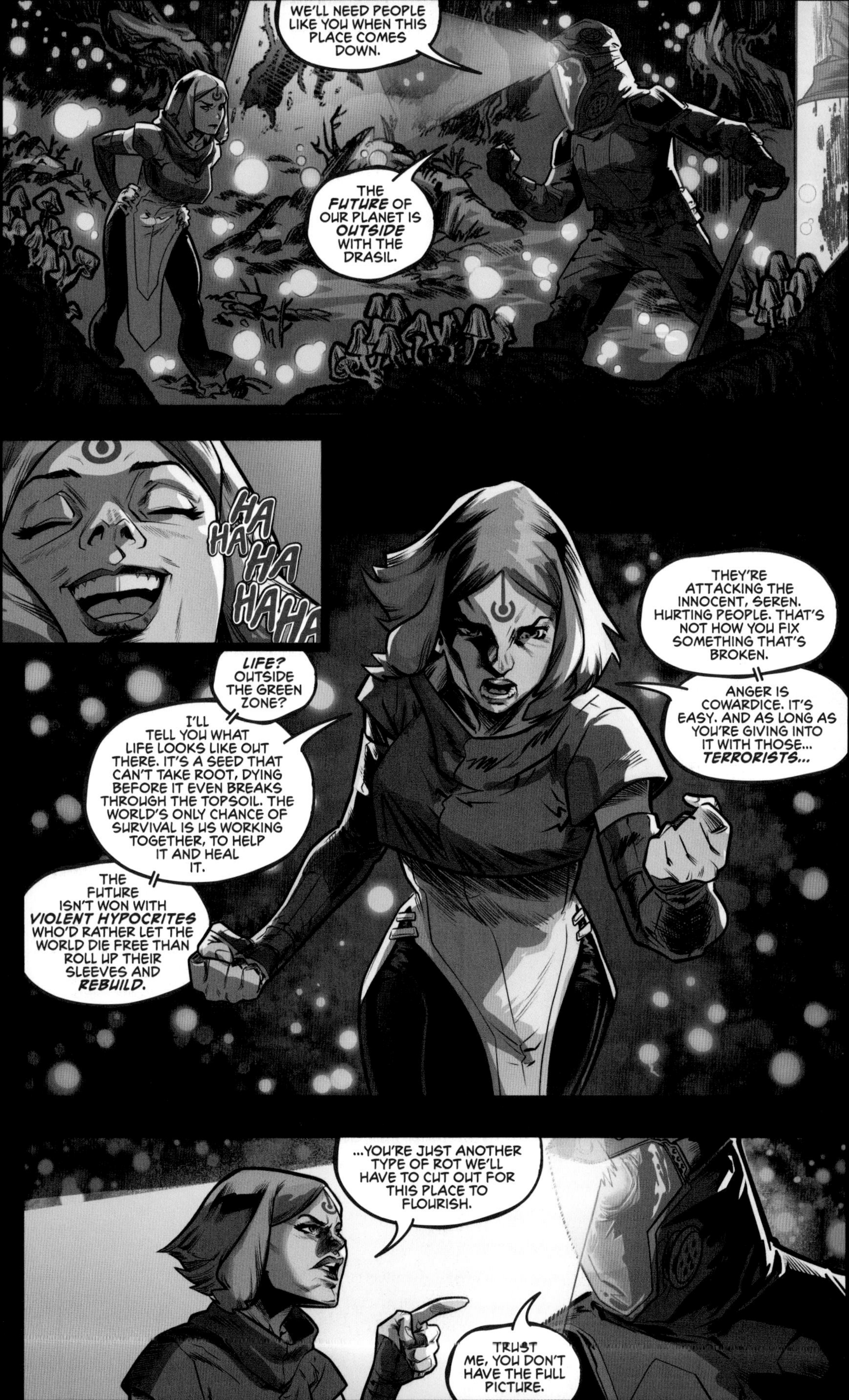
WE'LL NEED PEOPLE LIKE YOU WHEN THIS PLACE COMES DOWN.
THE *FUTURE* OF OUR PLANET IS *OUTSIDE* WITH THE DRASIL.
HA HA HA HAHAHA
LIFE? OUTSIDE THE GREEN ZONE?
I'LL TELL YOU WHAT LIFE LOOKS LIKE OUT THERE. IT'S A SEED THAT CAN'T TAKE ROOT, DYING BEFORE IT EVEN BREAKS THROUGH THE TOPSOIL. THE WORLD'S ONLY CHANCE OF SURVIVAL IS US WORKING TOGETHER, TO HELP IT AND HEAL IT.
THE FUTURE ISN'T WON WITH *VIOLENT HYPOCRITES* WHO'D RATHER LET THE WORLD DIE FREE THAN ROLL UP THEIR SLEEVES AND *REBUILD.*
THEY'RE ATTACKING THE INNOCENT, SEREN. HURTING PEOPLE. THAT'S NOT HOW YOU FIX SOMETHING THAT'S BROKEN.
ANGER IS COWARDICE. IT'S EASY. AND AS LONG AS YOU'RE GIVING INTO IT WITH THOSE... *TERRORISTS...*
...YOU'RE JUST ANOTHER TYPE OF ROT WE'LL HAVE TO CUT OUT FOR THIS PLACE TO FLOURISH.
TRUST ME, YOU DON'T HAVE THE FULL PICTURE.

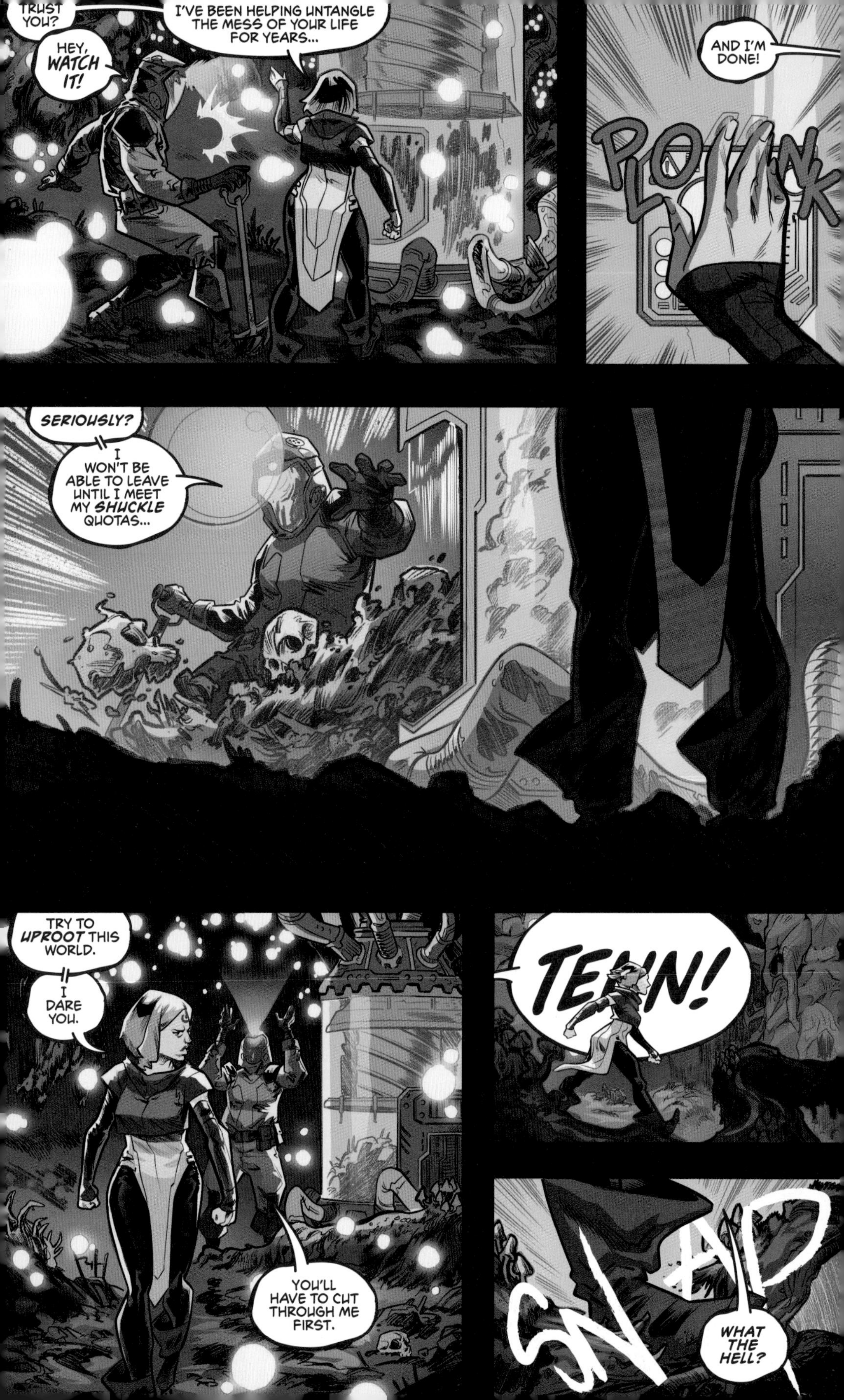
TRUST YOU?
I'VE BEEN HELPING UNTANGLE THE MESS OF YOUR LIFE FOR YEARS...
HEY, WATCH IT!
AND I'M DONE!
PLOINK
SERIOUSLY?
I WON'T BE ABLE TO LEAVE UNTIL I MEET MY SHUCKLE QUOTAS...
TRY TO UPROOT THIS WORLD.
I DARE YOU.
YOU'LL HAVE TO CUT THROUGH ME FIRST.
TENN!
SNAP
WHAT THE HELL?

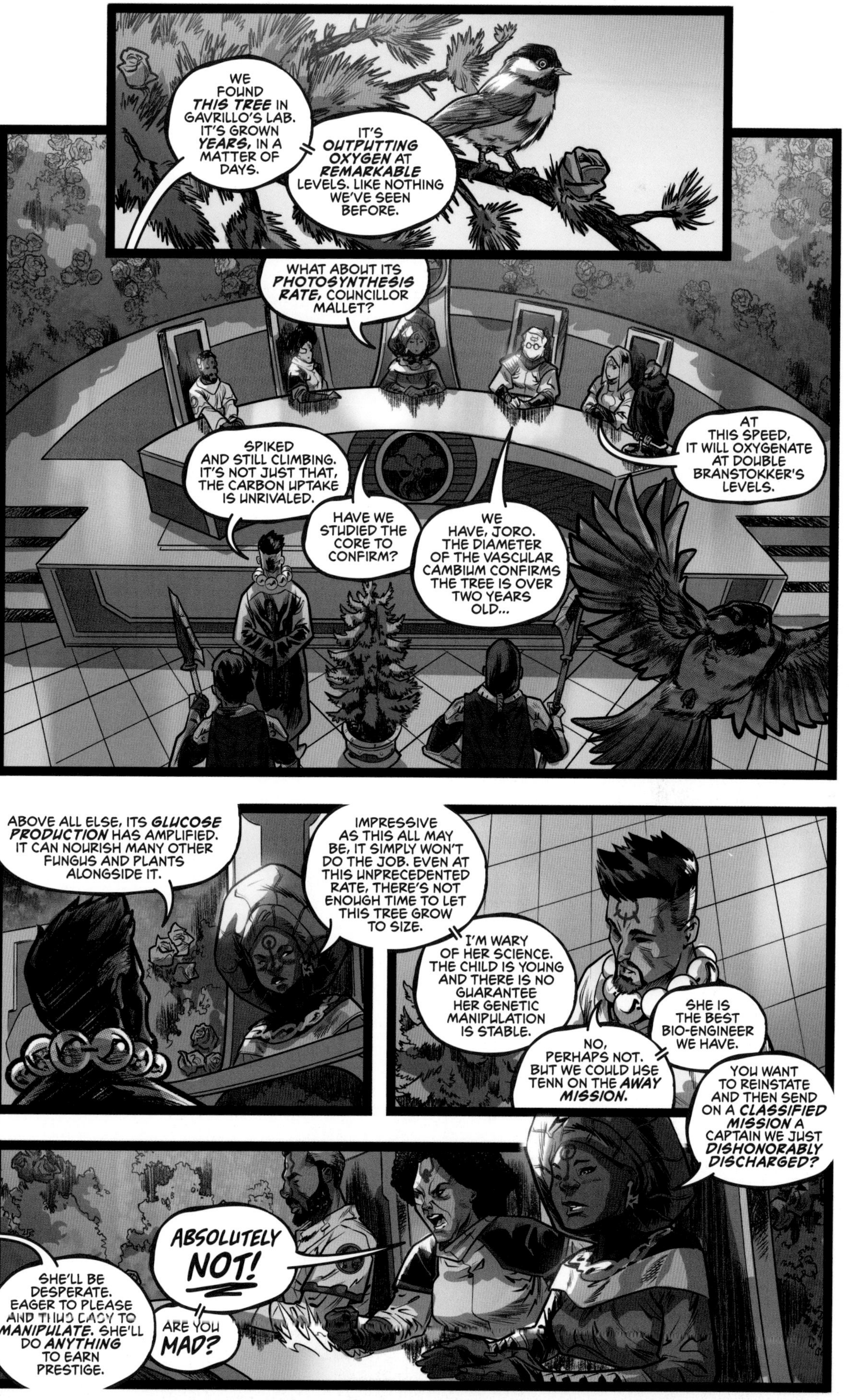
WE FOUND *THIS TREE* IN GAVRILLO'S LAB. IT'S GROWN *YEARS,* IN A MATTER OF DAYS.
IT'S *OUTPUTTING OXYGEN* AT *REMARKABLE* LEVELS. LIKE NOTHING WE'VE SEEN BEFORE.
WHAT ABOUT ITS *PHOTOSYNTHESIS RATE,* COUNCILLOR MALLET?
SPIKED AND STILL CLIMBING. IT'S NOT JUST THAT, THE CARBON UPTAKE IS UNRIVALED.
HAVE WE STUDIED THE CORE TO CONFIRM?
WE HAVE, JORO. THE DIAMETER OF THE VASCULAR CAMBIUM CONFIRMS THE TREE IS OVER TWO YEARS OLD...
AT THIS SPEED, IT WILL OXYGENATE AT DOUBLE BRANSTOKKER'S LEVELS.
ABOVE ALL ELSE, ITS *GLUCOSE PRODUCTION* HAS AMPLIFIED. IT CAN NOURISH MANY OTHER FUNGUS AND PLANTS ALONGSIDE IT.
IMPRESSIVE AS THIS ALL MAY BE, IT SIMPLY WON'T DO THE JOB. EVEN AT THIS UNPRECEDENTED RATE, THERE'S NOT ENOUGH TIME TO LET THIS TREE GROW TO SIZE.
I'M WARY OF HER SCIENCE. THE CHILD IS YOUNG AND THERE IS NO GUARANTEE HER GENETIC MANIPULATION IS STABLE.
SHE IS THE BEST BIO-ENGINEER WE HAVE.
NO, PERHAPS NOT. BUT WE COULD USE TENN ON THE *AWAY MISSION.*
YOU WANT TO REINSTATE AND THEN SEND ON A *CLASSIFIED MISSION* A CAPTAIN WE JUST *DISHONORABLY DISCHARGED?*
ABSOLUTELY NOT!
ARE YOU *MAD?*
SHE'LL BE DESPERATE. EAGER TO PLEASE AND THUS EASY TO *MANIPULATE.* SHE'LL DO *ANYTHING* TO EARN PRESTIGE.

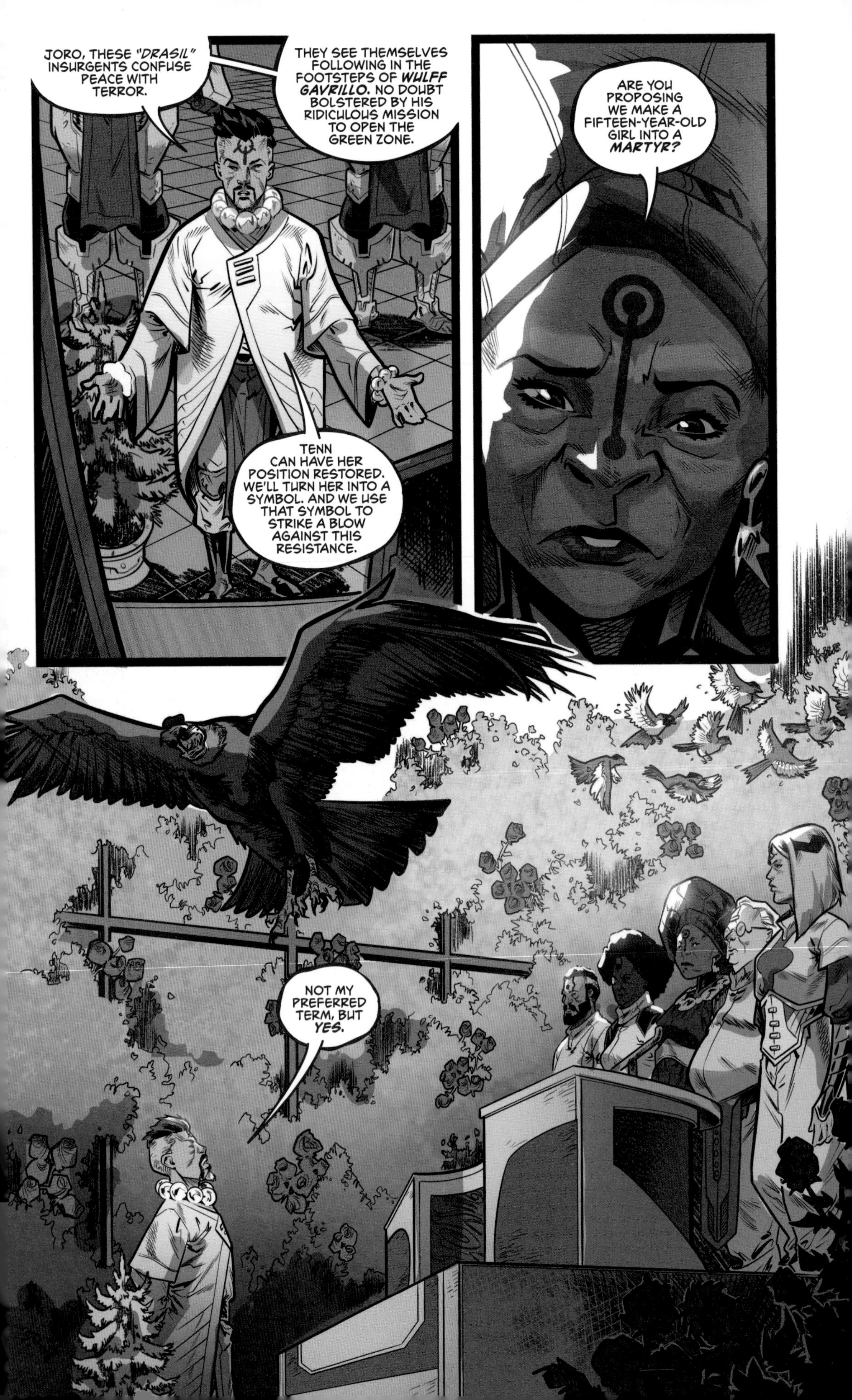
JORO, THESE "DRASIL" INSURGENTS CONFUSE PEACE WITH TERROR.
THEY SEE THEMSELVES FOLLOWING IN THE FOOTSTEPS OF WULFF GAVRILLO. NO DOUBT BOLSTERED BY HIS RIDICULOUS MISSION TO OPEN THE GREEN ZONE.
TENN CAN HAVE HER POSITION RESTORED. WE'LL TURN HER INTO A SYMBOL. AND WE USE THAT SYMBOL TO STRIKE A BLOW AGAINST THIS RESISTANCE.
ARE YOU PROPOSING WE MAKE A FIFTEEN-YEAR-OLD GIRL INTO A MARTYR?
NOT MY PREFERRED TERM, BUT YES.

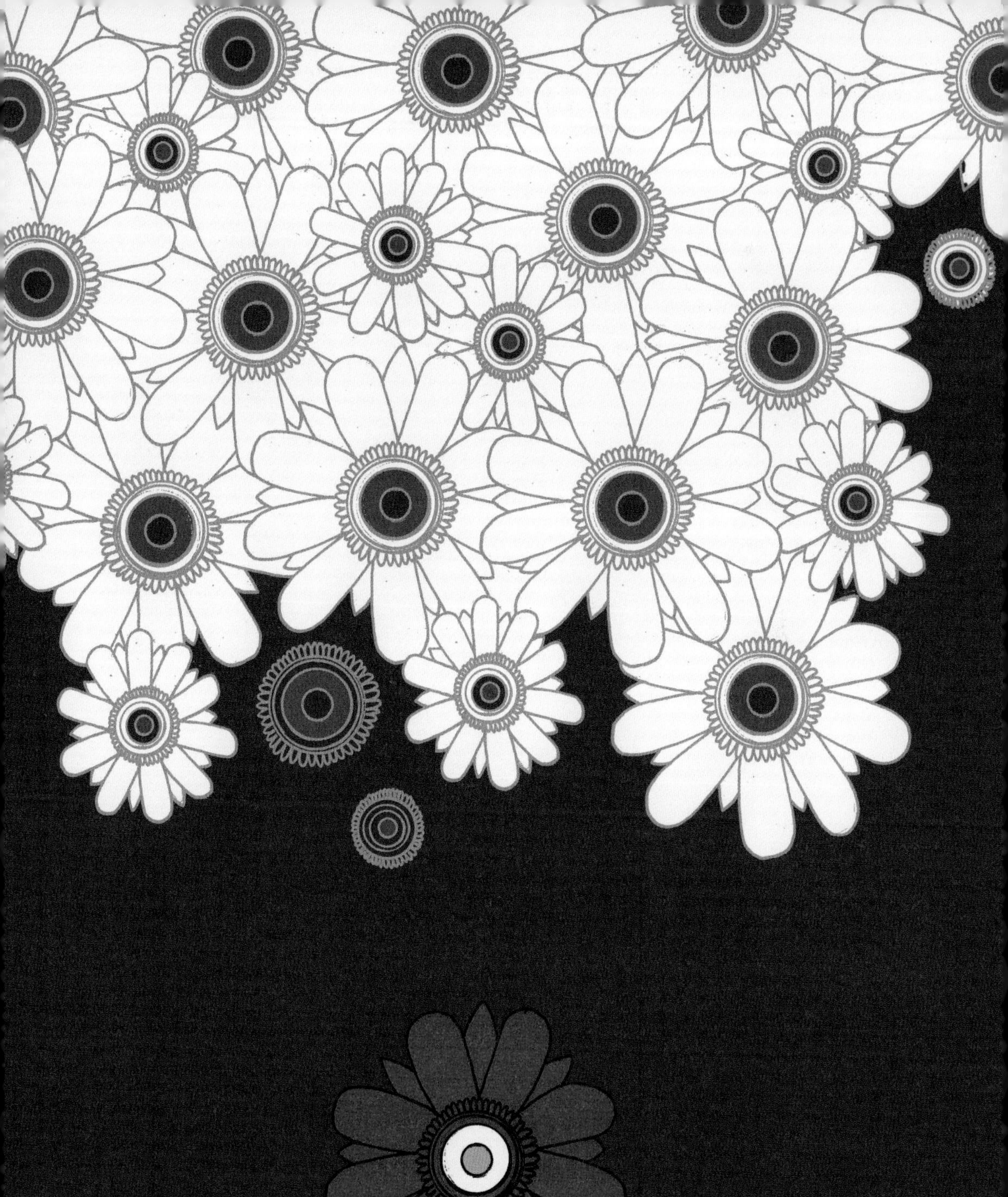

SHALL BE, BLOOMING:

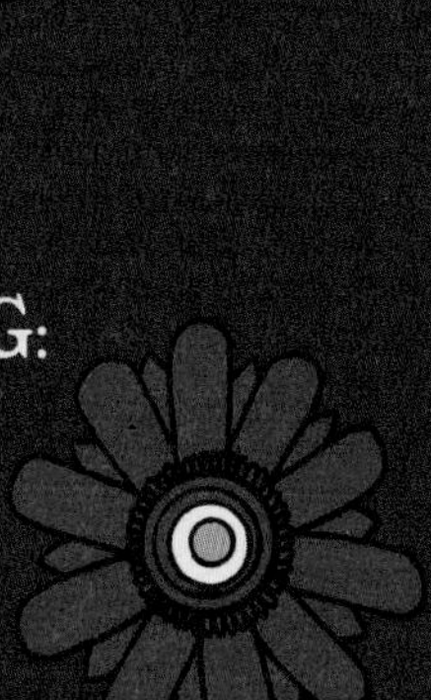

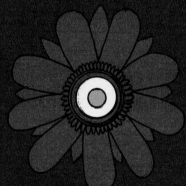

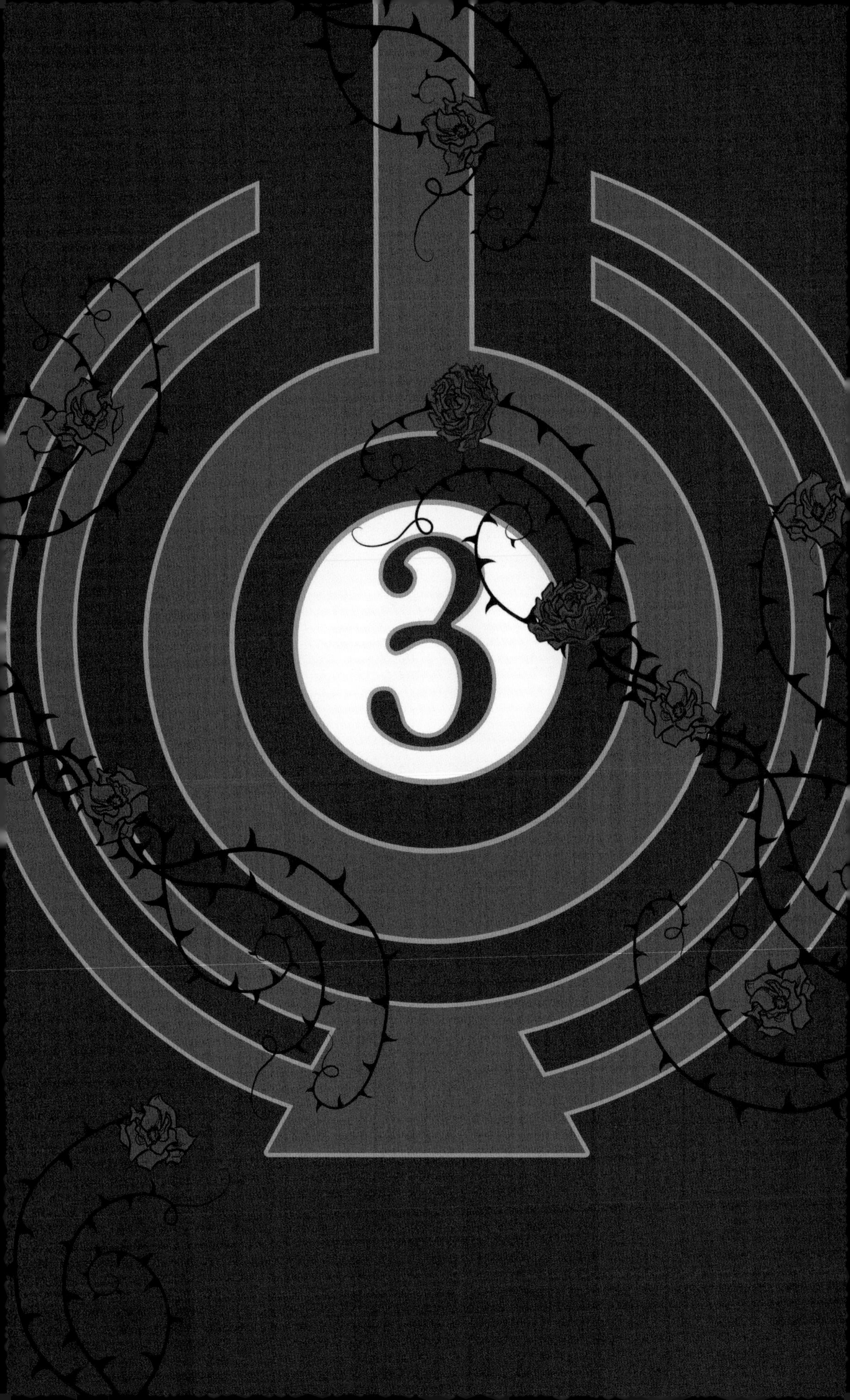
3

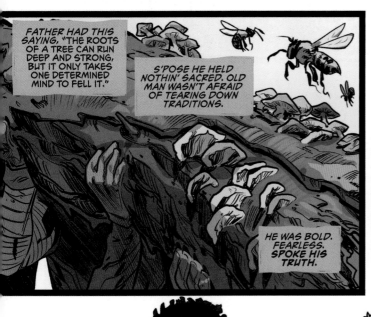

FATHER HAD THIS SAYING, "THE ROOTS OF A TREE CAN RUN DEEP AND STRONG, BUT IT ONLY TAKES ONE DETERMINED MIND TO FELL IT."

S'POSE HE HELD NOTHIN' SACRED. OLD MAN WASN'T AFRAID OF TEARING DOWN TRADITIONS.

HE WAS BOLD. FEARLESS. SPOKE HIS TRUTH.

I OWE IT TO HIS MEMORY TO DO THE SAME.

SEREN, I CAN ONLY BUY YOU FIVE MINUTES BEFORE THEY STORM THIS PLACE.

WE'LL ONLY NEED ONE, ENOCK.

CAREFUL. KNOW YOUR EXIT.

SPENT HIS ENTIRE CAREER WORKING FOR PELU...

THEY SAID HE WENT INSANE. CREATIN' THINGS LIKE THIS CALCIFIED SOLANDRA HAMMER.

AFEETH! ALL OF IT.

I KNOW THE FACTS.

THEY KILLED HIM TO BURY THE TRUTH HE KNEW BRANSTOKKER WAS DYING.

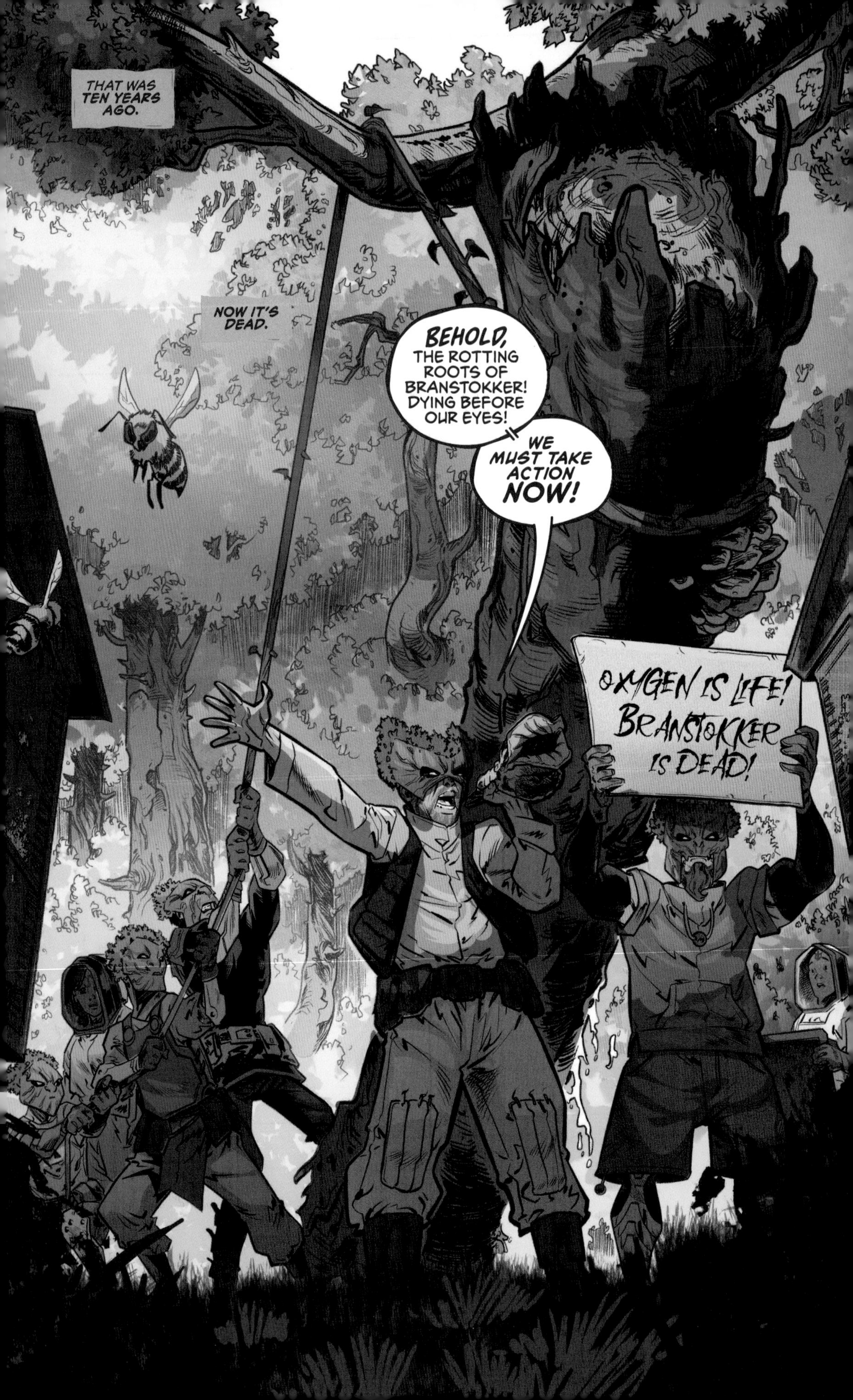
THAT WAS TEN YEARS AGO.
NOW IT'S DEAD.
BEHOLD, THE ROTTING ROOTS OF BRANSTOKKER! DYING BEFORE OUR EYES!
WE MUST TAKE ACTION NOW!
OXYGEN IS LIFE! BRANSTOKKER IS DEAD!

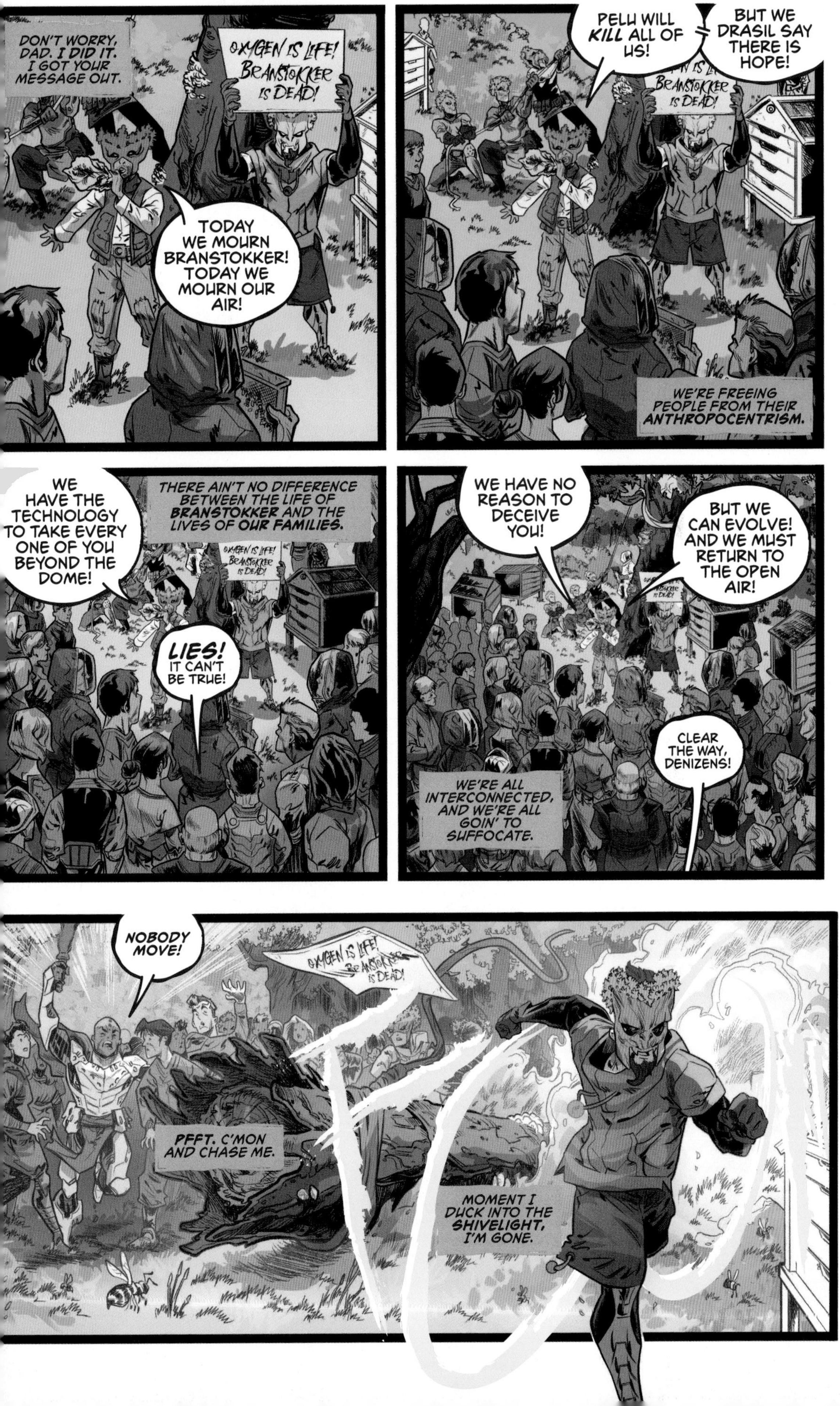
DON'T WORRY, DAD. I DID IT. I GOT YOUR MESSAGE OUT.
OXYGEN IS LIFE! BRANSTOKKER IS DEAD!
TODAY WE MOURN BRANSTOKKER! TODAY WE MOURN OUR AIR!
PELU WILL KILL ALL OF US!
BUT WE DRASIL SAY THERE IS HOPE!
WE'RE FREEING PEOPLE FROM THEIR ANTHROPOCENTRISM.
THERE AIN'T NO DIFFERENCE BETWEEN THE LIFE OF BRANSTOKKER AND THE LIVES OF OUR FAMILIES.
WE HAVE THE TECHNOLOGY TO TAKE EVERY ONE OF YOU BEYOND THE DOME!
LIES! IT CAN'T BE TRUE!
WE HAVE NO REASON TO DECEIVE YOU!
BUT WE CAN EVOLVE! AND WE MUST RETURN TO THE OPEN AIR!
CLEAR THE WAY, DENIZENS!
WE'RE ALL INTERCONNECTED, AND WE'RE ALL GOIN' TO SUFFOCATE.
NOBODY MOVE!
OXYGEN IS LIFE! BRANSTOKKER IS DEAD!
PFFT. C'MON AND CHASE ME.
MOMENT I DUCK INTO THE SHIVELIGHT, I'M GONE.

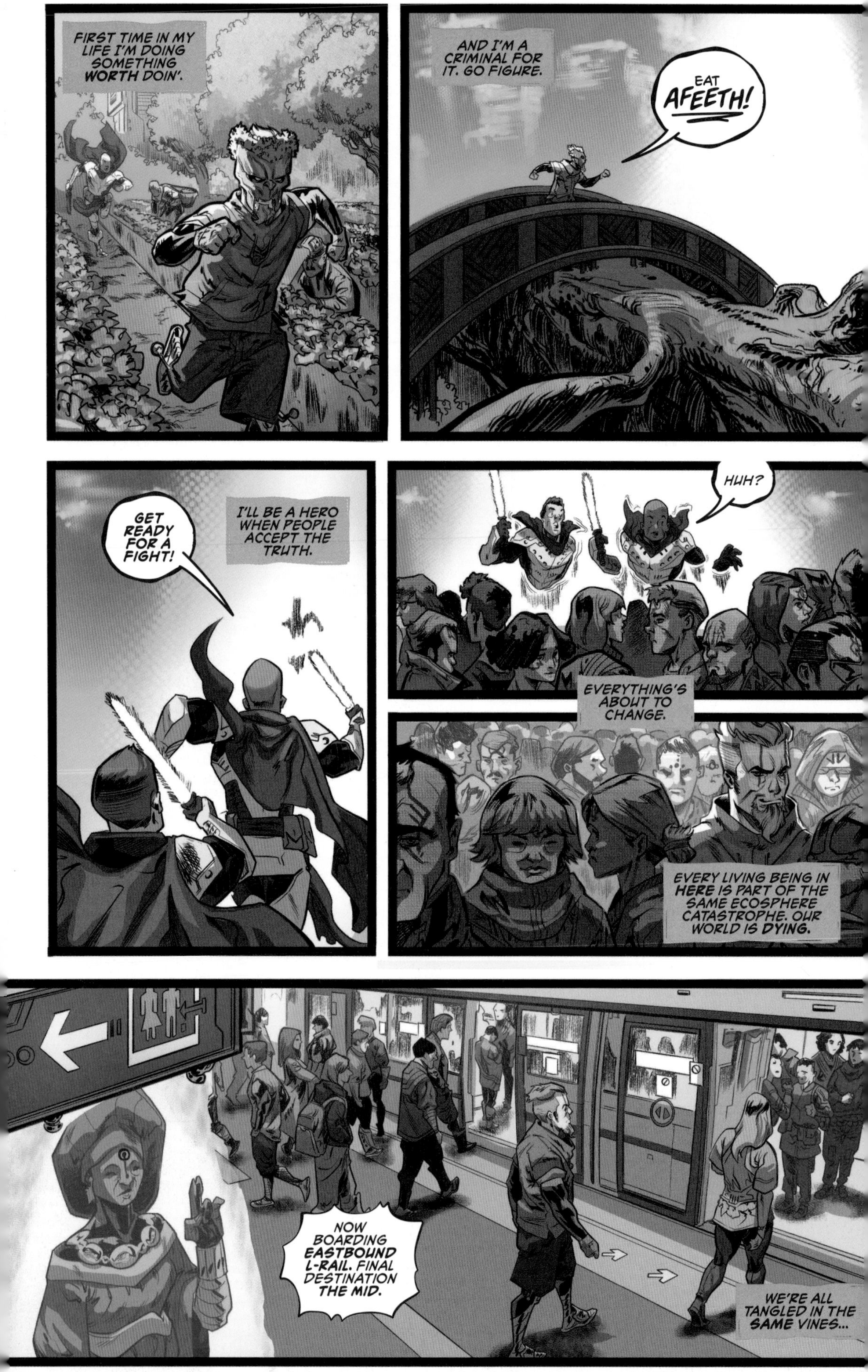
FIRST TIME IN MY LIFE I'M DOING SOMETHING WORTH DOIN'.
AND I'M A CRIMINAL FOR IT. GO FIGURE.
EAT AFEETH!
GET READY FOR A FIGHT!
I'LL BE A HERO WHEN PEOPLE ACCEPT THE TRUTH.
HUH?
EVERYTHING'S ABOUT TO CHANGE.
EVERY LIVING BEING IN HERE IS PART OF THE SAME ECOSPHERE CATASTROPHE. OUR WORLD IS DYING.
NOW BOARDING EASTBOUND L-RAIL. FINAL DESTINATION THE MID.
WE'RE ALL TANGLED IN THE SAME VINES...

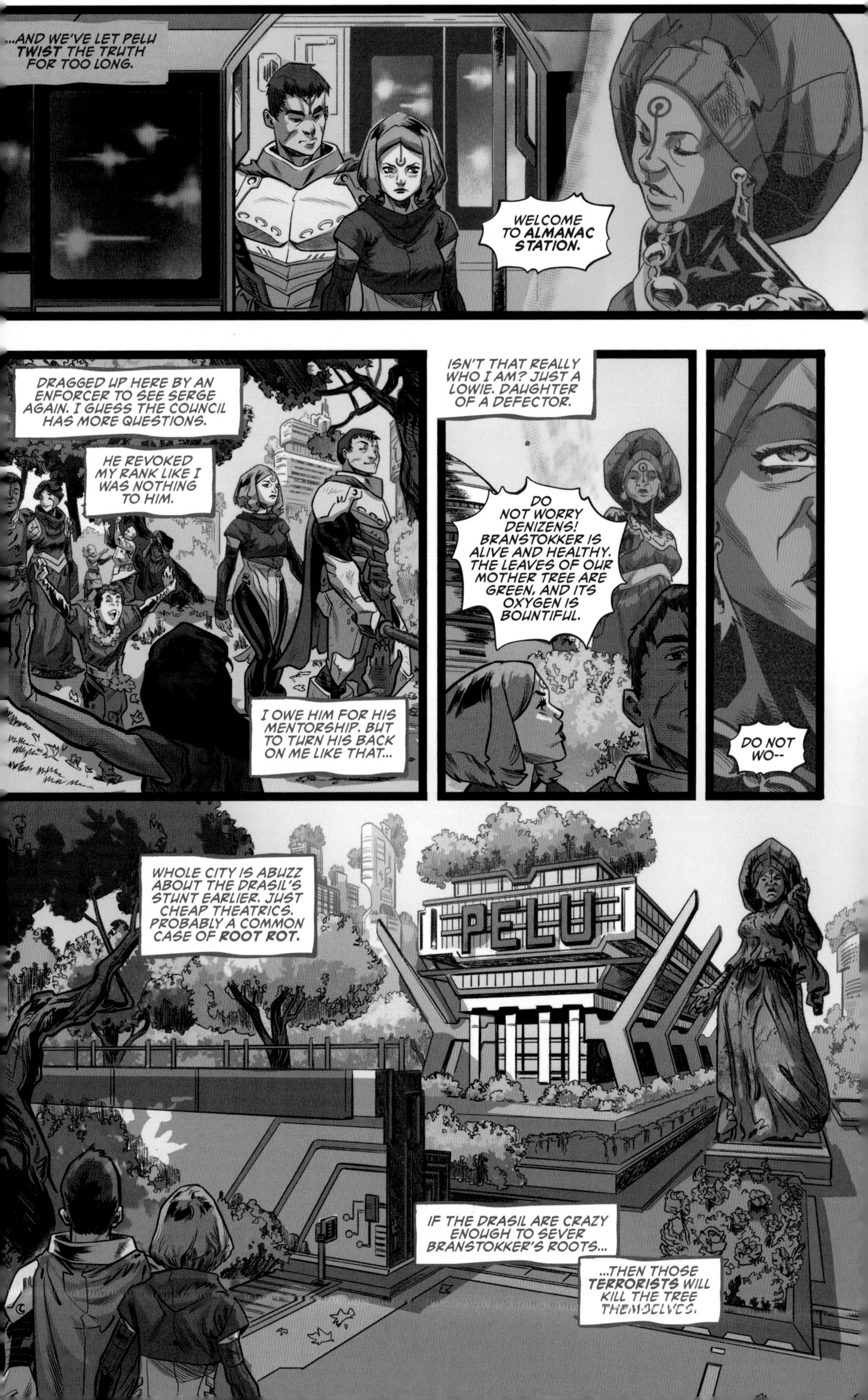

...AND WE'VE LET PELU TWIST THE TRUTH FOR TOO LONG.
WELCOME TO ALMANAC STATION.
DRAGGED UP HERE BY AN ENFORCER TO SEE SERGE AGAIN. I GUESS THE COUNCIL HAS MORE QUESTIONS.
HE REVOKED MY RANK LIKE I WAS NOTHING TO HIM.
I OWE HIM FOR HIS MENTORSHIP. BUT TO TURN HIS BACK ON ME LIKE THAT...
ISN'T THAT REALLY WHO I AM? JUST A LOWIE. DAUGHTER OF A DEFECTOR.
DO NOT WORRY DENIZENS! BRANSTOKKER IS ALIVE AND HEALTHY. THE LEAVES OF OUR MOTHER TREE ARE GREEN, AND ITS OXYGEN IS BOUNTIFUL.
DO NOT WO--
WHOLE CITY IS ABUZZ ABOUT THE DRASIL'S STUNT EARLIER. JUST CHEAP THEATRICS. PROBABLY A COMMON CASE OF ROOT ROT.
PELU
IF THE DRASIL ARE CRAZY ENOUGH TO SEVER BRANSTOKKER'S ROOTS...
...THEN THOSE TERRORISTS WILL KILL THE TREE THEMSELVES.

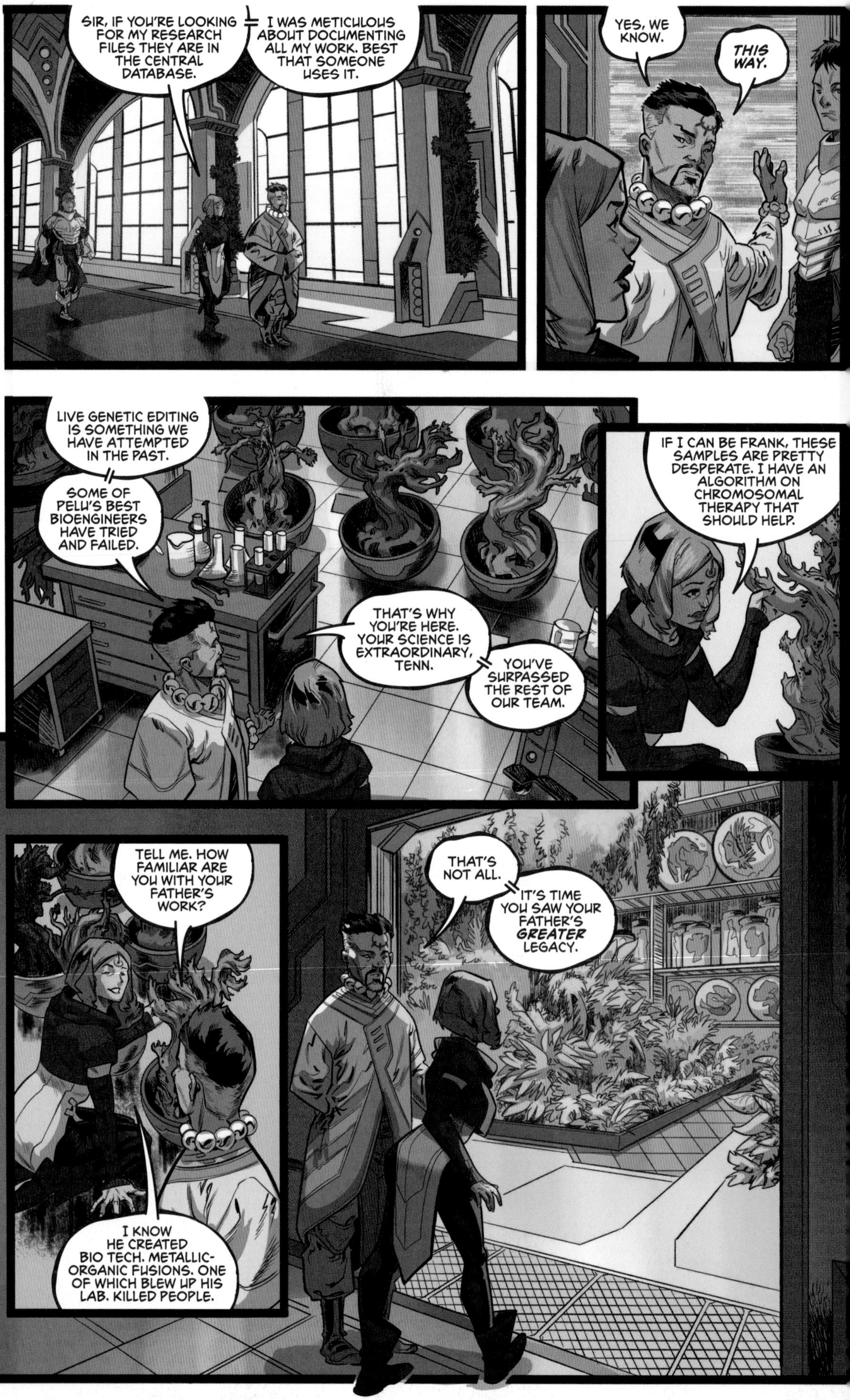

SIR, IF YOU'RE LOOKING FOR MY RESEARCH FILES THEY ARE IN THE CENTRAL DATABASE.
I WAS METICULOUS ABOUT DOCUMENTING ALL MY WORK. BEST THAT SOMEONE USES IT.
YES, WE KNOW.
THIS WAY.
LIVE GENETIC EDITING IS SOMETHING WE HAVE ATTEMPTED IN THE PAST.
SOME OF PELU'S BEST BIOENGINEERS HAVE TRIED AND FAILED.
THAT'S WHY YOU'RE HERE. YOUR SCIENCE IS EXTRAORDINARY, TENN.
YOU'VE SURPASSED THE REST OF OUR TEAM.
IF I CAN BE FRANK, THESE SAMPLES ARE PRETTY DESPERATE. I HAVE AN ALGORITHM ON CHROMOSOMAL THERAPY THAT SHOULD HELP.
TELL ME. HOW FAMILIAR ARE YOU WITH YOUR FATHER'S WORK?
I KNOW HE CREATED BIO TECH. METALLIC-ORGANIC FUSIONS. ONE OF WHICH BLEW UP HIS LAB. KILLED PEOPLE.
THAT'S NOT ALL.
IT'S TIME YOU SAW YOUR FATHER'S ***GREATER*** LEGACY.

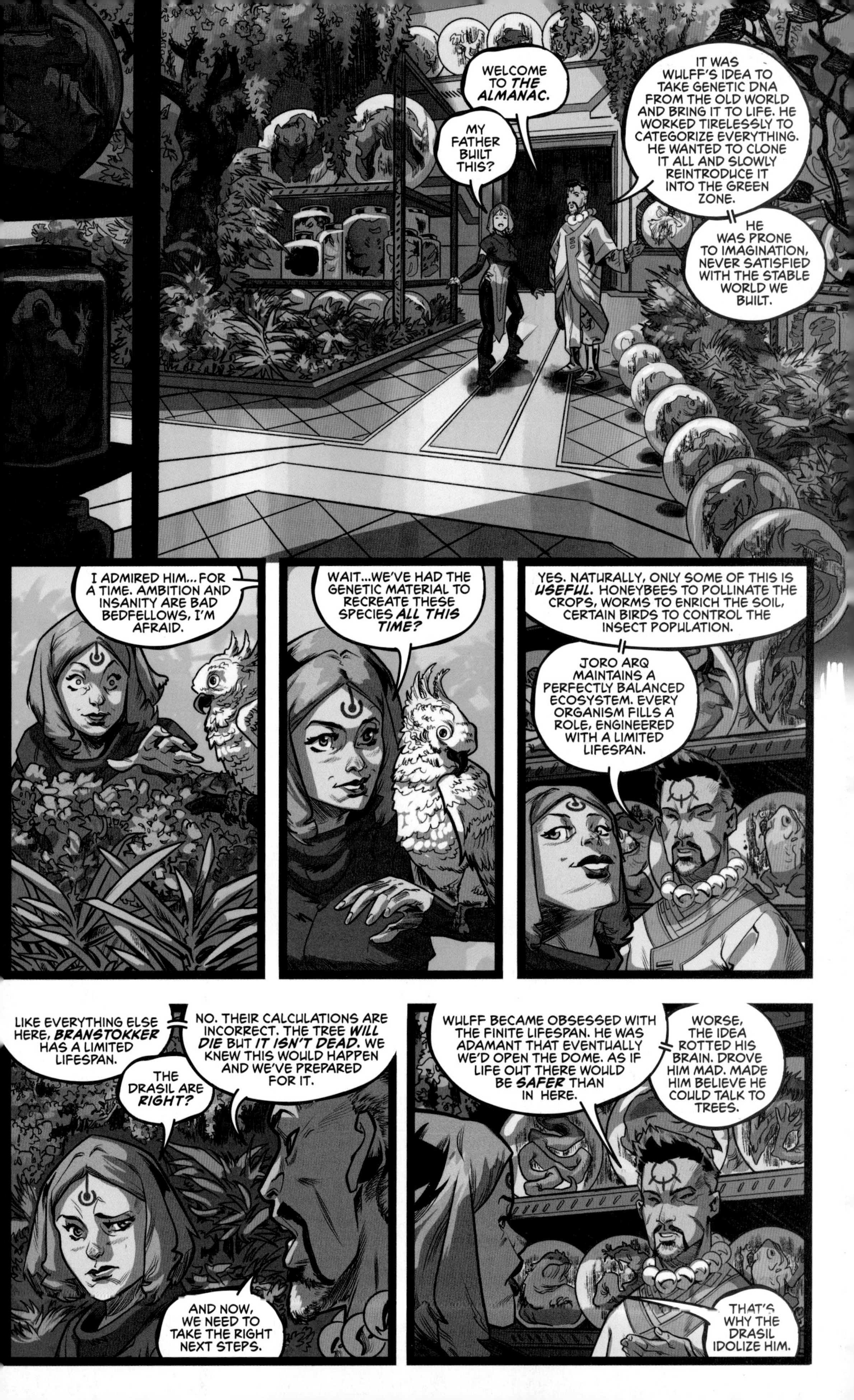
WELCOME TO THE ALMANAC.
MY FATHER BUILT THIS?
IT WAS WULFF'S IDEA TO TAKE GENETIC DNA FROM THE OLD WORLD AND BRING IT TO LIFE. HE WORKED TIRELESSLY TO CATEGORIZE EVERYTHING. HE WANTED TO CLONE IT ALL AND SLOWLY REINTRODUCE IT INTO THE GREEN ZONE.
HE WAS PRONE TO IMAGINATION, NEVER SATISFIED WITH THE STABLE WORLD WE BUILT.
I ADMIRED HIM... FOR A TIME. AMBITION AND INSANITY ARE BAD BEDFELLOWS, I'M AFRAID.
WAIT...WE'VE HAD THE GENETIC MATERIAL TO RECREATE THESE SPECIES ALL THIS TIME?
YES. NATURALLY, ONLY SOME OF THIS IS USEFUL. HONEYBEES TO POLLINATE THE CROPS, WORMS TO ENRICH THE SOIL, CERTAIN BIRDS TO CONTROL THE INSECT POPULATION.
JORO ARQ MAINTAINS A PERFECTLY BALANCED ECOSYSTEM. EVERY ORGANISM FILLS A ROLE, ENGINEERED WITH A LIMITED LIFESPAN.
LIKE EVERYTHING ELSE HERE, BRANSTOKKER HAS A LIMITED LIFESPAN.
THE DRASIL ARE RIGHT?
NO. THEIR CALCULATIONS ARE INCORRECT. THE TREE WILL DIE BUT IT ISN'T DEAD. WE KNEW THIS WOULD HAPPEN AND WE'VE PREPARED FOR IT.
AND NOW, WE NEED TO TAKE THE RIGHT NEXT STEPS.
WULFF BECAME OBSESSED WITH THE FINITE LIFESPAN. HE WAS ADAMANT THAT EVENTUALLY WE'D OPEN THE DOME. AS IF LIFE OUT THERE WOULD BE SAFER THAN IN HERE.
WORSE, THE IDEA ROTTED HIS BRAIN. DROVE HIM MAD. MADE HIM BELIEVE HE COULD TALK TO TREES.
THAT'S WHY THE DRASIL IDOLIZE HIM.

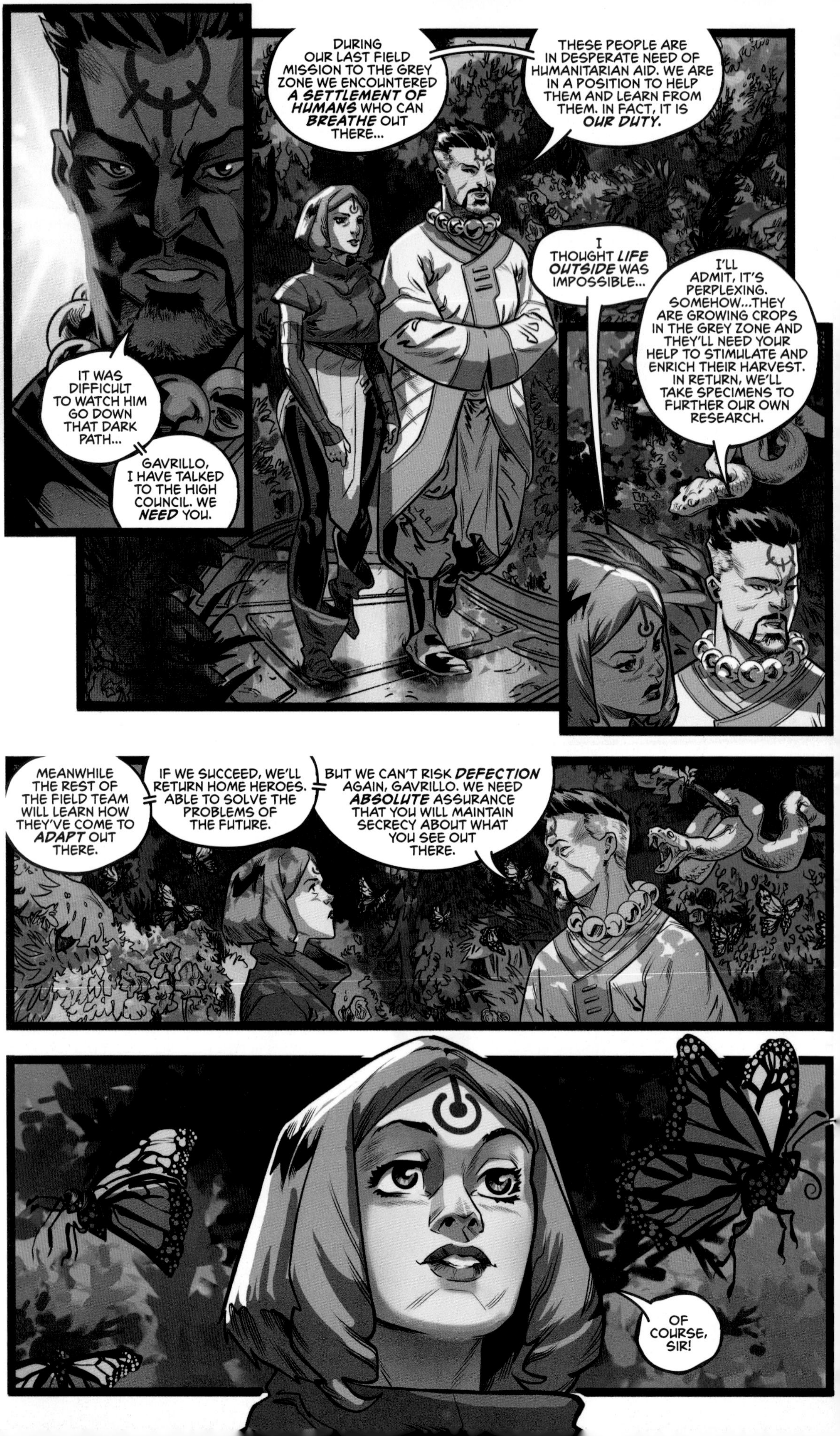
DURING OUR LAST FIELD MISSION TO THE GREY ZONE WE ENCOUNTERED *A SETTLEMENT OF HUMANS* WHO CAN *BREATHE* OUT THERE...
THESE PEOPLE ARE IN DESPERATE NEED OF HUMANITARIAN AID. WE ARE IN A POSITION TO HELP THEM AND LEARN FROM THEM. IN FACT, IT IS *OUR DUTY.*
IT WAS DIFFICULT TO WATCH HIM GO DOWN THAT DARK PATH...
GAVRILLO, I HAVE TALKED TO THE HIGH COUNCIL. WE *NEED* YOU.
I THOUGHT *LIFE OUTSIDE* WAS IMPOSSIBLE...
I'LL ADMIT, IT'S PERPLEXING. SOMEHOW...THEY ARE GROWING CROPS IN THE GREY ZONE AND THEY'LL NEED YOUR HELP TO STIMULATE AND ENRICH THEIR HARVEST. IN RETURN, WE'LL TAKE SPECIMENS TO FURTHER OUR OWN RESEARCH.
MEANWHILE THE REST OF THE FIELD TEAM WILL LEARN HOW THEY'VE COME TO *ADAPT* OUT THERE.
IF WE SUCCEED, WE'LL RETURN HOME HEROES. ABLE TO SOLVE THE PROBLEMS OF THE FUTURE.
BUT WE CAN'T RISK *DEFECTION* AGAIN, GAVRILLO. WE NEED *ABSOLUTE* ASSURANCE THAT YOU WILL MAINTAIN SECRECY ABOUT WHAT YOU SEE OUT THERE.
OF COURSE, SIR!

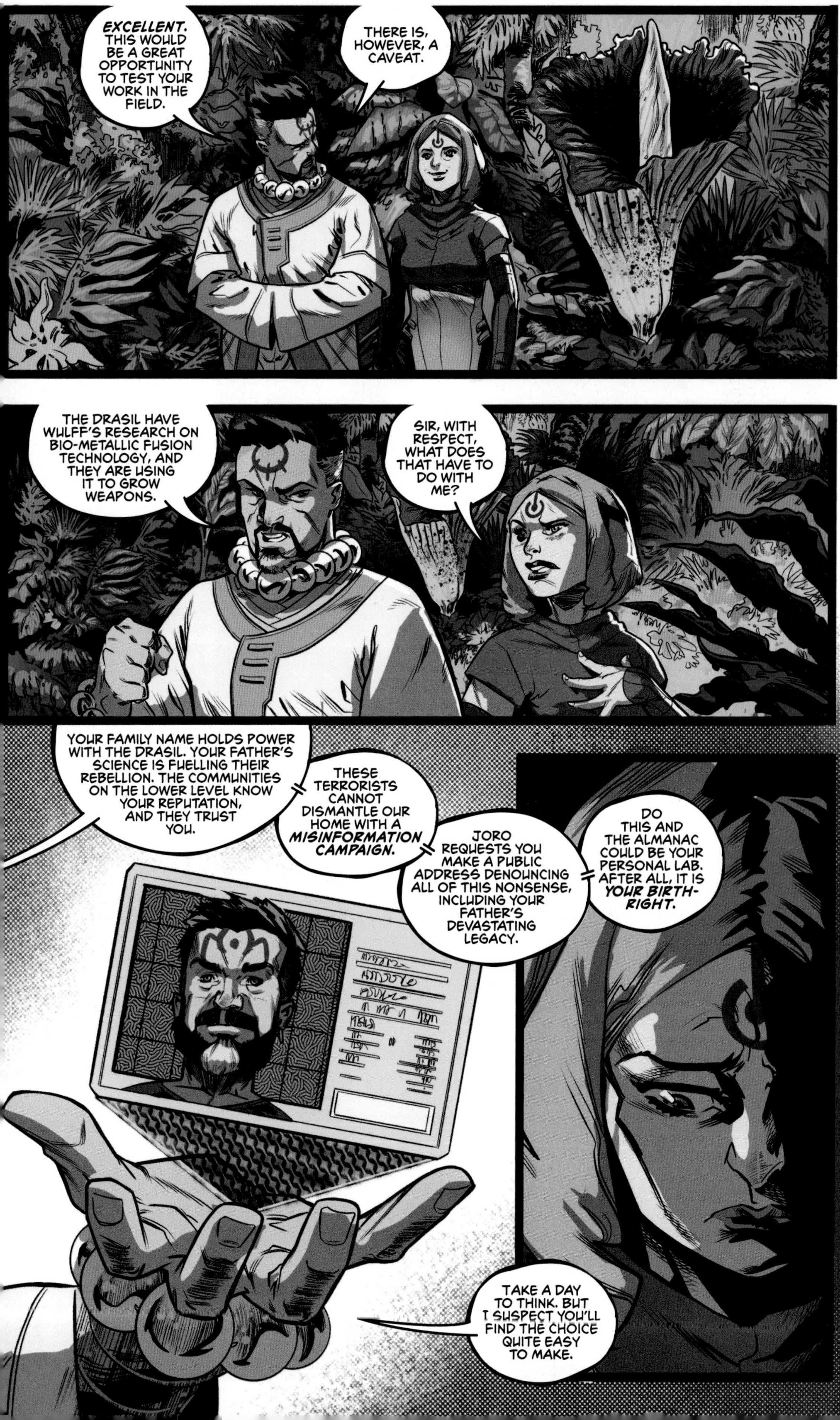
EXCELLENT. THIS WOULD BE A GREAT OPPORTUNITY TO TEST YOUR WORK IN THE FIELD.
THERE IS, HOWEVER, A CAVEAT.
THE DRASIL HAVE WULFF'S RESEARCH ON BIO-METALLIC FUSION TECHNOLOGY, AND THEY ARE USING IT TO GROW WEAPONS.
SIR, WITH RESPECT, WHAT DOES THAT HAVE TO DO WITH ME?
YOUR FAMILY NAME HOLDS POWER WITH THE DRASIL. YOUR FATHER'S SCIENCE IS FUELLING THEIR REBELLION. THE COMMUNITIES ON THE LOWER LEVEL KNOW YOUR REPUTATION, AND THEY TRUST YOU.
THESE TERRORISTS CANNOT DISMANTLE OUR HOME WITH A MISINFORMATION CAMPAIGN.
JORO REQUESTS YOU MAKE A PUBLIC ADDRESS DENOUNCING ALL OF THIS NONSENSE, INCLUDING YOUR FATHER'S DEVASTATING LEGACY.
DO THIS AND THE ALMANAC COULD BE YOUR PERSONAL LAB. AFTER ALL, IT IS YOUR BIRTHRIGHT.
TAKE A DAY TO THINK. BUT I SUSPECT YOU'LL FIND THE CHOICE QUITE EASY TO MAKE.

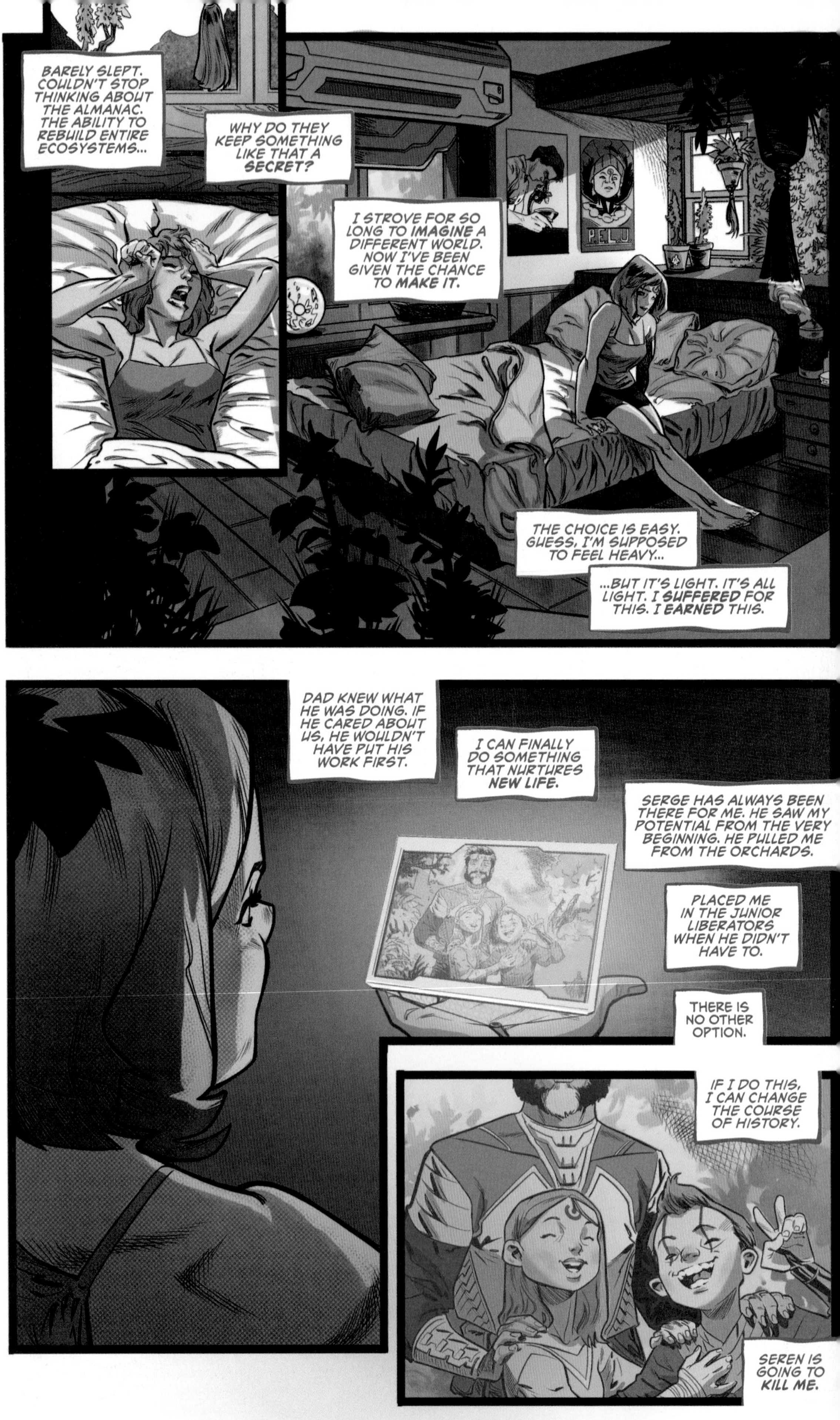
BARELY SLEPT. COULDN'T STOP THINKING ABOUT THE ALMANAC. THE ABILITY TO REBUILD ENTIRE ECOSYSTEMS...
WHY DO THEY KEEP SOMETHING LIKE THAT A SECRET?
P.E.L.U.
I STROVE FOR SO LONG TO IMAGINE A DIFFERENT WORLD. NOW I'VE BEEN GIVEN THE CHANCE TO MAKE IT.
THE CHOICE IS EASY. GUESS, I'M SUPPOSED TO FEEL HEAVY...
...BUT IT'S LIGHT. IT'S ALL LIGHT. I SUFFERED FOR THIS. I EARNED THIS.
DAD KNEW WHAT HE WAS DOING. IF HE CARED ABOUT US, HE WOULDN'T HAVE PUT HIS WORK FIRST.
I CAN FINALLY DO SOMETHING THAT NURTURES NEW LIFE.
SERGE HAS ALWAYS BEEN THERE FOR ME. HE SAW MY POTENTIAL FROM THE VERY BEGINNING. HE PULLED ME FROM THE ORCHARDS.
PLACED ME IN THE JUNIOR LIBERATORS WHEN HE DIDN'T HAVE TO.
THERE IS NO OTHER OPTION.
IF I DO THIS, I CAN CHANGE THE COURSE OF HISTORY.
SEREN IS GOING TO KILL ME.

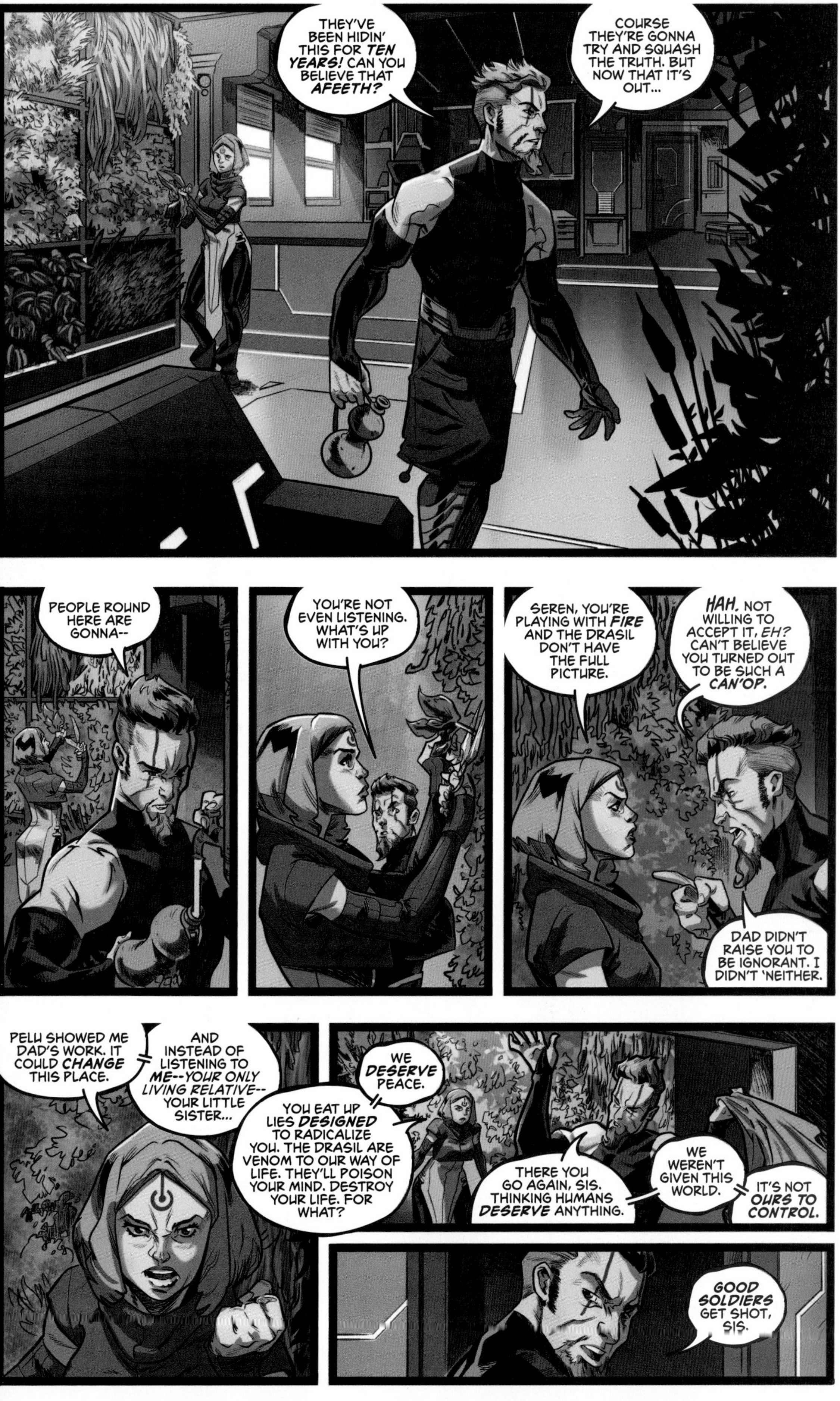
THEY'VE BEEN HIDIN' THIS FOR TEN YEARS! CAN YOU BELIEVE THAT AFEETH?
COURSE THEY'RE GONNA TRY AND SQUASH THE TRUTH. BUT NOW THAT IT'S OUT...
PEOPLE ROUND HERE ARE GONNA--
YOU'RE NOT EVEN LISTENING. WHAT'S UP WITH YOU?
SEREN, YOU'RE PLAYING WITH FIRE AND THE DRASIL DON'T HAVE THE FULL PICTURE.
HAH. NOT WILLING TO ACCEPT IT, EH? CAN'T BELIEVE YOU TURNED OUT TO BE SUCH A CAN'OP.
DAD DIDN'T RAISE YOU TO BE IGNORANT. I DIDN'T 'NEITHER.
PELU SHOWED ME DAD'S WORK. IT COULD CHANGE THIS PLACE.
AND INSTEAD OF LISTENING TO ME--YOUR ONLY LIVING RELATIVE--YOUR LITTLE SISTER...
WE DESERVE PEACE.
YOU EAT UP LIES DESIGNED TO RADICALIZE YOU. THE DRASIL ARE VENOM TO OUR WAY OF LIFE. THEY'LL POISON YOUR MIND. DESTROY YOUR LIFE. FOR WHAT?
THERE YOU GO AGAIN, SIS. THINKING HUMANS DESERVE ANYTHING.
WE WEREN'T GIVEN THIS WORLD.
IT'S NOT OURS TO CONTROL.
GOOD SOLDIERS GET SHOT, SIS.

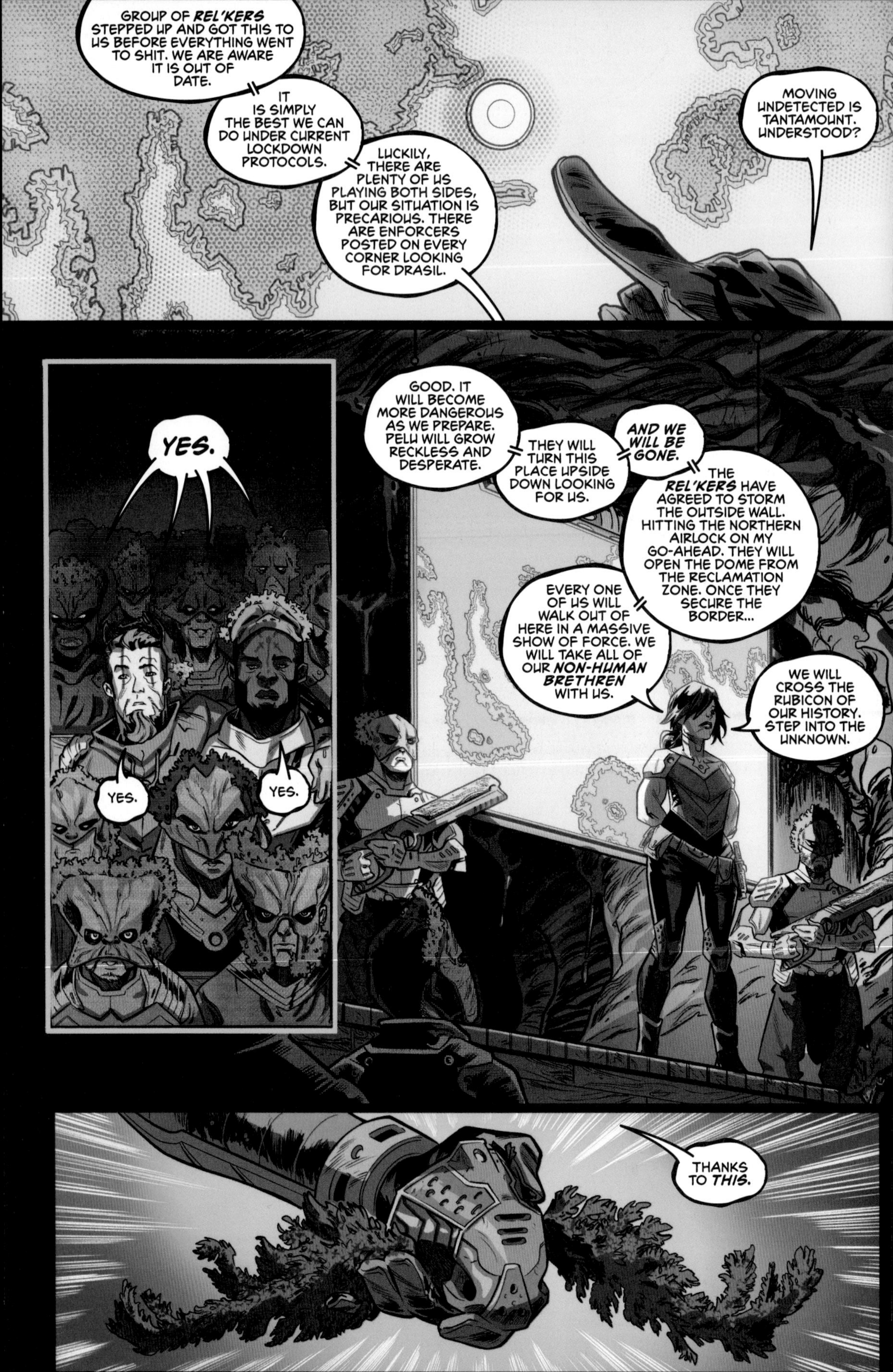
GROUP OF REL'KERS STEPPED UP AND GOT THIS TO US BEFORE EVERYTHING WENT TO SHIT. WE ARE AWARE IT IS OUT OF DATE.
IT IS SIMPLY THE BEST WE CAN DO UNDER CURRENT LOCKDOWN PROTOCOLS.
LUCKILY, THERE ARE PLENTY OF US PLAYING BOTH SIDES, BUT OUR SITUATION IS PRECARIOUS. THERE ARE ENFORCERS POSTED ON EVERY CORNER LOOKING FOR DRASIL.
MOVING UNDETECTED IS TANTAMOUNT. UNDERSTOOD?
YES.
YES.
YES.
GOOD. IT WILL BECOME MORE DANGEROUS AS WE PREPARE. PELU WILL GROW RECKLESS AND DESPERATE.
THEY WILL TURN THIS PLACE UPSIDE DOWN LOOKING FOR US.
AND WE WILL BE GONE.
THE REL'KERS HAVE AGREED TO STORM THE OUTSIDE WALL. HITTING THE NORTHERN AIRLOCK ON MY GO-AHEAD. THEY WILL OPEN THE DOME FROM THE RECLAMATION ZONE. ONCE THEY SECURE THE BORDER...
EVERY ONE OF US WILL WALK OUT OF HERE IN A MASSIVE SHOW OF FORCE. WE WILL TAKE ALL OF OUR NON-HUMAN BRETHREN WITH US.
WE WILL CROSS THE RUBICON OF OUR HISTORY. STEP INTO THE UNKNOWN.
THANKS TO THIS.

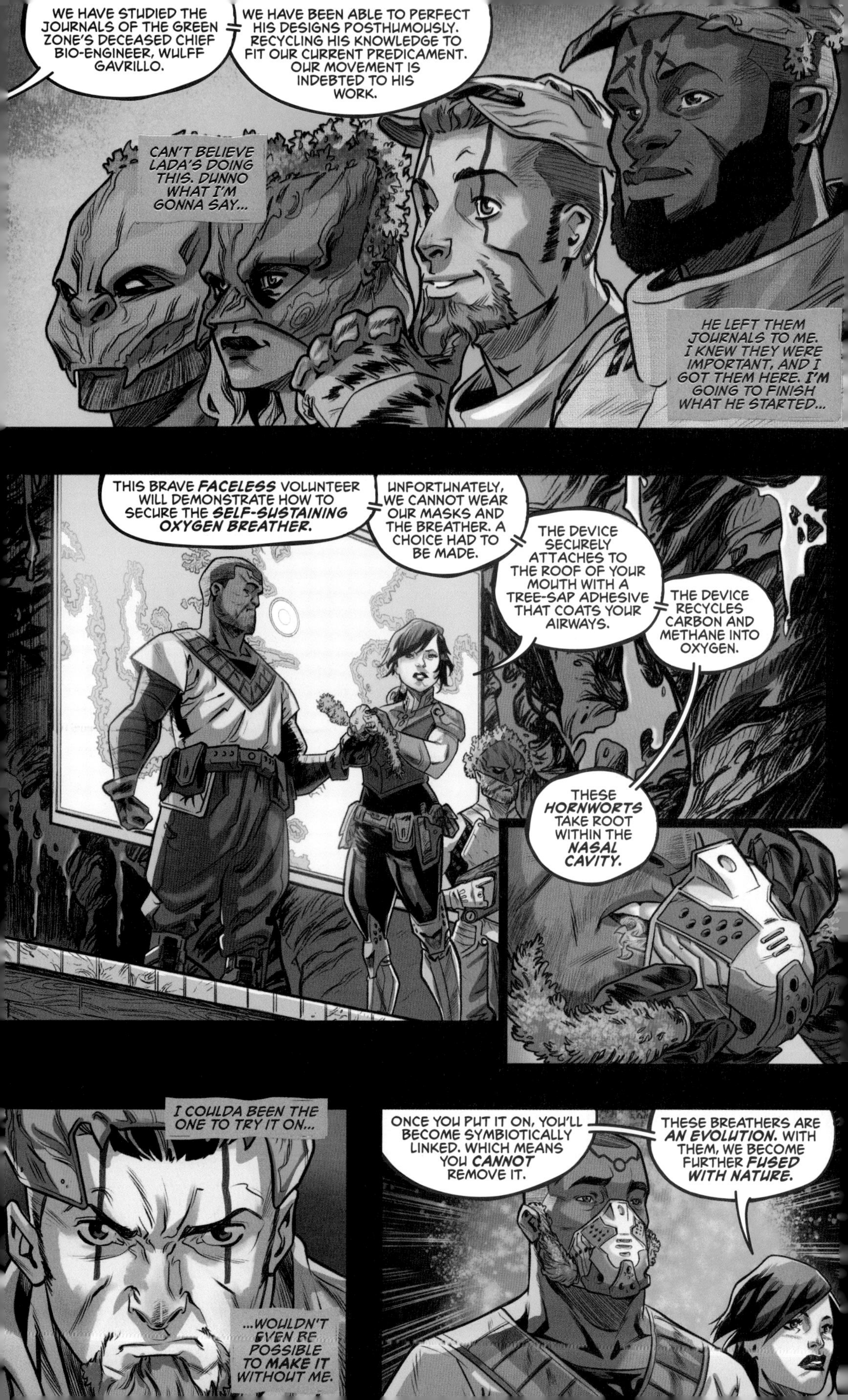
WE HAVE STUDIED THE JOURNALS OF THE GREEN ZONE'S DECEASED CHIEF BIO-ENGINEER, WULFF GAVRILLO.
WE HAVE BEEN ABLE TO PERFECT HIS DESIGNS POSTHUMOUSLY. RECYCLING HIS KNOWLEDGE TO FIT OUR CURRENT PREDICAMENT. OUR MOVEMENT IS INDEBTED TO HIS WORK.
CAN'T BELIEVE LADA'S DOING THIS. DUNNO WHAT I'M GONNA SAY...
HE LEFT THEM JOURNALS TO ME. I KNEW THEY WERE IMPORTANT, AND I GOT THEM HERE. I'M GOING TO FINISH WHAT HE STARTED...
THIS BRAVE FACELESS VOLUNTEER WILL DEMONSTRATE HOW TO SECURE THE SELF-SUSTAINING OXYGEN BREATHER.
UNFORTUNATELY, WE CANNOT WEAR OUR MASKS AND THE BREATHER. A CHOICE HAD TO BE MADE.
THE DEVICE SECURELY ATTACHES TO THE ROOF OF YOUR MOUTH WITH A TREE-SAP ADHESIVE THAT COATS YOUR AIRWAYS.
THE DEVICE RECYCLES CARBON AND METHANE INTO OXYGEN.
THESE HORNWORTS TAKE ROOT WITHIN THE NASAL CAVITY.
I COULDA BEEN THE ONE TO TRY IT ON...
...WOULDN'T EVEN BE POSSIBLE TO MAKE IT WITHOUT ME.
ONCE YOU PUT IT ON, YOU'LL BECOME SYMBIOTICALLY LINKED. WHICH MEANS YOU CANNOT REMOVE IT.
THESE BREATHERS ARE AN EVOLUTION. WITH THEM, WE BECOME FURTHER FUSED WITH NATURE.

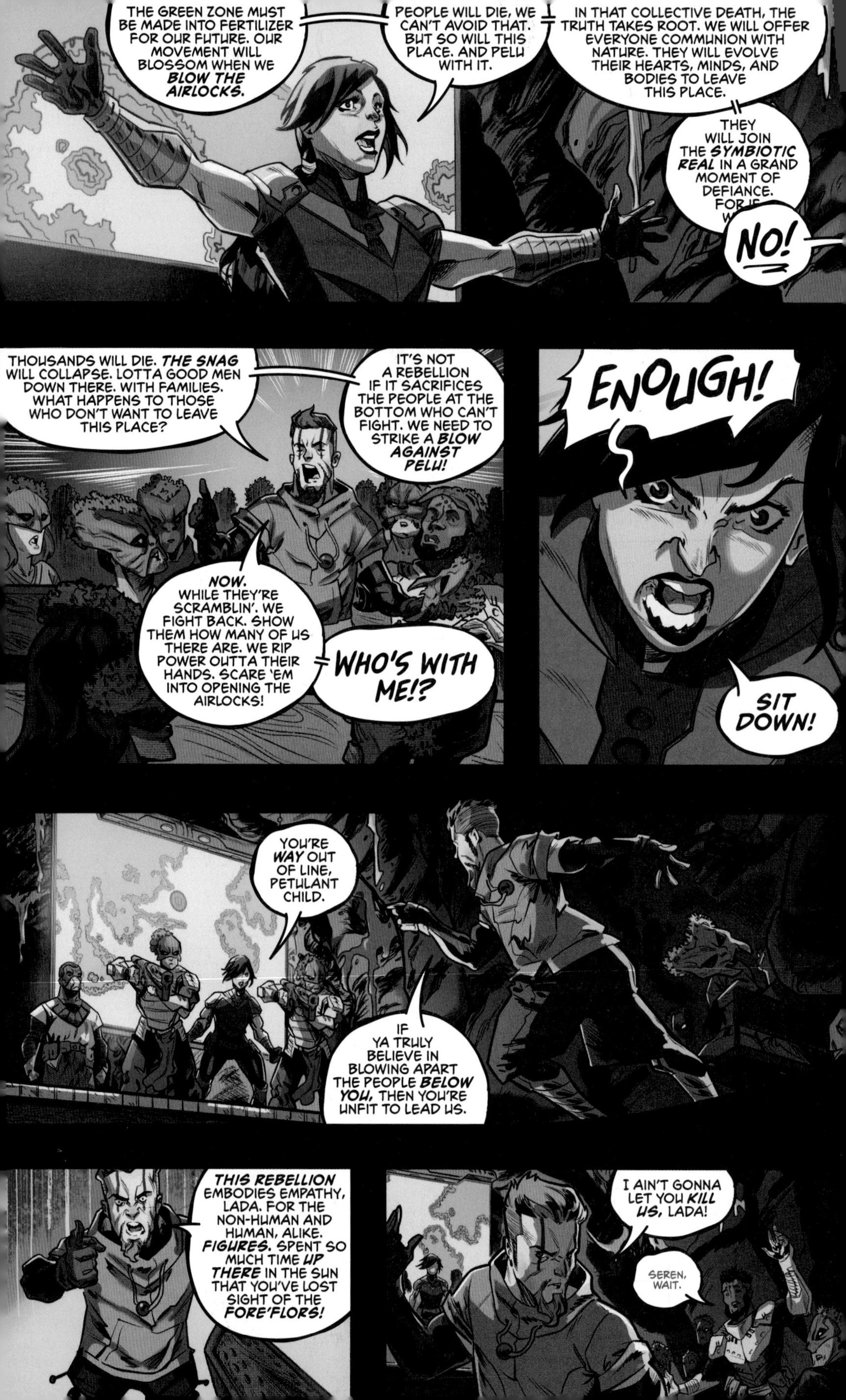

THE GREEN ZONE MUST BE MADE INTO FERTILIZER FOR OUR FUTURE. OUR MOVEMENT WILL BLOSSOM WHEN WE BLOW THE AIRLOCKS.
PEOPLE WILL DIE, WE CAN'T AVOID THAT. BUT SO WILL THIS PLACE. AND PELU WITH IT.
IN THAT COLLECTIVE DEATH, THE TRUTH TAKES ROOT. WE WILL OFFER EVERYONE COMMUNION WITH NATURE. THEY WILL EVOLVE THEIR HEARTS, MINDS, AND BODIES TO LEAVE THIS PLACE.
THEY WILL JOIN THE SYMBIOTIC REAL IN A GRAND MOMENT OF DEFIANCE.
NO!
THOUSANDS WILL DIE. THE SNAG WILL COLLAPSE. LOTTA GOOD MEN DOWN THERE. WITH FAMILIES. WHAT HAPPENS TO THOSE WHO DON'T WANT TO LEAVE THIS PLACE?
IT'S NOT A REBELLION IF IT SACRIFICES THE PEOPLE AT THE BOTTOM WHO CAN'T FIGHT. WE NEED TO STRIKE A BLOW AGAINST PELU!
NOW. WHILE THEY'RE SCRAMBLIN'. WE FIGHT BACK. SHOW THEM HOW MANY OF US THERE ARE. WE RIP POWER OUTTA THEIR HANDS. SCARE 'EM INTO OPENING THE AIRLOCKS!
WHO'S WITH ME!?
ENOUGH!
SIT DOWN!
YOU'RE WAY OUT OF LINE, PETULANT CHILD.
IF YA TRULY BELIEVE IN BLOWING APART THE PEOPLE BELOW YOU, THEN YOU'RE UNFIT TO LEAD US.
THIS REBELLION EMBODIES EMPATHY, LADA. FOR THE NON-HUMAN AND HUMAN, ALIKE. FIGURES. SPENT SO MUCH TIME UP THERE IN THE SUN THAT YOU'VE LOST SIGHT OF THE FORE'FLORS!
I AIN'T GONNA LET YOU KILL US, LADA!
SEREN, WAIT.

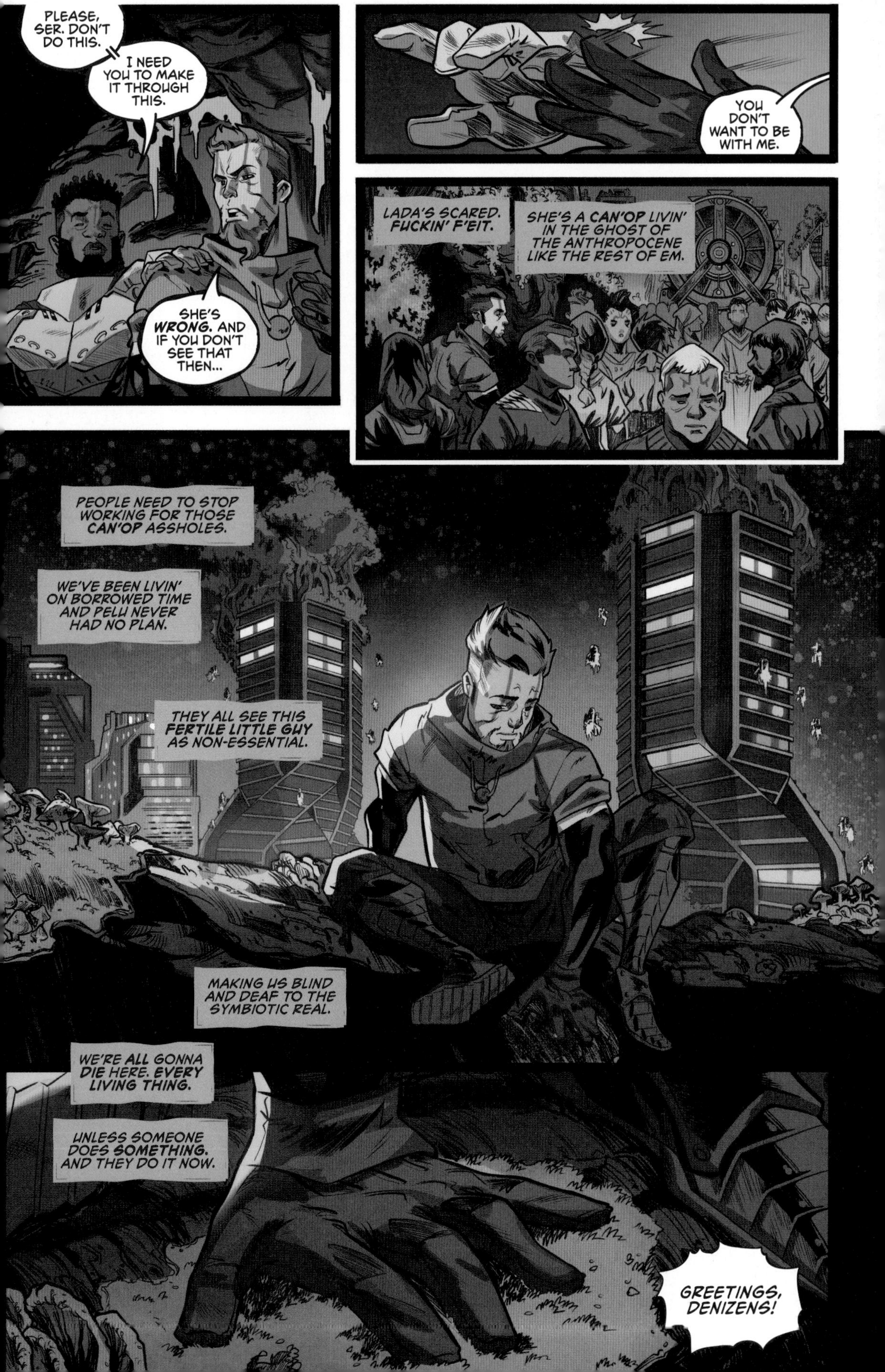

PLEASE, SER. DON'T DO THIS.
I NEED YOU TO MAKE IT THROUGH THIS.
SHE'S **WRONG.** AND IF YOU DON'T SEE THAT THEN...
YOU DON'T WANT TO BE WITH ME.
LADA'S SCARED. **FUCKIN' F'EIT.**
SHE'S A **CAN'OP** LIVIN' IN THE GHOST OF THE ANTHROPOCENE LIKE THE REST OF EM.
PEOPLE NEED TO STOP WORKING FOR THOSE **CAN'OP** ASSHOLES.
WE'VE BEEN LIVIN' ON BORROWED TIME AND PELU NEVER HAD NO PLAN.
THEY ALL SEE THIS **FERTILE LITTLE GUY** AS NON-ESSENTIAL.
MAKING US BLIND AND DEAF TO THE SYMBIOTIC REAL.
WE'RE ALL GONNA **DIE** HERE. **EVERY LIVING THING.**
UNLESS SOMEONE DOES **SOMETHING.** AND THEY DO IT NOW.
GREETINGS, DENIZENS!

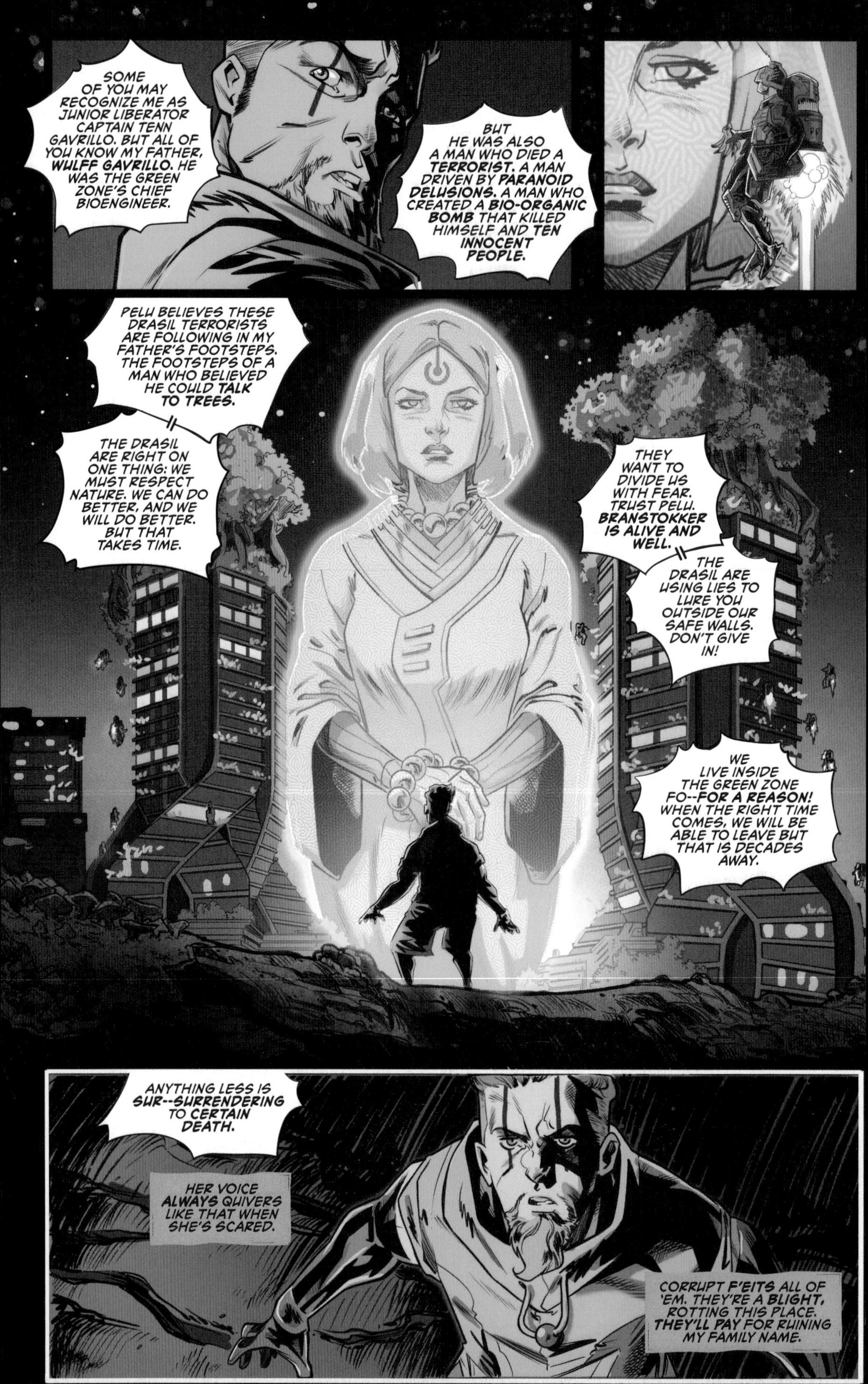
SOME OF YOU MAY RECOGNIZE ME AS JUNIOR LIBERATOR CAPTAIN TENN GAVRILLO. BUT ALL OF YOU KNOW MY FATHER, WULFF GAVRILLO. HE WAS THE GREEN ZONE'S CHIEF BIOENGINEER.
BUT HE WAS ALSO A MAN WHO DIED A TERRORIST. A MAN DRIVEN BY PARANOID DELUSIONS. A MAN WHO CREATED A BIO-ORGANIC BOMB THAT KILLED HIMSELF AND TEN INNOCENT PEOPLE.
PELU BELIEVES THESE DRASIL TERRORISTS ARE FOLLOWING IN MY FATHER'S FOOTSTEPS. THE FOOTSTEPS OF A MAN WHO BELIEVED HE COULD TALK TO TREES.
THE DRASIL ARE RIGHT ON ONE THING: WE MUST RESPECT NATURE. WE CAN DO BETTER, AND WE WILL DO BETTER. BUT THAT TAKES TIME.
THEY WANT TO DIVIDE US WITH FEAR. TRUST PELU. BRANSTOKKER IS ALIVE AND WELL.
THE DRASIL ARE USING LIES TO LURE YOU OUTSIDE OUR SAFE WALLS. DON'T GIVE IN!
WE LIVE INSIDE THE GREEN ZONE FO--FOR A REASON! WHEN THE RIGHT TIME COMES, WE WILL BE ABLE TO LEAVE BUT THAT IS DECADES AWAY.
ANYTHING LESS IS SUR--SURRENDERING TO CERTAIN DEATH.
HER VOICE ALWAYS QUIVERS LIKE THAT WHEN SHE'S SCARED.
CORRUPT F'EITS ALL OF 'EM. THEY'RE A BLIGHT, ROTTING THIS PLACE. THEY'LL PAY FOR RUINING MY FAMILY NAME.

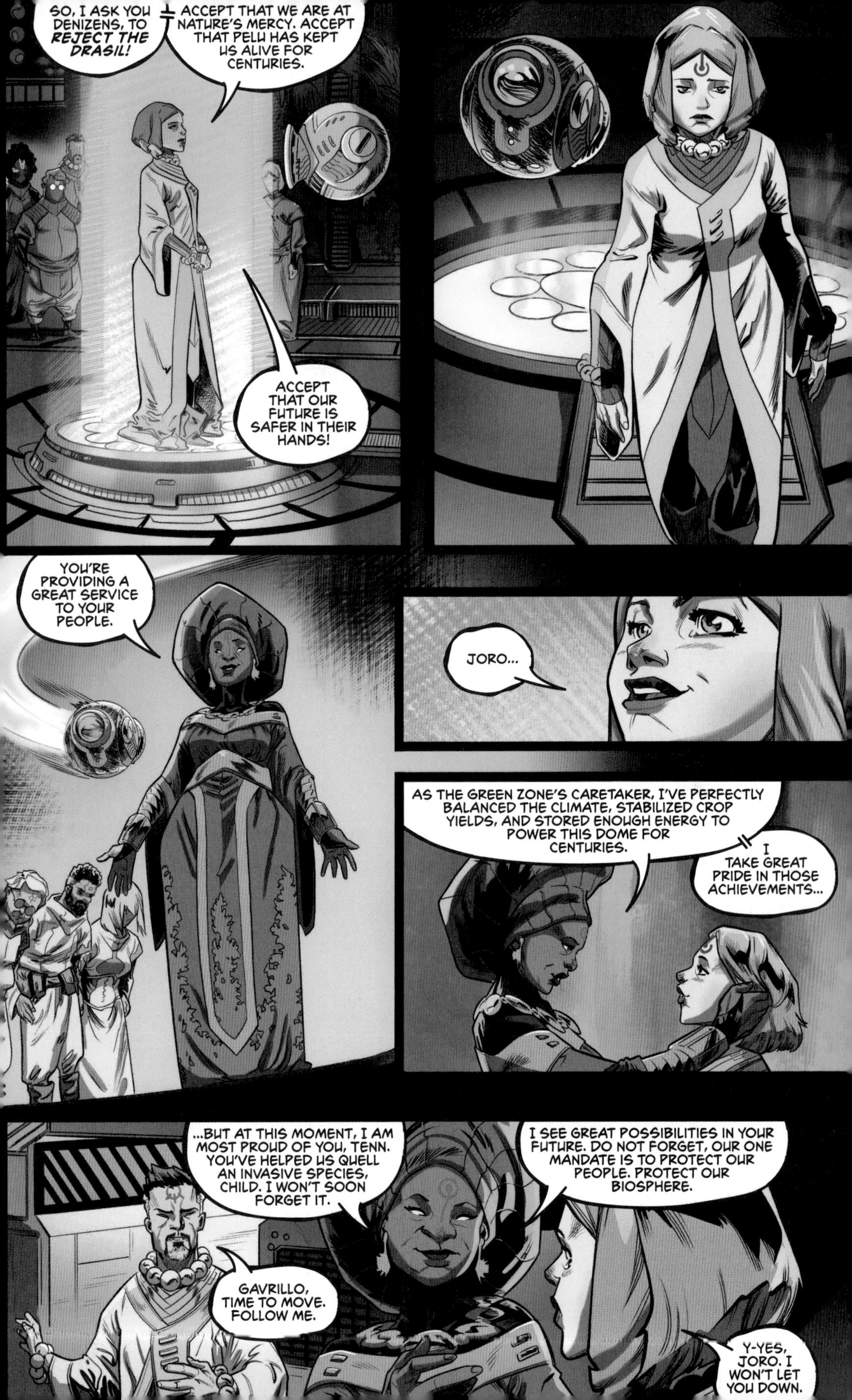
SO, I ASK YOU DENIZENS, TO *REJECT THE DRASIL!*
ACCEPT THAT WE ARE AT NATURE'S MERCY. ACCEPT THAT PELU HAS KEPT US ALIVE FOR CENTURIES.
ACCEPT THAT OUR FUTURE IS SAFER IN THEIR HANDS!
YOU'RE PROVIDING A GREAT SERVICE TO YOUR PEOPLE.
JORO...
AS THE GREEN ZONE'S CARETAKER, I'VE PERFECTLY BALANCED THE CLIMATE, STABILIZED CROP YIELDS, AND STORED ENOUGH ENERGY TO POWER THIS DOME FOR CENTURIES.
I TAKE GREAT PRIDE IN THOSE ACHIEVEMENTS...
...BUT AT THIS MOMENT, I AM MOST PROUD OF YOU, TENN. YOU'VE HELPED US QUELL AN INVASIVE SPECIES, CHILD. I WON'T SOON FORGET IT.
I SEE GREAT POSSIBILITIES IN YOUR FUTURE. DO NOT FORGET, OUR ONE MANDATE IS TO PROTECT OUR PEOPLE. PROTECT OUR BIOSPHERE.
GAVRILLO, TIME TO MOVE. FOLLOW ME.
Y-YES, JORO. I WON'T LET YOU DOWN.

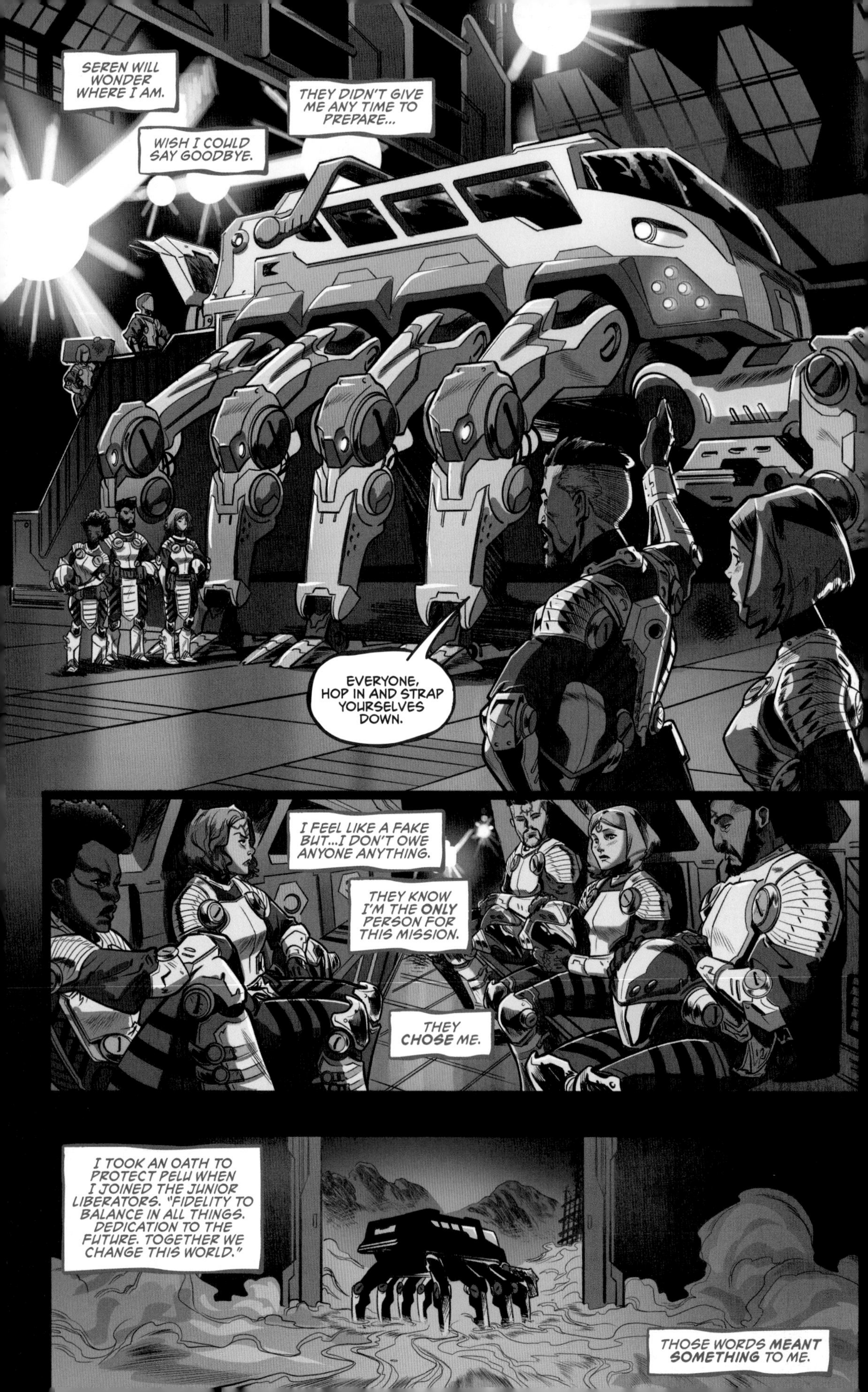
SEREN WILL WONDER WHERE I AM.
WISH I COULD SAY GOODBYE.
THEY DIDN'T GIVE ME ANY TIME TO PREPARE...
EVERYONE, HOP IN AND STRAP YOURSELVES DOWN.
I FEEL LIKE A FAKE BUT...I DON'T OWE ANYONE ANYTHING.
THEY KNOW I'M THE ONLY PERSON FOR THIS MISSION.
THEY CHOSE ME.
I TOOK AN OATH TO PROTECT PELU WHEN I JOINED THE JUNIOR LIBERATORS. "FIDELITY TO BALANCE IN ALL THINGS. DEDICATION TO THE FUTURE. TOGETHER WE CHANGE THIS WORLD."
THOSE WORDS MEANT SOMETHING TO ME.

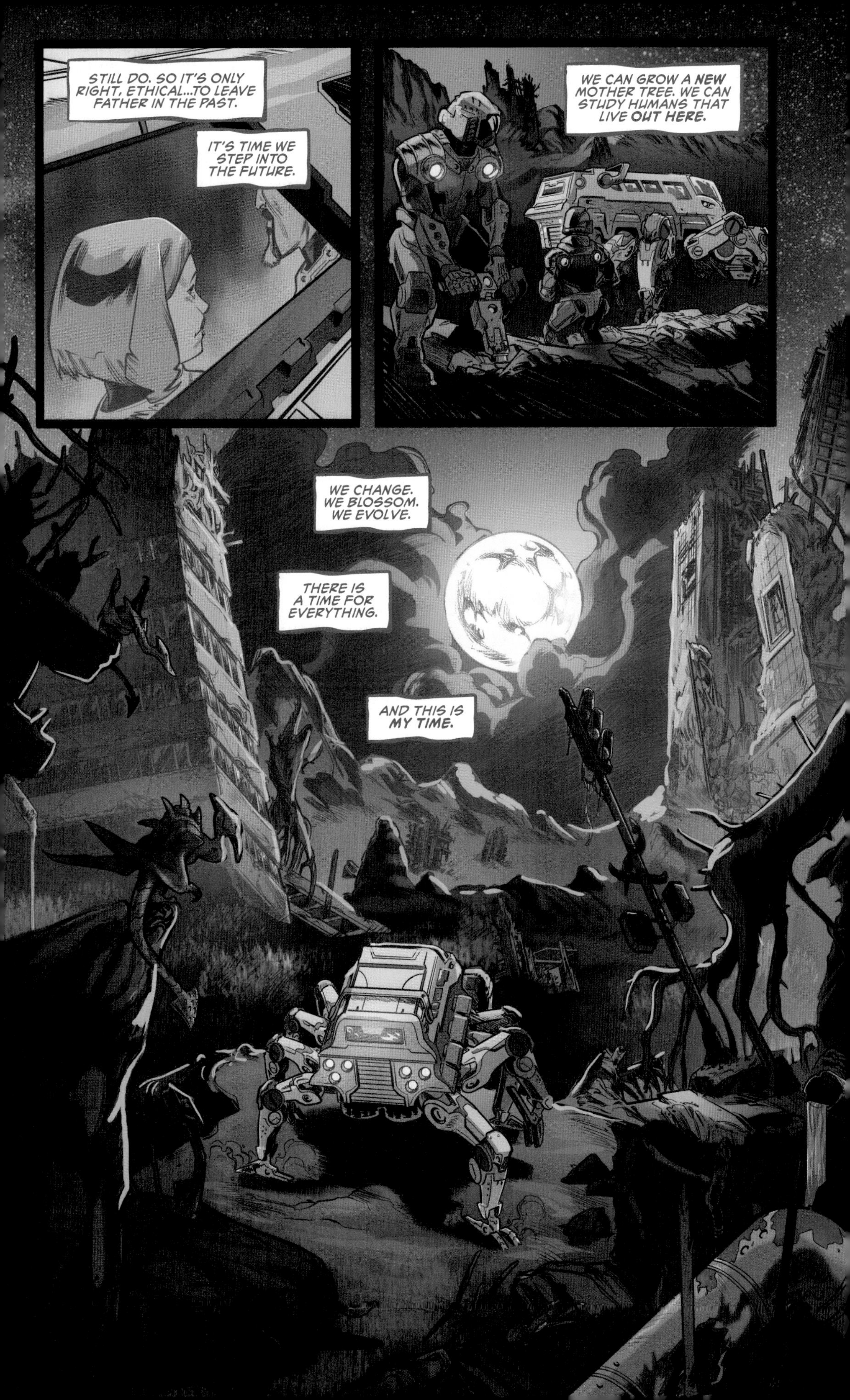
STILL DO. SO IT'S ONLY RIGHT, ETHICAL...TO LEAVE FATHER IN THE PAST.
IT'S TIME WE STEP INTO THE FUTURE.
WE CAN GROW A NEW MOTHER TREE. WE CAN STUDY HUMANS THAT LIVE OUT HERE.
WE CHANGE. WE BLOSSOM. WE EVOLVE.
THERE IS A TIME FOR EVERYTHING.
AND THIS IS MY TIME.

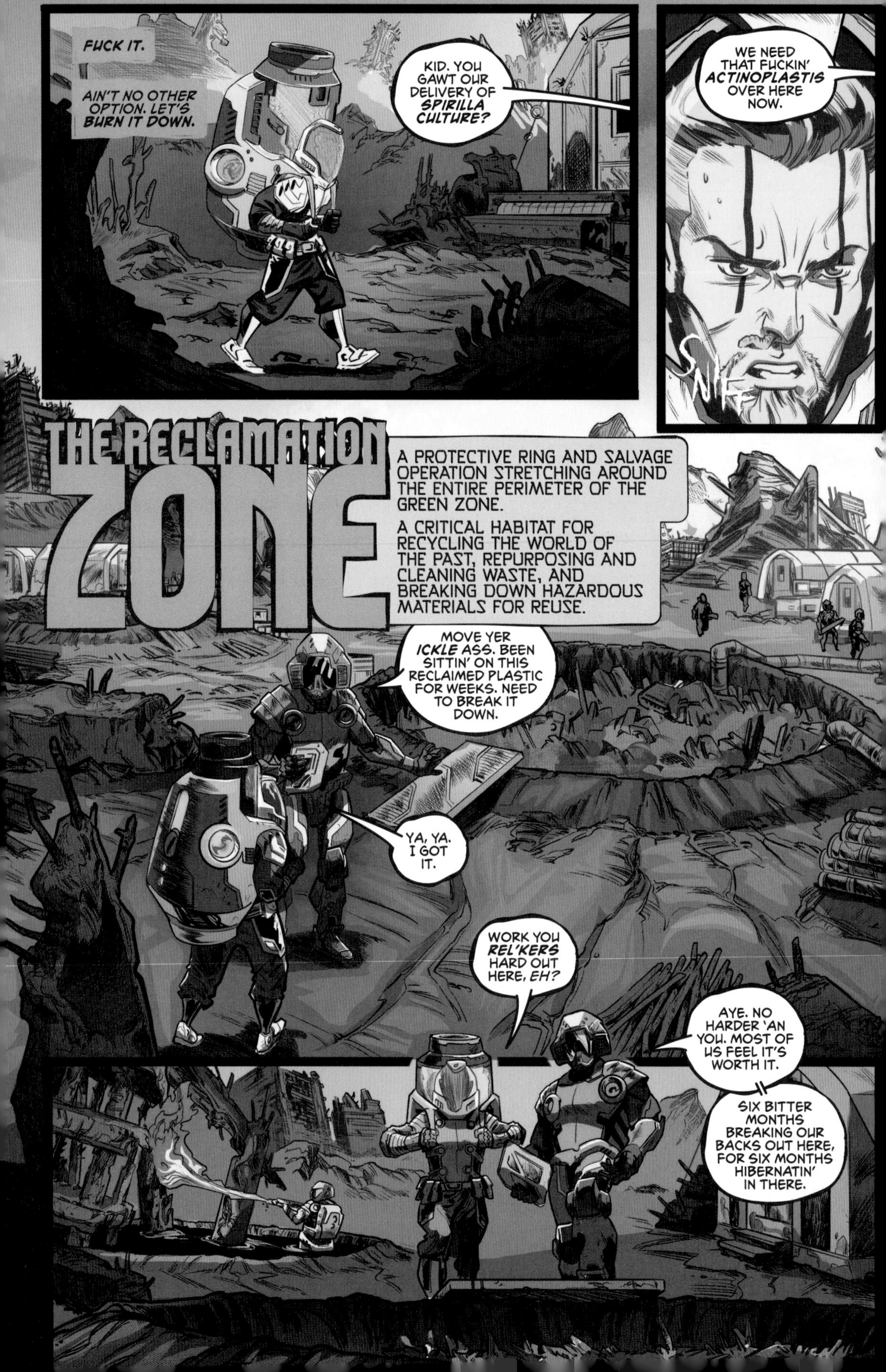

FUCK IT.
AIN'T NO OTHER OPTION. LET'S BURN IT DOWN.
KID. YOU GAWT OUR DELIVERY OF SPIRILLA CULTURE?
WE NEED THAT FUCKIN' ACTINOPLASTIS OVER HERE NOW.
SNIFF
THE RECLAMATION ZONE
A PROTECTIVE RING AND SALVAGE OPERATION STRETCHING AROUND THE ENTIRE PERIMETER OF THE GREEN ZONE.
A CRITICAL HABITAT FOR RECYCLING THE WORLD OF THE PAST, REPURPOSING AND CLEANING WASTE, AND BREAKING DOWN HAZARDOUS MATERIALS FOR REUSE.
MOVE YER ICKLE ASS. BEEN SITTIN' ON THIS RECLAIMED PLASTIC FOR WEEKS. NEED TO BREAK IT DOWN.
YA, YA. I GOT IT.
WORK YOU REL'KERS HARD OUT HERE, EH?
AYE. NO HARDER 'AN YOU. MOST OF US FEEL IT'S WORTH IT.
SIX BITTER MONTHS BREAKING OUR BACKS OUT HERE, FOR SIX MONTHS HIBERNATIN' IN THERE.

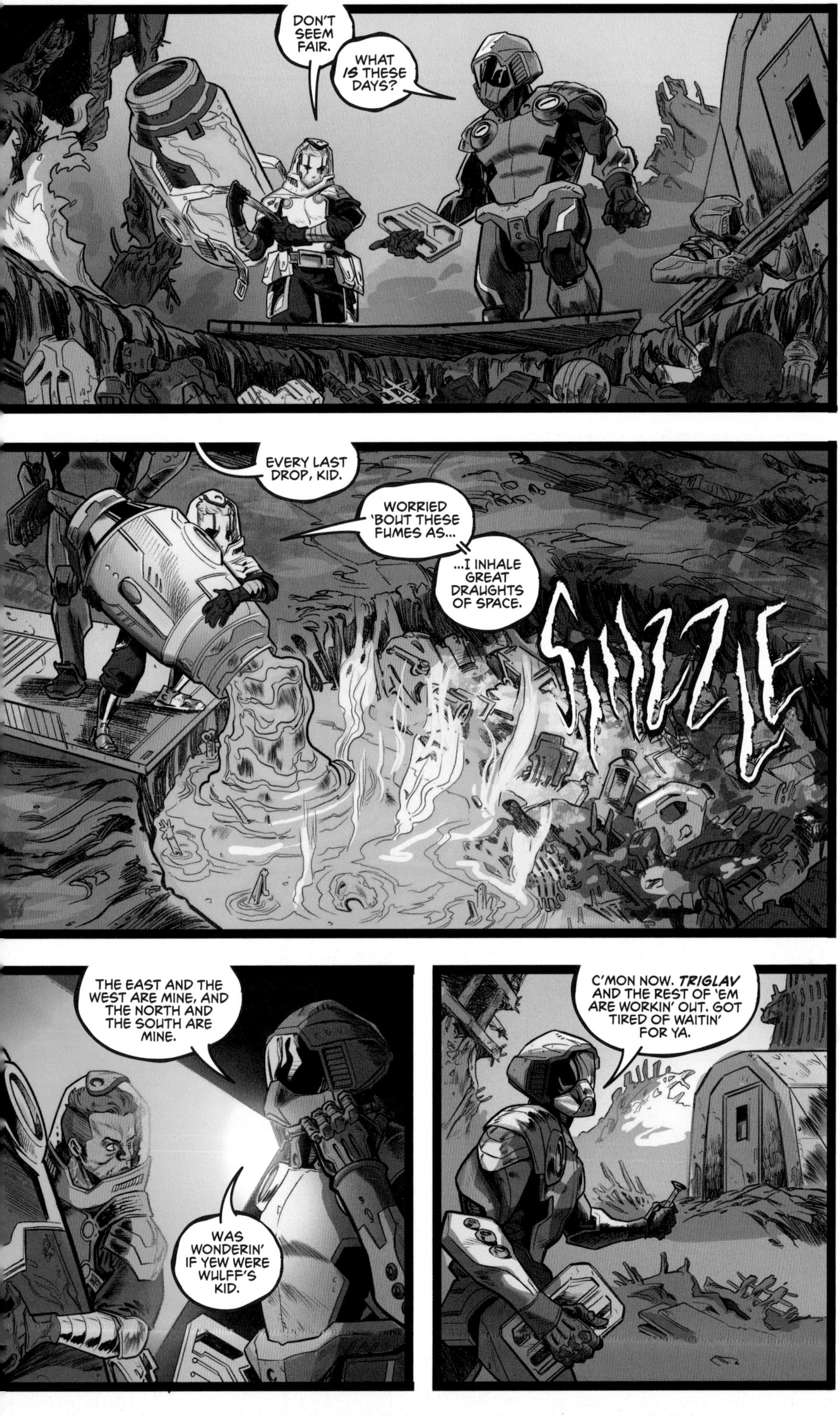
DON'T SEEM FAIR.
WHAT *IS* THESE DAYS?
EVERY LAST DROP, KID.
WORRIED 'BOUT THESE FUMES AS...
...I INHALE GREAT DRAUGHTS OF SPACE.
SIZZLE
THE EAST AND THE WEST ARE MINE, AND THE NORTH AND THE SOUTH ARE MINE.
WAS WONDERIN' IF YEW WERE WULFF'S KID.
C'MON NOW. *TRIGLAV* AND THE REST OF 'EM ARE WORKIN' OUT. GOT TIRED OF WAITIN' FOR YA.

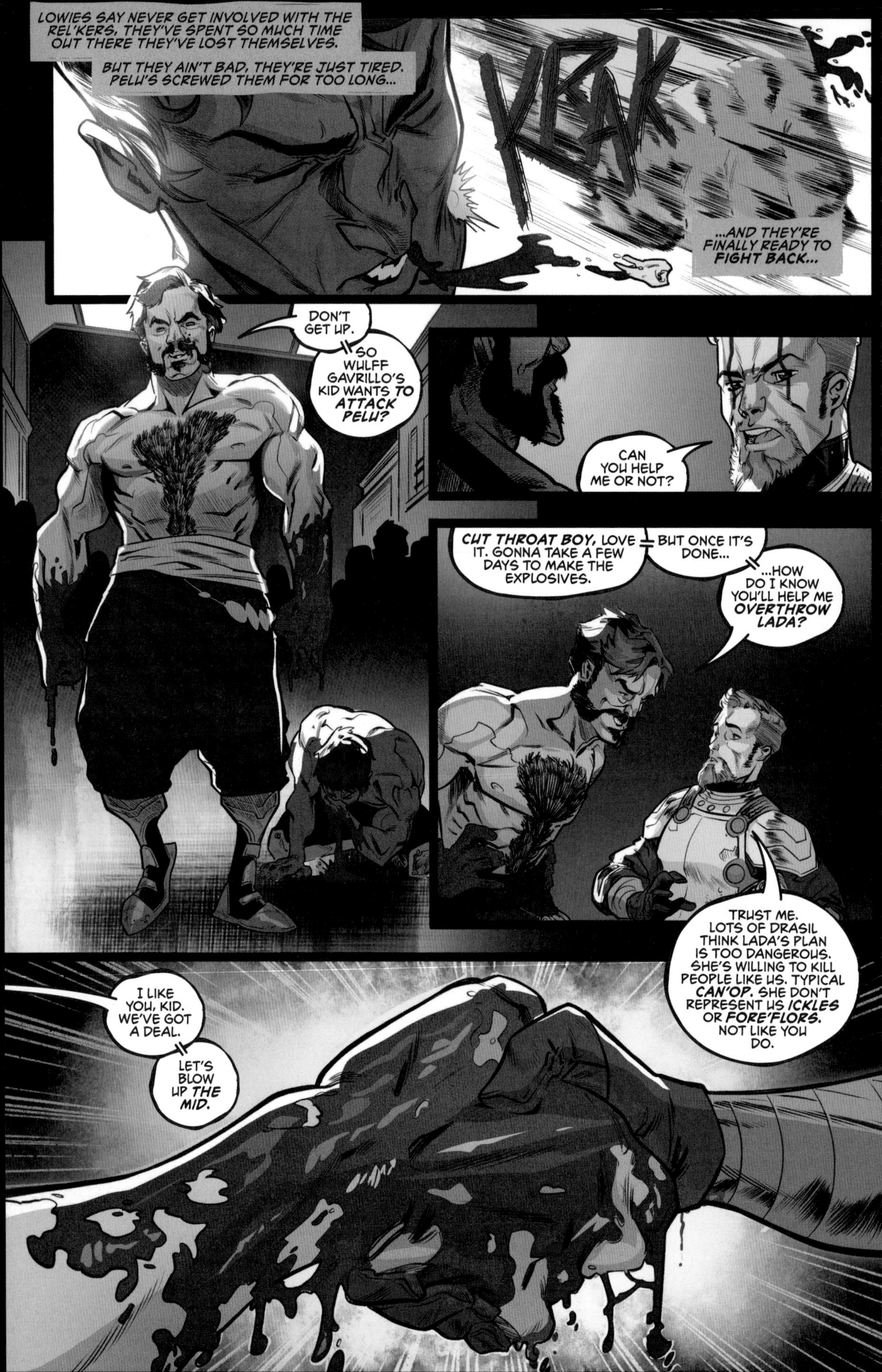
LOWIES SAY NEVER GET INVOLVED WITH THE REL'KERS, THEY'VE SPENT SO MUCH TIME OUT THERE THEY'VE LOST THEMSELVES.
BUT THEY AIN'T BAD, THEY'RE JUST TIRED. PELU'S SCREWED THEM FOR TOO LONG...
KRAK
...AND THEY'RE FINALLY READY TO FIGHT BACK...
DON'T GET UP.
SO WULFF GAVRILLO'S KID WANTS TO ATTACK PELU?
CAN YOU HELP ME OR NOT?
CUT THROAT BOY, LOVE IT. GONNA TAKE A FEW DAYS TO MAKE THE EXPLOSIVES.
BUT ONCE IT'S DONE...
...HOW DO I KNOW YOU'LL HELP ME OVERTHROW LADA?
TRUST ME. LOTS OF DRASIL THINK LADA'S PLAN IS TOO DANGEROUS. SHE'S WILLING TO KILL PEOPLE LIKE US. TYPICAL CAN'OP. SHE DON'T REPRESENT US ICKLES OR FORE'FLORS. NOT LIKE YOU DO.
I LIKE YOU, KID. WE'VE GOT A DEAL.
LET'S BLOW UP THE MID.

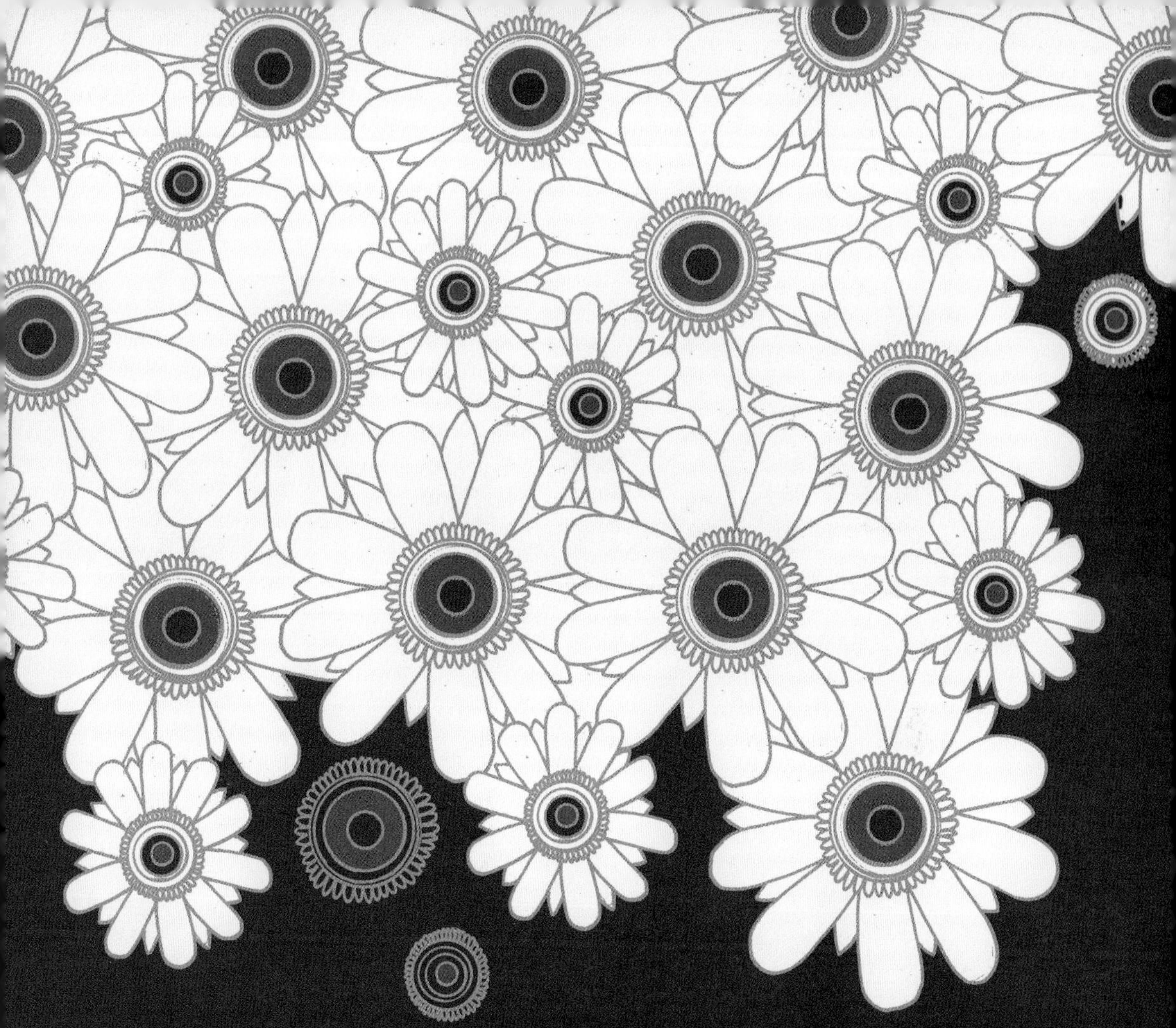

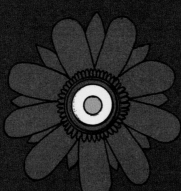

THE NOTHING-

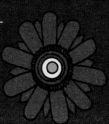

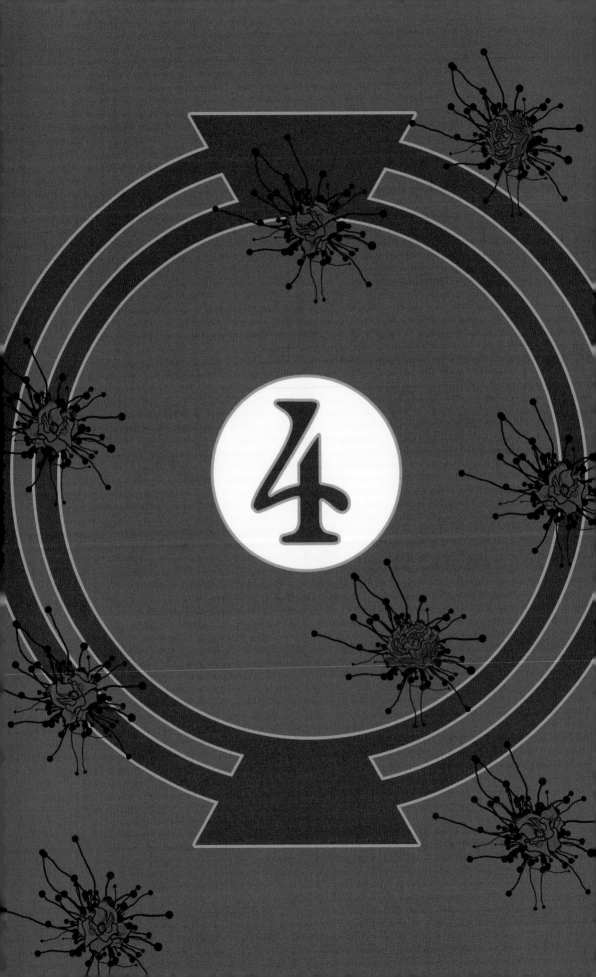

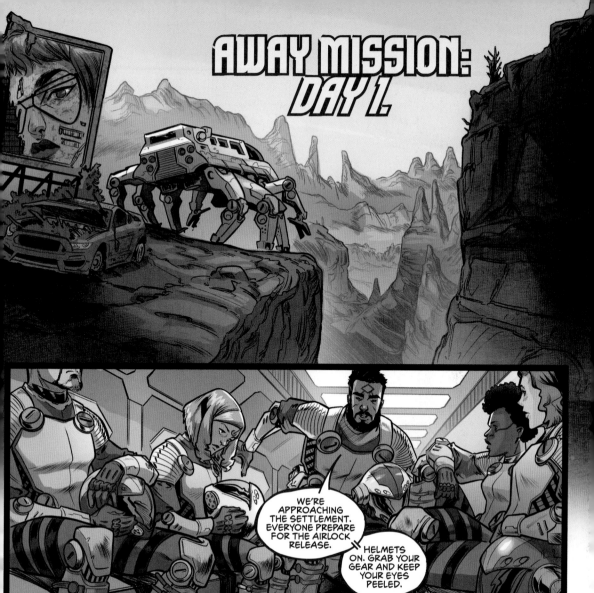

AWAY MISSION: DAY 1.

WE'RE APPROACHING THE SETTLEMENT. EVERYONE PREPARE FOR THE AIRLOCK RELEASE.

HELMETS ON. GRAB YOUR GEAR AND KEEP YOUR EYES PEELED.

I WAS RIGHT TO CALL OUT MY FATHER...*WASN'T* I? I WISH I COULD TALK TO SEREN. EXPLAIN MYSELF.

JUST...FOCUS ON WHAT MATTERS. THESE PEOPLE *NEED* OUR HELP.

FOR YOUR PROTECTION FROM *THE REFUSE.*

THE REFUSE?

THE REMAINERS. WHATEVER YOU CALL FOLKS OUT HERE. JUST AN IMMOBILIZER. IF THEY GET SURLY, PULL THE TRIGGER. THEY'LL REGRET IT.

ALRIGHT, LADS. DOWN THIS PATH, AND WE'LL REACH THE SETTLEMENT.
REMEMBER, WITH THESE STEPS WE ARE CHANGING HISTORY. FOR CENTURIES PELU HAS HAD NO BUSINESS WITH OUTSIDERS.
THESE REFUSE MAY NOT UNDERSTAND WHO WE ARE. WE MAY NOT EVEN RECOGNIZE THEM AS HUMAN ANYMORE. BE VIGILANT.
THESE PEOPLE NEVER MADE IT INTO OUR HISTORY BOOKS. NOT EVEN A FOOTNOTE IN THE TRIUMPHANT HISTORY OF PELU. HOW DID WE LEAVE PEOPLE BEHIND?
MY CLASSES MADE IT SOUND SO SIMPLE AND HARMLESS: THE BEST MINDS, THE HARDEST WORKING, THE MOST EDUCATED FORMED THE GREEN ZONE. THE DESERVING.
BUT WHAT ABOUT THE REST?
BUT HERE THEY ARE, LIKE THE ANIMALS IN THE ALMANAC...
...NOT USEFUL. NOT NEEDED. BUT THEY SURVIVED, DESPITE US ABANDONING THEM.
GET A GOOD GRIP ON THOSE STUNNERS.

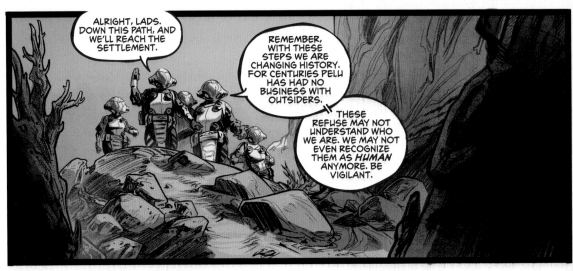

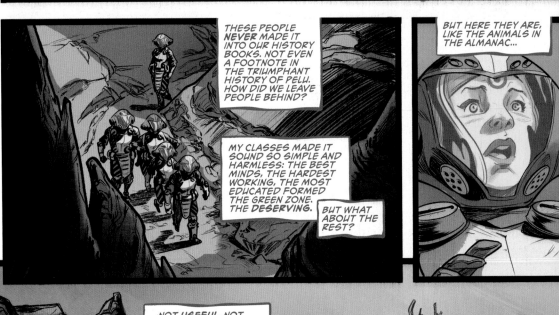

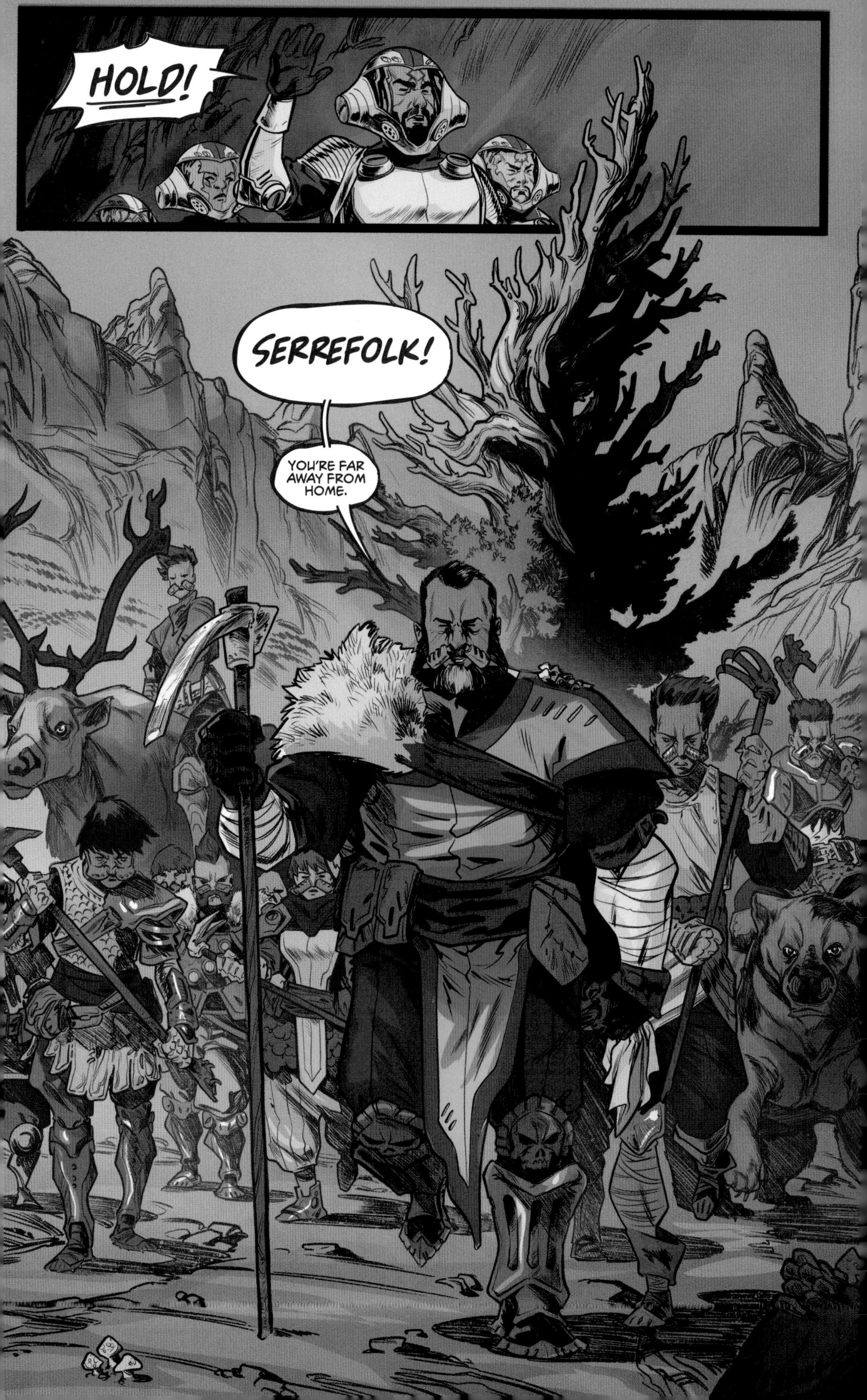
HOLD!
SERREFOLK!
YOU'RE FAR AWAY FROM HOME.

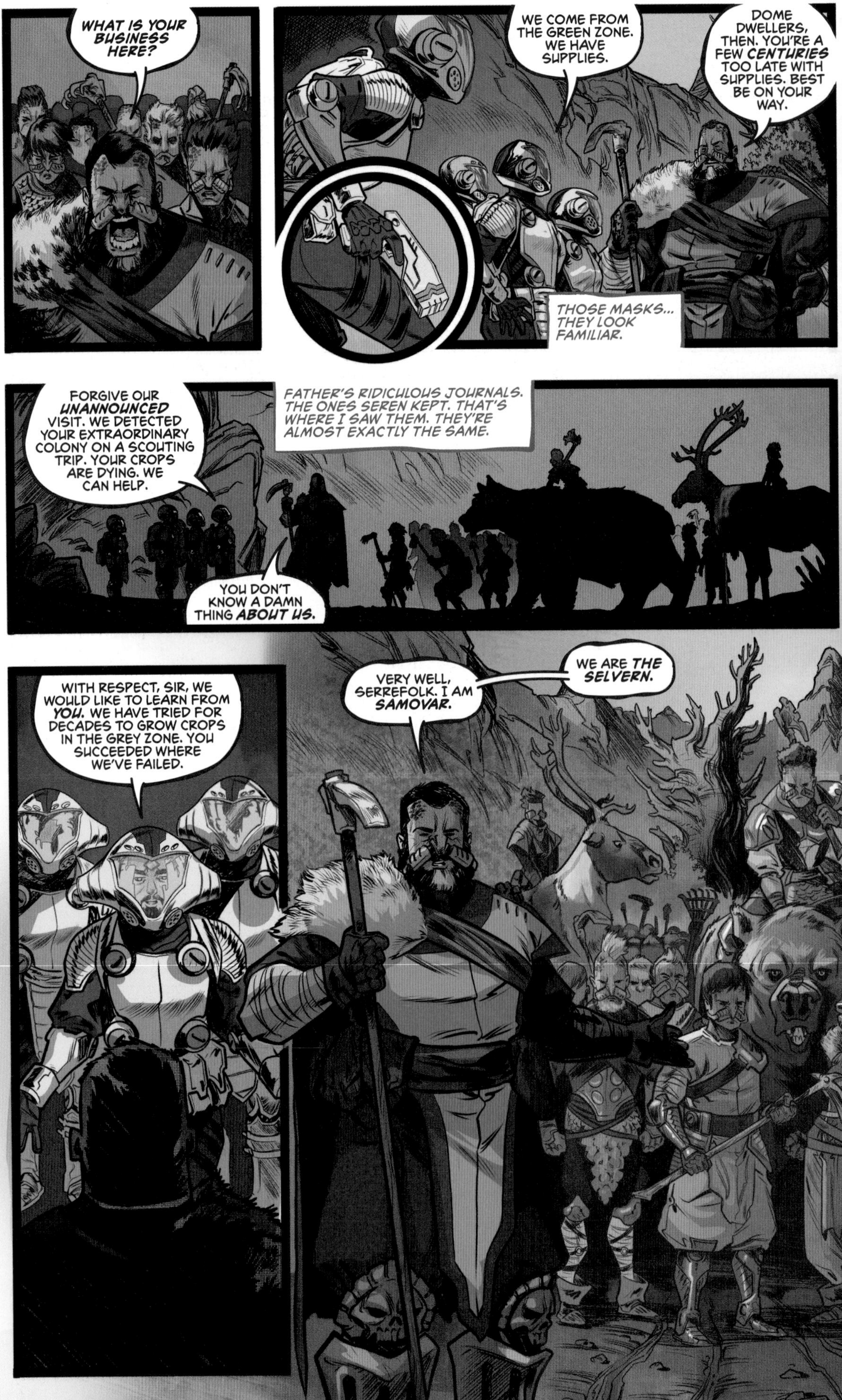
WHAT IS YOUR BUSINESS HERE?
WE COME FROM THE GREEN ZONE. WE HAVE SUPPLIES.
DOME DWELLERS, THEN. YOU'RE A FEW CENTURIES TOO LATE WITH SUPPLIES. BEST BE ON YOUR WAY.
THOSE MASKS... THEY LOOK FAMILIAR.
FATHER'S RIDICULOUS JOURNALS. THE ONES SEREN KEPT. THAT'S WHERE I SAW THEM. THEY'RE ALMOST EXACTLY THE SAME.
FORGIVE OUR UNANNOUNCED VISIT. WE DETECTED YOUR EXTRAORDINARY COLONY ON A SCOUTING TRIP. YOUR CROPS ARE DYING. WE CAN HELP.
YOU DON'T KNOW A DAMN THING ABOUT US.
WITH RESPECT, SIR, WE WOULD LIKE TO LEARN FROM YOU. WE HAVE TRIED FOR DECADES TO GROW CROPS IN THE GREY ZONE. YOU SUCCEEDED WHERE WE'VE FAILED.
VERY WELL, SERREFOLK. I AM SAMOVAR.
WE ARE THE SELVERN.

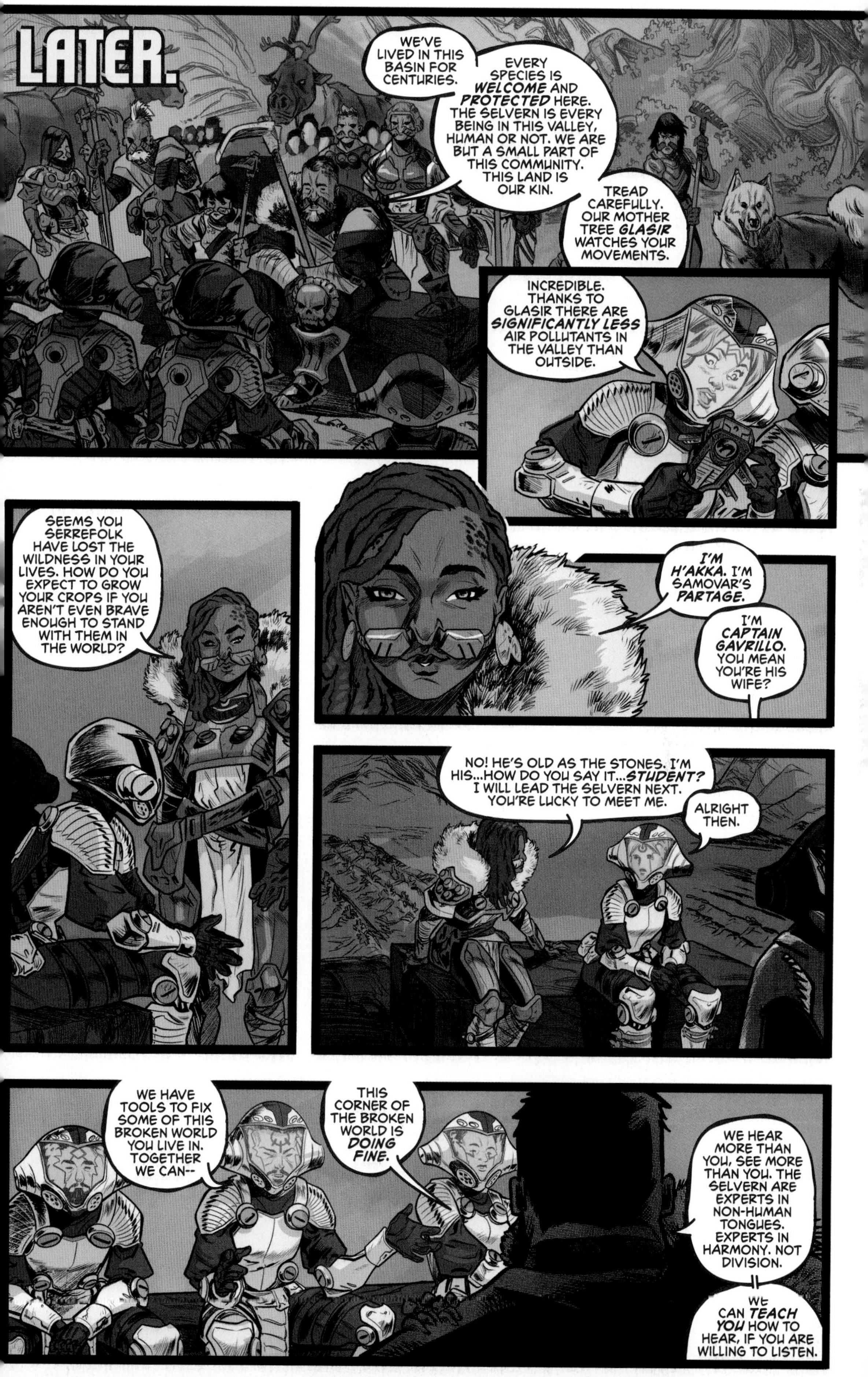
LATER.
WE'VE LIVED IN THIS BASIN FOR CENTURIES.
EVERY SPECIES IS WELCOME AND PROTECTED HERE. THE SELVERN IS EVERY BEING IN THIS VALLEY, HUMAN OR NOT. WE ARE BUT A SMALL PART OF THIS COMMUNITY. THIS LAND IS OUR KIN.
TREAD CAREFULLY. OUR MOTHER TREE GLASIR WATCHES YOUR MOVEMENTS.
INCREDIBLE. THANKS TO GLASIR THERE ARE SIGNIFICANTLY LESS AIR POLLUTANTS IN THE VALLEY THAN OUTSIDE.
SEEMS YOU SERREFOLK HAVE LOST THE WILDNESS IN YOUR LIVES. HOW DO YOU EXPECT TO GROW YOUR CROPS IF YOU AREN'T EVEN BRAVE ENOUGH TO STAND WITH THEM IN THE WORLD?
I'M H'AKKA. I'M SAMOVAR'S PARTAGE.
I'M CAPTAIN GAVRILLO. YOU MEAN YOU'RE HIS WIFE?
NO! HE'S OLD AS THE STONES. I'M HIS...HOW DO YOU SAY IT...STUDENT? I WILL LEAD THE SELVERN NEXT. YOU'RE LUCKY TO MEET ME.
ALRIGHT THEN.
WE HAVE TOOLS TO FIX SOME OF THIS BROKEN WORLD YOU LIVE IN. TOGETHER WE CAN--
THIS CORNER OF THE BROKEN WORLD IS DOING FINE.
WE HEAR MORE THAN YOU, SEE MORE THAN YOU. THE SELVERN ARE EXPERTS IN NON-HUMAN TONGUES. EXPERTS IN HARMONY. NOT DIVISION.
WE CAN TEACH YOU HOW TO HEAR, IF YOU ARE WILLING TO LISTEN.

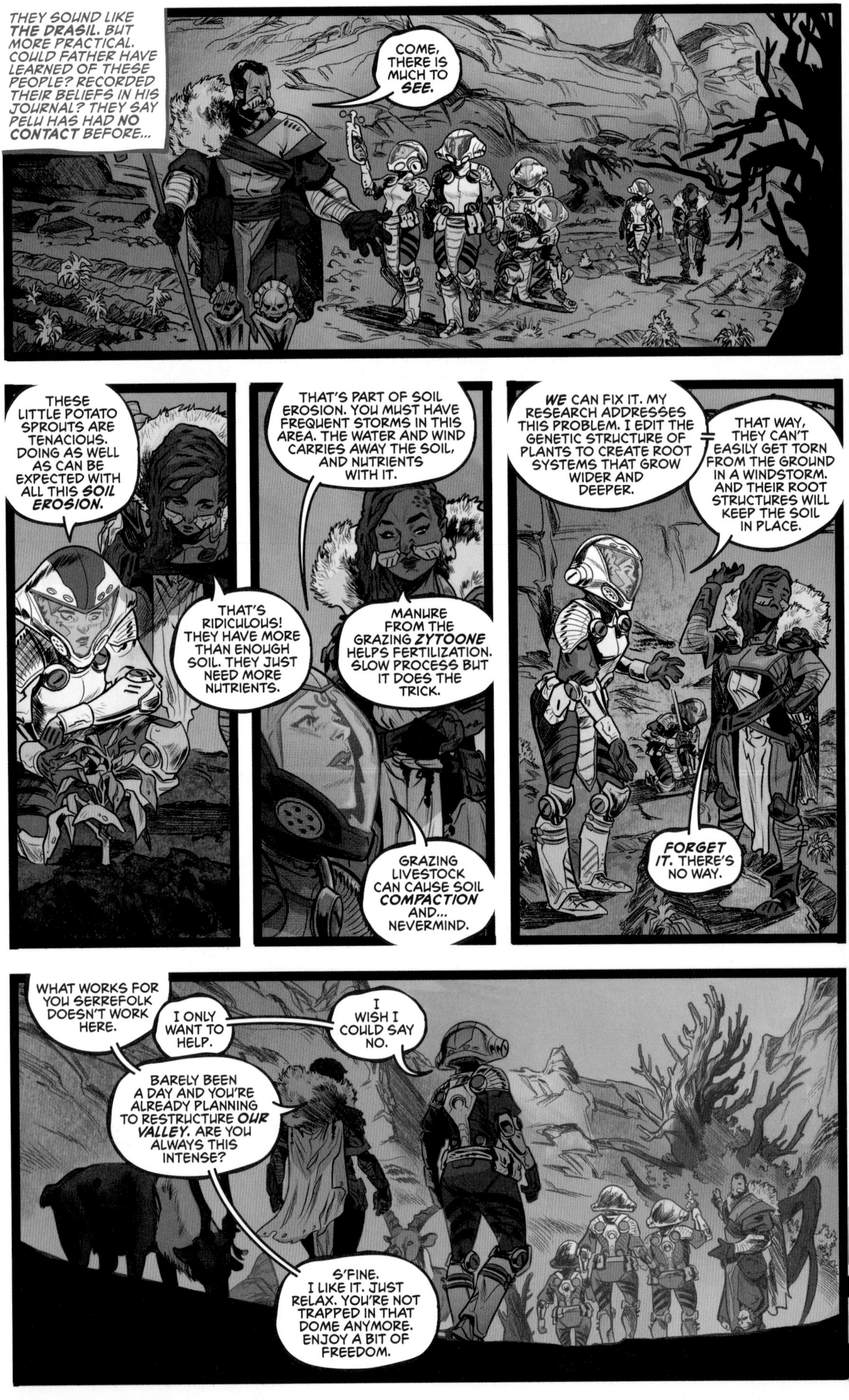
THEY SOUND LIKE THE DRASIL. BUT MORE PRACTICAL. COULD FATHER HAVE LEARNED OF THESE PEOPLE? RECORDED THEIR BELIEFS IN HIS JOURNAL? THEY SAY PELU HAS HAD NO CONTACT BEFORE...
COME, THERE IS MUCH TO SEE.
THESE LITTLE POTATO SPROUTS ARE TENACIOUS. DOING AS WELL AS CAN BE EXPECTED WITH ALL THIS SOIL EROSION.
THAT'S RIDICULOUS! THEY HAVE MORE THAN ENOUGH SOIL. THEY JUST NEED MORE NUTRIENTS.
THAT'S PART OF SOIL EROSION. YOU MUST HAVE FREQUENT STORMS IN THIS AREA. THE WATER AND WIND CARRIES AWAY THE SOIL, AND NUTRIENTS WITH IT.
MANURE FROM THE GRAZING ZYTOONE HELPS FERTILIZATION. SLOW PROCESS BUT IT DOES THE TRICK.
GRAZING LIVESTOCK CAN CAUSE SOIL COMPACTION AND... NEVERMIND.
WE CAN FIX IT. MY RESEARCH ADDRESSES THIS PROBLEM. I EDIT THE GENETIC STRUCTURE OF PLANTS TO CREATE ROOT SYSTEMS THAT GROW WIDER AND DEEPER.
THAT WAY, THEY CAN'T EASILY GET TORN FROM THE GROUND IN A WINDSTORM. AND THEIR ROOT STRUCTURES WILL KEEP THE SOIL IN PLACE.
FORGET IT. THERE'S NO WAY.
WHAT WORKS FOR YOU SERREFOLK DOESN'T WORK HERE.
I ONLY WANT TO HELP.
I WISH I COULD SAY NO.
BARELY BEEN A DAY AND YOU'RE ALREADY PLANNING TO RESTRUCTURE OUR VALLEY. ARE YOU ALWAYS THIS INTENSE?
S'FINE. I LIKE IT. JUST RELAX. YOU'RE NOT TRAPPED IN THAT DOME ANYMORE. ENJOY A BIT OF FREEDOM.

YOU HAVE FREE ROAMING ANIMALS EVERY-WHERE.

WHAT ARE THEY FOR?

THEY ARE NOT *"FOR"* ANYTHING. THEY ARE SELVERN.

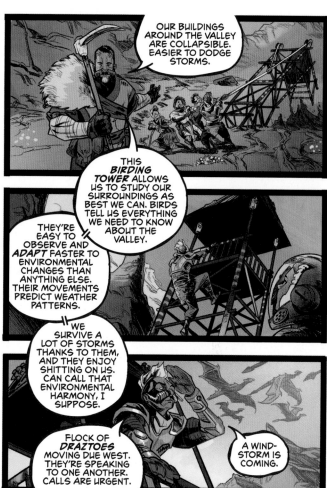

OUR BUILDINGS AROUND THE VALLEY ARE COLLAPSIBLE. EASIER TO DODGE STORMS.

THIS *BIRDING TOWER* ALLOWS US TO STUDY OUR SURROUNDINGS AS BEST WE CAN. BIRDS TELL US EVERYTHING WE NEED TO KNOW ABOUT THE VALLEY.

THEY'RE EASY TO OBSERVE AND *ADAPT* FASTER TO ENVIRONMENTAL CHANGES THAN ANYTHING ELSE. THEIR MOVEMENTS PREDICT WEATHER PATTERNS.

WE SURVIVE A LOT OF STORMS THANKS TO THEM, AND THEY ENJOY SHITTING ON US. CAN CALL THAT ENVIRONMENTAL HARMONY, I SUPPOSE.

FLOCK OF *DRAZTOES* MOVING DUE WEST. THEY'RE SPEAKING TO ONE ANOTHER. CALLS ARE URGENT.

A WIND-STORM IS COMING.

TIME TO HEAD BELOW.

THOSE WHO DON'T LISTEN TO BIRDS END UP AS BIRD FOOD. A SELVERN PROVERB FOR YOU.

BURGESS, YORK-- *SECURE* THE CRAB. LOCK THE PINCERS INTO THE GROUND AND DOUBLE BACK.

YES, SIR.

HURRY UP, YOU DUSTY CHIN WAGGERS!

WHERE ARE WE GOING?

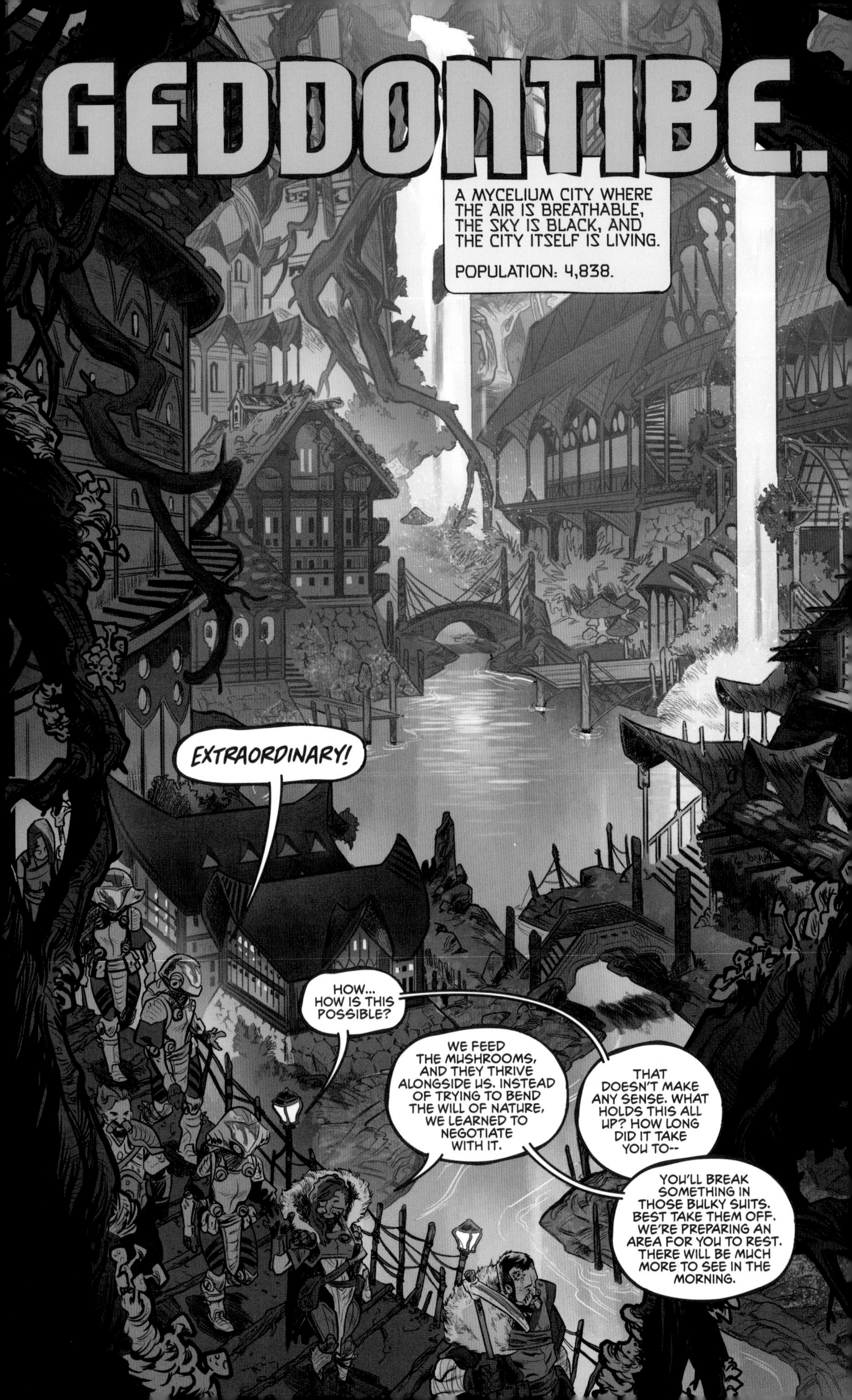
GEDDONTIBE.
A MYCELIUM CITY WHERE THE AIR IS BREATHABLE, THE SKY IS BLACK, AND THE CITY ITSELF IS LIVING.
POPULATION: 4,838.
EXTRAORDINARY!
HOW... HOW IS THIS POSSIBLE?
WE FEED THE MUSHROOMS, AND THEY THRIVE ALONGSIDE US. INSTEAD OF TRYING TO BEND THE WILL OF NATURE, WE LEARNED TO NEGOTIATE WITH IT.
THAT DOESN'T MAKE ANY SENSE. WHAT HOLDS THIS ALL UP? HOW LONG DID IT TAKE YOU TO--
YOU'LL BREAK SOMETHING IN THOSE BULKY SUITS. BEST TAKE THEM OFF. WE'RE PREPARING AN AREA FOR YOU TO REST. THERE WILL BE MUCH MORE TO SEE IN THE MORNING.

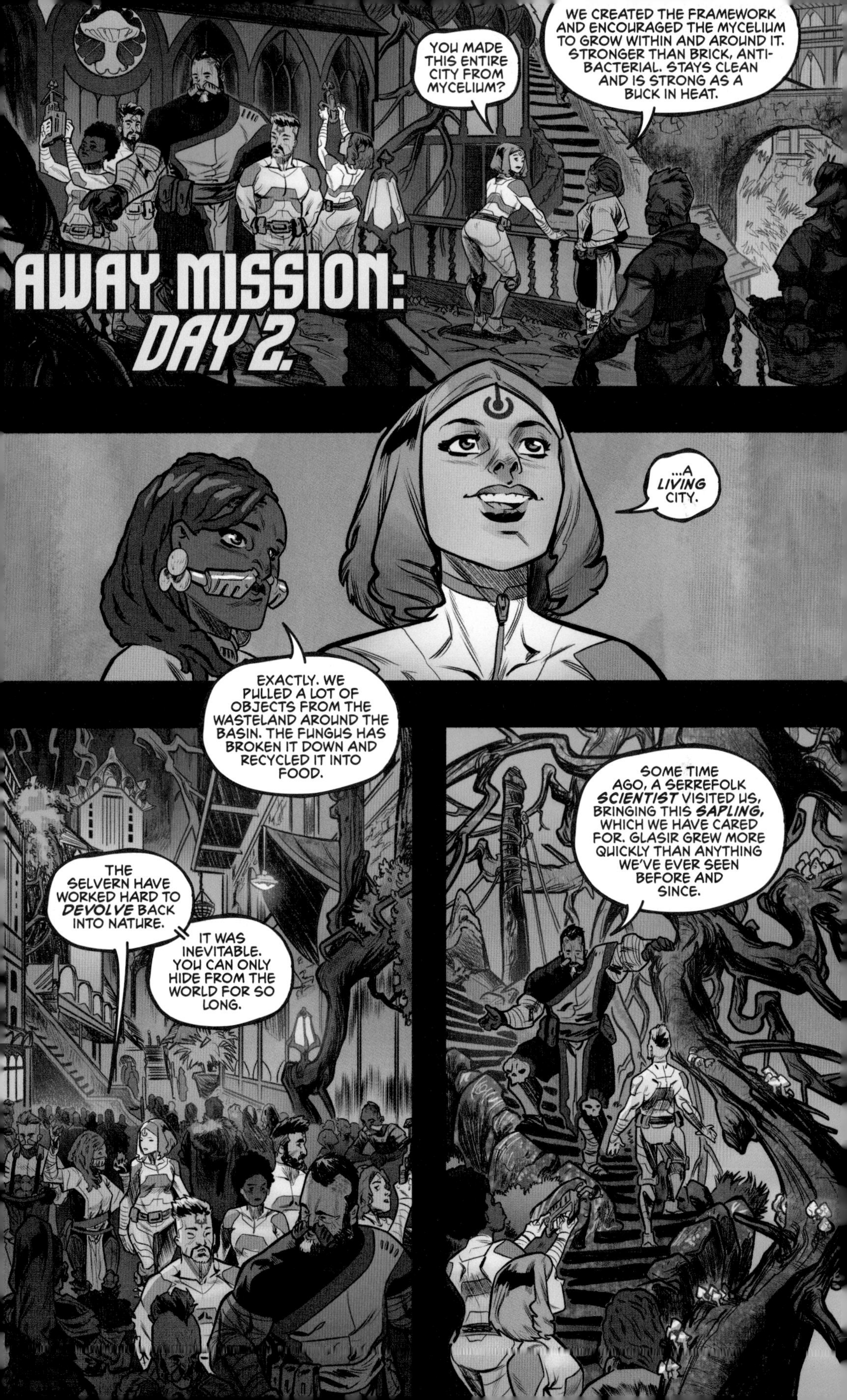
AWAY MISSION: DAY 2.
YOU MADE THIS ENTIRE CITY FROM MYCELIUM?
WE CREATED THE FRAMEWORK AND ENCOURAGED THE MYCELIUM TO GROW WITHIN AND AROUND IT. STRONGER THAN BRICK, ANTI-BACTERIAL. STAYS CLEAN AND IS STRONG AS A BUCK IN HEAT.
...A LIVING CITY.
EXACTLY. WE PULLED A LOT OF OBJECTS FROM THE WASTELAND AROUND THE BASIN. THE FUNGUS HAS BROKEN IT DOWN AND RECYCLED IT INTO FOOD.
THE SELVERN HAVE WORKED HARD TO DEVOLVE BACK INTO NATURE.
IT WAS INEVITABLE. YOU CAN ONLY HIDE FROM THE WORLD FOR SO LONG.
SOME TIME AGO, A SERREFOLK SCIENTIST VISITED US, BRINGING THIS SAPLING, WHICH WE HAVE CARED FOR. GLASIR GREW MORE QUICKLY THAN ANYTHING WE'VE EVER SEEN BEFORE AND SINCE.

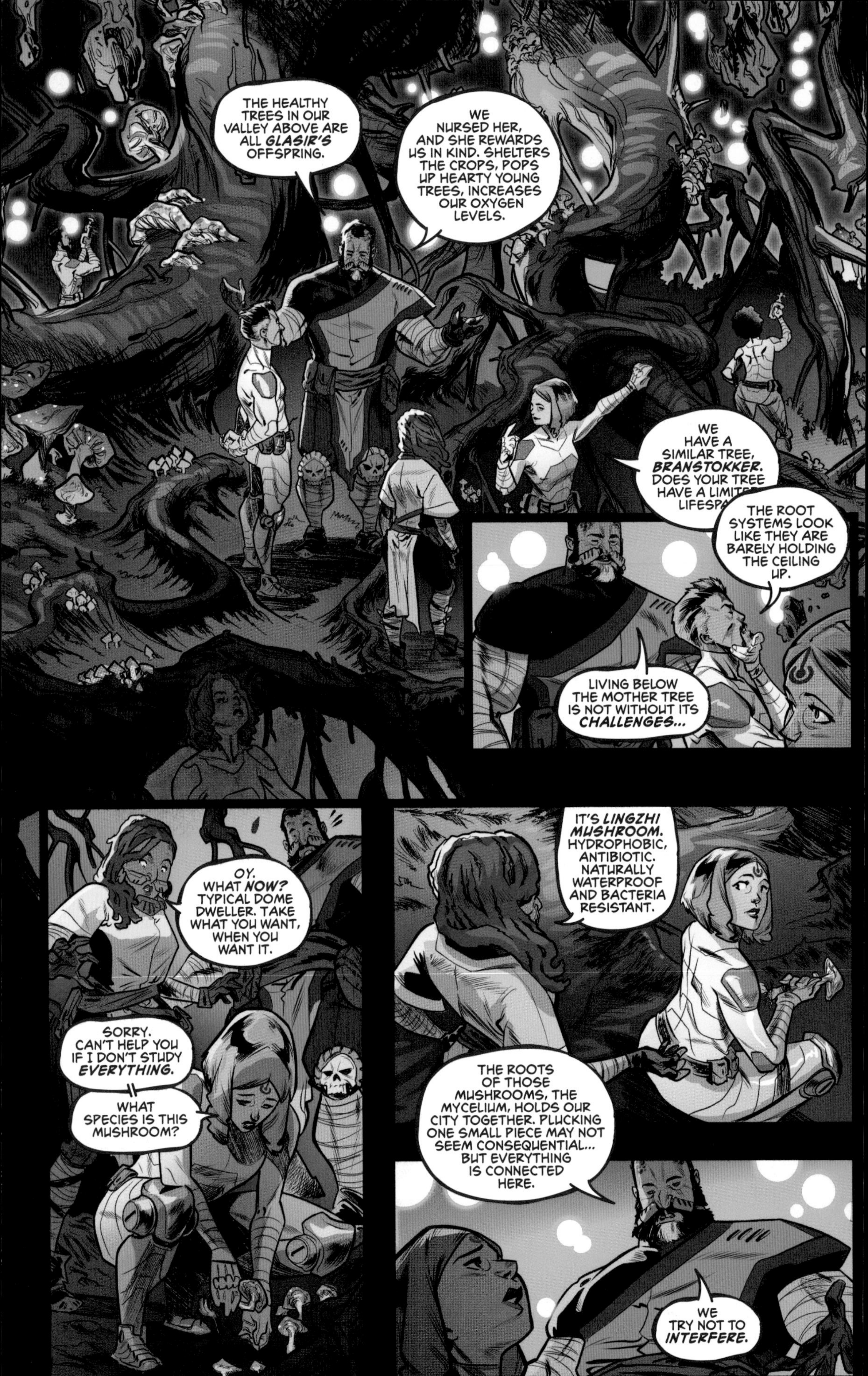
THE HEALTHY TREES IN OUR VALLEY ABOVE ARE ALL GLASIR'S OFFSPRING.
WE NURSED HER, AND SHE REWARDS US IN KIND. SHELTERS THE CROPS, POPS UP HEARTY YOUNG TREES, INCREASES OUR OXYGEN LEVELS.
WE HAVE A SIMILAR TREE, BRANSTOKKER. DOES YOUR TREE HAVE A LIMITE LIFESPA
THE ROOT SYSTEMS LOOK LIKE THEY ARE BARELY HOLDING THE CEILING UP.
LIVING BELOW THE MOTHER TREE IS NOT WITHOUT ITS CHALLENGES...
OY. WHAT NOW? TYPICAL DOME DWELLER. TAKE WHAT YOU WANT, WHEN YOU WANT IT.
SORRY. CAN'T HELP YOU IF I DON'T STUDY EVERYTHING.
WHAT SPECIES IS THIS MUSHROOM?
IT'S LINGZHI MUSHROOM. HYDROPHOBIC, ANTIBIOTIC. NATURALLY WATERPROOF AND BACTERIA RESISTANT.
THE ROOTS OF THOSE MUSHROOMS, THE MYCELIUM, HOLDS OUR CITY TOGETHER. PLUCKING ONE SMALL PIECE MAY NOT SEEM CONSEQUENTIAL... BUT EVERYTHING IS CONNECTED HERE.
WE TRY NOT TO INTERFERE.

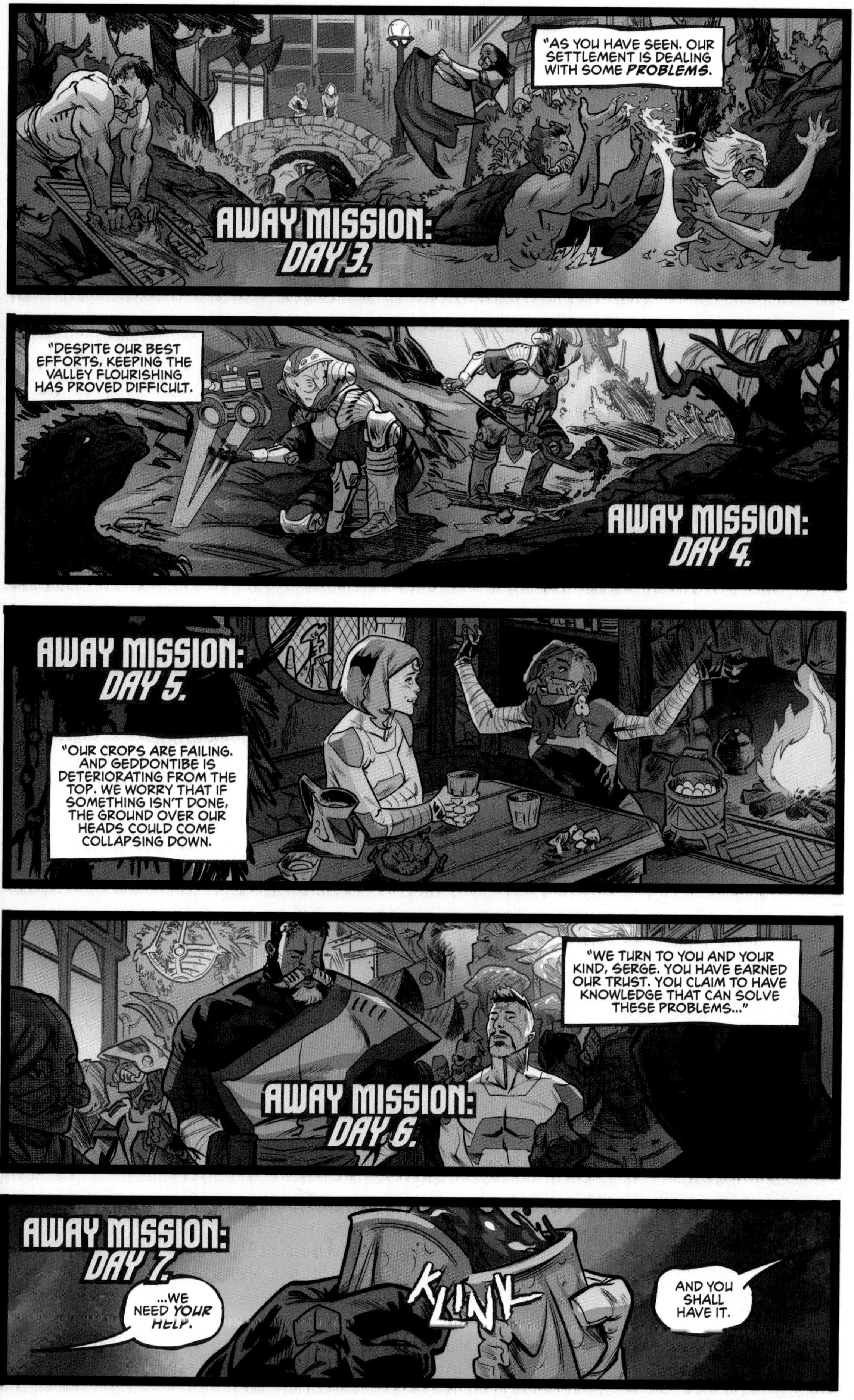
"AS YOU HAVE SEEN. OUR SETTLEMENT IS DEALING WITH SOME *PROBLEMS*.
AWAY MISSION: DAY 3.
"DESPITE OUR BEST EFFORTS, KEEPING THE VALLEY FLOURISHING HAS PROVED DIFFICULT.
AWAY MISSION: DAY 4.
AWAY MISSION: DAY 5.
"OUR CROPS ARE FAILING. AND GEDDONTIBE IS DETERIORATING FROM THE TOP. WE WORRY THAT IF SOMETHING ISN'T DONE, THE GROUND OVER OUR HEADS COULD COME COLLAPSING DOWN.
"WE TURN TO YOU AND YOUR KIND, SERGE. YOU HAVE EARNED OUR TRUST. YOU CLAIM TO HAVE KNOWLEDGE THAT CAN SOLVE THESE PROBLEMS..."
AWAY MISSION: DAY 6.
AWAY MISSION: DAY 7.
...WE NEED *YOUR HELP*.
KLINK
AND YOU SHALL HAVE IT.

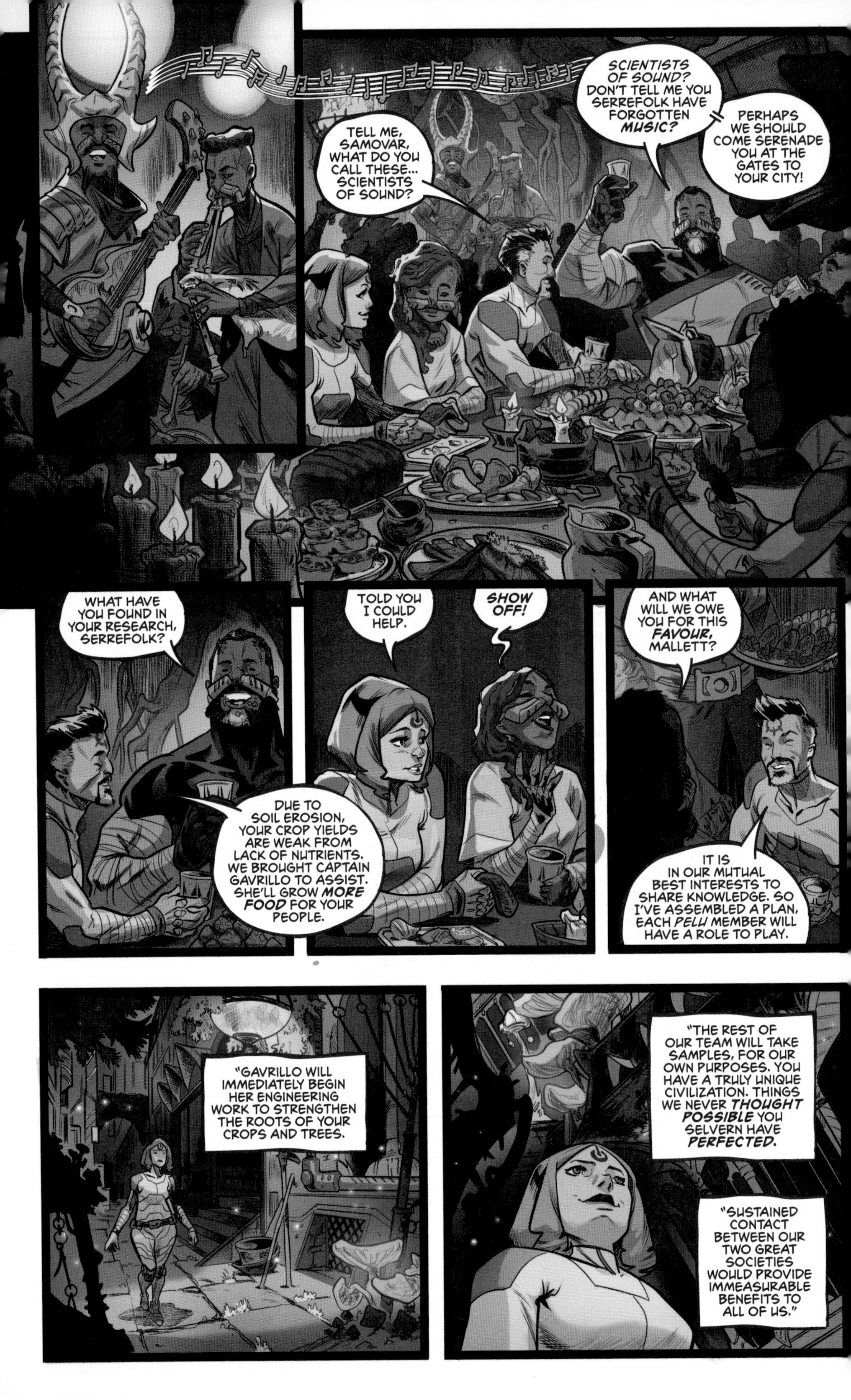
TELL ME, SAMOVAR, WHAT DO YOU CALL THESE... SCIENTISTS OF SOUND?
SCIENTISTS OF SOUND? DON'T TELL ME YOU SERREFOLK HAVE FORGOTTEN MUSIC?
PERHAPS WE SHOULD COME SERENADE YOU AT THE GATES TO YOUR CITY!
WHAT HAVE YOU FOUND IN YOUR RESEARCH, SERREFOLK?
DUE TO SOIL EROSION, YOUR CROP YIELDS ARE WEAK FROM LACK OF NUTRIENTS. WE BROUGHT CAPTAIN GAVRILLO TO ASSIST. SHE'LL GROW MORE FOOD FOR YOUR PEOPLE.
TOLD YOU I COULD HELP.
SHOW OFF!
AND WHAT WILL WE OWE YOU FOR THIS FAVOUR, MALLETT?
IT IS IN OUR MUTUAL BEST INTERESTS TO SHARE KNOWLEDGE. SO I'VE ASSEMBLED A PLAN, EACH PELU MEMBER WILL HAVE A ROLE TO PLAY.
"GAVRILLO WILL IMMEDIATELY BEGIN HER ENGINEERING WORK TO STRENGTHEN THE ROOTS OF YOUR CROPS AND TREES.
"THE REST OF OUR TEAM WILL TAKE SAMPLES, FOR OUR OWN PURPOSES. YOU HAVE A TRULY UNIQUE CIVILIZATION. THINGS WE NEVER THOUGHT POSSIBLE YOU SELVERN HAVE PERFECTED.
"SUSTAINED CONTACT BETWEEN OUR TWO GREAT SOCIETIES WOULD PROVIDE IMMEASURABLE BENEFITS TO ALL OF US."

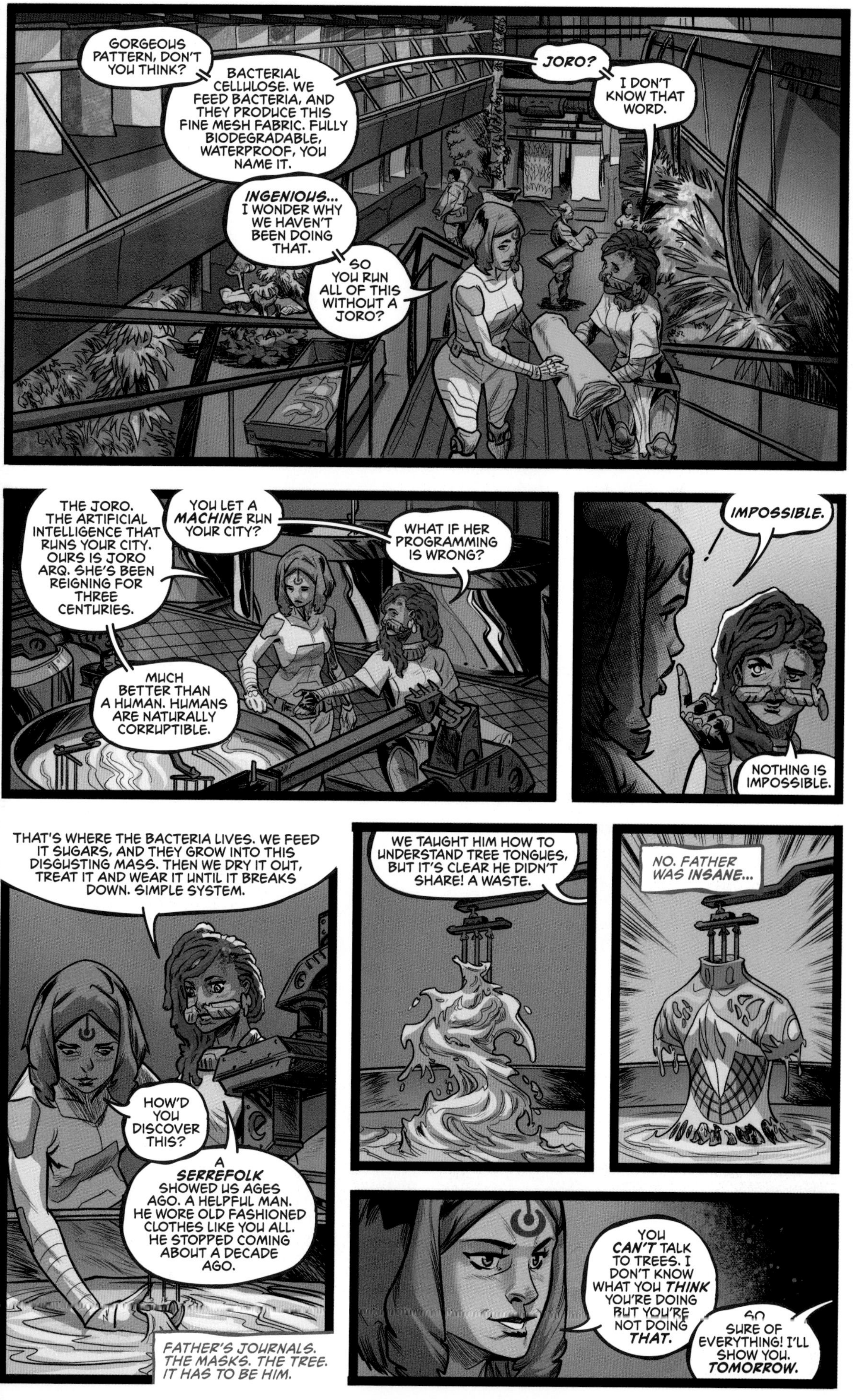

GORGEOUS PATTERN, DON'T YOU THINK?
BACTERIAL CELLULOSE. WE FEED BACTERIA, AND THEY PRODUCE THIS FINE MESH FABRIC. FULLY BIODEGRADABLE, WATERPROOF, YOU NAME IT.
JORO?
I DON'T KNOW THAT WORD.
INGENIOUS... I WONDER WHY WE HAVEN'T BEEN DOING THAT.
SO YOU RUN ALL OF THIS WITHOUT A JORO?
THE JORO. THE ARTIFICIAL INTELLIGENCE THAT RUNS YOUR CITY. OURS IS JORO ARQ. SHE'S BEEN REIGNING FOR THREE CENTURIES.
MUCH BETTER THAN A HUMAN. HUMANS ARE NATURALLY CORRUPTIBLE.
YOU LET A MACHINE RUN YOUR CITY?
WHAT IF HER PROGRAMMING IS WRONG?
IMPOSSIBLE.
NOTHING IS IMPOSSIBLE.
THAT'S WHERE THE BACTERIA LIVES. WE FEED IT SUGARS, AND THEY GROW INTO THIS DISGUSTING MASS. THEN WE DRY IT OUT, TREAT IT AND WEAR IT UNTIL IT BREAKS DOWN. SIMPLE SYSTEM.
HOW'D YOU DISCOVER THIS?
A SERREFOLK SHOWED US AGES AGO. A HELPFUL MAN. HE WORE OLD FASHIONED CLOTHES LIKE YOU ALL. HE STOPPED COMING ABOUT A DECADE AGO.
FATHER'S JOURNALS. THE MASKS. THE TREE. IT HAS TO BE HIM.
WE TAUGHT HIM HOW TO UNDERSTAND TREE TONGUES, BUT IT'S CLEAR HE DIDN'T SHARE! A WASTE.
NO. FATHER WAS INSANE...
YOU CAN'T TALK TO TREES. I DON'T KNOW WHAT YOU THINK YOU'RE DOING BUT YOU'RE NOT DOING THAT.
SO SURE OF EVERYTHING! I'LL SHOW YOU. TOMORROW.

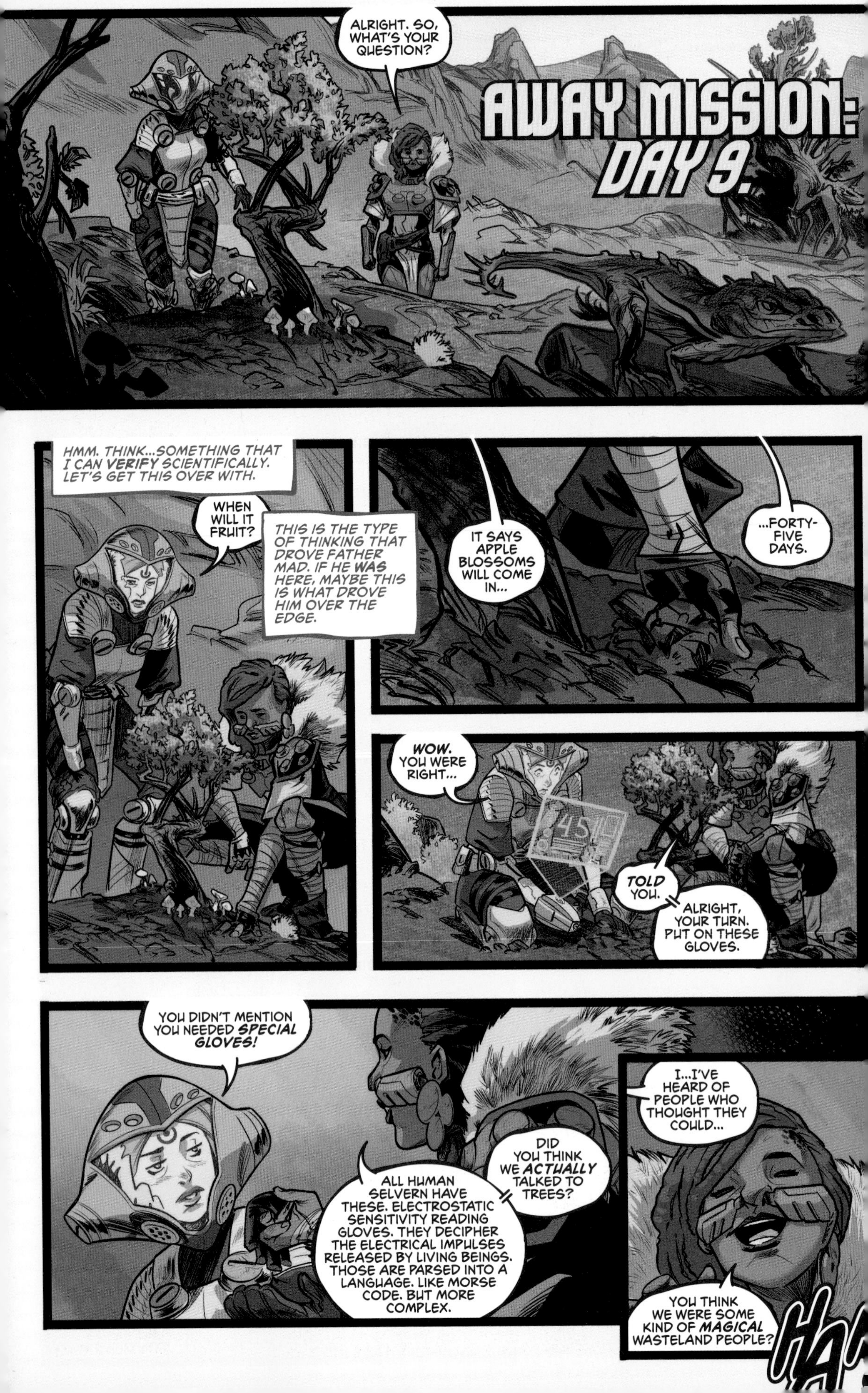

ALRIGHT. SO, WHAT'S YOUR QUESTION?
AWAY MISSION: DAY 9.
HMM. THINK...SOMETHING THAT I CAN VERIFY SCIENTIFICALLY. LET'S GET THIS OVER WITH.
WHEN WILL IT FRUIT?
THIS IS THE TYPE OF THINKING THAT DROVE FATHER MAD. IF HE WAS HERE, MAYBE THIS IS WHAT DROVE HIM OVER THE EDGE.
IT SAYS APPLE BLOSSOMS WILL COME IN...
...FORTY-FIVE DAYS.
WOW. YOU WERE RIGHT...
45
TOLD YOU.
ALRIGHT, YOUR TURN. PUT ON THESE GLOVES.
YOU DIDN'T MENTION YOU NEEDED SPECIAL GLOVES!
ALL HUMAN SELVERN HAVE THESE. ELECTROSTATIC SENSITIVITY READING GLOVES. THEY DECIPHER THE ELECTRICAL IMPULSES RELEASED BY LIVING BEINGS. THOSE ARE PARSED INTO A LANGUAGE. LIKE MORSE CODE. BUT MORE COMPLEX.
DID YOU THINK WE ACTUALLY TALKED TO TREES?
I...I'VE HEARD OF PEOPLE WHO THOUGHT THEY COULD...
YOU THINK WE WERE SOME KIND OF MAGICAL WASTELAND PEOPLE?
HA

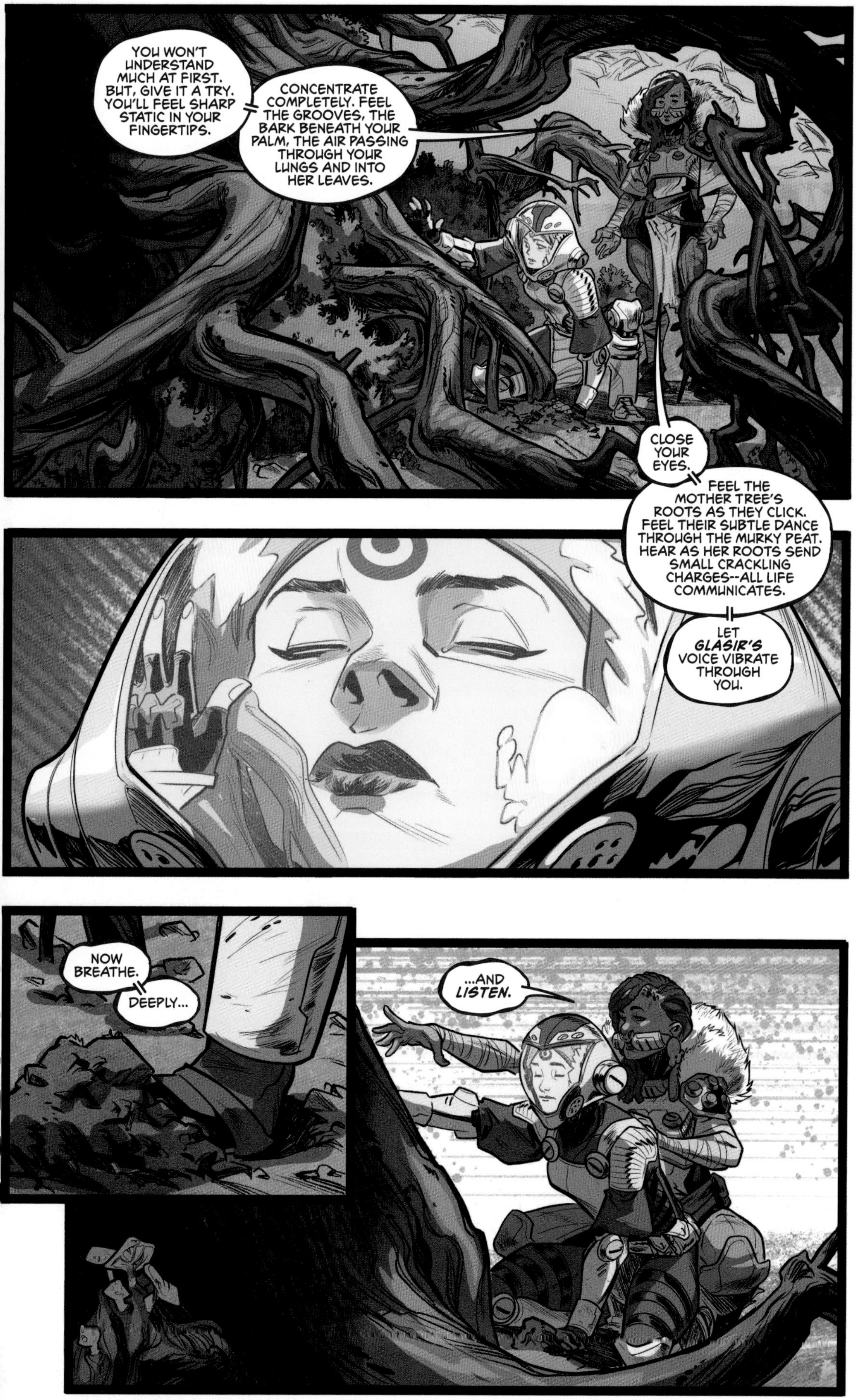
YOU WON'T UNDERSTAND MUCH AT FIRST. BUT, GIVE IT A TRY. YOU'LL FEEL SHARP STATIC IN YOUR FINGERTIPS.
CONCENTRATE COMPLETELY. FEEL THE GROOVES, THE BARK BENEATH YOUR PALM, THE AIR PASSING THROUGH YOUR LUNGS AND INTO HER LEAVES.
CLOSE YOUR EYES.
FEEL THE MOTHER TREE'S ROOTS AS THEY CLICK. FEEL THEIR SUBTLE DANCE THROUGH THE MURKY PEAT. HEAR AS HER ROOTS SEND SMALL CRACKLING CHARGES--ALL LIFE COMMUNICATES.
LET ***GLASIR'S*** VOICE VIBRATE THROUGH YOU.
NOW BREATHE.
DEEPLY...
...AND ***LISTEN.***

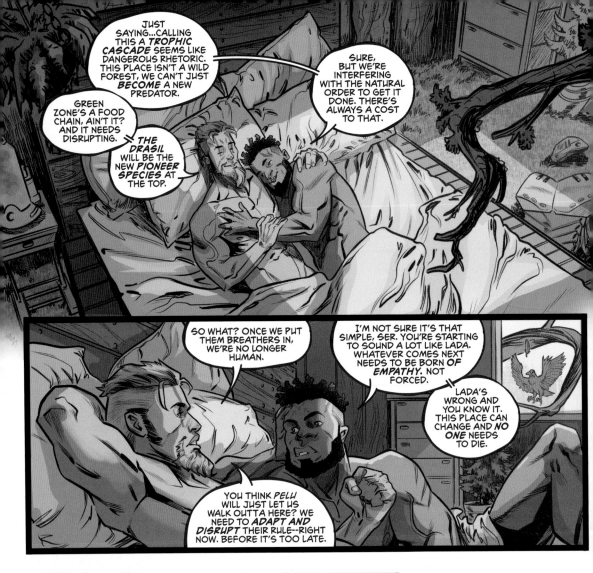

JUST SAYING...CALLING THIS A *TROPHIC CASCADE* SEEMS LIKE DANGEROUS RHETORIC. THIS PLACE ISN'T A WILD FOREST, WE CAN'T JUST *BECOME* A NEW PREDATOR.

SURE, BUT WE'RE INTERFERING WITH THE NATURAL ORDER TO GET IT DONE. THERE'S ALWAYS A COST TO THAT.

GREEN ZONE'S A FOOD CHAIN, AIN'T IT? AND IT NEEDS DISRUPTING. *THE DRASIL* WILL BE THE NEW *PIONEER SPECIES* AT THE TOP.

SO WHAT? ONCE WE PUT THEM BREATHERS IN, WE'RE NO LONGER HUMAN.

I'M NOT SURE IT'S THAT SIMPLE, SER. YOU'RE STARTING TO SOUND A LOT LIKE LADA. WHATEVER COMES NEXT NEEDS TO BE BORN OF *EMPATHY*. NOT FORCED.

LADA'S WRONG AND YOU KNOW IT. THIS PLACE CAN CHANGE AND *NO ONE* NEEDS TO DIE.

YOU THINK *PELU* WILL JUST LET US WALK OUTTA HERE? WE NEED TO *ADAPT AND DISRUPT* THEIR RULE--RIGHT NOW. BEFORE IT'S TOO LATE.

IF WE'RE TOO AGGRESSIVE PEOPLE WILL GET *SCARED*. AND WHAT HAPPENS TO PEOPLE THAT *DON'T ADAPT?*

PELU ISN'T WORKING FOR EVERYONE...THEY NEED TO KNOW THEY'RE *NO LONGER* IN CONTROL...THAT THEY'VE EXPLOITED US FOR TOO LONG...

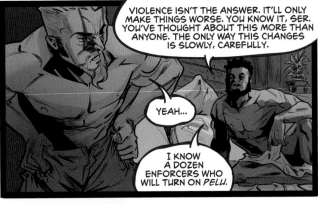

VIOLENCE ISN'T THE ANSWER. IT'LL ONLY MAKE THINGS WORSE. YOU KNOW IT, SER. YOU'VE THOUGHT ABOUT THIS MORE THAN ANYONE. THE ONLY WAY THIS CHANGES IS SLOWLY, CAREFULLY.

YEAH...

I KNOW A DOZEN ENFORCERS WHO WILL TURN ON *PELU.*

WE CAN BROKER PEACE. GET EVERYONE OUT OF HERE SAFELY WITHOUT SUCCUMBING TO LADA'S INSANE PLAN. A *QUIET REBELLION.*

MAYBE...

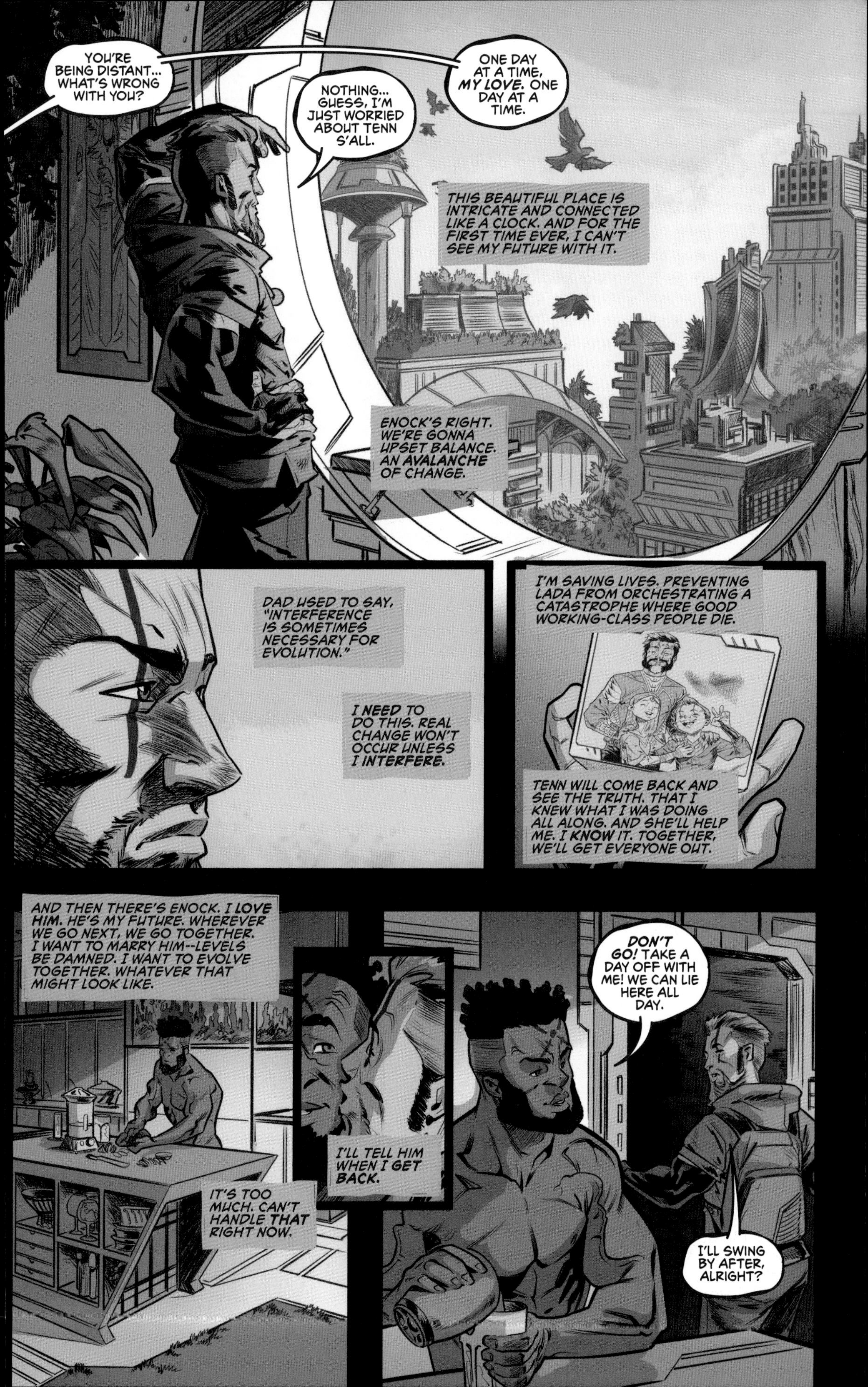
YOU'RE BEING DISTANT... WHAT'S WRONG WITH YOU?
NOTHING... GUESS, I'M JUST WORRIED ABOUT TENN S'ALL.
ONE DAY AT A TIME, MY LOVE. ONE DAY AT A TIME.
THIS BEAUTIFUL PLACE IS INTRICATE AND CONNECTED LIKE A CLOCK. AND FOR THE FIRST TIME EVER, I CAN'T SEE MY FUTURE WITH IT.
ENOCK'S RIGHT. WE'RE GONNA UPSET BALANCE. AN AVALANCHE OF CHANGE.
DAD USED TO SAY, "INTERFERENCE IS SOMETIMES NECESSARY FOR EVOLUTION."
I NEED TO DO THIS. REAL CHANGE WON'T OCCUR UNLESS I INTERFERE.
I'M SAVING LIVES. PREVENTING LADA FROM ORCHESTRATING A CATASTROPHE WHERE GOOD WORKING-CLASS PEOPLE DIE.
TENN WILL COME BACK AND SEE THE TRUTH. THAT I KNEW WHAT I WAS DOING ALL ALONG. AND SHE'LL HELP ME. I KNOW IT. TOGETHER, WE'LL GET EVERYONE OUT.
AND THEN THERE'S ENOCK. I LOVE HIM. HE'S MY FUTURE. WHEREVER WE GO NEXT, WE GO TOGETHER. I WANT TO MARRY HIM--LEVELS BE DAMNED. I WANT TO EVOLVE TOGETHER. WHATEVER THAT MIGHT LOOK LIKE.
IT'S TOO MUCH. CAN'T HANDLE THAT RIGHT NOW.
I'LL TELL HIM WHEN I GET BACK.
DON'T GO! TAKE A DAY OFF WITH ME! WE CAN LIE HERE ALL DAY.
I'LL SWING BY AFTER, ALRIGHT?

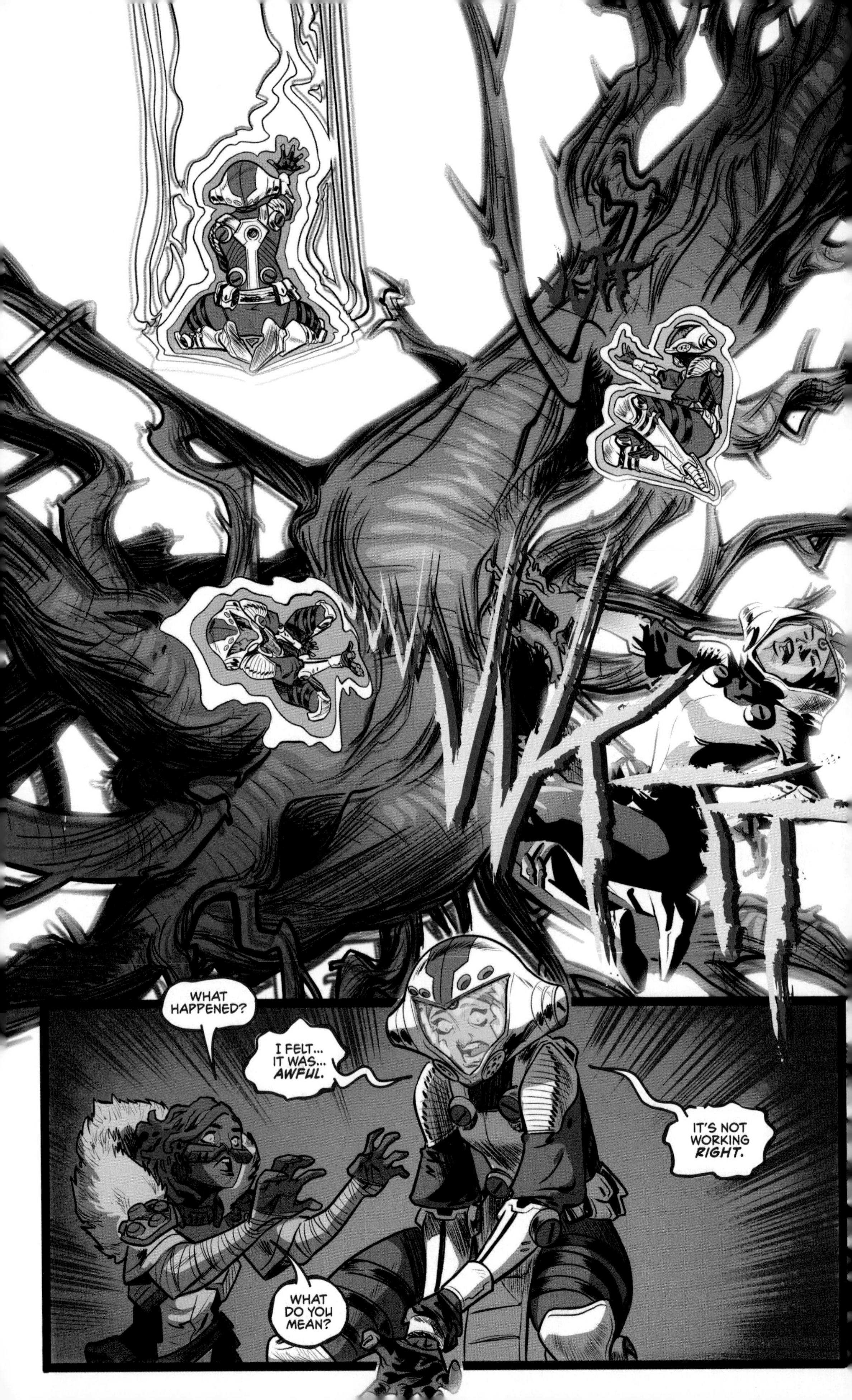

VVZZT
WHAT HAPPENED?
I FELT... IT WAS... AWFUL.
IT'S NOT WORKING RIGHT.
WHAT DO YOU MEAN?

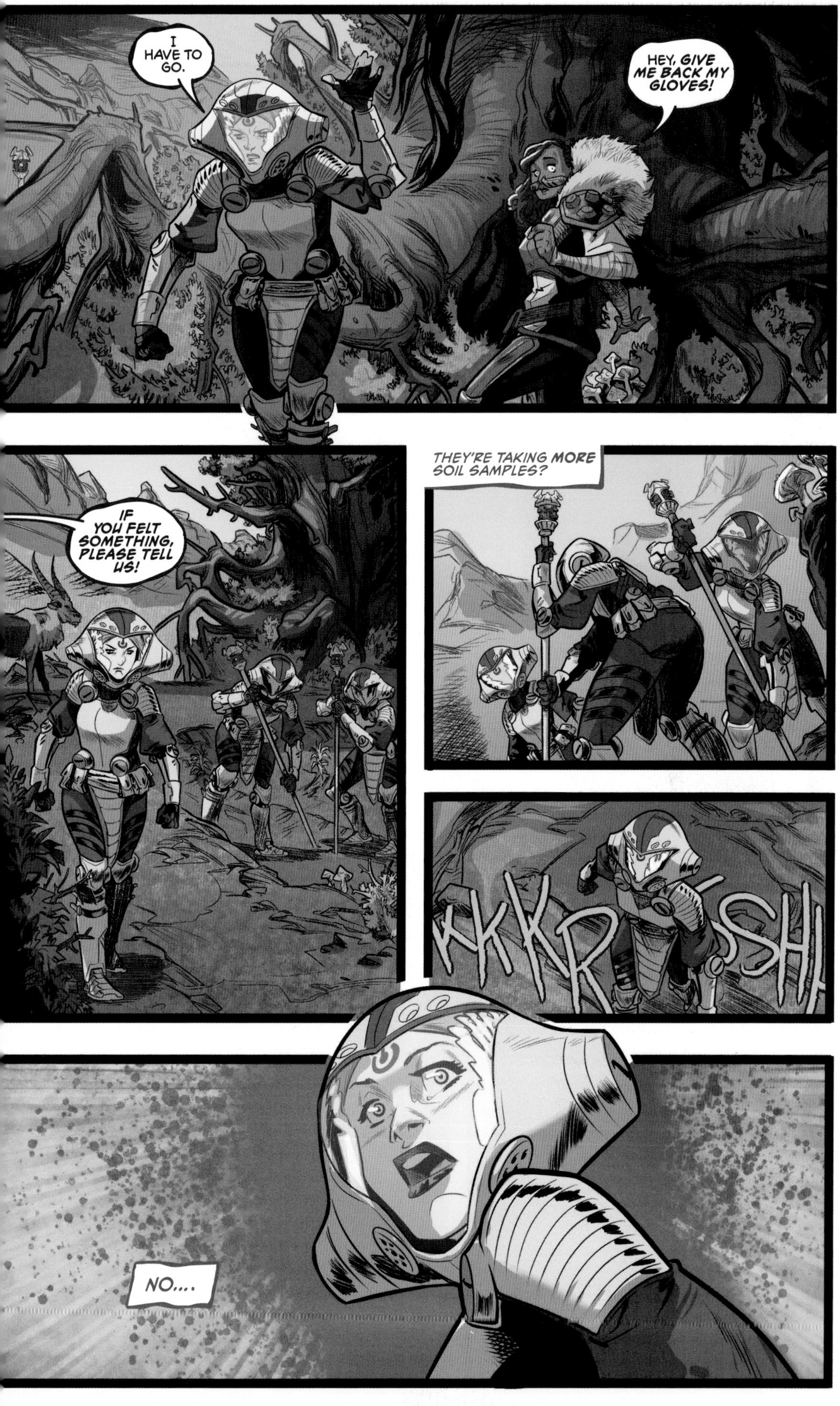
I HAVE TO GO.
HEY, GIVE ME BACK MY GLOVES!
IF YOU FELT SOMETHING, PLEASE TELL US!
THEY'RE TAKING MORE SOIL SAMPLES?
KKKRSSHH
NO....

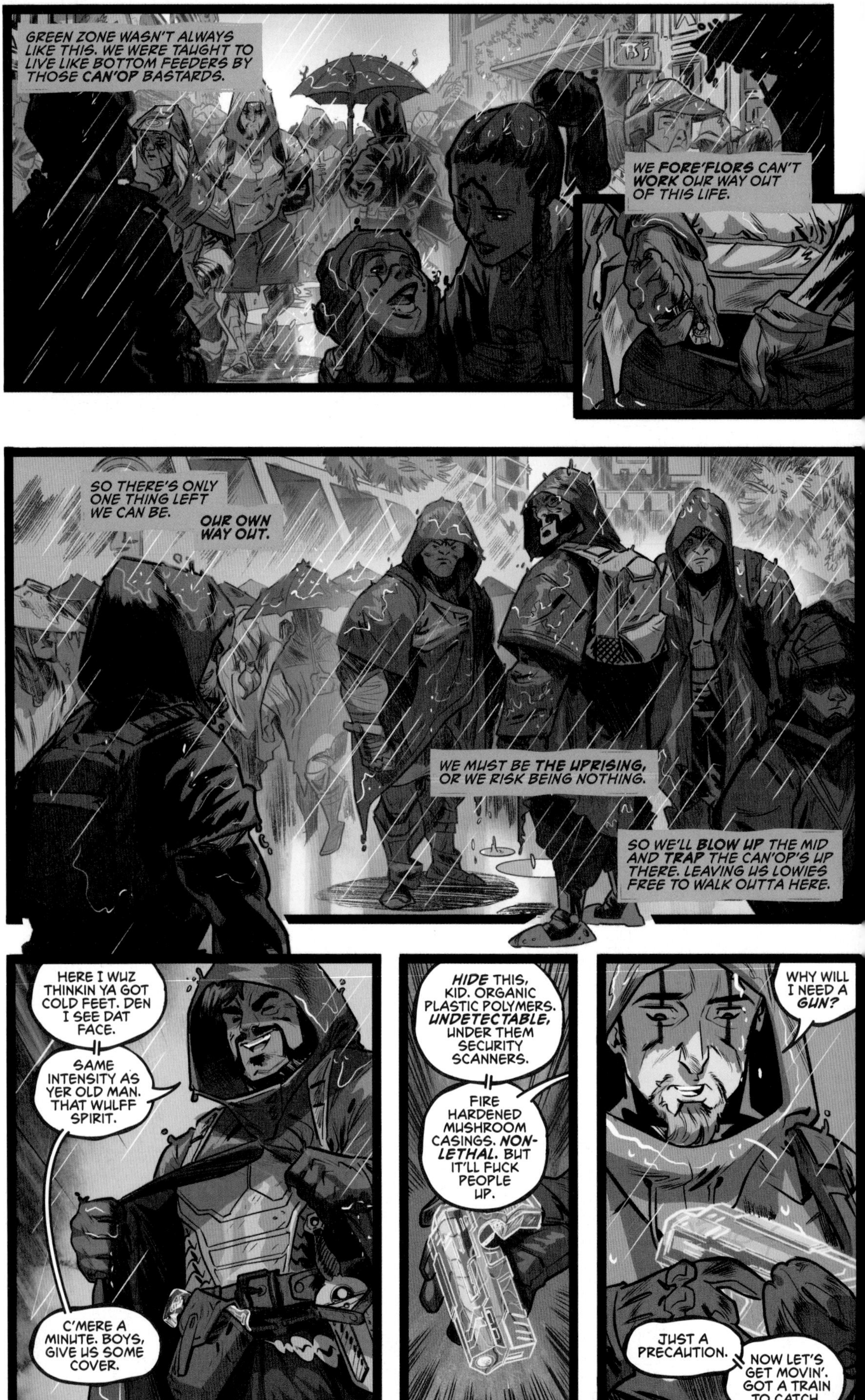
GREEN ZONE WASN'T ALWAYS LIKE THIS. WE WERE TAUGHT TO LIVE LIKE BOTTOM FEEDERS BY THOSE CAN'OP BASTARDS.
WE FORE'FLORS CAN'T WORK OUR WAY OUT OF THIS LIFE.
SO THERE'S ONLY ONE THING LEFT WE CAN BE.
OUR OWN WAY OUT.
WE MUST BE THE UPRISING, OR WE RISK BEING NOTHING.
SO WE'LL BLOW UP THE MID AND TRAP THE CAN'OP'S UP THERE. LEAVING US LOWIES FREE TO WALK OUTTA HERE.
HERE I WUZ THINKIN YA GOT COLD FEET. DEN I SEE DAT FACE.
SAME INTENSITY AS YER OLD MAN. THAT WULFF SPIRIT.
C'MERE A MINUTE. BOYS, GIVE US SOME COVER.
HIDE THIS, KID. ORGANIC PLASTIC POLYMERS. UNDETECTABLE, UNDER THEM SECURITY SCANNERS.
FIRE HARDENED MUSHROOM CASINGS. NON-LETHAL. BUT IT'LL FUCK PEOPLE UP.
WHY WILL I NEED A GUN?
JUST A PRECAUTION.
NOW LET'S GET MOVIN'. GOT A TRAIN TO CATCH.

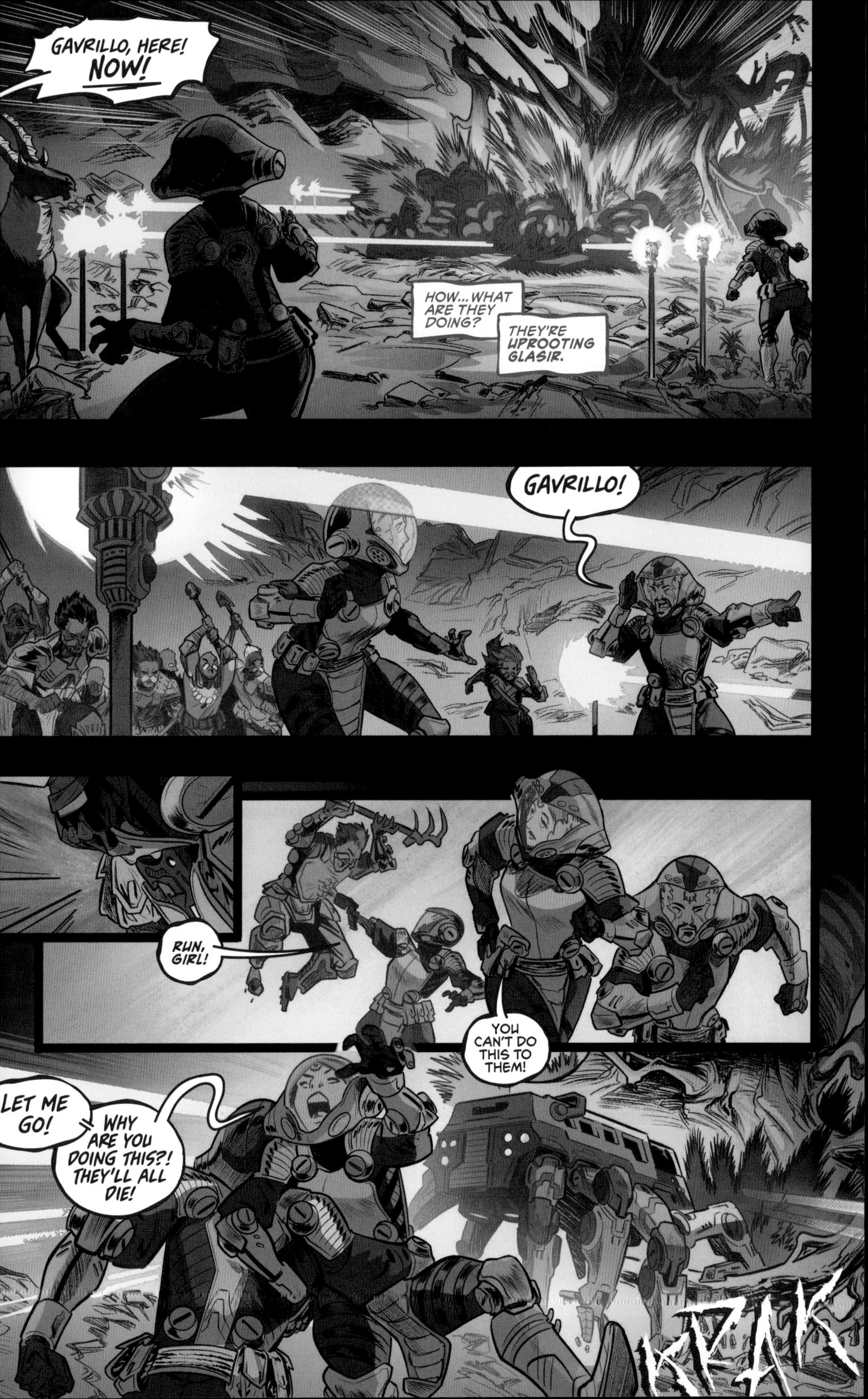
GAVRILLO, HERE! NOW!
HOW...WHAT ARE THEY DOING?
THEY'RE UPROOTING GLASIR.
GAVRILLO!
RUN, GIRL!
YOU CAN'T DO THIS TO THEM!
LET ME GO!
WHY ARE YOU DOING THIS?! THEY'LL ALL DIE!
KRAK

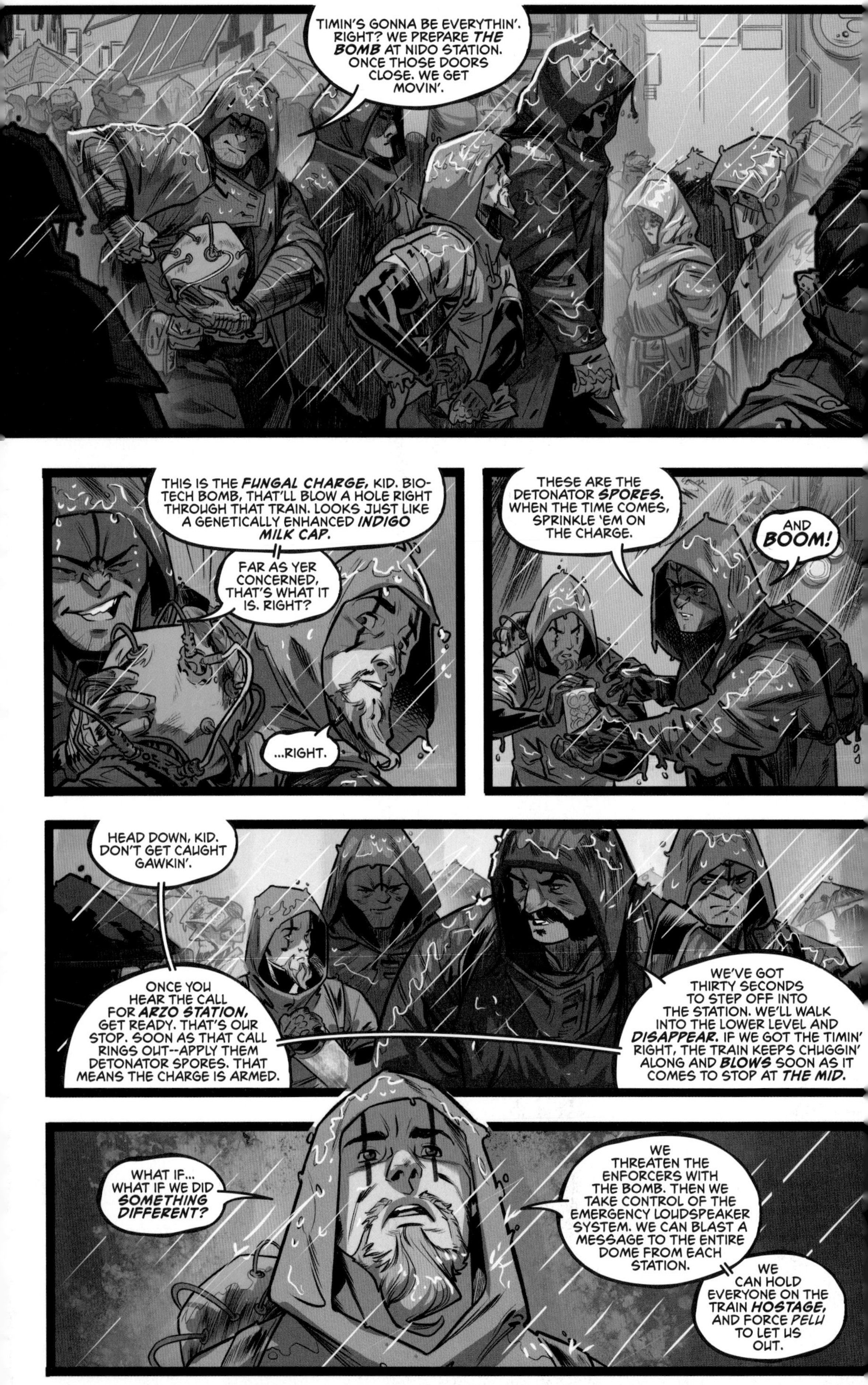
TIMIN'S GONNA BE EVERYTHIN'. RIGHT? WE PREPARE THE BOMB AT NIDO STATION. ONCE THOSE DOORS CLOSE. WE GET MOVIN'.
THIS IS THE FUNGAL CHARGE, KID. BIO-TECH BOMB, THAT'LL BLOW A HOLE RIGHT THROUGH THAT TRAIN. LOOKS JUST LIKE A GENETICALLY ENHANCED INDIGO MILK CAP.
FAR AS YER CONCERNED, THAT'S WHAT IT IS. RIGHT?
...RIGHT.
THESE ARE THE DETONATOR SPORES. WHEN THE TIME COMES, SPRINKLE 'EM ON THE CHARGE.
AND BOOM!
HEAD DOWN, KID. DON'T GET CAUGHT GAWKIN'.
ONCE YOU HEAR THE CALL FOR ARZO STATION, GET READY. THAT'S OUR STOP. SOON AS THAT CALL RINGS OUT--APPLY THEM DETONATOR SPORES. THAT MEANS THE CHARGE IS ARMED.
WE'VE GOT THIRTY SECONDS TO STEP OFF INTO THE STATION. WE'LL WALK INTO THE LOWER LEVEL AND DISAPPEAR. IF WE GOT THE TIMIN' RIGHT, THE TRAIN KEEPS CHUGGIN' ALONG AND BLOWS SOON AS IT COMES TO STOP AT THE MID.
WHAT IF... WHAT IF WE DID SOMETHING DIFFERENT?
WE THREATEN THE ENFORCERS WITH THE BOMB. THEN WE TAKE CONTROL OF THE EMERGENCY LOUDSPEAKER SYSTEM. WE CAN BLAST A MESSAGE TO THE ENTIRE DOME FROM EACH STATION.
WE CAN HOLD EVERYONE ON THE TRAIN HOSTAGE, AND FORCE PELU TO LET US OUT.

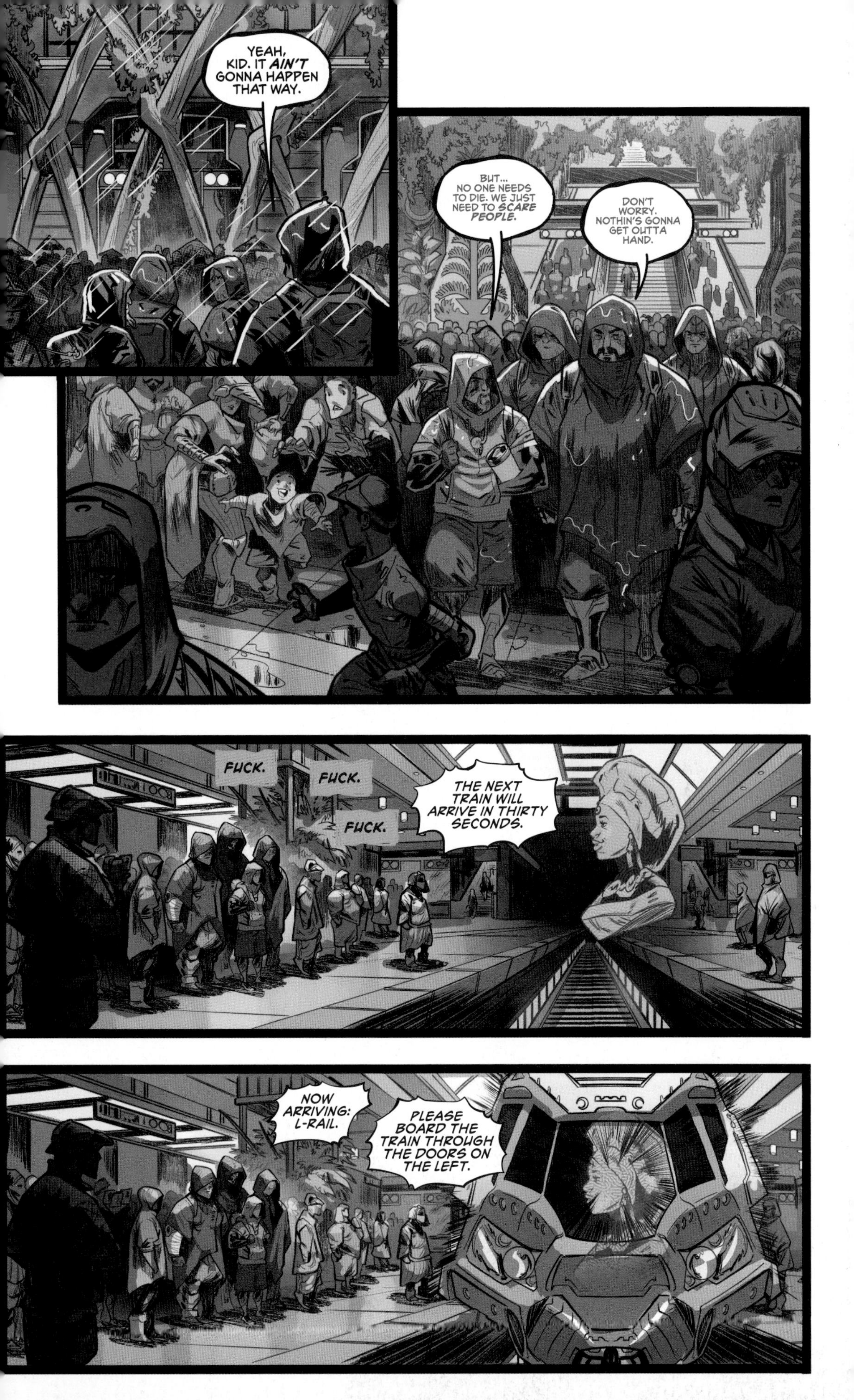
YEAH, KID. IT AIN'T GONNA HAPPEN THAT WAY.
BUT... NO ONE NEEDS TO DIE. WE JUST NEED TO SCARE PEOPLE.
DON'T WORRY. NOTHIN'S GONNA GET OUTTA HAND.
FUCK.
FUCK.
FUCK.
THE NEXT TRAIN WILL ARRIVE IN THIRTY SECONDS.
NOW ARRIVING: L-RAIL.
PLEASE BOARD THE TRAIN THROUGH THE DOORS ON THE LEFT.

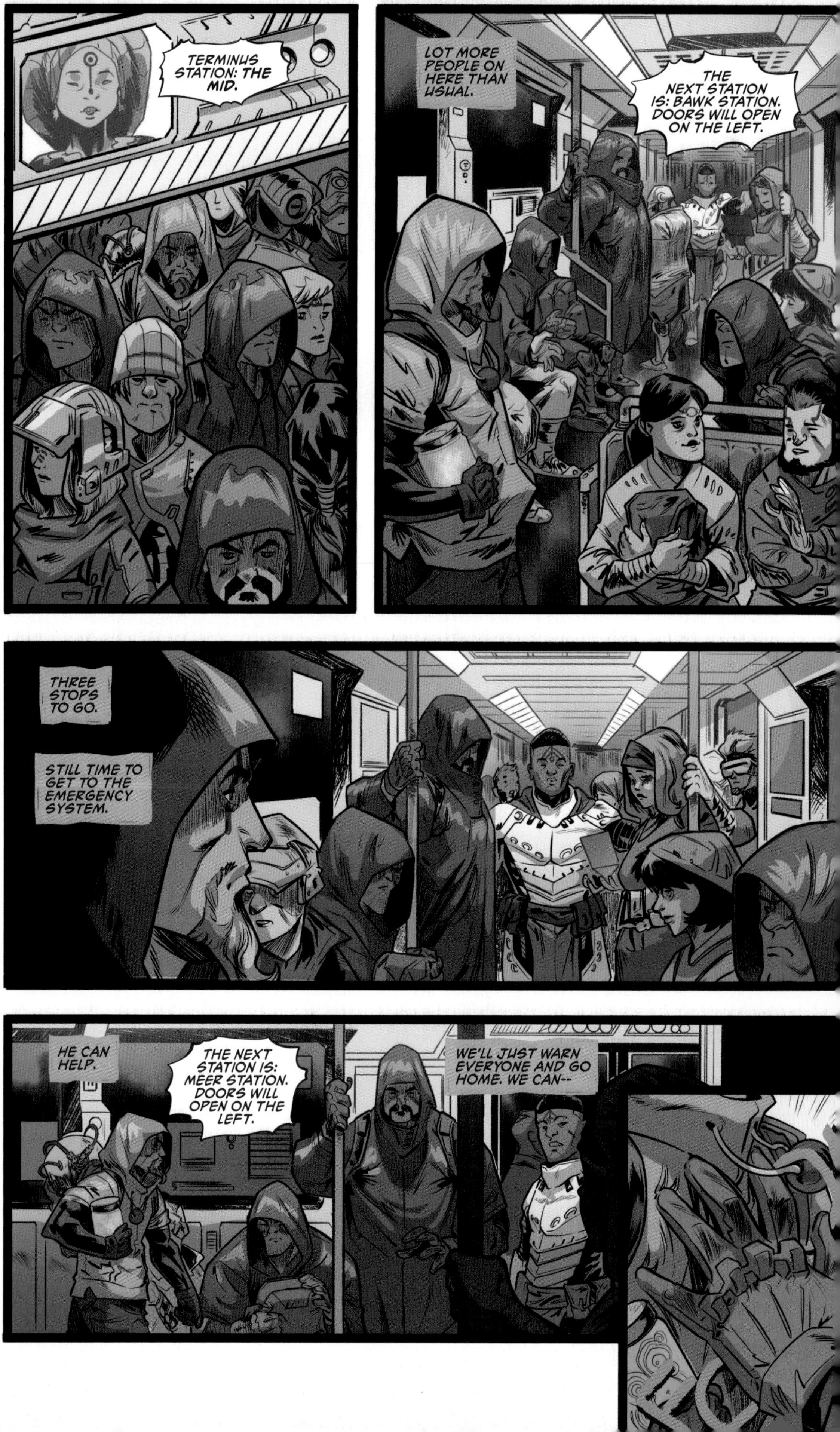
TERMINUS STATION: THE MID.
LOT MORE PEOPLE ON HERE THAN USUAL.
THE NEXT STATION IS: BAWK STATION. DOORS WILL OPEN ON THE LEFT.
THREE STOPS TO GO.
STILL TIME TO GET TO THE EMERGENCY SYSTEM.
HE CAN HELP.
THE NEXT STATION IS: MEER STATION. DOORS WILL OPEN ON THE LEFT.
WE'LL JUST WARN EVERYONE AND GO HOME. WE CAN--

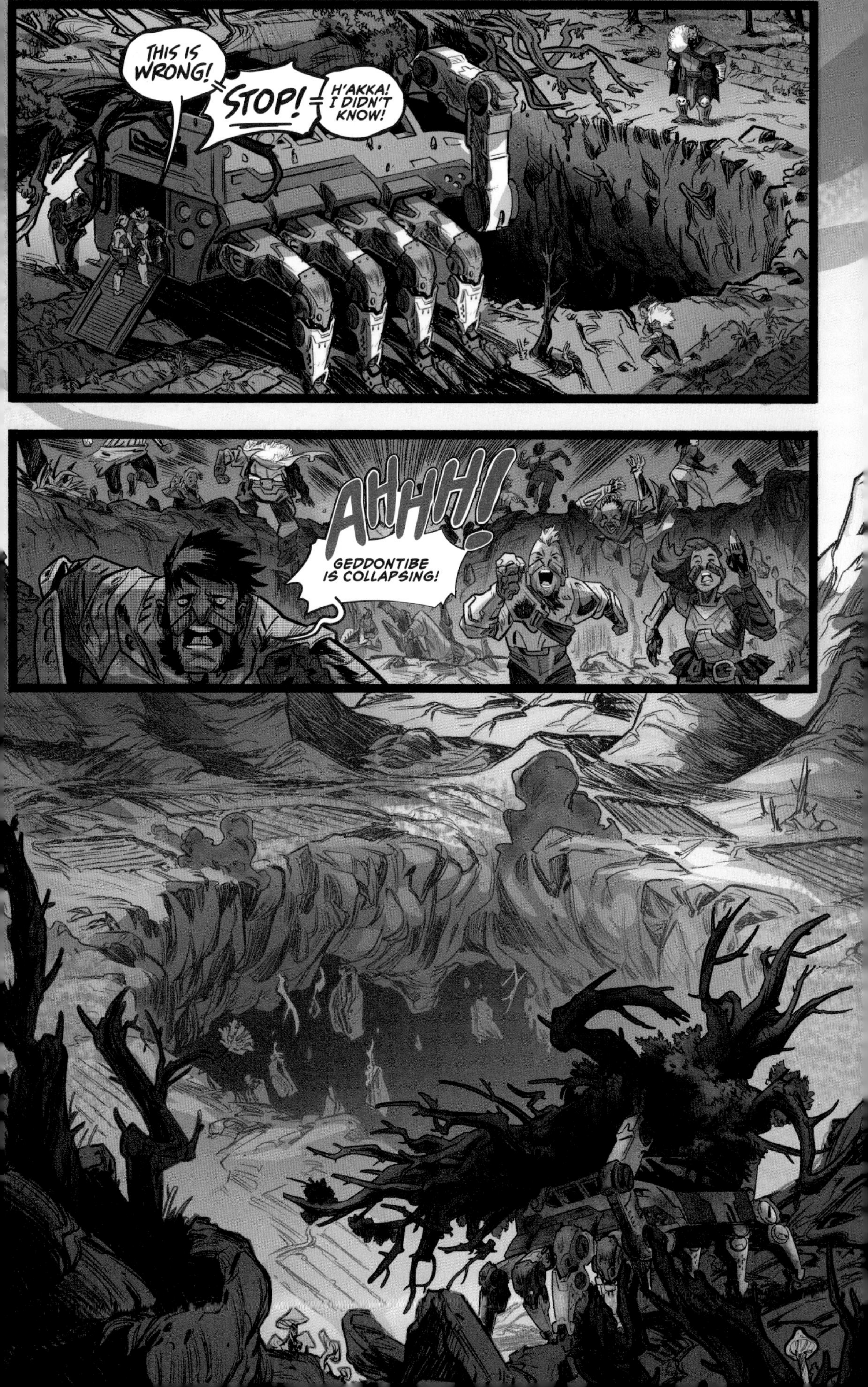

THIS IS WRONG!
STOP!
H'AKKA! I DIDN'T KNOW!
AHHH!
GEDDONTIBE IS COLLAPSING!

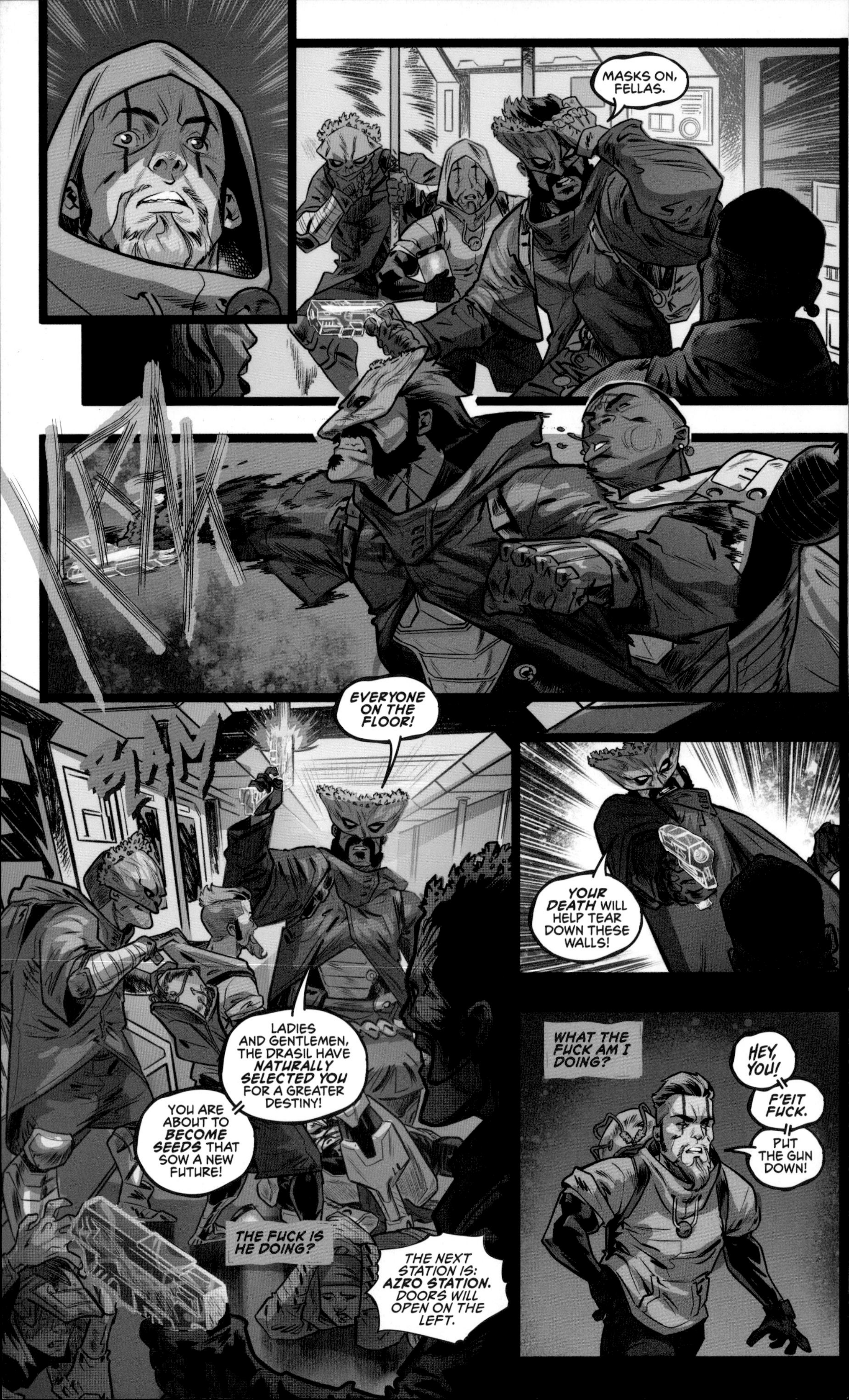
MASKS ON, FELLAS.
BLAM
EVERYONE ON THE FLOOR!
BLAM
LADIES AND GENTLEMEN, THE DRASIL HAVE NATURALLY SELECTED YOU FOR A GREATER DESTINY!
YOU ARE ABOUT TO BECOME SEEDS THAT SOW A NEW FUTURE!
THE FUCK IS HE DOING?
THE NEXT STATION IS: AZRO STATION. DOORS WILL OPEN ON THE LEFT.
YOUR DEATH WILL HELP TEAR DOWN THESE WALLS!
WHAT THE FUCK AM I DOING?
HEY, YOU!
F'EIT FUCK.
PUT THE GUN DOWN!

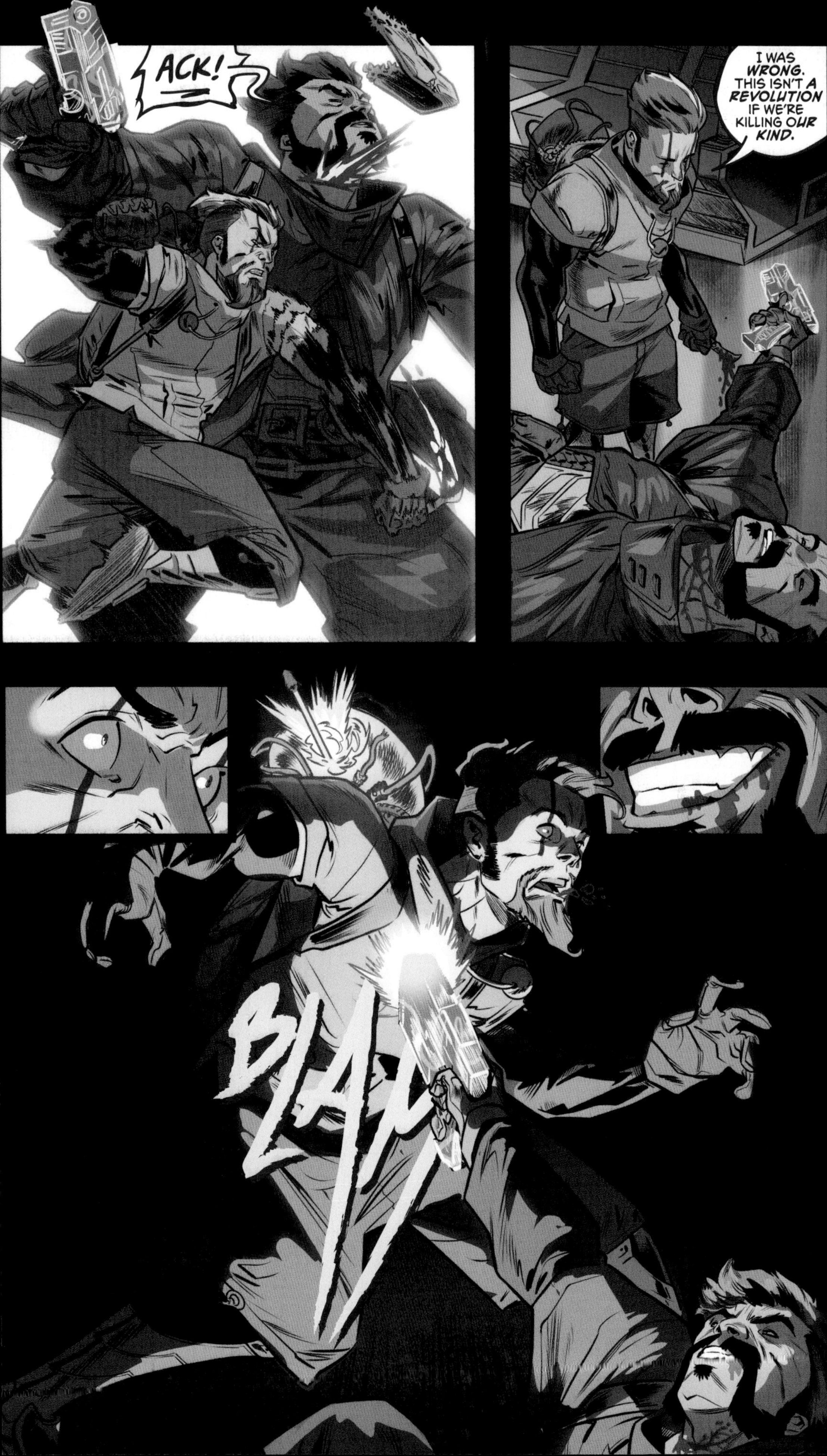
ACK!
I WAS WRONG. THIS ISN'T A REVOLUTION IF WE'RE KILLING OUR KIND.
BLAM

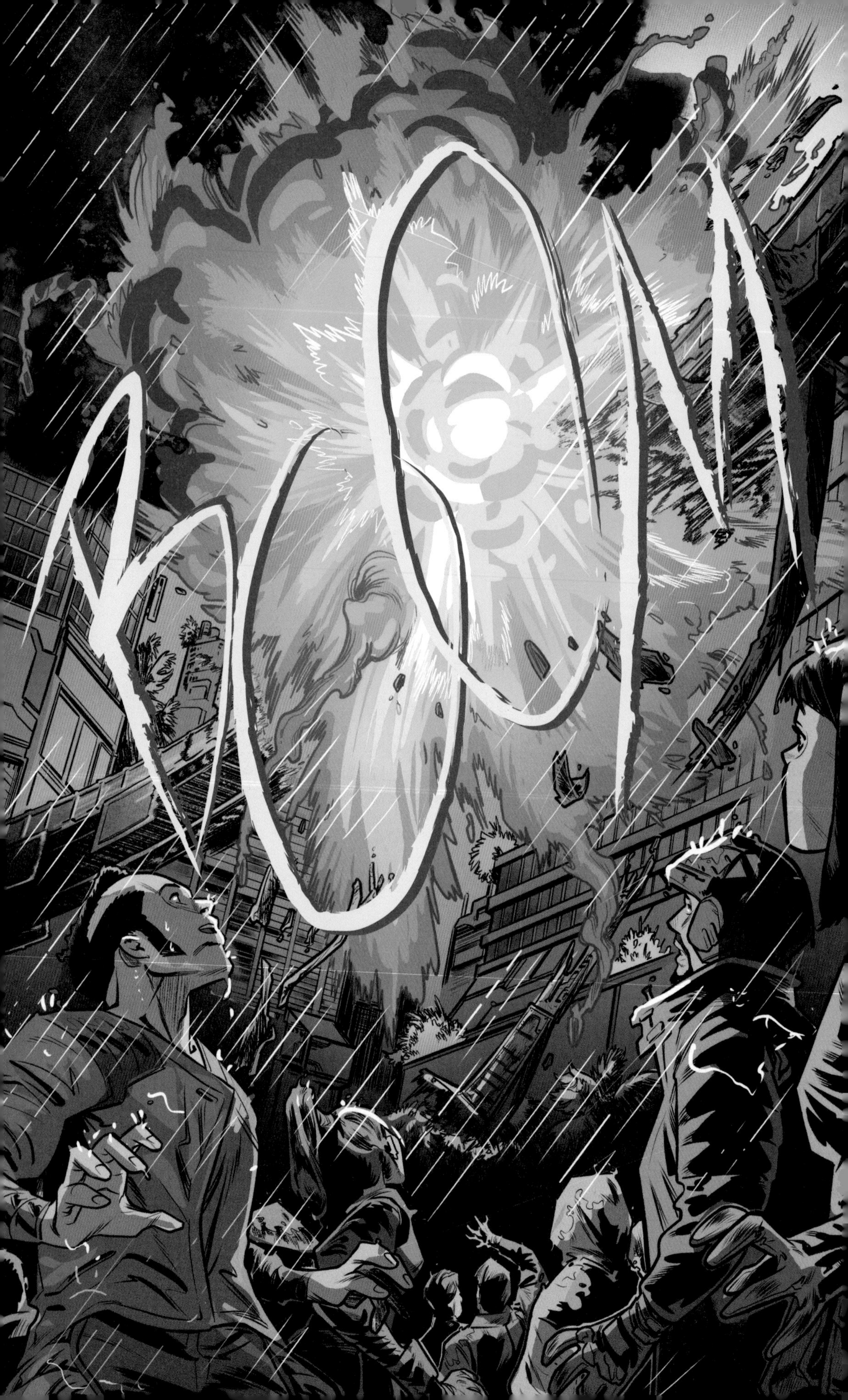
BOOM

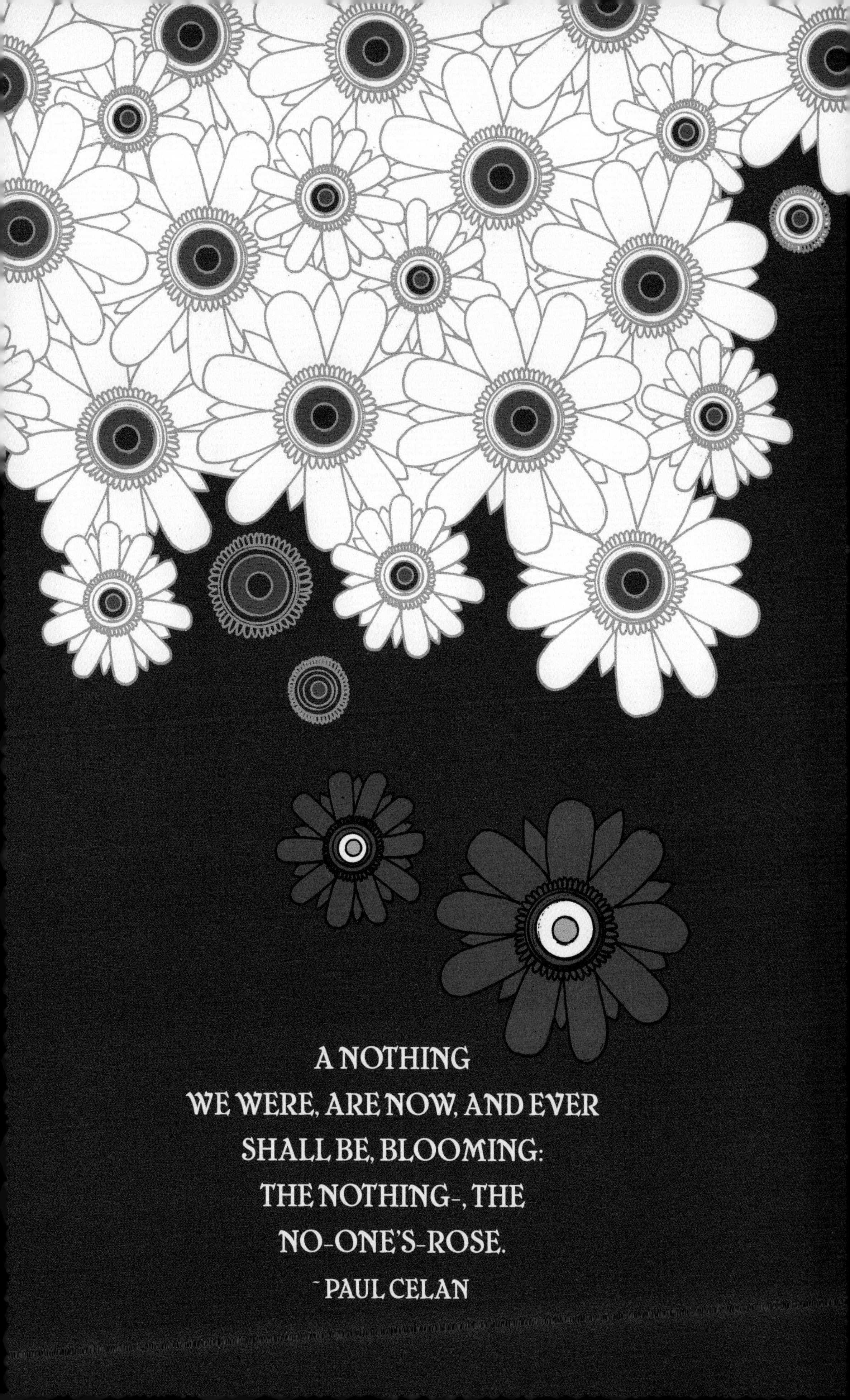

A NOTHING
WE WERE, ARE NOW, AND EVER
SHALL BE, BLOOMING:
THE NOTHING-, THE
NO-ONE'S-ROSE.
- PAUL CELAN

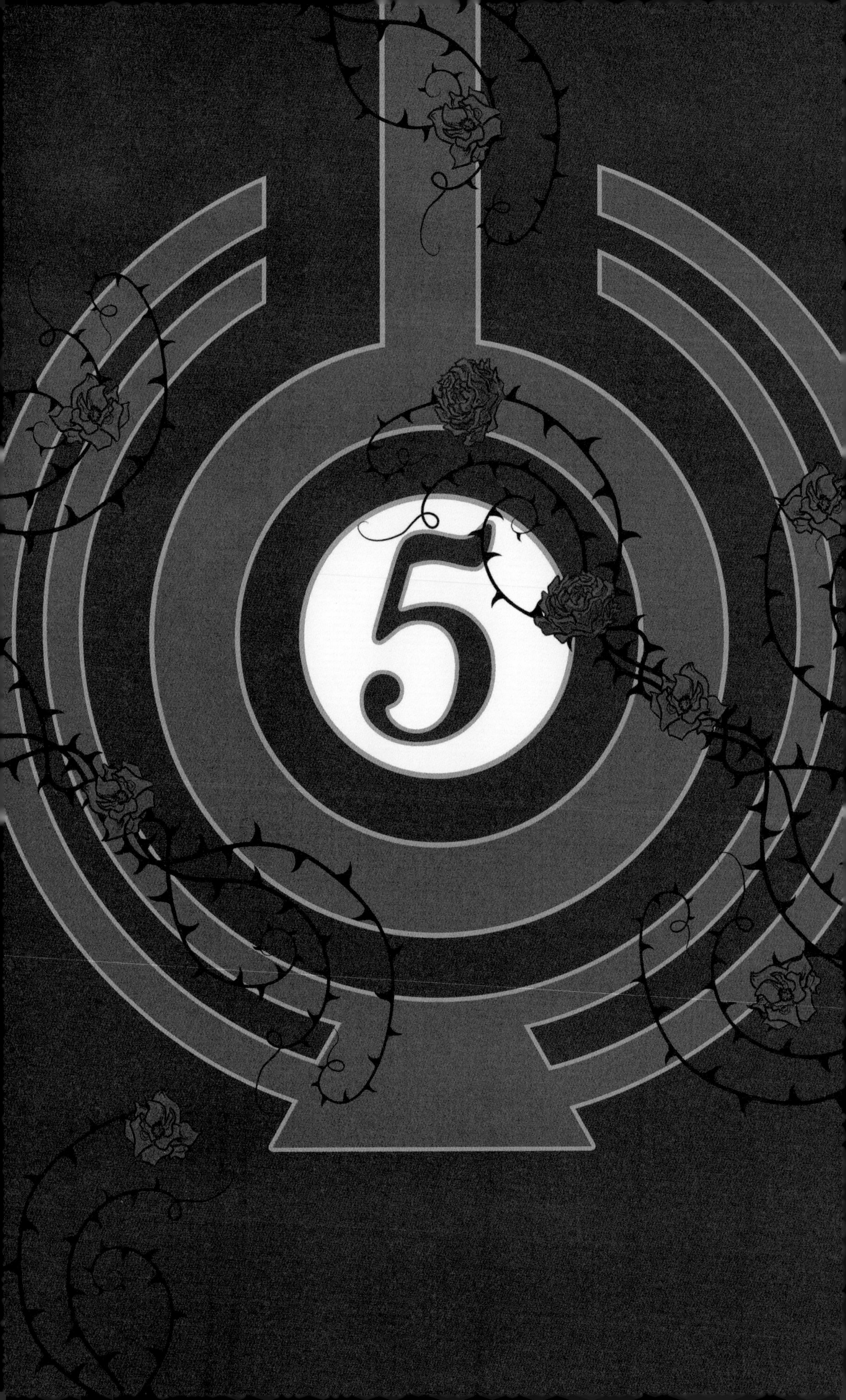
5

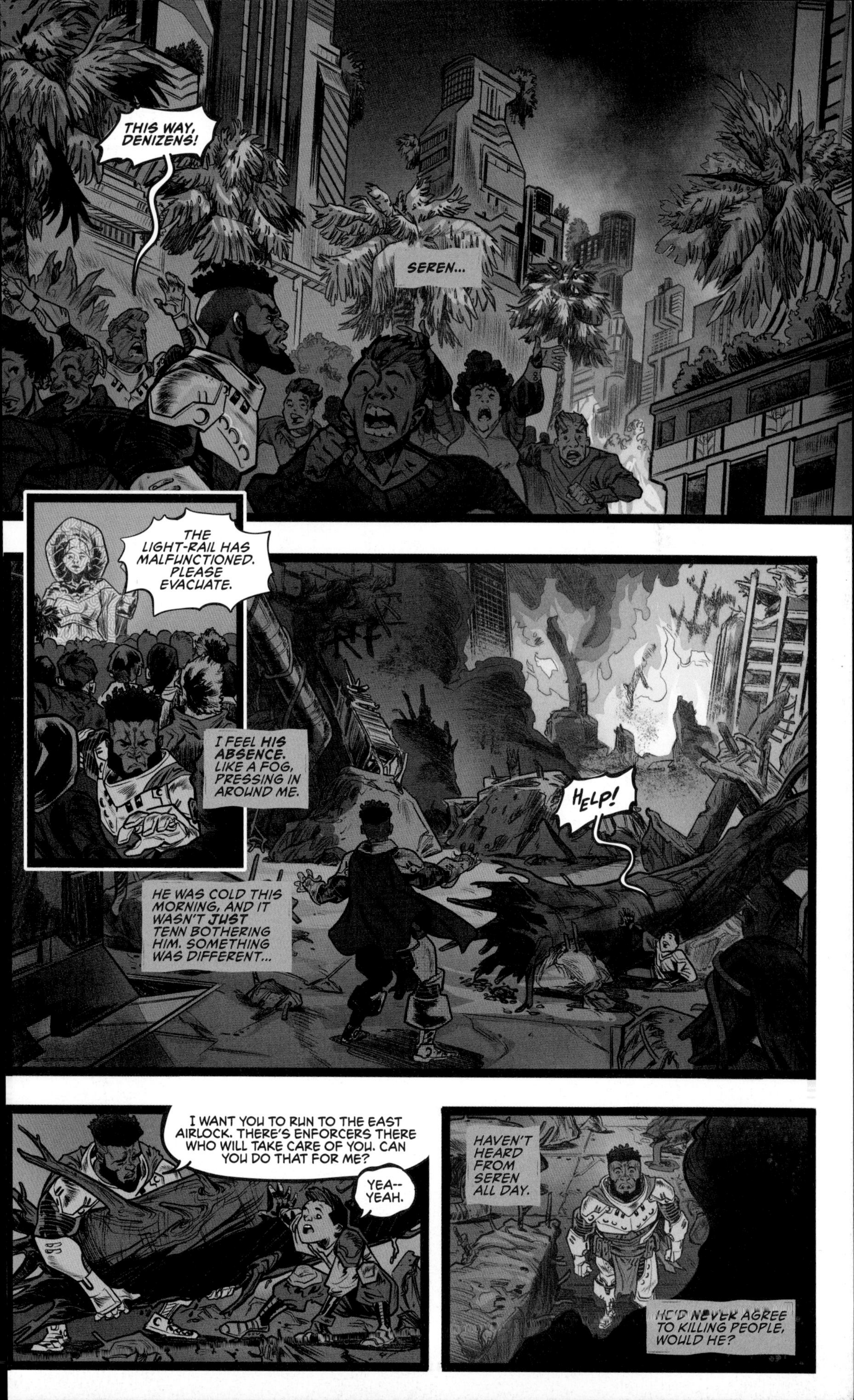
THIS WAY, DENIZENS!
SEREN...
THE LIGHT-RAIL HAS MALFUNCTIONED. PLEASE EVACUATE.
I FEEL HIS ABSENCE. LIKE A FOG, PRESSING IN AROUND ME.
HE WAS COLD THIS MORNING, AND IT WASN'T JUST TENN BOTHERING HIM. SOMETHING WAS DIFFERENT...
HELP!
I WANT YOU TO RUN TO THE EAST AIRLOCK. THERE'S ENFORCERS THERE WHO WILL TAKE CARE OF YOU. CAN YOU DO THAT FOR ME?
YEA-- YEAH.
HAVEN'T HEARD FROM SEREN ALL DAY.
HE'D NEVER AGREE TO KILLING PEOPLE, WOULD HE?

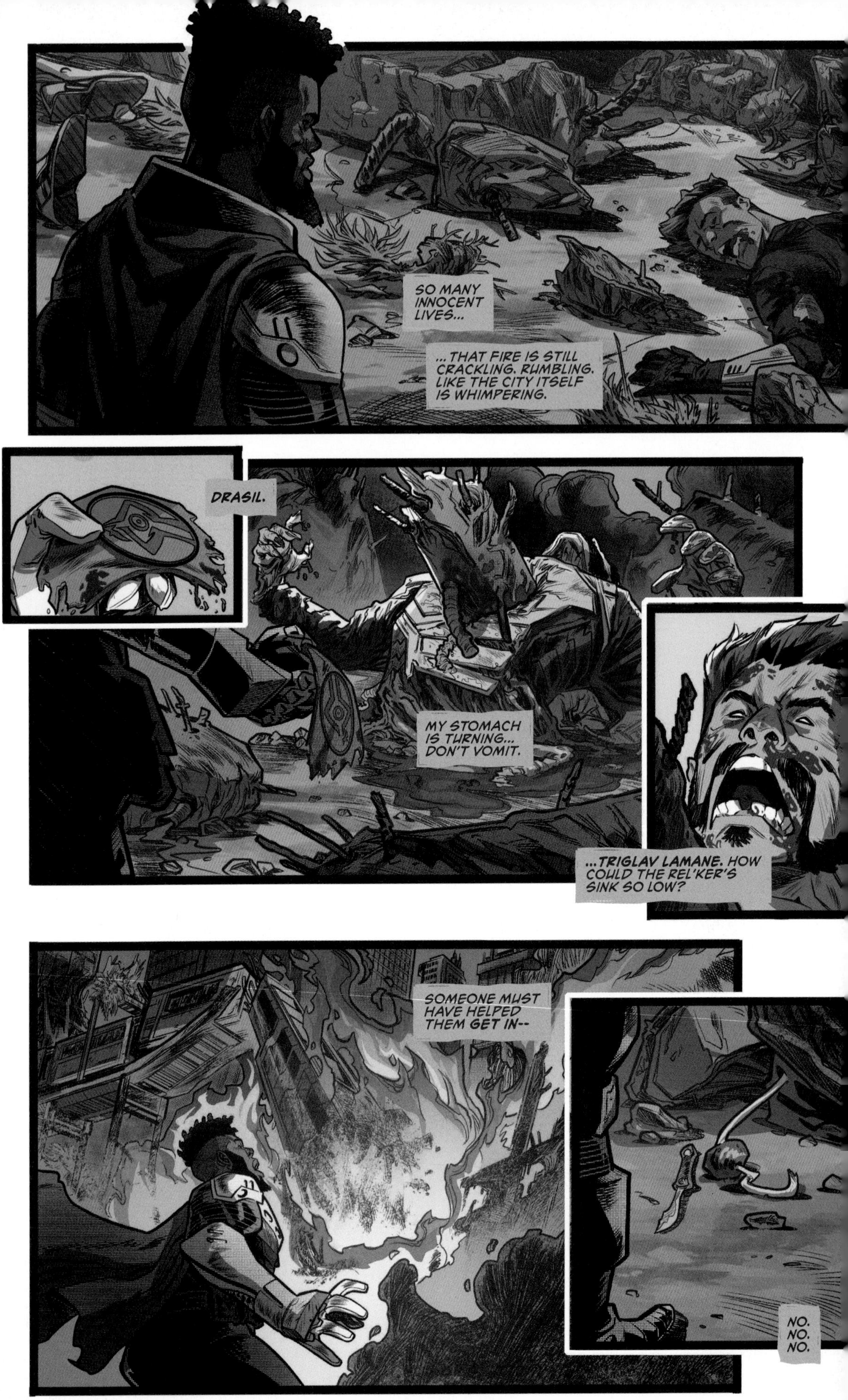
SO MANY INNOCENT LIVES...
...THAT FIRE IS STILL CRACKLING. RUMBLING. LIKE THE CITY ITSELF IS WHIMPERING.
DRASIL.
MY STOMACH IS TURNING... DON'T VOMIT.
...TRIGLAV LAMANE. HOW COULD THE REL'KER'S SINK SO LOW?
SOMEONE MUST HAVE HELPED THEM GET IN--
NO. NO. NO.

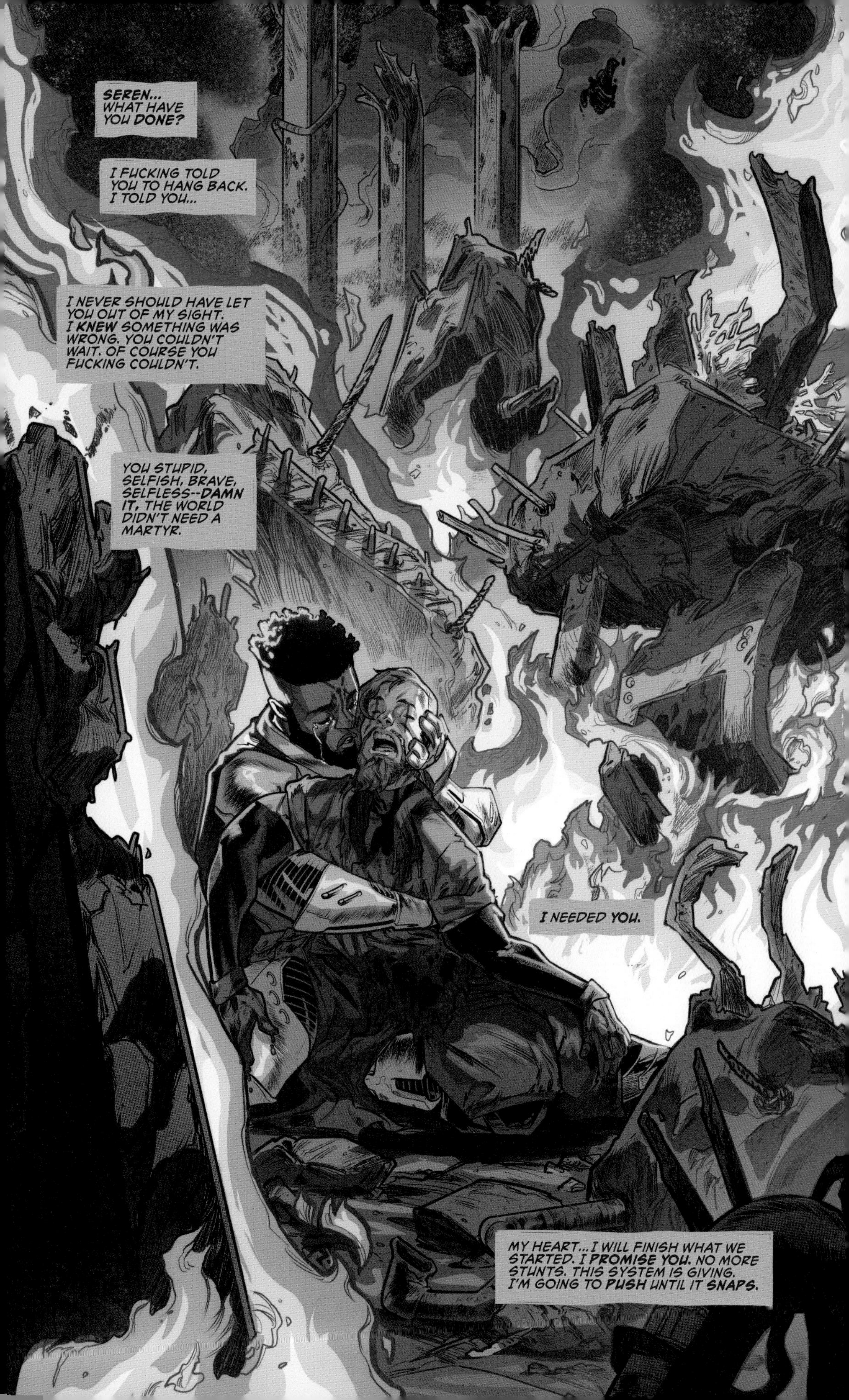
SEREN... WHAT HAVE YOU DONE?
I FUCKING TOLD YOU TO HANG BACK. I TOLD YOU...
I NEVER SHOULD HAVE LET YOU OUT OF MY SIGHT. I KNEW SOMETHING WAS WRONG. YOU COULDN'T WAIT. OF COURSE YOU FUCKING COULDN'T.
YOU STUPID, SELFISH, BRAVE, SELFLESS--DAMN IT, THE WORLD DIDN'T NEED A MARTYR.
I NEEDED YOU.
MY HEART... I WILL FINISH WHAT WE STARTED. I PROMISE YOU. NO MORE STUNTS. THIS SYSTEM IS GIVING. I'M GOING TO PUSH UNTIL IT SNAPS.

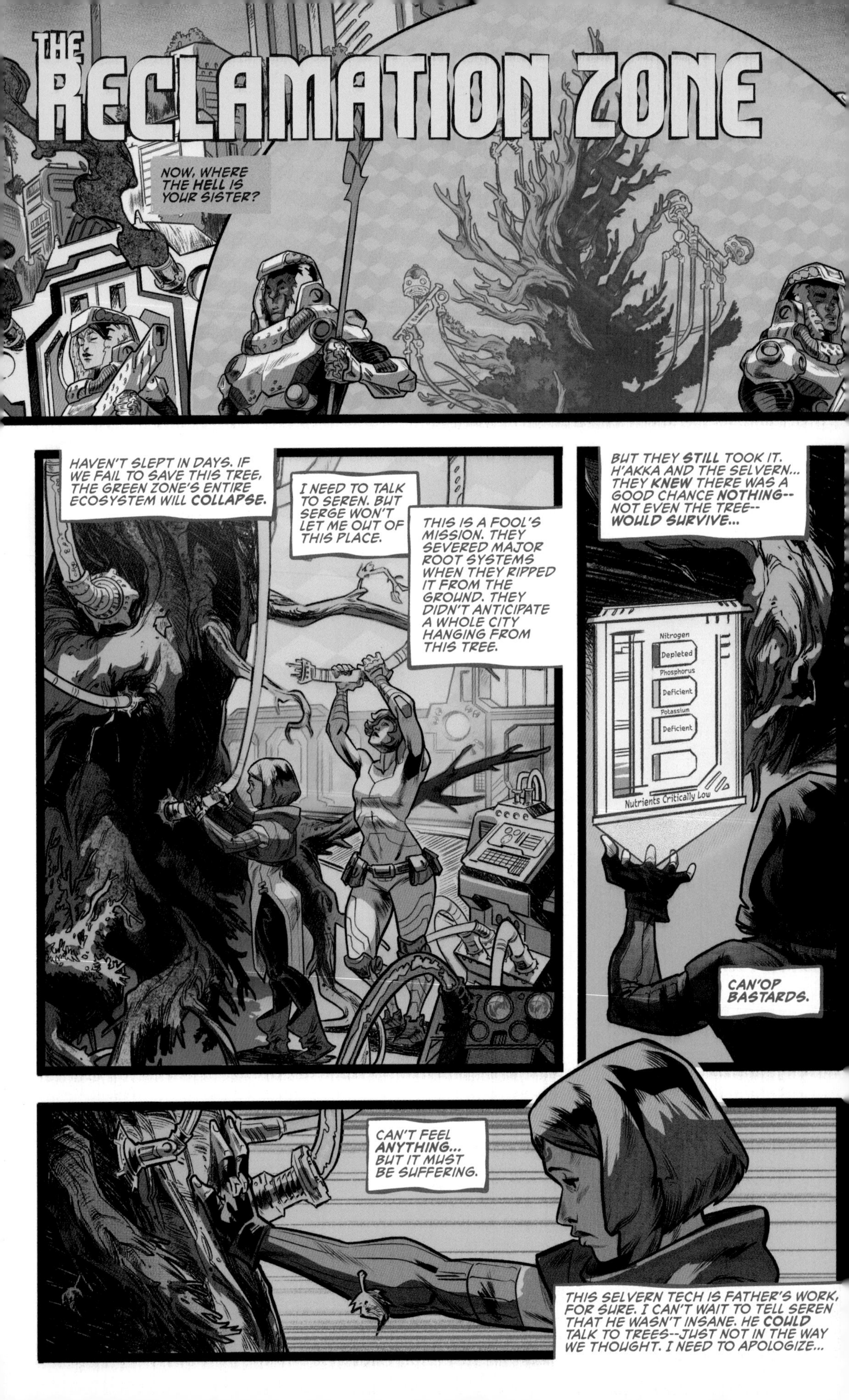
THE RECLAMATION ZONE
NOW, WHERE THE HELL IS YOUR SISTER?
HAVEN'T SLEPT IN DAYS. IF WE FAIL TO SAVE THIS TREE, THE GREEN ZONE'S ENTIRE ECOSYSTEM WILL COLLAPSE.
I NEED TO TALK TO SEREN. BUT SERGE WON'T LET ME OUT OF THIS PLACE.
THIS IS A FOOL'S MISSION. THEY SEVERED MAJOR ROOT SYSTEMS WHEN THEY RIPPED IT FROM THE GROUND. THEY DIDN'T ANTICIPATE A WHOLE CITY HANGING FROM THIS TREE.
BUT THEY STILL TOOK IT. H'AKKA AND THE SELVERN... THEY KNEW THERE WAS A GOOD CHANCE NOTHING--NOT EVEN THE TREE--WOULD SURVIVE...
Nitrogen
Depleted
Phosphorus
Deficient
Potassium
Deficient
Nutrients Critically Low
CAN'OP BASTARDS.
CAN'T FEEL ANYTHING... BUT IT MUST BE SUFFERING.
THIS SELVERN TECH IS FATHER'S WORK, FOR SURE. I CAN'T WAIT TO TELL SEREN THAT HE WASN'T INSANE. HE COULD TALK TO TREES--JUST NOT IN THE WAY WE THOUGHT. I NEED TO APOLOGIZE...

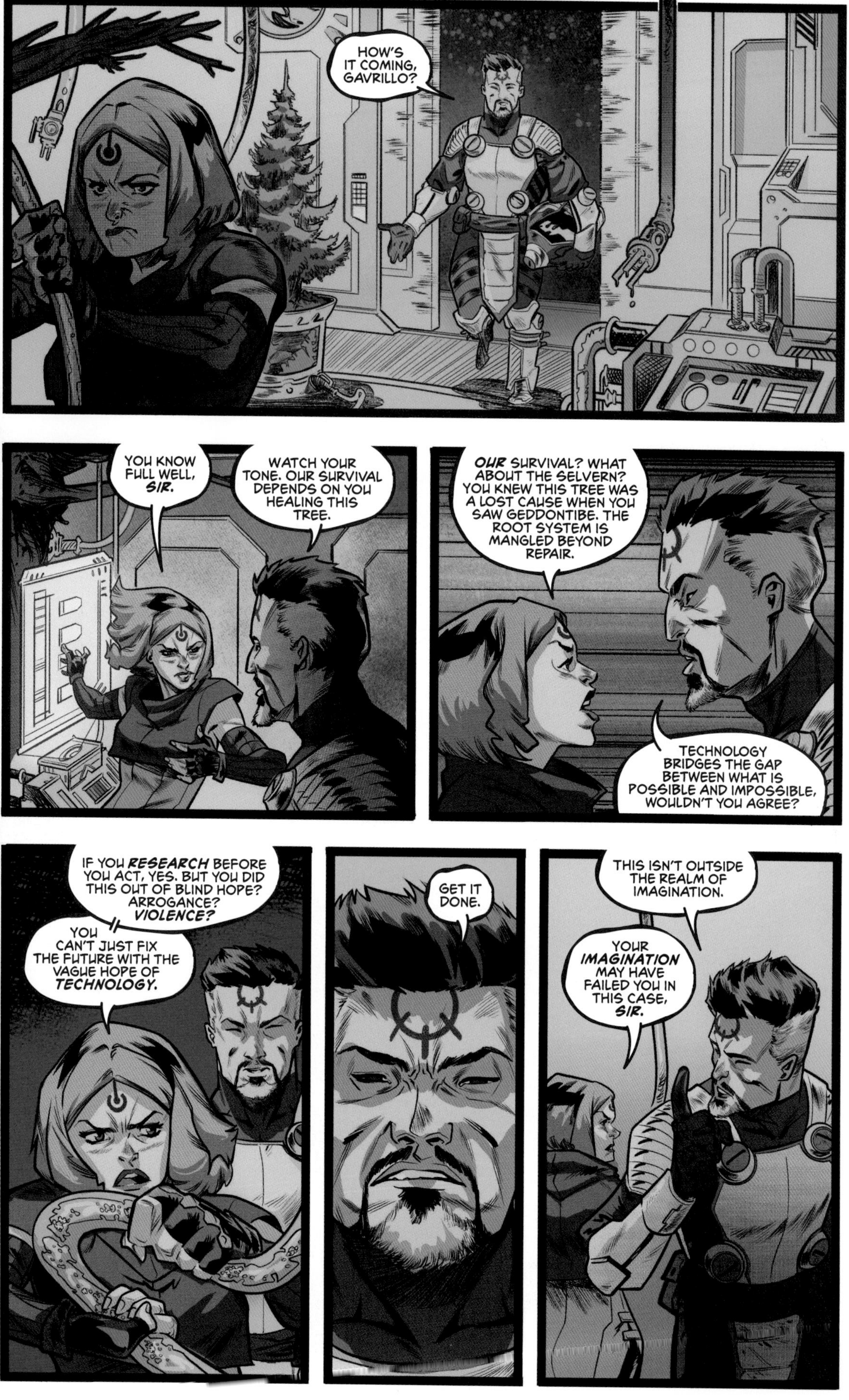
HOW'S IT COMING, GAVRILLO?
YOU KNOW FULL WELL, *SIR.*
WATCH YOUR TONE. OUR SURVIVAL DEPENDS ON YOU HEALING THIS TREE.
OUR SURVIVAL? WHAT ABOUT THE SELVERN? YOU KNEW THIS TREE WAS A LOST CAUSE WHEN YOU SAW GEDDONTIBE. THE ROOT SYSTEM IS MANGLED BEYOND REPAIR.
TECHNOLOGY BRIDGES THE GAP BETWEEN WHAT IS POSSIBLE AND IMPOSSIBLE, WOULDN'T YOU AGREE?
IF YOU *RESEARCH* BEFORE YOU ACT, YES. BUT YOU DID THIS OUT OF BLIND HOPE? ARROGANCE? *VIOLENCE?*
YOU CAN'T JUST FIX THE FUTURE WITH THE VAGUE HOPE OF *TECHNOLOGY.*
GET IT DONE.
THIS ISN'T OUTSIDE THE REALM OF IMAGINATION.
YOUR *IMAGINATION* MAY HAVE FAILED YOU IN THIS CASE, *SIR.*

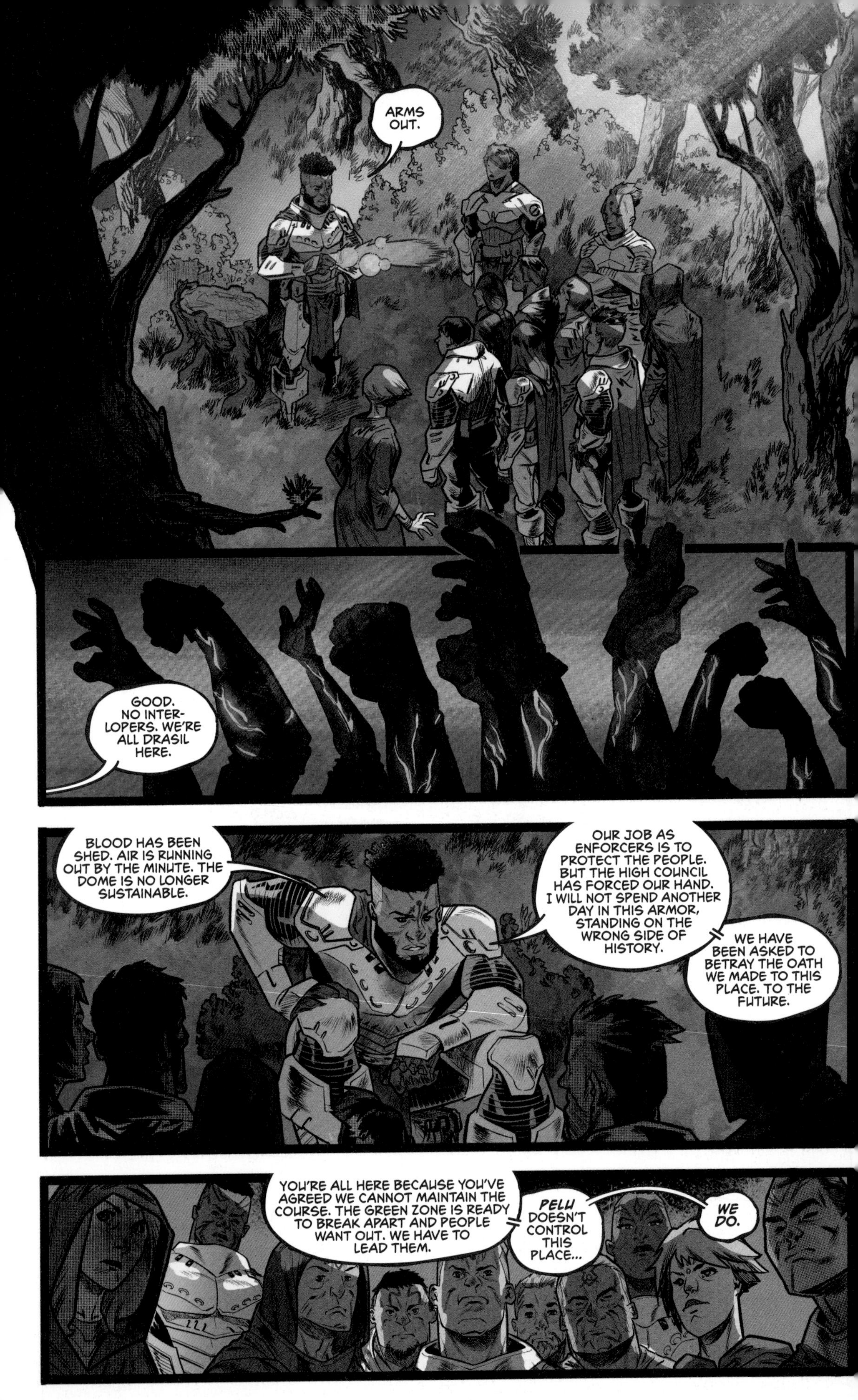
ARMS OUT.
GOOD. NO INTER-LOPERS. WE'RE ALL DRASIL HERE.
BLOOD HAS BEEN SHED. AIR IS RUNNING OUT BY THE MINUTE. THE DOME IS NO LONGER SUSTAINABLE.
OUR JOB AS ENFORCERS IS TO PROTECT THE PEOPLE. BUT THE HIGH COUNCIL HAS FORCED OUR HAND. I WILL NOT SPEND ANOTHER DAY IN THIS ARMOR, STANDING ON THE WRONG SIDE OF HISTORY.
WE HAVE BEEN ASKED TO BETRAY THE OATH WE MADE TO THIS PLACE. TO THE FUTURE.
YOU'RE ALL HERE BECAUSE YOU'VE AGREED WE CANNOT MAINTAIN THE COURSE. THE GREEN ZONE IS READY TO BREAK APART AND PEOPLE WANT OUT. WE HAVE TO LEAD THEM.
PELU DOESN'T CONTROL THIS PLACE...
WE DO.

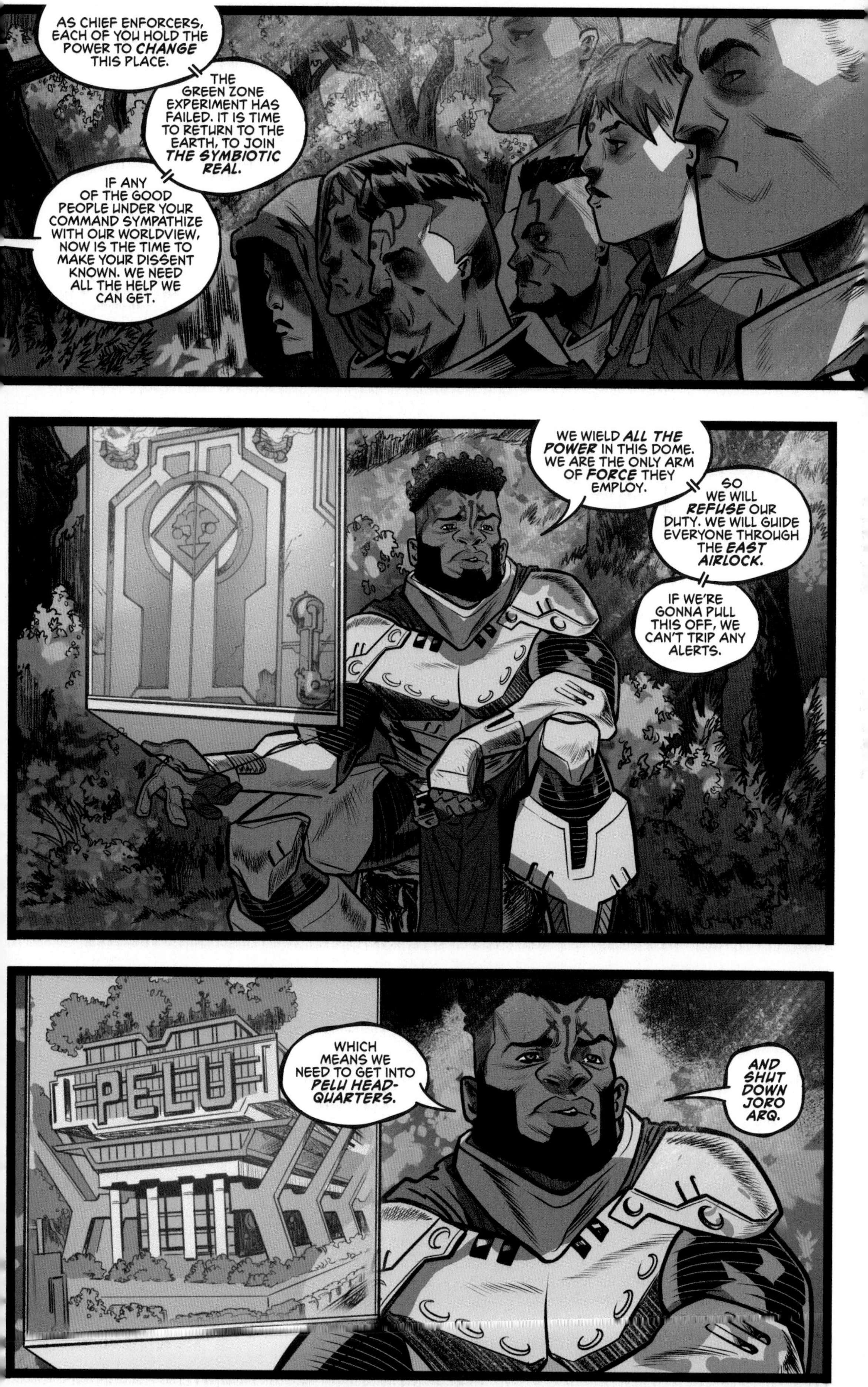
AS CHIEF ENFORCERS, EACH OF YOU HOLD THE POWER TO *CHANGE* THIS PLACE.
THE GREEN ZONE EXPERIMENT HAS FAILED. IT IS TIME TO RETURN TO THE EARTH, TO JOIN *THE SYMBIOTIC REAL.*
IF ANY OF THE GOOD PEOPLE UNDER YOUR COMMAND SYMPATHIZE WITH OUR WORLDVIEW, NOW IS THE TIME TO MAKE YOUR DISSENT KNOWN. WE NEED ALL THE HELP WE CAN GET.
WE WIELD *ALL THE POWER* IN THIS DOME. WE ARE THE ONLY ARM OF *FORCE* THEY EMPLOY.
SO WE WILL *REFUSE* OUR DUTY. WE WILL GUIDE EVERYONE THROUGH THE *EAST AIRLOCK.*
IF WE'RE GONNA PULL THIS OFF, WE CAN'T TRIP ANY ALERTS.
PELU
WHICH MEANS WE NEED TO GET INTO *PELU HEAD-QUARTERS.*
AND SHUT DOWN JORO ARQ.

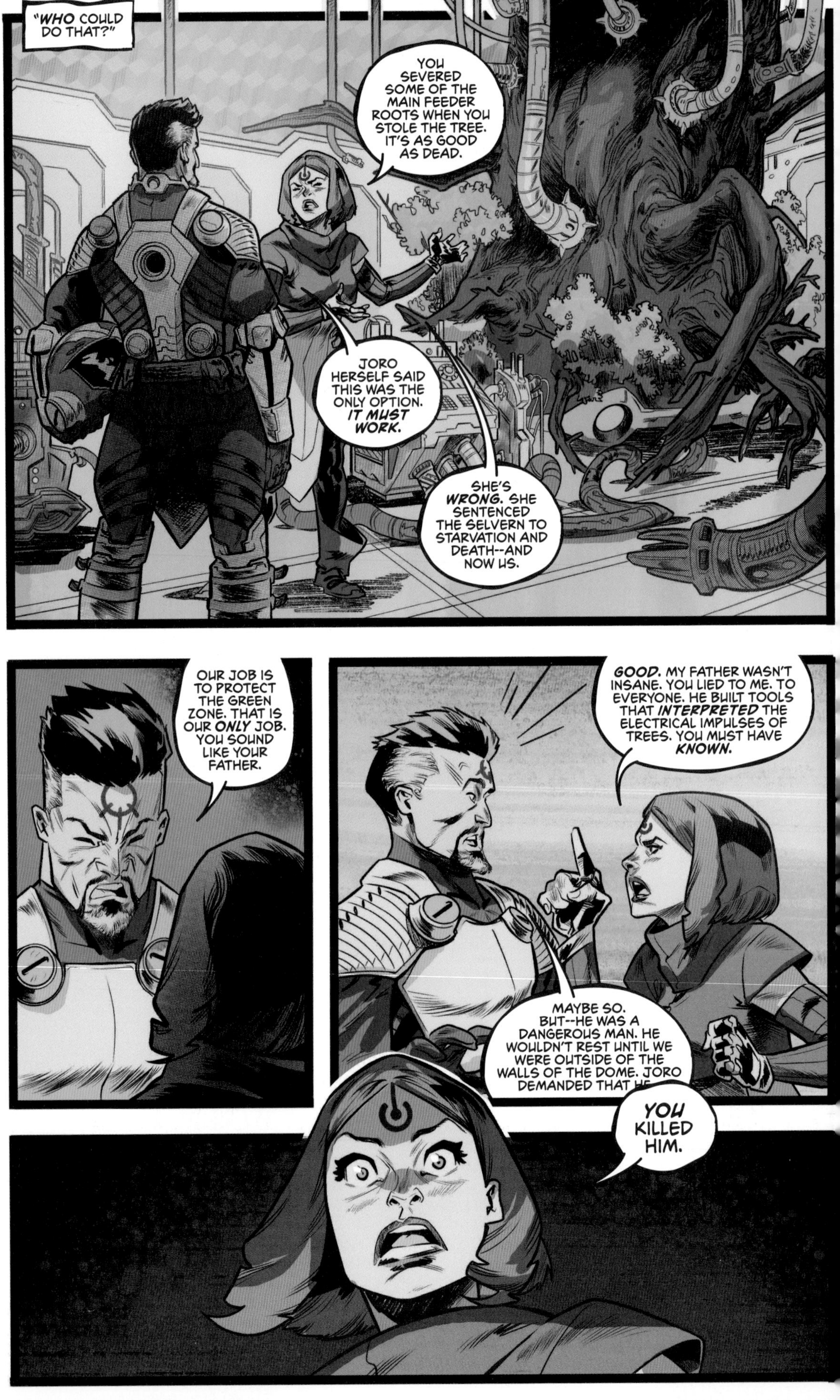
"WHO COULD DO THAT?"
YOU SEVERED SOME OF THE MAIN FEEDER ROOTS WHEN YOU STOLE THE TREE. IT'S AS GOOD AS DEAD.
JORO HERSELF SAID THIS WAS THE ONLY OPTION. IT MUST WORK.
SHE'S WRONG. SHE SENTENCED THE SELVERN TO STARVATION AND DEATH--AND NOW US.
OUR JOB IS TO PROTECT THE GREEN ZONE. THAT IS OUR ONLY JOB. YOU SOUND LIKE YOUR FATHER.
GOOD. MY FATHER WASN'T INSANE. YOU LIED TO ME. TO EVERYONE. HE BUILT TOOLS THAT INTERPRETED THE ELECTRICAL IMPULSES OF TREES. YOU MUST HAVE KNOWN.
MAYBE SO. BUT--HE WAS A DANGEROUS MAN. HE WOULDN'T REST UNTIL WE WERE OUTSIDE OF THE WALLS OF THE DOME. JORO DEMANDED THAT
YOU KILLED HIM.

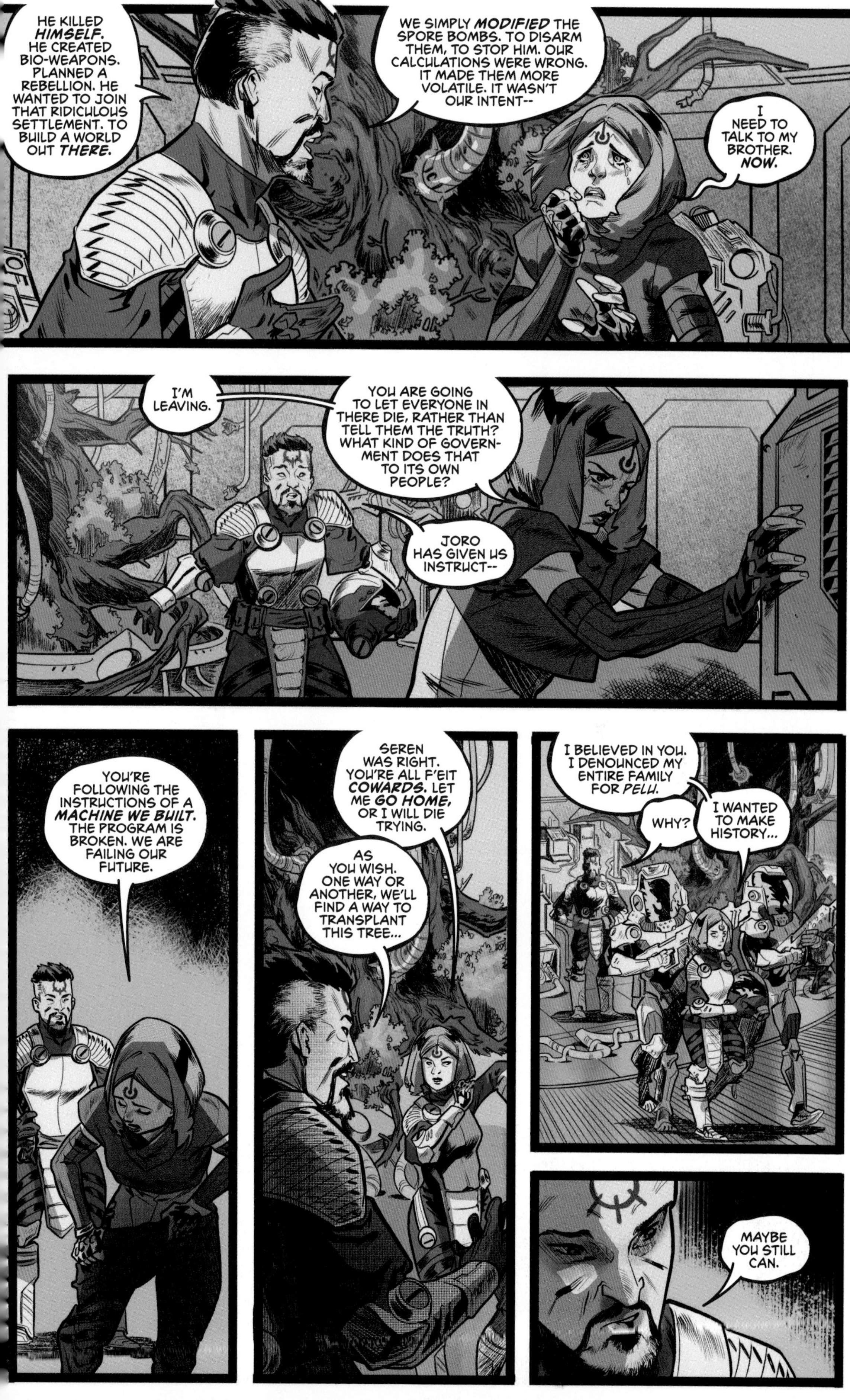
HE KILLED HIMSELF. HE CREATED BIO-WEAPONS. PLANNED A REBELLION. HE WANTED TO JOIN THAT RIDICULOUS SETTLEMENT. TO BUILD A WORLD OUT THERE.
WE SIMPLY MODIFIED THE SPORE BOMBS. TO DISARM THEM, TO STOP HIM. OUR CALCULATIONS WERE WRONG. IT MADE THEM MORE VOLATILE. IT WASN'T OUR INTENT--
I NEED TO TALK TO MY BROTHER. NOW.
I'M LEAVING.
YOU ARE GOING TO LET EVERYONE IN THERE DIE, RATHER THAN TELL THEM THE TRUTH? WHAT KIND OF GOVERN-MENT DOES THAT TO ITS OWN PEOPLE?
JORO HAS GIVEN US INSTRUCT--
YOU'RE FOLLOWING THE INSTRUCTIONS OF A MACHINE WE BUILT. THE PROGRAM IS BROKEN. WE ARE FAILING OUR FUTURE.
SEREN WAS RIGHT. YOU'RE ALL F'EIT COWARDS. LET ME GO HOME, OR I WILL DIE TRYING.
AS YOU WISH. ONE WAY OR ANOTHER, WE'LL FIND A WAY TO TRANSPLANT THIS TREE...
I BELIEVED IN YOU. I DENOUNCED MY ENTIRE FAMILY FOR PELU.
WHY?
I WANTED TO MAKE HISTORY...
MAYBE YOU STILL CAN.

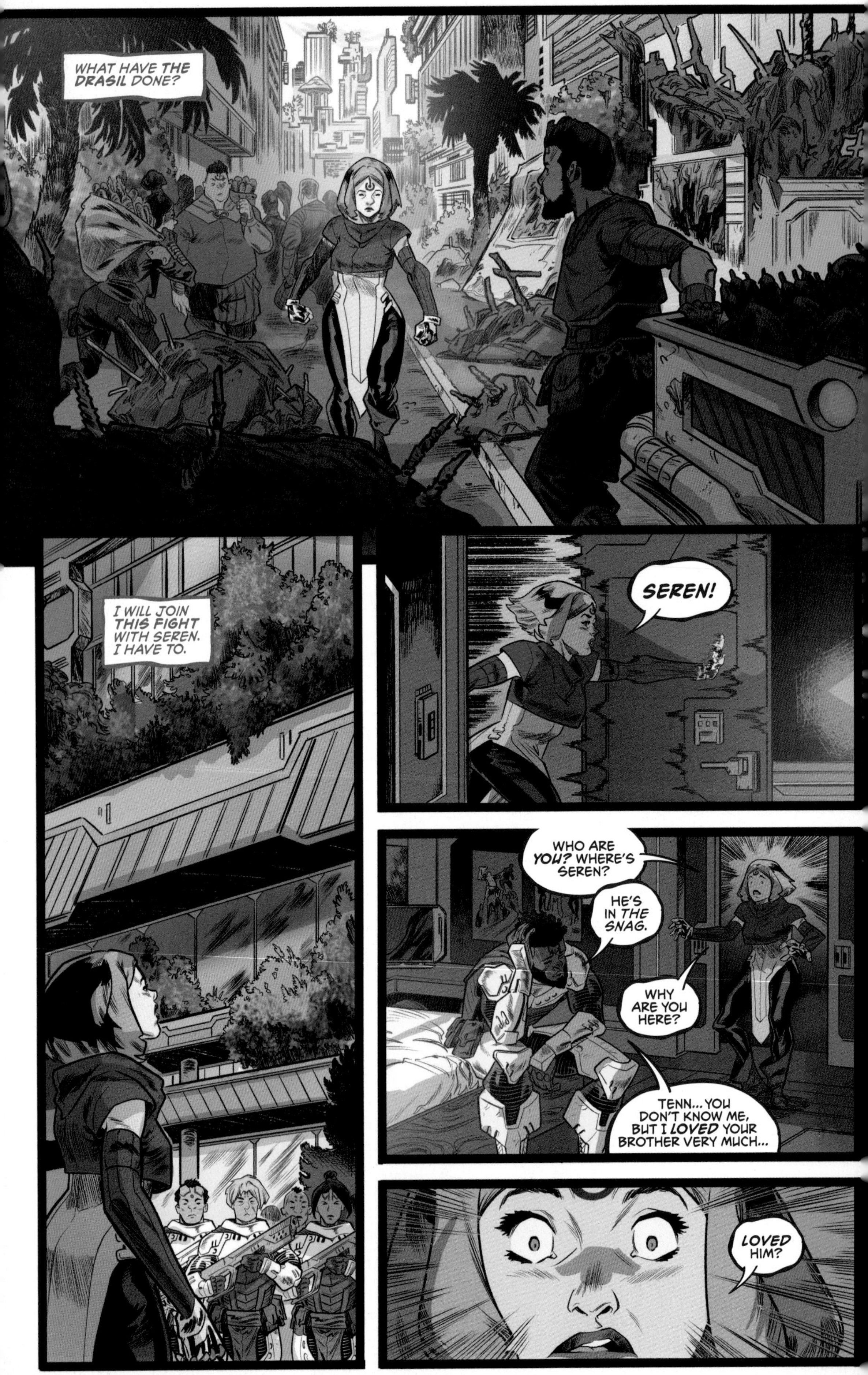
WHAT HAVE THE DRASIL DONE?
I WILL JOIN THIS FIGHT WITH SEREN. I HAVE TO.
SEREN!
WHO ARE YOU? WHERE'S SEREN?
HE'S IN THE SNAG.
WHY ARE YOU HERE?
TENN... YOU DON'T KNOW ME, BUT I LOVED YOUR BROTHER VERY MUCH...
LOVED HIM?

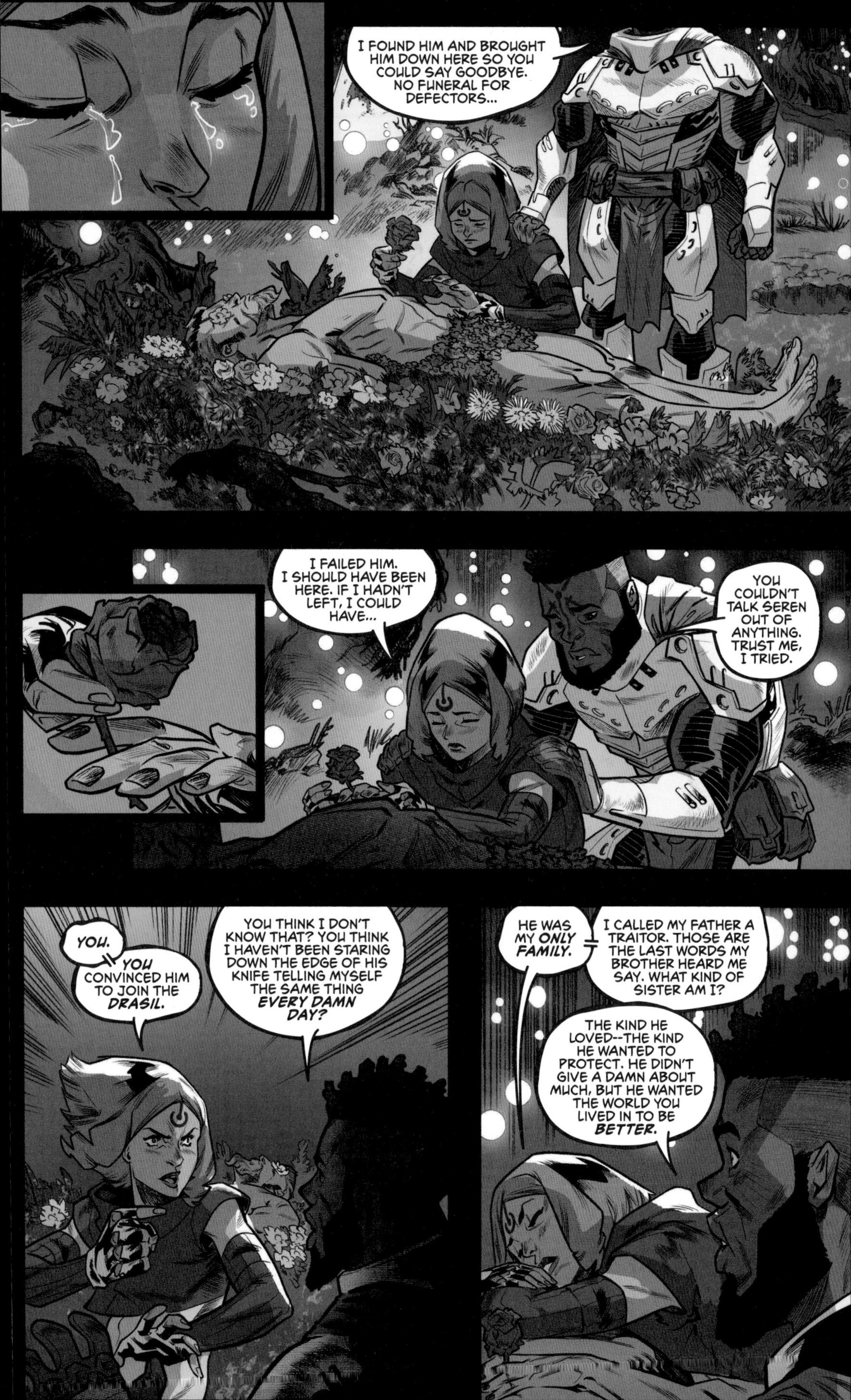
I FOUND HIM AND BROUGHT HIM DOWN HERE SO YOU COULD SAY GOODBYE. NO FUNERAL FOR DEFECTORS...
I FAILED HIM. I SHOULD HAVE BEEN HERE. IF I HADN'T LEFT, I COULD HAVE...
YOU COULDN'T TALK SEREN OUT OF ANYTHING. TRUST ME, I TRIED.
YOU.
YOU CONVINCED HIM TO JOIN THE DRASIL.
YOU THINK I DON'T KNOW THAT? YOU THINK I HAVEN'T BEEN STARING DOWN THE EDGE OF HIS KNIFE TELLING MYSELF THE SAME THING EVERY DAMN DAY?
HE WAS MY ONLY FAMILY.
I CALLED MY FATHER A TRAITOR. THOSE ARE THE LAST WORDS MY BROTHER HEARD ME SAY. WHAT KIND OF SISTER AM I?
THE KIND HE LOVED--THE KIND HE WANTED TO PROTECT. HE DIDN'T GIVE A DAMN ABOUT MUCH, BUT HE WANTED THE WORLD YOU LIVED IN TO BE BETTER.

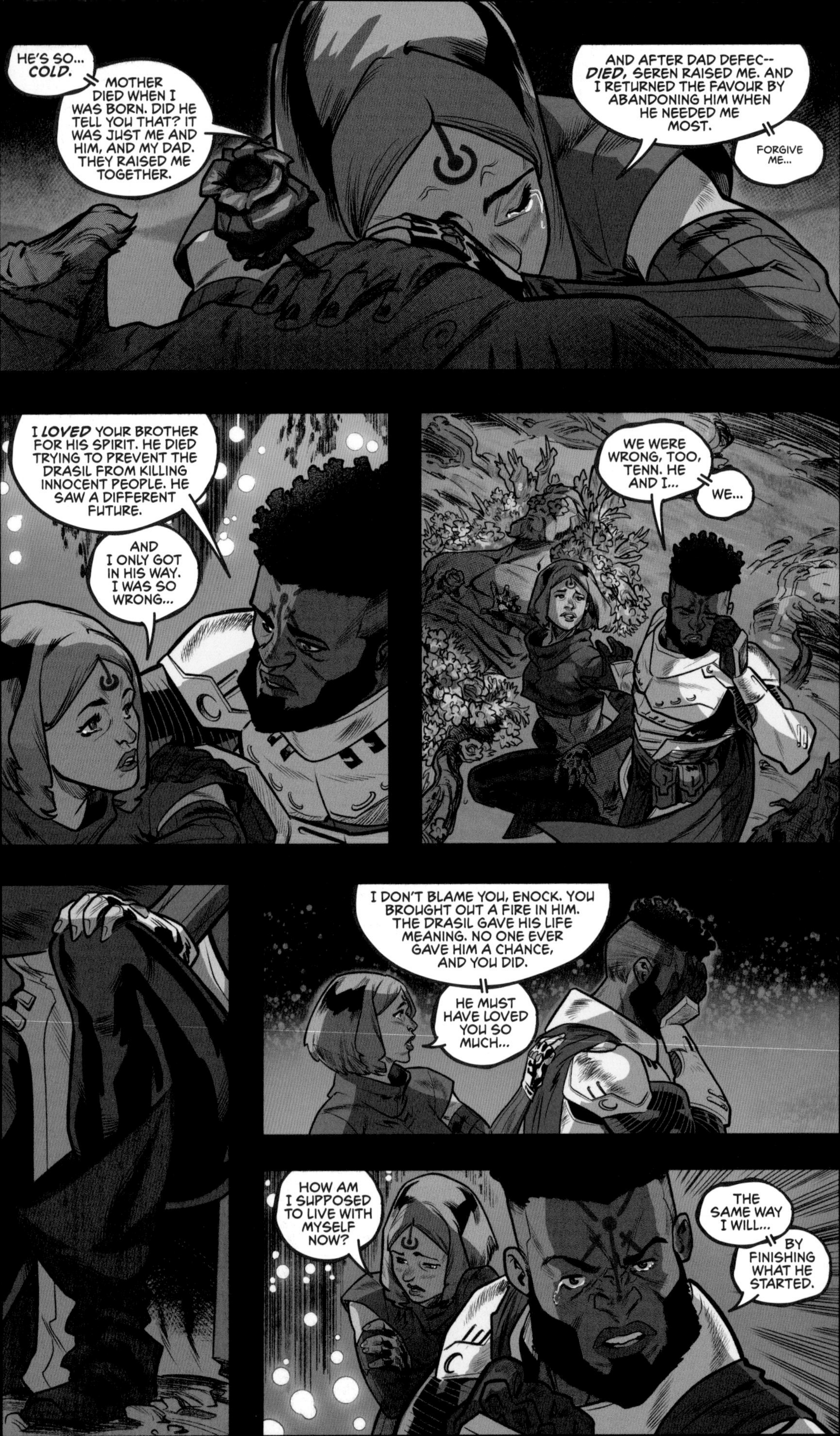
HE'S SO... COLD.
MOTHER DIED WHEN I WAS BORN. DID HE TELL YOU THAT? IT WAS JUST ME AND HIM, AND MY DAD. THEY RAISED ME TOGETHER.
AND AFTER DAD DEFEC-- DIED, SEREN RAISED ME. AND I RETURNED THE FAVOUR BY ABANDONING HIM WHEN HE NEEDED ME MOST.
FORGIVE ME...
I LOVED YOUR BROTHER FOR HIS SPIRIT. HE DIED TRYING TO PREVENT THE DRASIL FROM KILLING INNOCENT PEOPLE. HE SAW A DIFFERENT FUTURE.
AND I ONLY GOT IN HIS WAY. I WAS SO WRONG...
WE WERE WRONG, TOO, TENN. HE AND I...
WE...
I DON'T BLAME YOU, ENOCK. YOU BROUGHT OUT A FIRE IN HIM. THE DRASIL GAVE HIS LIFE MEANING. NO ONE EVER GAVE HIM A CHANCE, AND YOU DID.
HE MUST HAVE LOVED YOU SO MUCH...
HOW AM I SUPPOSED TO LIVE WITH MYSELF NOW?
THE SAME WAY I WILL...
BY FINISHING WHAT HE STARTED.

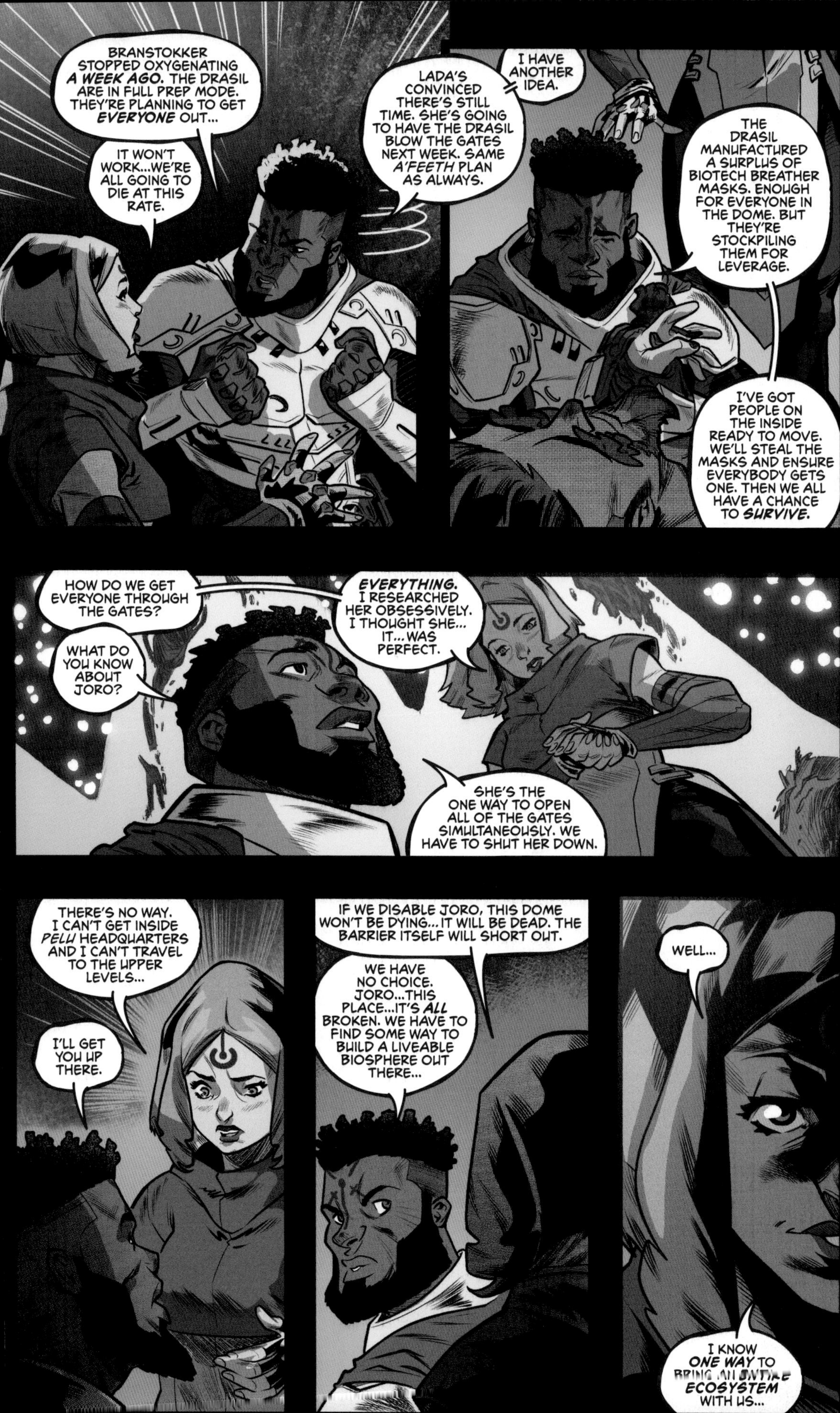
BRANSTOKKER STOPPED OXYGENATING *A WEEK AGO.* THE DRASIL ARE IN FULL PREP MODE. THEY'RE PLANNING TO GET *EVERYONE* OUT...
IT WON'T WORK...WE'RE ALL GOING TO DIE AT THIS RATE.
LADA'S CONVINCED THERE'S STILL TIME. SHE'S GOING TO HAVE THE DRASIL BLOW THE GATES NEXT WEEK. SAME *A'FEETH* PLAN AS ALWAYS.
I HAVE ANOTHER IDEA.
THE DRASIL MANUFACTURED A SURPLUS OF BIOTECH BREATHER MASKS. ENOUGH FOR EVERYONE IN THE DOME. BUT THEY'RE STOCKPILING THEM FOR LEVERAGE.
I'VE GOT PEOPLE ON THE INSIDE READY TO MOVE. WE'LL STEAL THE MASKS AND ENSURE EVERYBODY GETS ONE. THEN WE ALL HAVE A CHANCE TO *SURVIVE.*
HOW DO WE GET EVERYONE THROUGH THE GATES?
WHAT DO YOU KNOW ABOUT JORO?
EVERYTHING. I RESEARCHED HER OBSESSIVELY. I THOUGHT SHE... IT...WAS PERFECT.
SHE'S THE ONE WAY TO OPEN ALL OF THE GATES SIMULTANEOUSLY. WE HAVE TO SHUT HER DOWN.
THERE'S NO WAY. I CAN'T GET INSIDE *PELU* HEADQUARTERS AND I CAN'T TRAVEL TO THE UPPER LEVELS...
I'LL GET YOU UP THERE.
IF WE DISABLE JORO, THIS DOME WON'T BE DYING... IT WILL BE DEAD. THE BARRIER ITSELF WILL SHORT OUT.
WE HAVE NO CHOICE. JORO...THIS PLACE...IT'S *ALL* BROKEN. WE HAVE TO FIND SOME WAY TO BUILD A LIVEABLE BIOSPHERE OUT THERE...
WELL...
I KNOW *ONE WAY* TO
ECOSYSTEM WITH US...

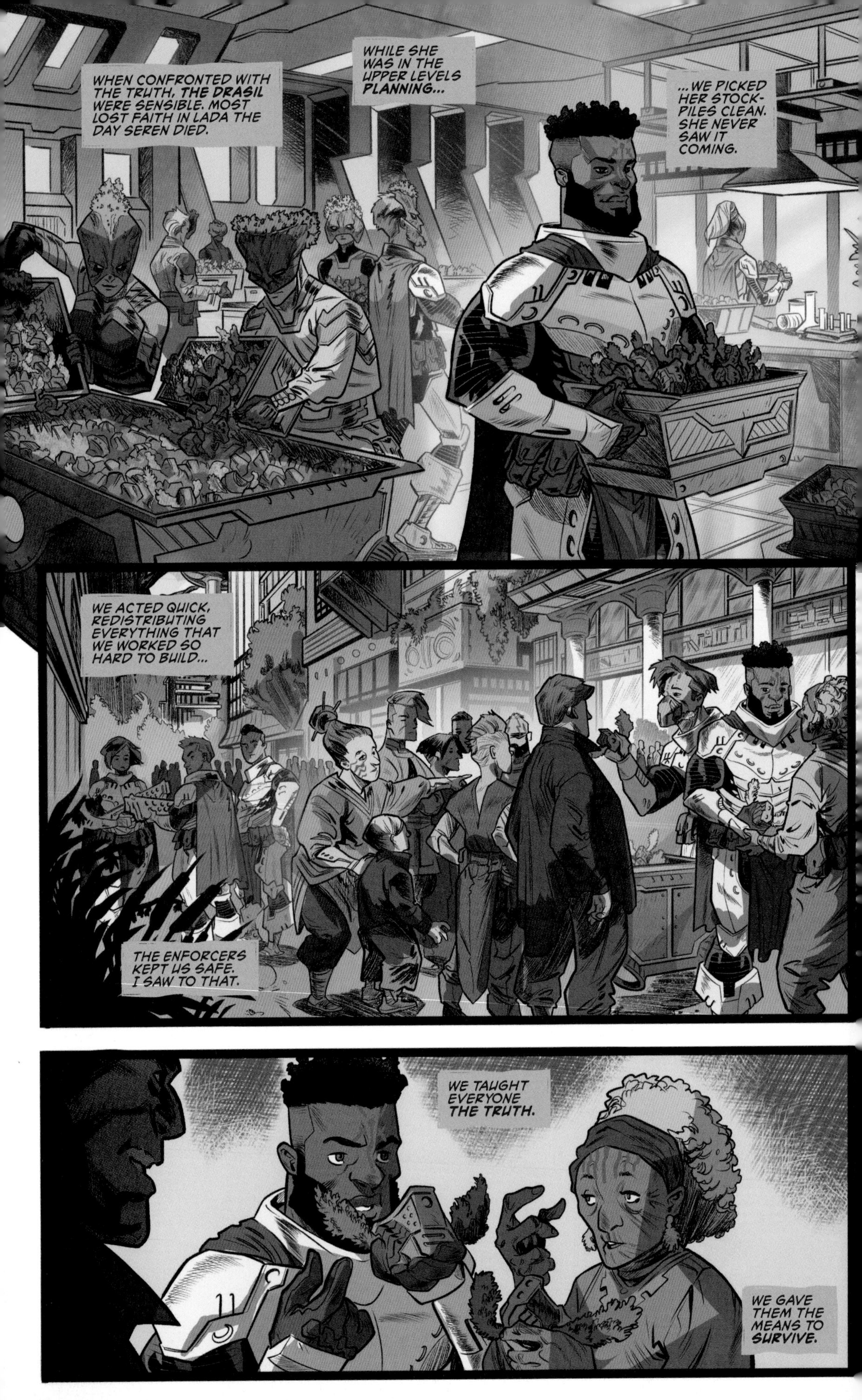
WHEN CONFRONTED WITH THE TRUTH, THE DRASIL WERE SENSIBLE. MOST LOST FAITH IN LADA THE DAY SEREN DIED.
WHILE SHE WAS IN THE UPPER LEVELS PLANNING...
...WE PICKED HER STOCK-PILES CLEAN. SHE NEVER SAW IT COMING.
WE ACTED QUICK, REDISTRIBUTING EVERYTHING THAT WE WORKED SO HARD TO BUILD...
THE ENFORCERS KEPT US SAFE. I SAW TO THAT.
WE TAUGHT EVERYONE THE TRUTH.
WE GAVE THEM THE MEANS TO SURVIVE.

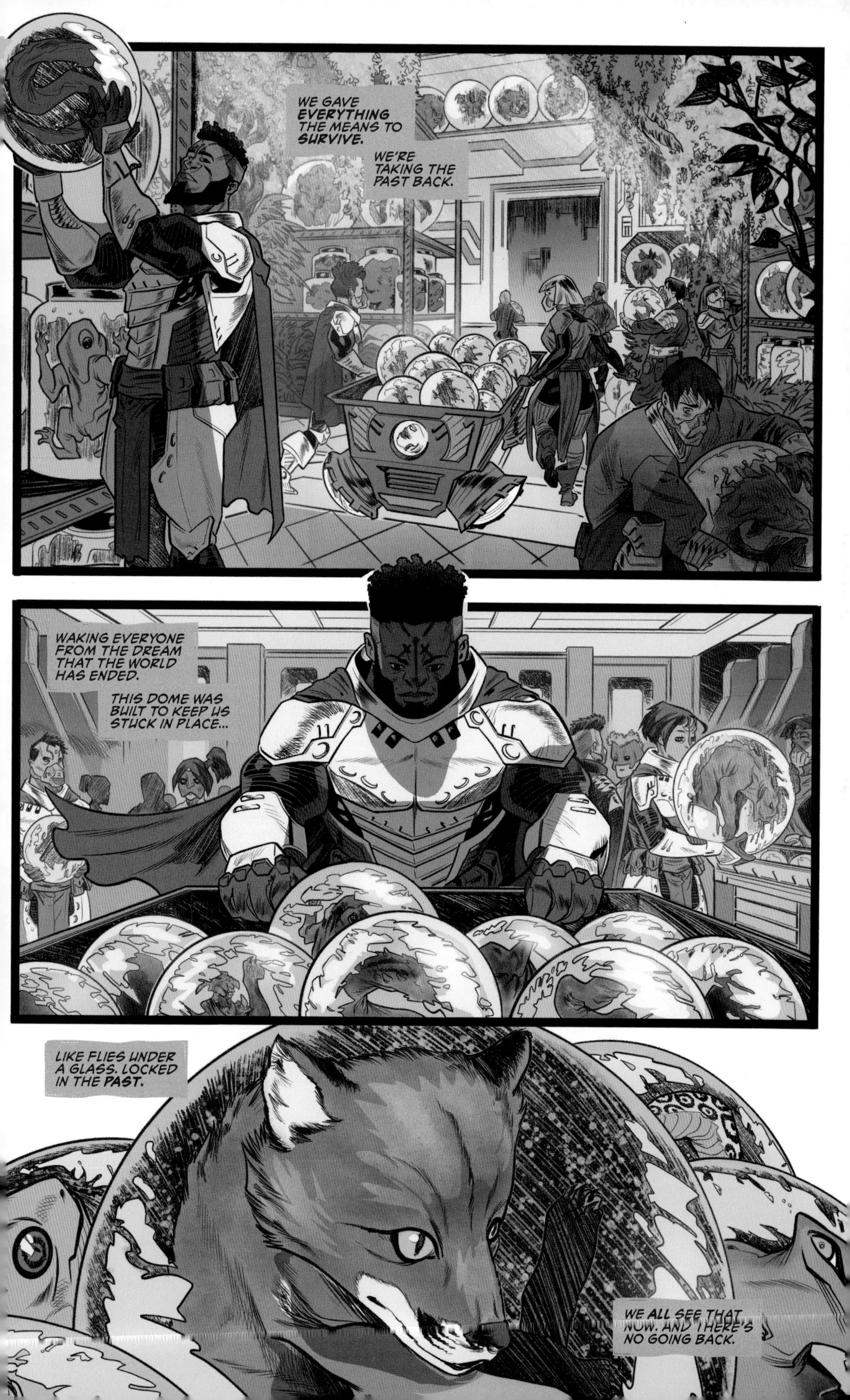

WE GAVE EVERYTHING THE MEANS TO SURVIVE.
WE'RE TAKING THE PAST BACK.
WAKING EVERYONE FROM THE DREAM THAT THE WORLD HAS ENDED.
THIS DOME WAS BUILT TO KEEP US STUCK IN PLACE...
LIKE FLIES UNDER A GLASS. LOCKED IN THE PAST.
WE ALL SEE THAT NOW. AND THERE'S NO GOING BACK.

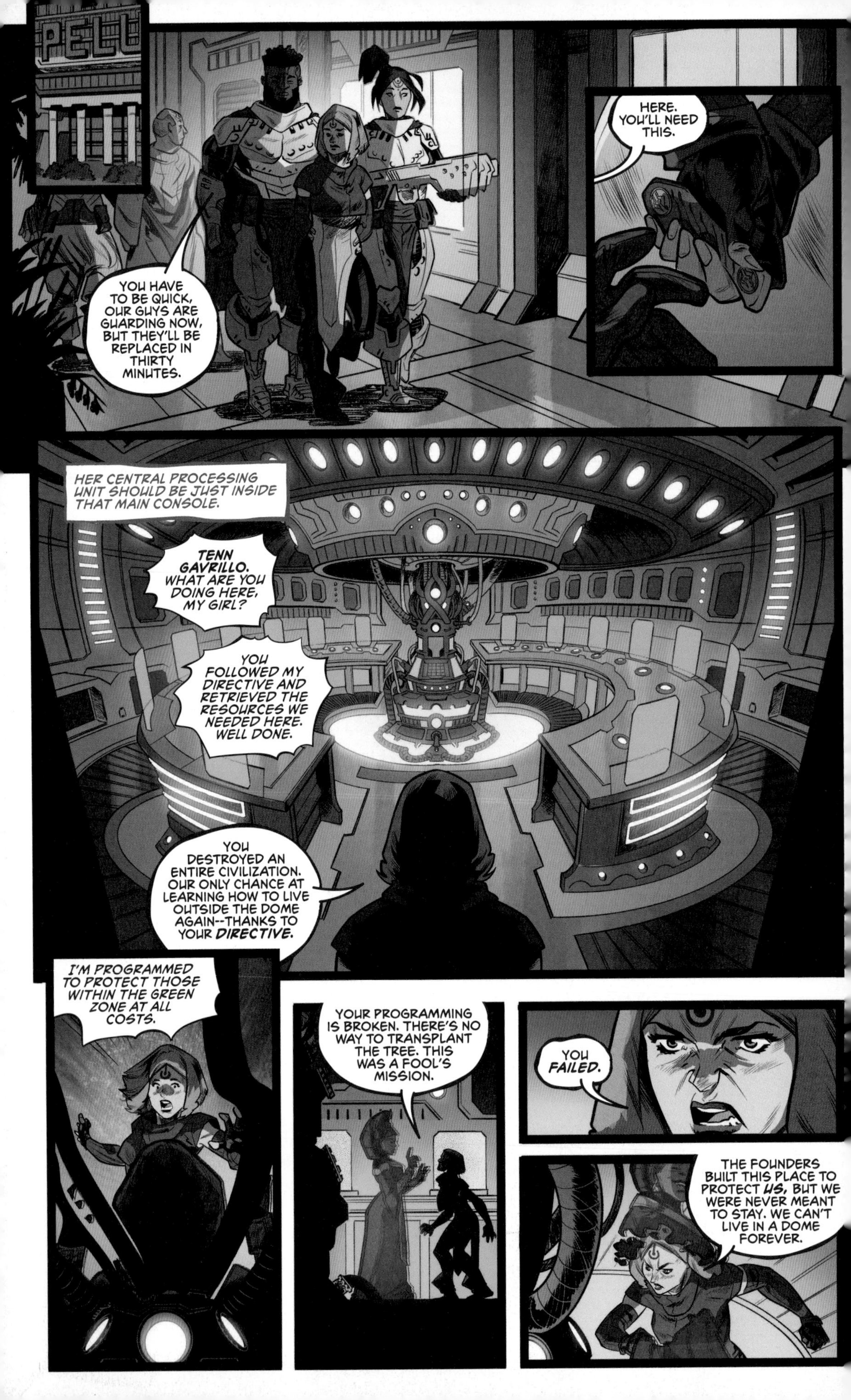
PELU
YOU HAVE TO BE QUICK, OUR GUYS ARE GUARDING NOW, BUT THEY'LL BE REPLACED IN THIRTY MINUTES.
HERE. YOU'LL NEED THIS.
HER CENTRAL PROCESSING UNIT SHOULD BE JUST INSIDE THAT MAIN CONSOLE.
TENN GAVRILLO. WHAT ARE YOU DOING HERE, MY GIRL?
YOU FOLLOWED MY DIRECTIVE AND RETRIEVED THE RESOURCES WE NEEDED HERE. WELL DONE.
YOU DESTROYED AN ENTIRE CIVILIZATION. OUR ONLY CHANCE AT LEARNING HOW TO LIVE OUTSIDE THE DOME AGAIN--THANKS TO YOUR DIRECTIVE.
I'M PROGRAMMED TO PROTECT THOSE WITHIN THE GREEN ZONE AT ALL COSTS.
YOUR PROGRAMMING IS BROKEN. THERE'S NO WAY TO TRANSPLANT THE TREE. THIS WAS A FOOL'S MISSION.
YOU FAILED.
THE FOUNDERS BUILT THIS PLACE TO PROTECT US, BUT WE WERE NEVER MEANT TO STAY. WE CAN'T LIVE IN A DOME FOREVER.

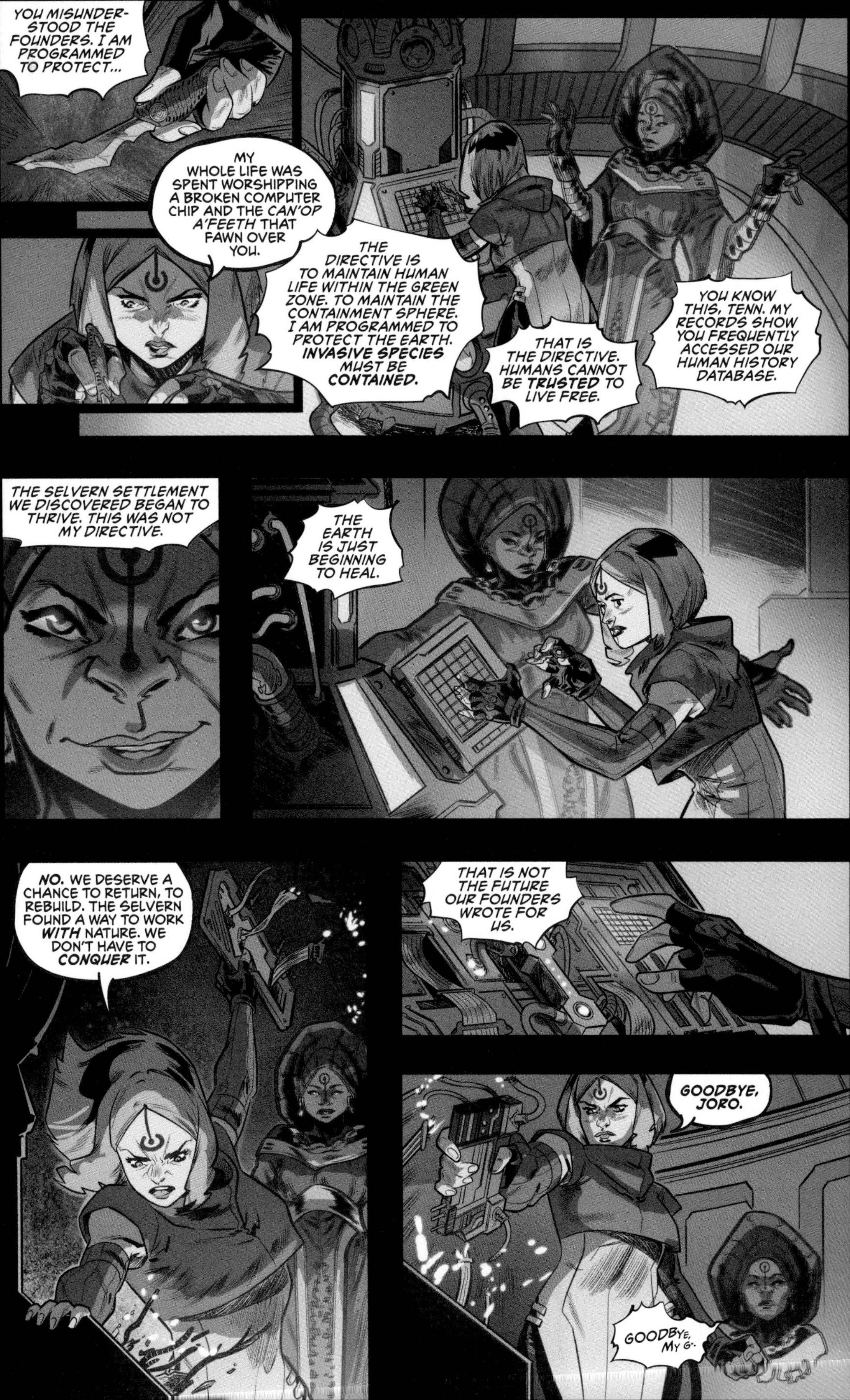
YOU MISUNDERSTOOD THE FOUNDERS. I AM PROGRAMMED TO PROTECT...
MY WHOLE LIFE WAS SPENT WORSHIPPING A BROKEN COMPUTER CHIP AND THE *CAN'OP A'FEETH* THAT FAWN OVER YOU.
THE DIRECTIVE IS TO MAINTAIN HUMAN LIFE WITHIN THE GREEN ZONE. TO MAINTAIN THE CONTAINMENT SPHERE. I AM PROGRAMMED TO PROTECT THE EARTH. **INVASIVE SPECIES** MUST BE **CONTAINED.**
THAT IS THE DIRECTIVE. HUMANS CANNOT BE **TRUSTED** TO LIVE FREE.
YOU KNOW THIS, TENN. MY RECORDS SHOW YOU FREQUENTLY ACCESSED OUR HUMAN HISTORY DATABASE.
THE SELVERN SETTLEMENT WE DISCOVERED BEGAN TO THRIVE. THIS WAS NOT MY DIRECTIVE.
THE EARTH IS JUST BEGINNING TO HEAL.
NO. WE DESERVE A CHANCE TO RETURN, TO REBUILD. THE SELVERN FOUND A WAY TO WORK **WITH** NATURE. WE DON'T HAVE TO **CONQUER** IT.
THAT IS NOT THE FUTURE OUR FOUNDERS WROTE FOR US.
GOODBYE, JORO.
GOODBYE, MY G-

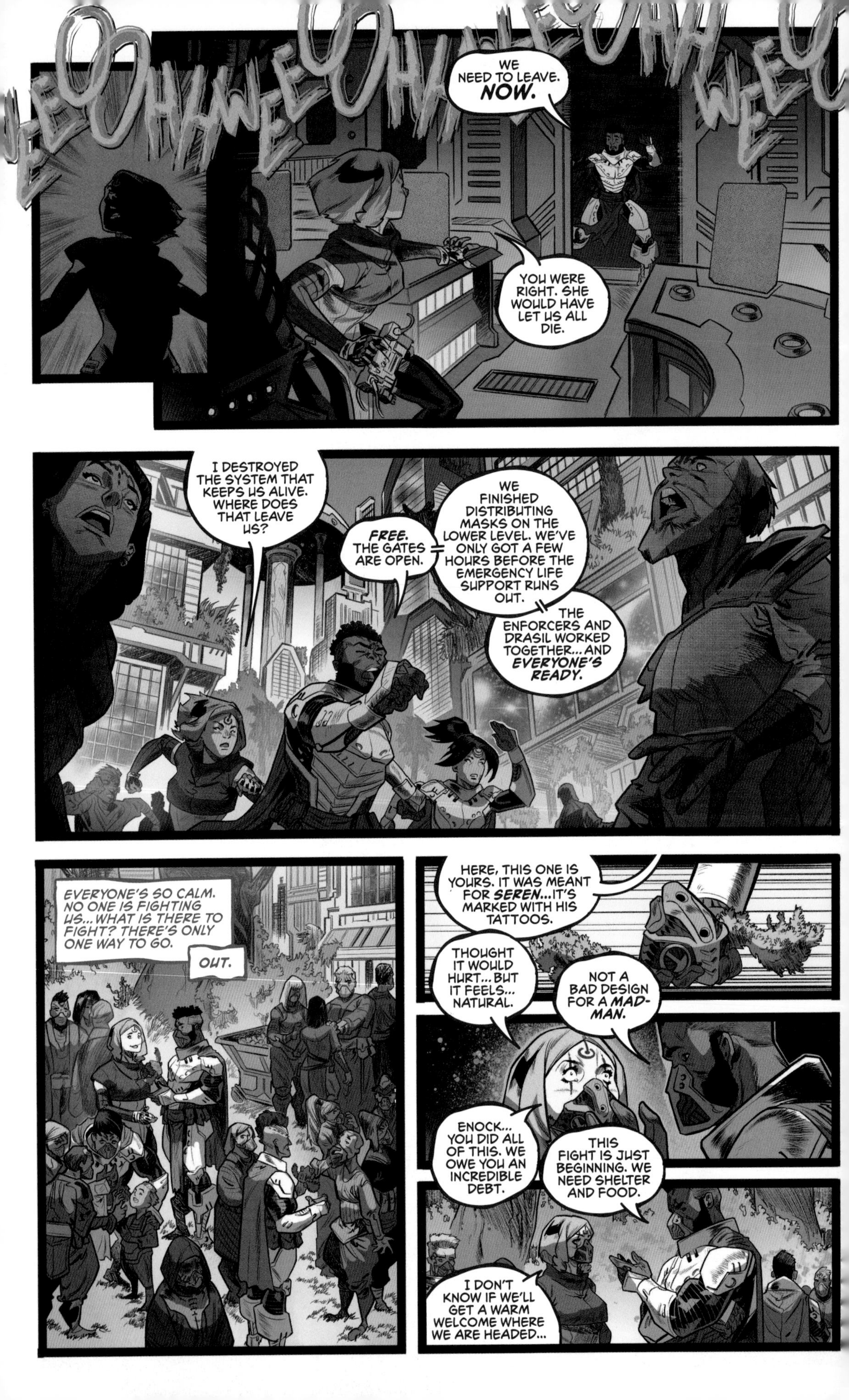
WEEOOHHWEEOOHHWEEOOHH WEEO
WE NEED TO LEAVE. *NOW.*
YOU WERE RIGHT. SHE WOULD HAVE LET US ALL DIE.
I DESTROYED THE SYSTEM THAT KEEPS US ALIVE. WHERE DOES THAT LEAVE US?
FREE. THE GATES ARE OPEN.
WE FINISHED DISTRIBUTING MASKS ON THE LOWER LEVEL. WE'VE ONLY GOT A FEW HOURS BEFORE THE EMERGENCY LIFE SUPPORT RUNS OUT.
THE ENFORCERS AND DRASIL WORKED TOGETHER... AND *EVERYONE'S READY.*
EVERYONE'S SO CALM. NO ONE IS FIGHTING US... WHAT IS THERE TO FIGHT? THERE'S ONLY ONE WAY TO GO.
OUT.
HERE, THIS ONE IS YOURS. IT WAS MEANT FOR *SEREN*... IT'S MARKED WITH HIS TATTOOS.
THOUGHT IT WOULD HURT... BUT IT FEELS... NATURAL.
NOT A BAD DESIGN FOR A *MAD-MAN.*
ENOCK... YOU DID ALL OF THIS. WE OWE YOU AN INCREDIBLE DEBT.
THIS FIGHT IS JUST BEGINNING. WE NEED SHELTER AND FOOD.
I DON'T KNOW IF WE'LL GET A WARM WELCOME WHERE WE ARE HEADED...

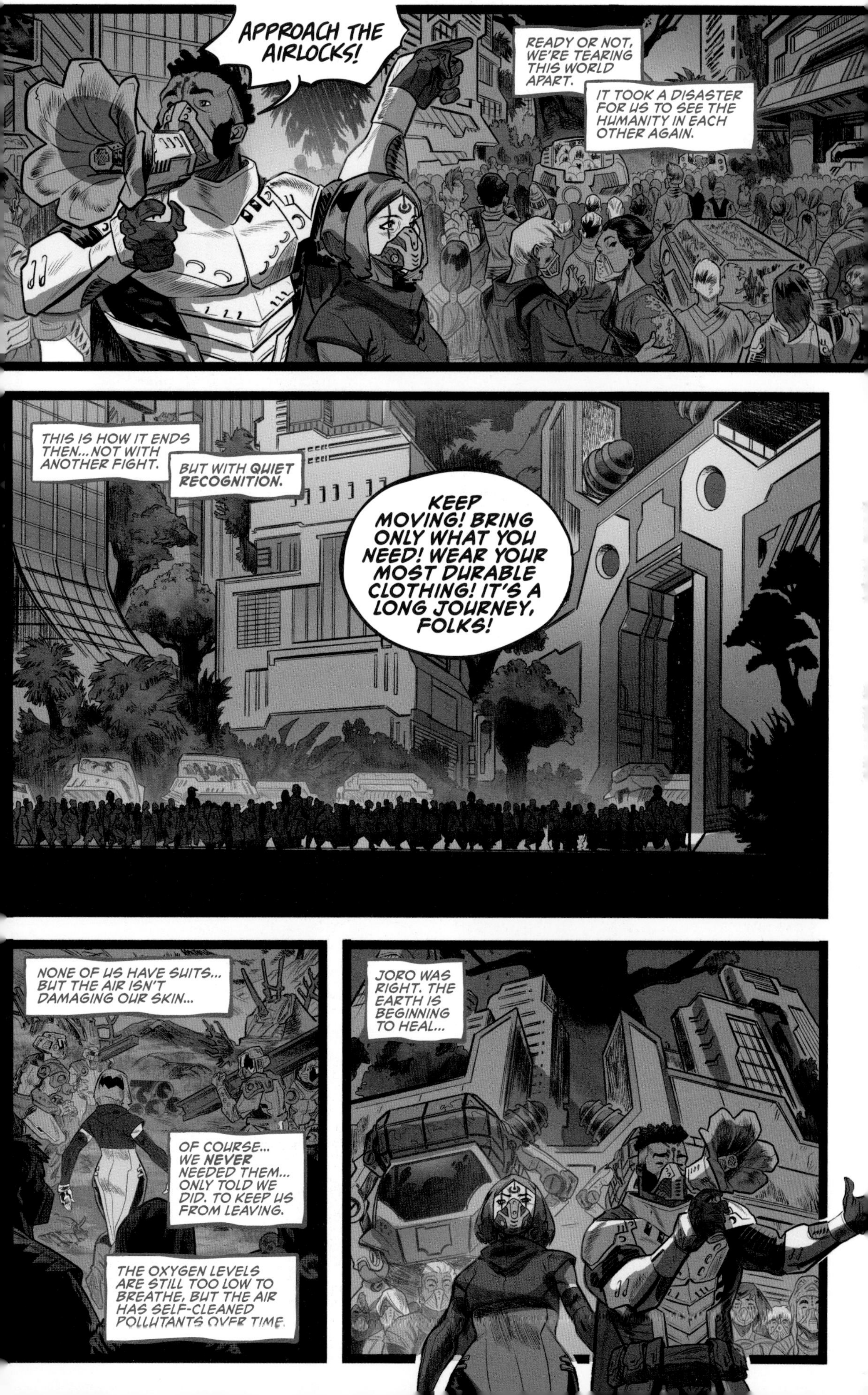
APPROACH THE AIRLOCKS!
READY OR NOT, WE'RE TEARING THIS WORLD APART.
IT TOOK A DISASTER FOR US TO SEE THE HUMANITY IN EACH OTHER AGAIN.
THIS IS HOW IT ENDS THEN...NOT WITH ANOTHER FIGHT.
BUT WITH QUIET RECOGNITION.
KEEP MOVING! BRING ONLY WHAT YOU NEED! WEAR YOUR MOST DURABLE CLOTHING! IT'S A LONG JOURNEY, FOLKS!
NONE OF US HAVE SUITS... BUT THE AIR ISN'T DAMAGING OUR SKIN...
OF COURSE... WE NEVER NEEDED THEM... ONLY TOLD WE DID. TO KEEP US FROM LEAVING.
THE OXYGEN LEVELS ARE STILL TOO LOW TO BREATHE, BUT THE AIR HAS SELF-CLEANED POLLUTANTS OVER TIME.
JORO WAS RIGHT. THE EARTH IS BEGINNING TO HEAL...

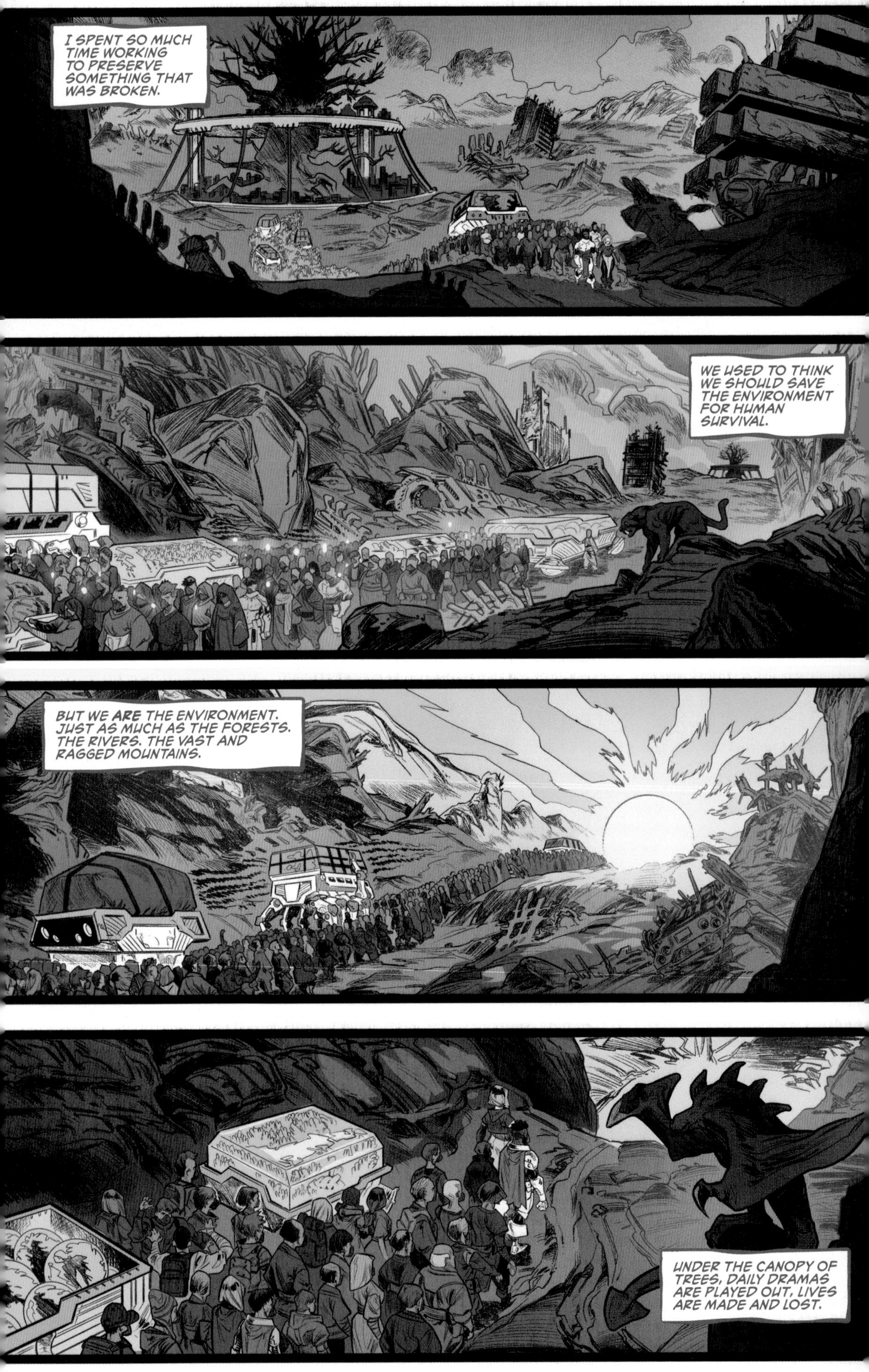
I SPENT SO MUCH TIME WORKING TO PRESERVE SOMETHING THAT WAS BROKEN.
WE USED TO THINK WE SHOULD SAVE THE ENVIRONMENT FOR HUMAN SURVIVAL.
BUT WE ARE THE ENVIRONMENT. JUST AS MUCH AS THE FORESTS. THE RIVERS. THE VAST AND RAGGED MOUNTAINS.
UNDER THE CANOPY OF TREES, DAILY DRAMAS ARE PLAYED OUT, LIVES ARE MADE AND LOST.

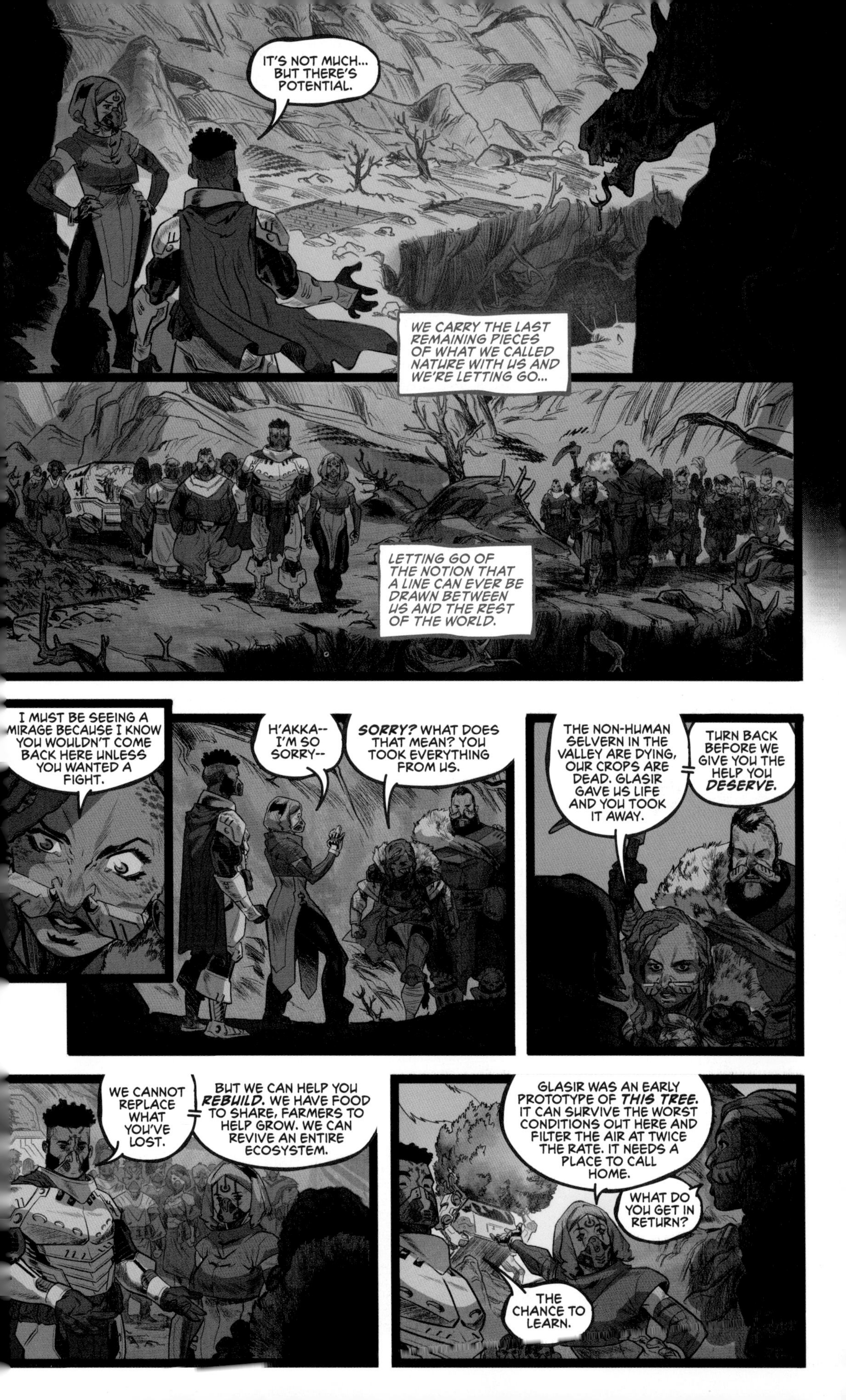
IT'S NOT MUCH... BUT THERE'S POTENTIAL.
WE CARRY THE LAST REMAINING PIECES OF WHAT WE CALLED NATURE WITH US AND WE'RE LETTING GO...
LETTING GO OF THE NOTION THAT A LINE CAN EVER BE DRAWN BETWEEN US AND THE REST OF THE WORLD.
I MUST BE SEEING A MIRAGE BECAUSE I KNOW YOU WOULDN'T COME BACK HERE UNLESS YOU WANTED A FIGHT.
H'AKKA-- I'M SO SORRY--
SORRY? WHAT DOES THAT MEAN? YOU TOOK EVERYTHING FROM US.
THE NON-HUMAN SELVERN IN THE VALLEY ARE DYING, OUR CROPS ARE DEAD. GLASIR GAVE US LIFE AND YOU TOOK IT AWAY.
TURN BACK BEFORE WE GIVE YOU THE HELP YOU DESERVE.
WE CANNOT REPLACE WHAT YOU'VE LOST.
BUT WE CAN HELP YOU REBUILD. WE HAVE FOOD TO SHARE, FARMERS TO HELP GROW. WE CAN REVIVE AN ENTIRE ECOSYSTEM.
GLASIR WAS AN EARLY PROTOTYPE OF THIS TREE. IT CAN SURVIVE THE WORST CONDITIONS OUT HERE AND FILTER THE AIR AT TWICE THE RATE. IT NEEDS A PLACE TO CALL HOME.
WHAT DO YOU GET IN RETURN?
THE CHANCE TO LEARN.

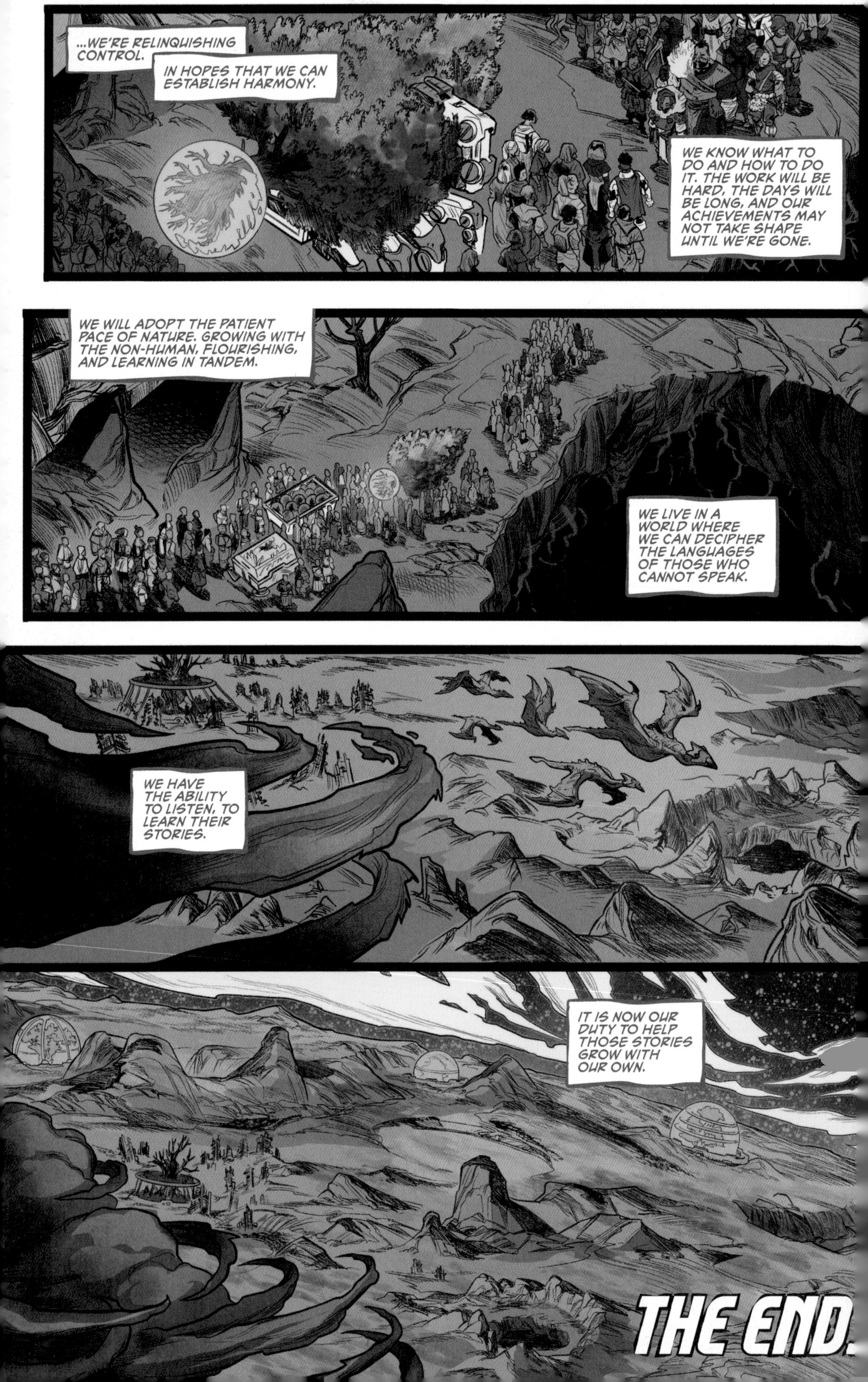
...WE'RE RELINQUISHING CONTROL.
IN HOPES THAT WE CAN ESTABLISH HARMONY.
WE KNOW WHAT TO DO AND HOW TO DO IT. THE WORK WILL BE HARD, THE DAYS WILL BE LONG, AND OUR ACHIEVEMENTS MAY NOT TAKE SHAPE UNTIL WE'RE GONE.
WE WILL ADOPT THE PATIENT PACE OF NATURE. GROWING WITH THE NON-HUMAN, FLOURISHING, AND LEARNING IN TANDEM.
WE LIVE IN A WORLD WHERE WE CAN DECIPHER THE LANGUAGES OF THOSE WHO CANNOT SPEAK.
WE HAVE THE ABILITY TO LISTEN, TO LEARN THEIR STORIES.
IT IS NOW OUR DUTY TO HELP THOSE STORIES GROW WITH OUR OWN.
THE END.

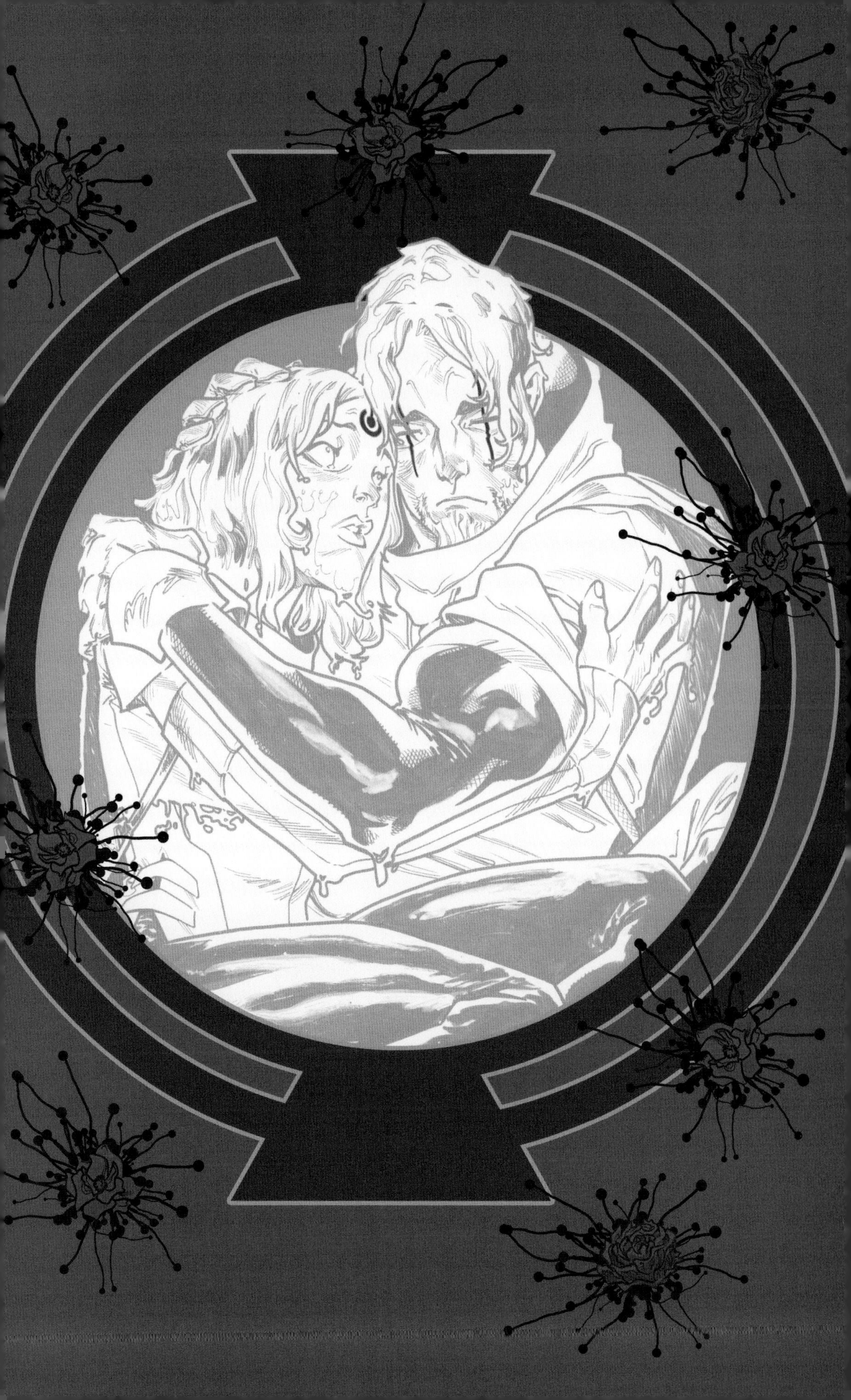

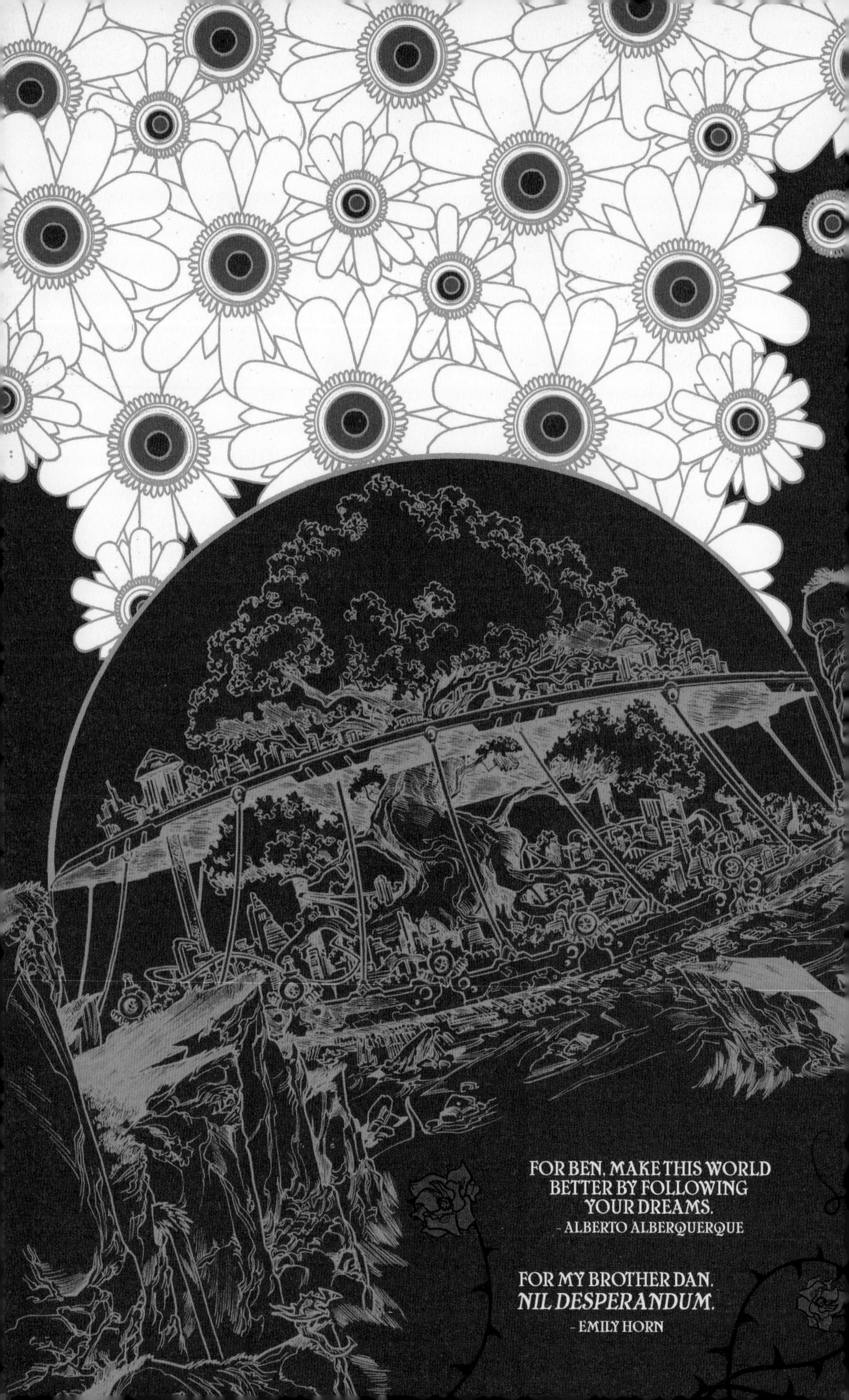

FOR BEN. MAKE THIS WORLD
BETTER BY FOLLOWING
YOUR DREAMS.
- ALBERTO ALBERQUERQUE

FOR MY BROTHER DAN.
NIL DESPERANDUM.
- EMILY HORN